William Allingham, Thomas Campbell, William Alfred Hill

The Poetical Works of Thomas Campbell

William Allingham, Thomas Campbell, William Alfred Hill

The Poetical Works of Thomas Campbell

ISBN/EAN: 9783337396152

Printed in Europe, USA, Canada, Australia, Japan

Cover: Foto ©Andreas Hilbeck / pixelio.de

More available books at **www.hansebooks.com**

THE POETICAL WORKS OF THOMAS CAMPBELL.

EDITED BY HIS NEPHEW-IN-LAW,

THE REV. W. ALFRED HILL, M.A.,

WORCESTER COLLEGE, OXFORD; VICAR OF THROWLEY.

WITH A SKETCH OF HIS LIFE

BY WILLIAM ALLINGHAM.

LONDON:

GEORGE BELL AND SONS, YORK STREET,

COVENT GARDEN.

1875.

ADVERTISEMENT.

BY arrangement with the representatives of the late poet, the publishers are enabled to include in this edition the poems of which the copyright has not yet expired.

CONTENTS.

CONTENTS.

vii

CONTENTS.

SKETCH OF THE LIFE OF
THOMAS CAMPBELL.

Born at Glasgow, July 27, 1777; died at Boulogne,
June 15, 1844.

 REMEMBER saying to a school-fellow, "Campbell is dead." "Who is Campbell?" "The poet—author of 'Hohenlinden,' you know, in *The Elocutionist;* and the 'Exile of Erin,' and 'Lord Ullin's Daughter,' and the 'Battle of the Baltic,' and the 'Soldier's Dream.' He died last Saturday at Boulogne."

The gods had not made my friend poetical, and he could not be made to care; but to me it seemed natural to take an interest in the life and personality of one whose pen had a charm, and I should have thanked anyone for bringing before my eyes some credible picture, bodily and mental, of the Poet.

That is now sufficiently attainable. The external facts of his history are simple and distinct. His character is nowise hard of comprehension; the testimony, however tinged in transmission, of all the witnesses that have spoken of him being essentially the same. His faculties—though we cannot settle them with all the precision that will probably in such cases be in the power of our

sons or grandsons, when scientific analysis shall
have thoroughly learned how to deal with mental
as with other forms of force, and to express any
possible combination of memory, conscientious-
ness, logicality, imagination, religiosity, &c. by a
simple formula—Campbell's faculties, too, while
undoubtedly those of a superior mind, are not
of a mysterious order.   To anyone who looks with
average care and insight, Thomas Campbell and
the life he had in this troublesome world are as
intelligible as need be.

Every man's story is worth hearing if properly
told; if not worth, the fault lies in the telling.
It is customary to apologize for the want of incidents in a literary life, but nothing is more tedious
than incident unconnected with nature and character, and shown in relation to these no incident
is unimportant.   A great point, always, is to be
duly brief; and at least by this quality the present
sketch hopes to commend itself to the reader.

Thomas Campbell's career was, in a sense,
entirely that of a literary man; not that he
was an assiduous scholar or a diligent writer,
but inasmuch as he had no other occupation.
His very first publication was a great popular hit,
and at an early age, by means of this 'Pleasures
of Hope' and half-a-dozen lyrics, he had won almost his full fame as a writer.   This early fame
appeared to hold him back.   Having won a garland, he was unwilling to take the chances of the
arena again.   The sense of owning a reputation,
which to some men would have been an incite-
ment to activity, for him, who was of lazy tem-
perament and of fastidious taste, clogged his ink
and wrapt his pen with cobwebs.   Considering
his natural abilities and bent, his education,
leisure, and life-term, he did but little work

after his kind. But let us now take up the records (Dr. Beattie's chiefly, the staunch and devoted friend of the poet;[1] Mr. Cyrus Redding's;[2] and scattered up and down elsewhere in contemporary memoirs and notices), adding to them a few gleanings of trustworthy oral testimony; and see what picture they give us of Thomas Campbell, and the scenes he passed through in his pilgrimage from mother's bosom in High Street, Glasgow, to last pillow in the upper town of Boulogne; the final resting-place for his shape of clay being Westminster Abbey.

At the beginning of the last century there was a certain Scottish laird, Archibald Campbell by name, living on his small estate at Kirnan, near Inverary; which estate descended, at his death, in more or less out-at-elbows condition to the eldest son Robert. Robert sinking ever further into debt, at last went up to London to try to do something for himself, and tried writing, as one resource, taking the side of Sir Robert Walpole; but died after a short and unmemorable career. The second son, Archibald, was made a Presbyterian minister, went to Jamaica, finally settled in Virginia, and died there old and respected. Alexander Campbell, the laird's third son, was brought up to what are vaguely called "mercantile pursuits"—went to America, there made close acquaintance with one Daniel Campbell, clansman but not relation, and returned with him to Glasgow, where the two started as Virginia traders (tobacco, sugar, rum); a busy

[1] Life and Letters of Thomas Campbell. Edited by William Beattie, M.D., one of his Executors. 3 vols. Second Edition. London, 1850.

[2] Literary Reminiscences and Memoirs of Thomas Campbell. 2 vols. London, 1860.

city then too, Glasgow, but quiet and small
(perhaps 50,000 in population), compared with
the wealthy, filthy, huge, horrible place of to-day.

Now, Daniel had a sister, about twenty years
of age, by name Margaret, a slight shapely girl
with neat features, brownish complexion, dark hair,
and, specially, a pair of "piercing black eyes;"[1]
a girl vivacious, cordial, helpful, and withal
shrewd; showing in later days "a considerable
fund of anecdote;" musical too, fond of singing
Scottish songs, and better educated than usual in
her time and rank: and this pleasant Margaret,
appropinquity helping, was wooed and won by her
brother's partner, Alexander, an old bachelor of
five-and-forty. They were married in Glasgow
Cathedral, 12th of January, 1756, and set up house
in the High Street, a stirring dingy thoroughfare
at right angles with the river; somewhat narrow
and steep; with the big old gateway of the University opening into it midway. The Campbell
house has long since disappeared; and of late
years the University has moved to a wide-view-
ing suburban hill, and a railway station occupies
its old place.

For some twenty years after this, the firm
of A. and D. Campbell continued to flourish,
and Alexander's dwelling-house in High Street
became gradually filled and enlivened with a
numerous young generation. In 1775, there were
ten young Campbells there, seven sons and three
daughters; the eldest child, Mary, not yet nineteen. In that year burst out the American War;
Virginia trade broke down suddenly like a bridge
in flood; many business houses went bankrupt;
and A. and D. Campbell, as it were in a day, sank

---

[1] Dr. Beattie, from eye-witness.

from prosperity to almost poverty. On Alexander, with his sixty-five years and ten children, this must have borne very heavily; but he endured the spite of fortune "with equanimity, or even cheerfulness;" and in his wife's prudence, courage and activity, he found the best kind of help and consolation. She at once set to work upon a new and careful regimen of economy, drawing in all round and keeping strictly within the narrowed limits of their income; securing thus a decent roof over their heads, food and clothes sufficient, but of the plainest, and, above all, education for the children. Old Alexander, who now gave up business entirely,—a quiet, easy-going man, choosing rather to scrape together and make the most of the fragments of his wrecked wealth, than, at his age, adventure again,—was an indulgent parent, as elderly parents often are; and his good wife found it expedient, *per contra*, to keep up a rigid system in household matters,—is said to have been at times "severe, or even harsh." But the Campbell children long afterwards could look back with entire gratitude to the pious and faithful government of their early days, their father's mild wisdom and equanimity, their mother's loving strictness and supervision : a better inheritance than much fine gold.

This old Glasgow merchant, grave mild man, now retired from market bustle with the wrecks of his savings, was fond of reading theology and history, and had some acquaintance among the college professors ; Adam Smith for one, and Thomas Reid another. He "could sing a good naval song," moreover, but was no encourager of poetry or any sort of light literature. He held strictly to the Kirk of Scotland, and punctually kept up the usage of family worship, praying *extem-*

pore, and sometimes with fervour that made a life-long impression on his children's memory. It was a household characteristically *Scotch*—serious, orthodox, orderly, frugal; with voice of song heard now and again in the form of some national melody; living in good repute and neighbour-liness; mercantile status not hindering some contact with the learned professorial world; nay, the portal of an ancient university, and all that this may admit to, lying conveniently open to the boys of the family, as it did and does to Scotch lads of even much humbler class.

Some two years after the retiring from business, Mrs. Campbell brought her husband, who was then about sixty-seven, an eighth son, born July 27, 1777, and named Thomas, after Dr. Reid, Professor of Moral Philosophy, who christened him. There were now eleven children, from Mary and Isabella, young women of nineteen and twenty, to Baby Tom, prescriptive pet of the household.

Mary, by and by, taught the little fellow to read; and at about the age of eight he began to attend the Grammar School, of which a worthy and diligent Mr. Allison was master. Little Tom decidedly *took* to learning, usually stood at the top of his class, and proudly brought home many a good mark and no few prizes. But, being naturally of a delicate constitution, and perhaps overdoing his book-work, the child after a time fell ill, and was sent out to a cottage on the banks of the river Cart, some miles from Glasgow, to the charge of an old "webster" (weaver) and his wife, doubtless well known to the Campbell family. Here, among wild flowers, cornfields, and clear-flowing waters, the boy spent six happy summer weeks, and returned to home and day-school with improved health, and a store of pleasant images in his memory.

At this time, while passing through his ninth and tenth years, little Tom was trying his hand at rhyming. He composed a 'Poem on the Seasons':—

> " Lo, smiling May doth now return at last,
>   But ah! she runs, she ruus along too fast," &c.

'Poem on Finishing the Versions':—

> " So adieu to rebukes, and also to Versions,
>   I hope I'll now have some time for diversions."

'Poem on the Death of a Favourite Parrot':—

> " In Caledonia lives a youth
>   Of genius and of fame,
>   Whose company yields me delight,
>   Will Irvine is his name.

> " A chattering parrot he possess'd,
>   Whose each diverting jest
>   For weary lessons cheer'd him up,
>   And sooth'd his anxious breast," &c.

But Death's dart was lately thrown; and

> " None can escape his powerful arm,
>   Or shun the fatal blow,
>   Thus powerful kings as well as Poll
>   His victims are laid low."

A natural impulse to rhyme was also shown in the readiness with which he produced metrical 'versions' (his were usually metrical) of passages given out to the class for translation; and at home he used to declaim, when he could get any one to listen, lines of Horace and Virgil which he had learned by heart. At twelve, he was getting on with Greek, and tried his hand at Anacreon. He took warmly to the noble tongue of Homer and Sophocles, and was all his life glad to keep up and proud to show his acquaintance with it.

On the whole, although he disliked routine and

had frequent fits of idleness, young Campbell was a highly promising schoolboy, and entered Glasgow University (in October, 1791, aged fourteen years and three months) attended by the hopes and expectations of his family: a boy of rather short stature, trimly built, vivacious and excitable, with pleasant face and a pair of bright eyes under his college cap, fond of declaiming Greek hexameters and English couplets, of chopping logic with his chosen companions; and, by and by, of making speeches in students' discussion meetings, with remarkable fluency and in a strong Glasgow brogue. The boy's favourite English books were the poems of Milton, Pope, Thomson, Gray, and Goldsmith; and he did not fail to go on with his own experiments in verse-making; showing (nearly all that can be shown therein at such a time of life) a decided metrical instinct. Among these juvenilia has been preserved 'The Pons Asinorum,—a song, written in Mr. J. Miller's Mathematical Class,' which has a spirited swing :—

" As Miller's Hussars march'd up to the wars,
     With the captain in person before 'em,
     It happen'd one day that they met on their way
       With the dangerous *Pons Asinorum!*

" Now see the bold band, each a sword in his hand,
     And his Euclid for target before him!
     Not a soul of them all could the dangers appall
       Of the hazardous *Pons Asinorum!*

" While the streamers wide flew and the loud trumpets blew,
     And the drum beat responsive before 'em;
     Then Miller, their chief, thus harangued them in brief,
       'bout the dangerous *Pons Asinorum!*

" ' My soldiers,' said he, ' though dangers there be,
     Yet behave with a proper decorum ;
     Dismiss every fear, and with boldness draw near
       To the dangerous *Pons Asinorum!* " &c.

On one occasion he obtained a holiday for the Greek class by a poetic petition to the professor. In his second session he won the prize for English poetry by a more grave and elaborate effort, entitled 'A description of the Distribution of Prizes in the Common Hall of the University of Glasgow on the 1st of May, 1793.' The two first lines and two last will suffice as specimens :—

> " Phœbus has risen; and many a glittering ray
> Diffuses splendour o'er the auspicious day.
>
> * * * * * *
>
> Now go, ye prosp'rous, be not too elate,
> And let contentment soothe the adverse fate!"

The drillings of the Glasgow Volunteers (making ready "to baffle Gallia's boastful crew") inspired the lad into a lyric which made his name known to a wider Glasgow circle :—

> " Hark! hark! the fife's shrill notes arise,
> And ardour beats the martial drum;
> And broad the silken banner flies,
> Where Clutha's native squadrons come!"

And 'Verses on the Queen of France,' signed T. C., appeared in the Poet's Corner of a Glasgow newspaper :—

> " Behold, where Gallia's captive queen,
> With steady eye, and look serene,
> In life's last awful, awful scene,
> Slow leaves her sad captivity," &c.

—in the metre of which sounds a note premonitory of 'Hohenlinden.' Meanwhile he went on with his Greek and Latin, attended lectures on Logic and Belles-Lettres; spoke often at a college debating club called 'The Discursive;' wrote satirical verses on the members of it; and, moreover, gained a little much-needed cash by giving occasional lessons to less advanced students or pupils.

The gay and cheerful lad, fond of talk, anecdote and jest, was moreover able to play some on the German flute,—"but his collection of airs was very limited and generally of a plaintive character."[1]

Thus the pleasant hopeful years went by: home life; college life; literary essayings both in prose and verse;—also (not so pleasant) the beginnings of a legal career, in the humble form of clerking in the office of a Glasgow solicitor, kinsman of his mother. It was very necessary that each one of the reduced merchant's many sons should as soon as possible begin to earn something, and this clerking was frugally combined with Tom's college course. At first the Church had been thought of, then Medicine; but each in turn was given up; and, after no long trial, Law, too, was abandoned, for Commerce; and in his seventeenth year we find the youth engaged in a merchant's office, though still a University student. A letter of his at this time [2] to a friend of the name of James Thomson living in London, is written in an amusingly didactic style. He asserts that "in the metropolis of England, human nature is seen in its most variegated states and employments. The concourse of characters to be met with there, have given scope to the contemplative geniuses of many distinguished men." He thinks "it admits of no doubt that commerce humanizes society"—adding, "In your next, however, I expect to hear a more complete review of the benefits of commerce than my narrow observation has permitted me to make. If you are at present in London, I request the favour of a few remarks upon the general cast of its inhabitants. I have heard

---

[1] Dr. Beattie, i. 68.   [2] *Ibid.*, i. 108.

several accounts of its edifices, curiosities, manners, &c.; but, I assure you, your observations, on whatever part of it you have hitherto seen, would afford me much pleasure," (May 17, 1794.) In a letter to Thomson about a month later he writes, " I believe I shall spend no more winters in this country, as my purpose is to join my brothers in America." But fate had it otherwise.

His father, now near eighty-five, and already poor (depending mainly on what he received from two small commercial Benefit Societies) became suddenly poorer by the decision against him of a long-pending Chancery suit; debts pressed; poor Mrs. Campbell was weighed down with anxieties. At this crisis, a temporary situation of tutor was offered to young Thomas in the family of a namesake, Mrs. Campbell, residing in the Island of Mull, and by the advice of friends he accepted it, much urged by the consideration of *res angusta domi*. Just before starting, he was gladdened with three prizes for as many verse translations, one from Claudian, one from Aristophanes, and one from the ' Choephoræ' of Æschylus, of which latter take a specimen :—

" Hail! sacred dead! a maiden weeps for you;
   For you I wake the madness of despair!
The deep-struck wounds of woe my cheeks bedew;
   I feed my bosom with eternal care."

That is enough.

Young Thomas Campbell, now seventeen years and nine months old, set out from Glasgow for the Western Highlands on the 18th of May, 1795, in company with a class-fellow, one Joseph Finlayson, who was also going as tutor. " I was so little proud of it," wrote T. C. in later life,[1] " that in passing through Greenock I pur-

[1] Dr. Beattie, i. 127, 128.

posely omitted to call on my mother's cousin, Mr. Robert Sinclair, at that time a wealthy merchant and first magistrate of the town, with a family of handsome daughters, one of whom I married some nine years afterwards." The two lads walked about Greenock quay all the evening, then repaired to the little inn where they had bespoken beds, and finding themselves ravenously hungry, ventured (not without fear and trembling for the cost) to order beefsteaks and ale, which set them singing and reciting poetry. " I still retain the opinion that life is pleasanter in the real transition than in the retrospect; but still I am bound to regard this part of my recollections of life as very agreeable. [Yes, one can believe that!] I was, it is true, very poor; [poor at seventeen!] but I was gay as a lark, and hardy as the Highland heather." They crossed the Frith of Clyde to Argyllshire (trunks sent by land to Inverary) each with his whole travelling kit tied in handkerchief and slung on stick over shoulder. " The wide world contained not two merrier boys. We sang and recited poetry throughout the long wild Highland glens"— Ossian among other things. So they walked along; fed on herrings and potatoes, with whisky, and sleeping on chairs by the peat fire,—inn beds being worse than suspectable. " Nevertheless, the roaring streams and torrents, with the yellow primroses and chanting cuckoos on their banks— the heathery mountains, with the sound of the goats bleating at their tops, delighted me beyond measure. I felt a soul in every muscle of my body." At Inverary the companions separated, and young Campbell went on by himself to Oban and thence crossed to Mull. In a long summer's day he walked the whole length of the island without a guide save the westering sun, and with seldom even a footpath, and at twilight reached the house of Sunipol, standing on the solitary northern shore of Mull near the centre of a bay.

Mrs. Campbell the young tutor found to be " a worthy, sensible widow lady," and very kind. Towards his pupils, he says,—" I made a conscience of duty;" adding, " I never beat them —remembering how much I loved my father for having never beaten me." At first he was melancholy in this solitude and among strangers, and wrote an Elegy of twenty-six lines, beginning,—

" The tempest blackens on the dusky moor,
　And billows lash the long-resounding shore ;"

which perhaps shows some movement, however timid, towards individuality of expression. But before his five months' stay was ended he had discovered much to interest him in Mull, and its neighbours the basaltic Staffa and saintly Iona; and a great part of his stock of original poetic imagery was unconsciously gathered at this time. In youth we reckon the days and ourselves cheap: the Future will bring something worth while. But the Future, too often, brings cares and bewilderments, and a sad looking-back to those bright days of forward-looking. Many a time, be sure, did the famous author of ' The Pleasures of Hope,' first-class literary lion, diner at Holland House, and so forth, see visions of that wild western island, its gray-blue rocks, grassy glens, heathery mountains, and waves of " tumultuous roar;" often think with a sigh of the lad of seventeen who once wandered in those landscapes, and could fancy himself miserable, in spite of health, poetry, and all

" The promised joys of life's unmeasured way."

To this short residence in Mull, and to the military scenes which came before him when he first visited the Continent, may be traced nearly all the poetic imagery and many of the themes of Campbell's poetry. The sensibility of his mind to similar impressions seems to have dulled long before he had reached even middle life.

Amidst his duties as tutor young Campbell found time to employ his pen both in translations from the Greek and in original verses. Those addressed to ' Caroline ' are believed to have been inspired by a pretty young lady of seventeen, a clergyman's daughter, who came on a visit to Mrs. Campbell's house; but were most likely polished up at a later time into their present state of rather formal elegance, scarcely rising after all beyond the mark of a very good drawing-school performance in pictorial art: *e. g.*

> " Where'er thy morning breath has play'd,
>   Whatever isles of ocean fann'd,
>   Come to my blossom-woven shade,
>   Thou wandering wind of fairy-land ! "

One thing noticeable in Campbell's verses from the very first, is the care with which they are written.

Near the end of October (1795) young Campbell, his term of teaching ended, took leave of the Sunipol household, and of their lonely island, now white-topt with snow, white-girt with angry breakers; and again in company with his friend Joe Finlayson, *his* task likewise over, journeyed homewards four days by land and water. They lost their way once, between Oban and Loch Awe, and passed the cold night in their plaids under the lee of a whinstone wall; but this apparently did them no harm; and they briskly entered Glasgow, rejoicing to behold the kirk-steeples and feel the familiar pavement underfoot instead of heath and bent.

Campbell went immediately to his old work of tuition, preparing younger college lads; also going on with his own studies and University course. At this time we hear, in his letters, of illness (perhaps from that night under the wall), a month's confinement to the house, and excessive low spirits; but he soon rallied and went on. Next to poetry, his great delight was in oratory, especially when it denounced tyranny and oppression. One of his pupils was a youth of the name of Cunninghame, who long afterwards (when a Scotch judge) gave Dr. Beattie some reminiscences of this Glasgow time, worth noting by whoso is curious to trace on chart the voyage of that soul-ship known as the *Thomas Campbell*, of Glasgow. Thomas used to repeat, with the greatest enthusiasm, the more impassioned passages of Lord Chatham's speeches in favour of American freedom; while at other times he poured forth, with great rapture, Mr. Burke's declamation against Warren Hastings, and Mr. Wilberforce's heart-rending description of the ' Middle Passage.' It cannot appear surprising that these sentiments, often dwelt upon, produced a strong conviction both in master and pupil —ages 18 and 14—that " the governors of the world were in league against mankind, and that a time would come for the vindication of the wrongs of society." Both Thomas Campbell and his brother Daniel, Lord Cunninghame adds, exulted in the French Revolution; and in many a hot juvenile discussion declared that even the Reign of Terror was as nothing " compared with the manifold evils that would ensue, if the allied powers were successful in restoring despotism in

France, or in subjugating and dividing that country, as they had shortly before partitioned Poland—a country for which he [Thomas] always expressed the deepest sympathy." We all of us owe much of the furniture and dominant colour of our minds to the images and thoughts of our teens : Campbell appears to have fully furnished his mental house in this early period, and afterwards added or altered as little as possible. External lodging he changed often (too often); but in that Inner Apartment always remained the old Greek busts in their places, the sketches of Highland scenery, the somewhat ideal portraits of Koskiusco and William Tell, certain battle-pictures by land and sea, and a few pencil sketches of female beauty, with more grace than individuality.

In June 1796 Campbell quitted Glasgow University, and went as tutor to the eight-year-old son of Colonel Napier (great-grandson of Napier of the logarithms), then living at Downie, a lonely farm-house on the shore of the Sound of Jura, within an hour's walk of the canal from Loch Fyne. His work occupied but a few hours a day ; he had time for reading, chiefly (in the regular part of it) jurisprudence and history, for at this time he had a strong wish to go to the bar ; but alas! no money to help. But much of his reading was of the desultory sort ; and he passed many hours in scrambling about the rocky mountainous shores, where his mind received pictures that were afterwards embodied in poetry. Nor did he neglect the practice of literary composition ; finished a translation of the 'Choephoræ,' and sent a copy of the MS. to a friend in London, "with some faint hope of having it published ;" wrote or finished, moreover, certain short poems, one of which is called 'Love and Madness.' In the collected poems it is said to have been " Written in 1795," but if so it was probably polished up afterwards, for the author sends it in September, 1796, in a letter from Downie, to his friend Mr. James Thomson, as " lately finished." The incident that gave rise to it was a murder done in Warwickshire, by a Miss Broderick, on her faithless lover, named Errington. As a matter of style, the piece is worth looking at. Pope mainly seems to be the model, and not for metre only :—

> " Once more I view thy sheeted spectre stand,
>   Roll the dim eye, and wave the paly hand !
> Soon let this fluttering spark of vital flame
> Forsake its languid, melancholy frame," &c.

A production less promising, and the less so for its completeness of a sort, it would be hard to find from the pen of a young man destined to really add something to the treasures of English poetry. It is usual for a poet to begin by admiring, perhaps worshipping, some one or more of his immediate predecessors—of those to whose song the actual world is ringing and replying. Among the oddest things in Campbell is his apathy, all through life, for the poetry of his own era. To all appearance he never cared to give it any attention.

In this summer of 1796 (a season of bright fine weather), and in a Scottish town not far distant from Glasgow, a life-tragedy was going through its last sad scene; one to which men's eyes still turn, and fill with tears; nor is it likely to lose its interest and pathos in many future centuries, for all who speak the English tongue. A great poet, scarcely in the prime of his years, but whose songs had already been added to the heritage of the human race, was dying in poverty and wretchedness. " On the 21st of July at Dumfries, Robert Burns, aged 37 years and 6 months." If he and his songs had been Chinese, young Campbell, so far as we can see, could not have been less interested about them. There is, however, just one mention of the Ayrshire poet, namely in an 'Epistle to Three Ladies,' written about this time—

> " Or list the lays of Burns, untimely starred,
>   Or weep for ' Auburn,' with its sweetest bard—" [1]

and in later years came a not highly successful ' Ode to the Memory of Burns.'

Campbell drew imagery from Scottish scenery, and has let slip a few provincialisms ; but on the whole his muse, instead of displaying a Scottish nationality, puts it aside as far as she can. The young Inverary tutor's ambition was to reside in London. His literary models were of the school of Dryden, Pope, Addison, Johnson, and Goldsmith. In the latter part of his college time his fellow-students had often spoken of him as " the Pope of Glasgow." Here at Downie he was trying his hand among other things on the decasyllabic couplet—from which came results not as yet dreamed of.

In March, 1797, he writes to a Glasgow friend from Downie, in a despondent mood, " I find, to my sad experience, the disadvantage of not being early educated to one employment or other "—he had fixed upon the law, had promises of help in that direction, but found he could not manage it, must either " follow the profession of a teacher, or emigrate to my brothers in America. . . . . I leave this place in five weeks ; I cannot say pre-

<hr>

[1] Life, &c., i. 219.

cisely where, whether to Glasgow or Edinburgh."
We catch, however, a hint of solacement : " My
evening walks are sometimes accompanied by *one*,
who, for a twelvemonth past, has won my purest,
but most ardent affection."

Campbell returned to his old father's house
in low health and very bad spirits, poor fellow;
sensitive, anxious, without money or occupation,
no suitable life-path to be discovered.   He would
not enter the Church ; of tutorship he was tired.
He had some vague hopes of combining law with
literature, but how to make a practical beginning ?

One day early in May he set off on foot for
Edinburgh.   His friend and former pupil, Cunninghame, was settled there, in the office of a
writer to the signet.   Through him, but with
difficulty, young Campbell got employment as
a copying clerk in the Register House, a post of
dreary drudgery and scanty pay; moving after
some weeks to a somewhat better place of the
same sort in the office of a Mr. Whytt.

But Minerva comes unexpectedly to her children's help. In Edinburgh young Campbell met an
acquaintance, Mr. Hugh Park, a Glasgow school-
master ; and they used to walk together.   Now
Park knew Dr. Anderson, at that time a literary
' big-wig ' of the Scottish capital, and author of
' Lives of the British Poets ; ' and one day, going
to visit at the doctor's house, was immediately
called on by two young ladies of the family to
say who " that handsome lad " was, they had
seen taking leave of him in the street ?   " One
Thomas Campbell—only a lawyer's clerk, but was
distinguished at Glasgow University, and is really
something of a poet ! "—says Park ; and shows
the Elegy written in Mull, which is luckily in his
pocket.   On which followed an introduction, and

much kindness on Dr. Anderson's part. He recommended young Campbell to Mr. Mundell, a publisher, who engaged him to make for twenty pounds an abridgment of Bryan Edwards's 'West Indies.' With this (his first work for the press) in hand, Campbell quitted the odious law-copying desk, " the most accursed of all professions," he wrote to a friend; and returned in the end of July to his native Glasgow, as usual on foot, after an absence of some two months.

The next three months he spent in Glasgow, or in visiting friends; and from time to time continued his verse-making attempts. One of these, first appearing probably in a newspaper, speedily got into the budget of the street ballad-singers, and won a real popular success—'The Wounded Hussar.' For the first time, a new singer's voice, though as yet indistinguishable, was heard on the stage of the world; it was timid and conventional enough:—

" Alone to the banks of the dark-rolling Danube
    Fair Adelaide hied when the battle was o'er:
  ' Oh whither,' she cried, ' hast thou wander'd, my lover,
    Or here dost thou welter and bleed on the shore ? ' "

But the metre was telling; the little piece did not want clearness and compactness; and as a whole it was found to express the incident lyrically to common apprehensions. *To hit the mark* in art, any art, is, even in its humblest examples, a most curious feat—simply done, if at all; too subtle to be explained by any ingenuity of criticism. All the teaching and all the striving in the world will not do it; and yet it is far from being done by accident; when the right man appears, he can win battles, solve mathematic problems, write songs.

In the end of October or beginning of Nov-

ember (still 1797), young Campbell returned
to Edinburgh, again journeying on foot; baggage sent by carrier.   He had done his ' Abridgment' for the bookseller, and looked forward to
more and better literary work. In case of success,
or fair promise of it, his mother and aged father
were to move their scanty household gods to Edinburgh, at that day not only a more cultivated and
aristocratic, but a larger city than Glasgow;
which removal was, in fact, accomplished a year
or so later.

Again in the Scottish capital, the young man,
still without a profession or any regular employment, and having attempted and given up almost
in limine Church, Law, and Medicine, turned
his face once more towards the third of those
' three black Graces.'   He attended chemistry
and anatomy classes at the University of Edinburgh, very anxious to refute the galling charge of
"unsteadiness" now often brought against him by
his relatives.   But alas! the poor fellow found
Hygeia as unpropitious to him as her sisters.   He
was forced into literary hack-work again,—some
sort of geographical compiling, for very small pay;
and by and by, to take pupils for preparation in
Greek and Latin.   Just at this time, the post, one
day in January, 1798, brought an important letter
from Virginia ; containing a long looked-for in-
vitation from his brother Robert,—" Come over
to us, brother Tom, a situation is ready ;" which
he at once accepted, and arranged to quit Scotland
and Europe in the month of March, being thus
for the third time on tiptoe for flight to the
New World.   And once more came disappoint-
ment. His eldest brother disapproved: "Tom had
better stay and finish his education."   So the
plan that the parents should move to Edinburgh

was resumed, and carried out at Martinmas, 1798 ; Thomas meanwhile, with health and spirits improved by visits to friends in the country, going on with the booksellers, and the college grinding ; medical studies being again and finally abandoned.

In this desultory way young Campbell, now in his twenty-first year, made a tolerable livelihood, " so long (as he himself told or wrote to Dr. Beattie)[1] as I was industrious." But something interfered. When a tutor in Mull, Campbell had received a letter from a Glasgow friend, Mr. Hamilton Paul, ending thus : " We have now three ' Pleasures ' by first-rate men of genius, viz. the 'Pleasures of Imagination,' the 'Pleasures of Memory,' and the ' Pleasures of Solitude ! '[2] Let us cherish the ' Pleasures of Hope,' that we may meet soon in Alma Mater." This stray breath, perhaps, stirred into life, if it did not carry to its appropriate soil, the germ of a future poem ; and there seems reason to think that it began to sprout soon after. Certain, that now two years and a half later, in the month of March, namely, 1798, among other vernal burgeonings, a something called the ' Pleasures of Hope ' was definitely growing into shape in the mind of a young Scotchman, then lodging on a dingy *land* or flat in Rose Street. " I took long walks about Arthur's Seat, conning over my own (as I thought them) magnificent lines ; and as my ' Pleasures of Hope' got on, my pupils fell off."[3] His aunt, Mrs. Campbell, and her beautiful daughter Margaret, were his first two auditors ; from whom, naturally, he received " no small encouragement ;" and as the poem grew more complete it became known and applauded by other friends. How best

<hr>

[1] Life, i. 226.   [2] Zimmermann's.   [3] Life, i. 226.

to get it into print was an anxious question, solved by negotiation of Dr. Anderson with publisher Mundell. Campbell, probably in one of his alternate fits of despondency, made over his copyright for the consideration of 200 copies of the book ; and the poet's gain was thus about £50 only. But it must be added, that afterwards, when the adventure proved a notable success, he received many additional payments. The forthcoming new poem was discussed in the best literary coteries of Edinburgh ; urged and advised by Dr. Anderson, the author retouched his work over and over again with the most anxious care.

On the same or another dingy flat in Rose Street, lodged a landscape painter, of the name of Somerville, who one day was amazed to discover that his neighbour, young Campbell, of demeanour so unpretending, and whose ordinary conversation was quaint, queer, desultory, comic, occasionally querulous and sarcastic, but always rather the reverse of poetical,[1] was actually a poet ! sometimes, too, a very dejected poet, and almost at times as if going crazy ; and in such discontented moods he often wandered into the landscape painter's room—"to get away from myself," he used to say. Somerville tried to cheer him by praising his poem—"What a splendid thing! everybody says so;" but Campbell retorted in a bitter tone, "Ah, and suppose some day everybody finds out, as I did this morning, that it is mere *trash ?* " But "that very evening we supped together," and before one in the morning the despondent bard grew wildly merry ; then confessed he was really going to be a great man ; planned how to live and travel when the money

---

[1] From Mrs. Dugald Stewart, apparently. Life, i. 248.

came, and for the time was "quite serious in his plans." "I suspect," adds S., "that Campbell had, after his own wayward fashion, a great deal of ambition in him;" "a cross of the Spanish *hidalgo*" too, much pride and hauteur, ready to fire up at the remotest indication of a slight or affront.

At last the Poem was given to the world; and "public curiosity having been studiously kept awake for some months, the demand for copies was unprecedented." The 27th of April, 1799, was the birthday of Thomas Campbell's fame. "The 'Pleasures of Hope,'" he wrote in after-life, "appeared exactly when I was twenty-one years and nine months old. It gave me a general acquaintance in Edinburgh." Among others, the young poet became known to Dr. Gregory Mackenzie ('Man of Feeling'), Dugald Stewart, Archibald Alison, Telford the engineer, Henry Erskine, and Walter Scott. Mr. Walter Scott, advocate, was at this time known in Edinburgh society as a most genial and agreeable companion, and a man of literary tastes, who had published translations of a couple of Bürger's ballads in thin drawing-room quarto. He was now, in the spring of 1799, twenty-eight years o'd, a married man of some twelvemonth's experience, and had just brought out a translation of Goethe's 'Goetz von Berlichingen.' At Mr. Scott's house in Castle Street young Campbell came to a dinner-party; no introductions were made, but the conversation at table was easy and cultivated. After dinner Mr. Scott rising with a twinkle in his shrewd grey eyes, spoke to this effect: "Gentlemen, we have all been reading the 'Pleasures of Hope;' and now I have the honour to propose the health of the poet" (pointing to a young gentleman on his right), "Mr.

Thomas Campbell," which naturally made a pleasant sensation; nor was the blushing hero wanting in a fit reply,—a bright-eyed, smooth-cheeked, comely youth, rather short in stature, and still of boyish appearance.

In fact, the new poet now stood confessed, and not in Edinburgh alone, but in London, and, gradually, wherever such things could interest mankind. His poem was quoted in the House of Representatives at Washington, and in a thousand other places. It was praised on all sides for its moral, patriotic, literary merits. It became a favourite prize-book and gift-book. It was eloquent and sonorous, after the most accepted models; not without a flavour of novelty, too, in the style; and it took up various topics familiar and interesting to the public mind, and touched them artistically,—wrongs of Poland, wrongs of India, the French Revolution, negro slavery, mutiny of the *Bounty*, &c. Here is not the place to attempt a new criticism, were such required, on this well-known poem, still at hand in every house, and whose thousand and odd lines can be read in an hour. At the head of each of the two parts is an analysis, according to due form and precedent. It has some likeness to its predecessor, the 'Pleasures of Imagination,' in its marshalling of symbolic personages, Fancy, Truth, Genius, Mercy, Freedom, and an unconscionable number of rather vague "Spirits" of various kinds; all, for the nonce, under the sovereignty of Hope,—"primeval Hope," "congenial Hope," "Hope, the charmer," "Propitious Power," "eternal Hope," &c.; but Dr. Akenside's production is from beginning to end a mere phantasmagoria, in dull blank verse. The 'Pleasures of Memory,' published only seven years before, had evidently been much more suggestive to Campbell,—a poem of about the same length, in two parts, each with due analysis prefixed, written in couplets of the Pope-cum-Goldsmith school, and with a moderate allowance of personifications (Mercy, Fancy, Science, and Hope herself, keeping MEMORY company, the hostess on that occasion), but introducing human people and incidents throughout. In fact, the third poem of "Pleasures" is a child of the second, with unmistakeable family likeness in size and aspect, in structure and style; but with stronger muscles and more significant features. Byron, in a letter to Moore (Sept. 5, 1813), says, "I have been reading 'Memory' again, the other day, and 'Hope' together, and retain all my preference of the former. His elegance is really wonderful—there is no such thing as a vulgar line in his book." (Dr. Beattie, by the bye, mistakenly quotes this praise as though given to Campbell.) But neither is there one line of Rogers' poem that has become current coin in English literature; whereas Campbell, even by his first effort, secured what some one has called "an immortality of quotation." A reader of our own day, used to far wider scope and freer movement, is likely to feel himself hampered and trammelled by these stately stilted couplets, and to greet with laughter or derision the stuffed allegories (on the banks of the Clyde or Thames) which the showman thus pompously exhibits. "Extremely artificial from beginning to end!" one exclaims: but it is necessary, for all that, to recollect the force of fashion in poetry; and for a century past one fashion of English poetry had continued dominant. The bold Elizabethan style faded into affectation, frivolity, scragginess; then rose the Correct School and reigned supreme, as we have said, for a whole century. It aimed at and produced a refinement of general manners, so to speak, in poetry, and had at the same time the effect of discouraging and obliterating individuality. As people at a sermon expected—and, indeed, as many congregations still expect— their preacher to address them within the limits of certain well-known formalities, so when readers took up a poem (and the run was on didactic and reflective poetry) they expected everything there to be said after a particular manner, and nothing to be said which could not be so said gracefully. The best models were familiar; there was no doubt as to the standard of excellence; and every new aspirant to public favour naturally kept this before him and strove to reach it. It was at the end of a century of *literary* poetry that it befell Thomas Campbell to compete for a laurel wreath; he tried for it and won it, according to established literary rules; and, judged by these, the merits of his work are still easy to discern.

The signs of a poetic revolution, however, were already springing up; not first among colleges or literary coteries, but in a Scottish peasant's cottage, in the back parlour of a poor London engraver; and a certain shy melancholy recluse, of the richer class, had also jotted down with simplicity and freshness some of the musings of his rural walks. Soon after this Wordsworth and Coleridge boldly announced the new era, with the fervour and pugnacity of conscious apostles.

Campbell always detested "the Lake School;" but the freer air of the new era had its effect upon him, and without distinctly abandoning a jot of the old traditions he gave in more or less, and took advantage of the franker and easier manners which had ousted those of his youth. He came to resemble an old Tory, transformed by pressure of events into a 'moderate Conservative.'   But the 'Pleasures of Hope' belongs to the *ancien régime;* a dissertation in verse, studied, rhetorical, academic.   The clever finale might have come from the pen of Pope or Dryden :—

> " When wrapt in fire the realms of ether glow,
>   And heaven's last thunder shakes the world below,
>   Thou, undismay'd, shalt o'er the ruins smile,
>   And light thy torch at Nature's funeral pile."

It recalls in particular the closing lines of the 'Dunciad.'   But here and there the new poet shows a touch of his own, superior perhaps in nature, force, and picturesqueness, in combination with the all-needful artistic sense, to anything of a similar kind to be quoted from his classic predecessors.   The most popular lines in the poem were probably those on Poland :—

> " Oh ! bloodiest picture in the book of Time !
>   Sarmatia fell, unwept, without a crime," &c.

What degree of intimacy with Polish history and politics young Campbell had acquired at Glasgow and in the Island of Mull, it would be rash to guess; but we know that " patriotism " was a word of magic power in his youthful ear, and those lines on Koskiusco and his cause were vigorous and resonant, and with a little ingenuity on the writer's part, and a little allowance on the reader's, came reasonably well under the head of " Hope." They include, however, one of the worst of several glaring and easily remediable faults of taste which, in spite of frequent and anxious revision, still remain in the poem: the military music on the ramparts of Warsaw is thus described :—

> " Then peal'd the notes, omnipotent to charm,"

a rather too magniloquent phrase taken here by

itself, but glaringly wrong inasmuch as it destroys the effect of a passage some twenty lines down, where the weighty word would, if not already used, have fallen grandly on the ear :—

> " O righteous Heaven ! ere Freedom found a grave,
>   Why slept the sword, omnipotent to save ? "

Among other evils, it may here be hinted in passing, caused by the dismemberment of Poland, it was an unlucky event for Thomas Campbell ; " the Polish cause " proving one of those phantoms on which he afterwards wasted so much of his life.

The second part of the " Pleasures " is perhaps the better of the two. The long passage including that Wordsworthian line (shade of Campbell, forgive the manner of praise !)—

> " And muse on Nature with a poet's eye,"

has much charm, though it might be questioned whether Madame HOPE ought to have the credit of this series of pictures. The lines of most living interest, not by virtue of style or imagery, but of their substance, are those in which the Lucretian theory of Creation is rejected :—

> " I smile on death, if Heavenward HOPE remain.
>   But if the warring winds of Nature's strife
>   Be all the faithless charter of my life—
>   If Chance awaked, inexorable power,
>   This frail and feverish being of an hour,
>   Doom'd o'er the world's precarious scene to sweep
>   Swift as the tempest travels on the deep,
>   To know Delight but by her parting smile,
>   And toil, and wish, and weep a little while ;
>   Then melt, ye elements, that form'd in vain
>   This troubled pulse and visionary brain !"

It does not seem likely that our poets will return to the company of personified human qualities and passions, or to the stilted and conventional diction of "classical" English verse. But it is very possible that they may sooner or later, since our own fashions have no especial privilege of permanency, retrace their steps in the direction of clearness of meaning, succinctness and purity of expression, honest measure in metres, and general harmony of form, without loss of richness, boldness, or any happy variety of gift available within the natural limits of the poetic art—limits wide and unfixed, yet real; even like those of our planet's atmosphere. No boundary there whatever: but adventure in any direction a little too far, you find you cannot breathe; cannot fly, though more than eagle-winged.

Campbell was now "very much noticed and invited out," and spent a good part of the summer in visiting friends, old and new. The publishers, bringing out a new edition of 2,000, presented him with an additional £50. He again revised the work with care, and added several passages. It is curious to note, especially considering the young author's environment and early training, that in the first edition there was no reference whatever to Christianity, even in speaking of a life beyond the grave. HOPE was a heathen goddess. But in the second edition, acting, doubtless, on advice, the poet inserted the forty-six lines beginning,—

" Oh deep, enchanting prelude to repose,"

and ending,—

" Sprang to her source, the bosom of her God!"

He still, however, managed dexterously with the needful orthodoxy, and did not far commit himself :—

" Hark, as the spirit eyes with eagle gaze
The noon of heaven, undazzled by the blaze,

> On heavenly winds that waft her to the sky
> Float the sweet tones of star-born melody,
> Wild as that hallow'd anthem sent to hail
> Bethlehem's shepherds in the lonely vale,
> When Jordan hush'd her waves, and midnight still
> Watch'd on the holy towers of Zion's hill!"

Always fond of change of scene, the Poet longed to visit foreign countries, and having now some money in pocket determined on a continental tour. After various alterations of plan he sailed in the Leith packet for Hamburgh, June 1st, 1800. His notion was to travel, to study German literature, to go on at quiet intervals with a projected poem, the " Queen of the North" (namely, Edinburgh), to send short pieces to the "Morning Chronicle," where Perry had made him welcome; and to come back and give lectures on *belles-lettres*, in London or else in Dublin. At Hamburgh the poet was received with respect and hospitality by various British residents. He also made acquaintance, as a declared supporter of " patriotism," with several refugee Irishmen, who had been concerned in the Rebellion of '98, and to one of these, named Anthony McCann, " an honest, excellent man," he took a great fancy. " It was in consequence of meeting him one evening on the banks of the Elbe, lonely and pensive at the thoughts of his situation, that I wrote the 'Exile of Erin.'"[1] Warned of the dangers of travelling in time of war, he took advice which pointed to Ratisbon as a safe and suitable place to stay at; reached that city in August, but found it anything but peaceful. It was filled with troops; distant cannonade and musketry resounded, fighting was going on within sight of the walls; dead and wounded

---

[1] Autob. Notes, 1837, in Dr. Beattie, 1, 331.

soldiers were carried through the streets. In brief, the French, driving Klenau and his Austrians before them, entered Ratisbon three days after Campbell's arrival. He was suddenly in the midst of the exciting and dreadful realities of war. Writing to Dr. Anderson on the 10th of August, he says: "Since the arrival of the gallant Republicans, we have many specimens of military evolutions extremely striking. Such fiery countenances and rapid manœuvres as these active little fellows exhibit are only to be expected from the conquerors of Lodi. and Marengo. It would raise every . spark of enthusiasm in your heart to see them marching with stately and measured steps to the war-song of Liberty,"—that is, the *Marseillaise.* In his notes written in later life, he says, "This formed the most important epoch in my life, in point of impressions; but those impressions at seeing numbers of men strewn dead on the field, or, what was worse, seeing them in the act of dying, are so horrible in my memory that I study to banish them." Campbell also saw a charge of the Austrian cavalry on the French; but the battle of Hohenlinden, fought December 3, about twenty English miles east of Munich, he did not see, save in his mind's eye.

At Ratisbon, Campbell sojourned some two months and a half, taking advantage of an armistice to make excursions to Munich and elsewhere; then, hostilities on the point of breaking out anew, he returned northwards and reached Altona at the beginning of winter. There he remained till spring; very sad and gloomy at times, from want of company, feeling of exilement, fears—not groundless—of his money running dry, depression of health. But anon, the barometer rises again : the ' Queen of the North' will do wonders for his fame and pocket; a nine months' tour in Germany, Bohemia, &c., even Turkey, is looked forward to; and he does really go on studying German, and ·writing short poems, some of which he sends from time to time to the 'Morning Chronicle.'

In March all his continental plans were suddenly arrested by the breaking-out of war between England and Denmark. An English squadron appeared off the Sound. Altona was no place for an Englishman. Campbell, half expecting to be stopped, got away hastily in a small trading vessel, for Leith; chased by a Danish privateer, she put into Yarmouth, and there Campbell landed and travelled up to London by mail-coach, April 7, 1801.

He arrived in the great city with only a few shillings in his pocket; hastened to the 'Morning Chronicle' office in hopes of finding Mr. Perry, but was for the moment disappointed, and rather alarmed at his position. A day or two later, however, the sky looked brighter; he had found Perry, and a warm and cordial welcome; and was speedily introduced to some of the chief literary men, Mackintosh, Rogers, Sydney Smith, and others of the Holland House set.

Among the poems sent by Campbell from Germany, and published in the 'Morning Chronicle,' the first was 'Lines on Visiting a Scene in Argyleshire;' the second, 'The Beech-tree's Petition.' 'The Exile of Erin' was published in that journal on the 28th of January, 1801, with this preface, "The meeting of the Imperial Parliament, we trust, will be distinguished by acts of mercy. The following most interesting and pathetic song, it is hoped, will induce them to extend their benevolence to those unfortunate men, whom delusion and error have doomed to exile, but who sigh for a return to their native homes." Two days after this appeared the spirited ' Ode to Winter;' and a little later, ' Ye Mariners of England,' under this title— " Alteration of the old ballad ' Ye Gentlemen of England,' composed on the prospect of a Russian war ;" which old ballad Campbell used to hear with delight, and often ask for, at the house of one of his Edinburgh friends. To the same period, that of his first sojourn in Germany, belong the germs of ' Hohenlinden,' 'The Soldier's Dream,' and ' The Battle of the Baltic;' but these remained unpublished, probably unfinished, for some considerable time afterwards.

Ten days after reaching London he was grieved by the news of his father's death, ninety-one years old very nearly. Nevermore should the son see that pious and placid old face, feel the pressure of that affectionate venerable hand. When the news came, delayed by various accidents, even the funeral was over. The good Dr. Anderson had assisted Mrs. Campbell in soothing the patriarch's last hours, and arranging the burial, at which fate did not allow a single one of the seven sons to be present. Campbell left London by Leith packet, and went to his widowed mother's humble house in Edinburgh, where she and her three daughters, all more or less invalids, were struggling to subsist on the scantiest means ; and it is easy to imagine how welcome was Tom's advent. On his part, out of a small and uncertain income, at first flowing entirely from a not too ready pen, and managed without the least financial faculty, he did what he could, now and always, to help them.

In spite of troubles, the Poet was now

at times in high spirits. Old scenes renewed their charm; old friends rejoiced to see him; a new edition of the 'Pleasures' was called for. He went much into Edinburgh literary society, notable both as poet and as eye-witness returned from the actual scenes of war. Scott, Jeffrey, and Telford the engineer were among his most frequent associates. On the other hand, he had no profession, no fixed employment whatever, no assured source of income. He hoped for some engagement as professor or at least temporary lecturer; but none could be found, perhaps none was sought in any business-like fashion. To clear off some family debts, he borrowed a sum of money at usurious interest; and altogether this summer must have been an anxious one for Campbell.

Some time in the autumn another turn of fortune came. At the house of Dugald Stewart he was introduced to Lord Minto, peer and diplomatist, who, taking a fancy to the Poet, induced him to become his guest at Minto, and afterwards, in the early part of the next year, 1802, to occupy a room in his house in Hanover Square, London. There Campbell took up his residence for the season, half guest, half occasional secretary; seeing something of high life, which pleased him little, and much of the selectest literary society of the capital, enchanting at first by its ease and brilliancy, but soon found to be superficial, satiating, and more wearisome than honest dulness. His health and spirits in this unaccustomed London life were often low; and he discovered for himself once more the universal experience that external appliances can do little for a man's happiness. Happy at times he was, no doubt; not amidst the fireworks of aristocratic and literary

London, "this scene of hurry and absurdity,"[1] but in his solitary room and solitary walks, while 'Hohenlinden' and 'Lochiel's Warning' were taking shape in his mind. These he slowly finished, as his manner was; often reading them to friends, and reflecting on their suggestions. These two poems were intended to appear in a new quarto edition of the 'Pleasures,' but he changed his mind and printed them by themselves anonymously, chiefly, it would seem, for private circulation. 'Lochiel' was after this much enlarged and improved, before it was allowed to take its place finally among the finished works of the author.

This autumn he spent chiefly at Minto Castle, little contented by the luxury there and the smiling talk of lords and ladies; hoping fervently all the time that Lord Minto will be able to " do something for him;" his lordship indeed being willing enough, if he can see what and how. Campbell, at this time twenty-five years old, is described[2] as " scrupulously neat in his dress, which, agreeably to the fashion of the day, consisted of a blue coat, with bright gilt buttons, a white waistcoat and cravat, buff nankins and white stockings, with shoes and silver buckles. His hair was already falling off; and he adopted the peruke, which was never afterwards laid aside."

At the end of October Campbell left Minto Castle for Edinburgh, where he stayed through the winter, revising a new handsome edition of poems in quarto, and writing or attempting to write some jobwork for the publishers; but doing both,

---

[1] Letter to John Richardson, Esq., Dr. Beattie's Life, i. 386.
[2] Dr. Beattie, Life, i. 405.

we conceive,—the latter especially,—in a slow and lazy fashion that justified the name "Procrastination Tom," which his friends sometimes applied to him.

In the end of March, 1803, we find him again in London, but at a coffeehouse and afterwards in lodgings, not at Lord Minto's ; again plunging into " society," and declaring that this kind of life is " absolutely a burning fever :" "I have one eternal round of invitations. . . . I have not one day free of headaches, nor one night of tolerable rest. . . . The expense is enormous." June, however, brought some consolation. The new quarto subscription edition came out, handsomely printed, with engravings ; and ' The Exile of Erin,' ' Lochiel,' ' Hohenlinden,' and other pieces, added to the ' Pleasures of Hope,'—of which the publishers, with prudent liberality (it being well for them to keep up the connection) had not insisted on claiming full copyright. Campbell again found himself in the novel situation of having some money in hand. Moreover, he was *in love.*

Mr. Robert Sinclair, kinsman to the poet by the mother's side, at this time lived in London ; his " counting-house " (business not described) being in Trinity Square, City, and his private residence in Park Street, Westminster, at which latter house Thomas Campbell was a frequent and welcome guest,—welcome above all to his cousin Matilda Sinclair, a lively and lady-like young woman. Emboldened by " subscriptions to his quarto still pouring in," and an actual " fifty-pound bank-note in his desk," Campbell *proposed.* Mr. Sinclair had his natural business doubts, but allowed them to be overcome ; and, in short,—

" September 10, 1803, in St. Margaret's, Westminster, Thomas Campbell, Esq., author of the 'Pleasures of Hope,' to Matilda, youngest daughter of Robert Sinclair, Esq., of Park Street, Westminster."

After a short wedding trip, the happy pair settled in " an elegant suite of rooms," at 25, Upper Eaton Street, Pimlico ; and the poet began a new chapter of experiences as married man. The pen was to be his magic wand wherewith to conjure up the solid necessaries of life. Mrs. Campbell, whose age was much the same as her husband's, was smallish but graceful, dark, somewhat Spanish-looking, with much vivacity of manner, and " a sensibility, or rather irritability, which often impaired her health." She had travelled on the continent, was a lively converser ; and often, too, her dark eyes had an expression of tender melancholy. A good, gentle, loving wife she proved ; but a sufferer from the sad drawback of always feeble health.

A year or so later the establishment was increased by a plump young gentleman with blue eyes—a baby of nervous parentage, and hiding, alas ! the seeds of cerebral disorder under his healthy appearance. And shortly after, Campbell took a house at Sydenham, then a beautiful furzy common, tree-fringed, with shady lanes and wide prospects, on a lease of twenty-one years, and there planted his little household. He had had hopes of settling near Edinburgh, in " a cottage ;" but London, all things considered, offered the best chance of earning. And at Sydenham he did stay seventeen years, and there on the whole had the most contented part of his uneasy and fidgety life ; an affectionate attentive wife and " lovely boy " at home—after a time, two boys ; friendly neighbours ; London within easy reach, but its noise and smoke kept aloof. As to work, being settled at Sydenham, he went on compiling certain "Annals" (modern history, a kind of continuation of Smollett), which he had engaged to do for his Edinburgh publisher, and wrote anonymously in various periodicals. On the "Star" newspaper he had a regular engagement. But daily writing for bread did not suit him at all; he was slow, dilatory, and extremely fastidious; made countless erasures, and in the end often threw the painfully elaborated manuscript into the fire. However, he managed to pull through from month to month in some tolerable manner, and to send his mother £50 a year, although his anxieties were often increased by attacks of illness. " By orders of my *gravelist*, and from better motives, I have laid aside every propensity to take one glass more than does me good."[1] He suffered much from sleeplessness; but " the wolf was at the door," and besides current expenses he had to pay usurious interest on money borrowed to furnish his house with—£40 a year on a loan of £200.[2] *Per contra*, he continued to receive remittances out of the sale of the quarto edition of the poems; but without, it seems, ever accurately knowing how much. He was, in fact, one of the worst arithmeticians: " I am always ready to shoot myself when I come to the subject of cash accounts."

" Of the poetical pieces," says Dr. Beattie,[3] " cautiously elaborated in the course of this year [1804], three only were permitted to see the light. These were—' Lord Ullin's Daughter,'

[1] To John Richardson, Esq., Sept. 10, 1804.
[2] His own statement, Life, ii. 28.
[3] Life, ii. 32.

' The Soldier's Dream,' and 'The Turkish Lady,' all of which had been sketched among the scenes to which they refer—the first in the Island of Mull, and the two latter in Bavaria, but were not revised and finished until he had retired to Sydenham.   The next on the anvil was the ' Battle of the Baltic;' it was composed at short intervals during the winter, and finished in April, but reduced, before publication, to nearly one-half of the original stanzas, as preserved in his letter to [Sir] Walter Scott."

Indeed the metre of this famous poem was changed, as witness the first stanza of the early version :—

> " 1. Of Nelson and the north
>   Sing the day.
>   When, their haughty powers to vex,
>   He engaged the Danish decks,
>   And with twenty floating wrecks
>   Crowned the fray."

In the same letter to Scott, March 27, 1805, he broaches a plan for " a collection of the best specimens of English poetry," inviting the co-operation of his brother bard, whose " Lay of the Last Minstrel" had just made its triumphant appearance.

A fortnight later he writes to Scott that the sea-song " is to go along with ' Lochiel' and ' Hohenlinden,' with the poems at the end of my quarto volume, and a little Turkish story about the siege of Belgrade, of which I know not what, how much or how little, or how much less than little, I may make of it. I was always a dead bad hand at telling a story; and " [curious remark!] " if your own poetry be excepted, I know no one in Scotland born who has the narrative faculty." In the same letter he requests a loan of £50; and the good Scott immediately sends a draft on Longmans for 50 *guineas*,—a handsomer formula, which authors and artists, like physicians, would do well to retain. The notion of the ‘British Poets’ expanded itself into a scheme of fifteen volumes, and about fifty lives; pay, for Scott and self, say £500 apiece. But after various negotiations, this proposal fell through; and what did take shape was the work known as ‘Campbell’s Specimens.’

In October, 1805, an important and lasting relief came to the poet’s distressed economics. (Sydney Smith, probably about this time, had conveyed to him “a munificent present” from Lady Holland.)[1] He was placed on the Pension List for £200 a year (it was only £168 nett). Campbell said he “never could discover the precise individual” to whom he was indebted for it; but, not to speak of the interest of Lord Minto, Lord Holland, and others, Charles Fox, then prime minister, was a known admirer. Half of this pension Campbell set aside for his mother and sisters.

Moreover,—for strokes of good fortune, too, seldom come single,—the poet’s friends, to whom his straitened condition was no secret, had set busily to work on a subscription list for another quarto edition of the poems, with the object of forming a permanent fund for his family. Mr. Francis Horner, writing to Mr. John Richardson, December 31, 1805,[2] is glad to hear “the subscription for Campbell is going on so prosperously,” and mentions that Mr. Pitt has put his name to it; but he at the same time suggests that Mr. Richardson should

---

[1] His own statement, Life, ii. 69.
[2] Life, ii. 76. .

counsel economy in the future. "You will be of great service to Campbell in this respect when you come to London, for nobody here knows him domestically enough to speak freely to him on these subjects. You must teach him to consider this subscription as an exertion which cannot with propriety, nor even, perhaps, with success, be tried another time; and that from this time he must look forward to a plan of income and expense wholly depending upon himself, and most strictly adjusted. He gets four guineas a week for translating foreign gazettes at the 'Star' office; it is not quite the best employment for a man of genius, but it occupies him only four hours of the morning, and the payment ought to go a great length in defraying his annual expenses." Very reasonable remarks, no doubt; though Campbell would scarcely have relished them, nor perhaps have looked upon " only four hours " every morning of newspaper drudgery as so light a matter.

The next three years may be glided quickly over in such a slight biographical sketch as this. We find Campbell tasting country air among the lanes and gorses of Sydenham, and coming frequently to town, now to the newspaper office in Carey Street ('Star' and 'Philosophical Magazine,'—both long forgotten), now to dine at Holland House, and discuss classics with Charles Fox and other celebrities. He also crept lazily along with his 'Annals' and 'Specimens of English Poetry.' Moreover, another son was born to him, whom he named Alison. He had long been casting about in vain for "a subject" for a new poem ; and at last, by accident, did catch (it seems from a German novel) the floating germ of a subject, which settling in his mind, shaped itself, by slow process of incubation, into 'Gertrude of Wyoming.' In August, 1808, he writes to Mr. Richardson: "I have given some touches of my best kind to the Second Part. I have some stanzas on the anvil which enchant myself; and though they may not enchant others, I am by these new lines growing a great deal more sanguine about the poem, which shall be out at Christmas, D.V. I am in high love with the work." Afterwards, in January, he writes in another mood: "I have finished the stanzas of the last sheet of 'Gertrude' according to their *new* alteration. I am tired with the poem myself." Having been, as usual, submitted to the criticism of friends, and often re-touched, the new poem at length made its appearance in public in April, 1809, heralded (for the article appeared on the very day of publication) by an emphatic trumpet-blast of eulogy (blown by his friend Jeffrey) from that conspicuous tower of criticism, the 'Edinburgh Review.' Along with 'Gertrude,' in the handsome quarto, were printed the 'Mariners of England,' 'The Battle of the Baltic,' 'Glenara,' and 'Lord Ullin's Daughter;' and in a new edition, which appeared in the following spring, 'O'Connor's Child' was added.

'Gertrude' is an elegant and highly finished composition, "with those soft and skyish tints of purity and truth"—as Jeffrey said in a letter to the poet [1]—"which fall like enchantment on all minds that can make anything of such matters." The handling of the Spenserian stanza recalls the 'Castle of Indolence;' but while Thomson has with good effect imitated the antique fashion of the 'Faery Queen,' Campbell

---

[1] March 1, 1809.

has shown equal judgment in preferring a select
modern style, the few deviations from which are
perhaps blemishes — as "mickle glee" (part i.
st. 6), and "bower" (iii. 10).   A more pervading
fault (which runs, indeed, through nearly all
Campbell's poetry) is the use of hollow, conventional diction, and trite embellishments—"cherub
infancy," "unconscious fascinations," "nature's
fervid feelings,"

> " Adieu ! sweet scion of the setting sun !
>   But should affection's storms thy blossom mock,
>   Then come again, my own adopted one ! "

> " Roll on, ye days of raptured influence, shine ! "

and too many such.   It would, perhaps, be im-
possible to read ' Gertrude ' aloud and with due
emphasis to an audience of the present day without the risk of exciting risibility at least as often
as the nobler emotions.   It may be doubted
whether the culminating situation would convey
its intended deep pathos through these words
of the heroine, fatally wounded by an Indian
volley :—

> " And faltering, on her Waldegrave's bosom thrown,
>   ' Weep not, O love,' she cries, ' to see me bleed;
>   Thee, Gertrude's sad survivor, thee alone
>   Heaven's peace commiserate ! for scarce I heed
> These wounds—yet thee to leave is death, is death indeed !'"

A mixture of the extremely artificial and conventional with manly directness and vigour is
peculiar to Campbell, and perhaps traceable partly
to the anxiety with which he touched and re-
touched and polished his work.   The picture
was often too much worked upon,—to borrow an
illustration from the studio; though the charm
of spontaneity still survived in many happy passages. The landscapes in this poem, though vague,

have much sweetness of colour. Byron says ("Diary," Jan. 11, 1821), "'Gertrude' has no more locality in common with Pennsylvania than with Penmanmawr. It is notoriously full of grossly false scenery, as all Americans declare, though they praise parts of the poem." In a note to a subsequent edition Campbell apologised for his error in describing Brandt as a "monster;" but left the passage unaltered!

Lines from the poem have become "familiar quotations," as where Outalassi is called

> " The stoic of the woods—a man without a tear ;"

or Gertrude's eyes are pictured,

> " affectionate and glad,
> That seem'd to love whate'er they look'd upon ;"

or mortal happiness is described as

> " The torrent's smoothness ere it dash below."

The general form into which the poem is cast shows the hand of a true artist. He strikes at once, yet not abruptly, a premonitory note of pathos :—

> " On Susquehanna's side, fair Wyoming !
>   Although the wild flower on thy ruin'd wall,
>   And roofless homes, a sad remembrance bring
>   Of what thy gentle people did befall ;
>   Yet wert thou once the loveliest land of all
>   That see the Atlantic wave their morn restore.
>   Sweet land ! may I thy lost delights recall,
>   And paint thy Gertrude in her bower of yore,
> Whose beauty was the love of Pennsylvania's shore."

And ends tellingly with the Indian's lyrical burst of grief and expectation of revenge, leaving the action to be carried further in the reader's imagination :—

> " ' And I could weep,'—th' Oneyda chief
>   His descant wildly thus begun,—

> ' But that I may not stain with grief
>   The death-song of my father's son,
>   Or bow this head in woe!
> For by my wrongs, and by my wrath,
> To-morrow Areouski's breath
> (That fires yon heaven with storms of death)
>   Shall light us to the foe ;
> And we shall share, my Christian boy,
> The foeman's blood, the avenger's joy !' "

It may nevertheless be questioned, whether the piecing of a lyrical measure into the Spenserian, such as we find here (as in ' Childe Harold '), is entirely satisfactory. In spite of Campbell's fastidiousness, two somewhat glaring Scotticisms have crept into ' Gertrude.'—" We know not other," (ii. 6) instead of " each other ; " and " cataract " rhyming to " slack," " back," " rack " (iii. 14), which however is not so bad as rhyming it to "walk," as Mr. Moir did, the ' Delta,' of Blackwood's Magazine.

The rhyme " cataracts " " backs " occurs too in ' O'Connor's Child.' That exquisitely finished poem, added to the second edition of ' Gertrude,' is somewhat misty in its outlines. The time is in the earlier years of the English settlement in Ireland. The nameless heroine, a daughter of one of the royal O'Connors, has a lover of inferior rank; with whom she runs away. Her fierce brothers pursue, find their place of refuge, slay Connocht Moran, and drag their sister home again. She, distracted, utters a wild curse on her own family and clan as they issue forth to battle against the English chivalry, and to destruction. Then, out of her mind, sometimes raving, other times melancholy, " O'Connor's pale and lovely child " takes up her abode in a solitary shieling; and there, one day, to a passing stranger she tells her tragic story. Somewhat misty in outline, as we say, if not indeed a vapoury thing altogether. 'Castle-Connor,' and the rest of the scenery and decorations are about as truthful as those of a romantic opera. Yet it is dyed with delicate ethereal tints, and the versification is delicious.

If Geoffrey Chaucer or William Shakespeare, or John Milton, had died at the age of thirty-two, great indeed had been our unknown losses ; no 'Canterbury Tales,' no 'Paradise Lost,' no 'Lear,' 'Macbeth,' 'Tempest,' and many another $\kappa\tau\tilde{\eta}\mu\alpha$ $\grave{\epsilon}\varsigma$ $\dot{\alpha}\epsilon\acute{\iota}$. But if Thomas Campbell's mortal course had ended at that age, his fame would stand no hair-breadth lower than it does, nor were English poetry the poorer,—though he did afterwards write some fine lines.

His life at Sydenham flowed on, bringing its series of events, its gains and losses, domestic and other, more or less momentous to those concerned, but with little matter for record. In July 1810 his second little boy, Alison, died of scarlet fever ; and in February 1812 his good old mother breathed her last, near Edinburgh, at the age of seventy-six. In April of this year, Campbell began a series of five lectures on Poetry, at the Royal Institution, which were successfully accomplished (in spite of a tendency to Scotch accent), and made the poet a more prominent object *pro tem.* in London society. About the same time (killing two birds with one stone) he was engaged upon his 'Specimens of the British Poets,' for Mr. Murray. In the autumn of 1814, he made one of the crowd of English who ran to Paris ; where he met Madame de Staël, Denon, Schlegel, Humboldt, and other celebrities, saw a good deal of Mrs. Siddons, and was presented to the Duke himself.

As to finances, our Poet, always the same wretched arithmetician, and always rather free-handed, not alone to his mother and sisters, but often to strangers, had up to this time managed to scramble along, with the help of his wife's care and frugality; not seldom stopping a gap by the expensive method of money borrowed on exorbitant interest. Even with the pension, he had only just managed to keep going. The spring of 1815 did him a good turn; a bag of money tumbled at his feet, as though out of the clouds, on the death of a Highland cousin, MacArthur Stewart by name. The old man (one of his family reported) had said " little Tommy the Poet ought to have a legacy, because he had been so kind as to give his mother £60 a year out of his pension," and so put him down for £500; but Campbell luckily was also named a 'residuary legatee,' and there proved to be so much 'residue' to divide, that his share mounted altogether to close on £4,500 clear. Henceforward he had an assured annual income of between four and five hundred pounds, no bad backbone for a modest housekeeping.

After years of preparation, in his lazy and fastidious way (the fear of an uncorrected misprint would cause him a sleepless night), the ' Specimens of the British Poets ' were at length published, in the spring of 1816; with a prefatory essay coming down to Pope, and short lives of the later poets. Campbell's judgments appear to me sound and reasonable for the most part, sometimes acute; and are always clearly expressed. But there are singularly glaring errors; for example, " Herrick and Cowley stood at the head of Donne's metaphysical followers, were generally loose and rugged in their versification and preposterous in their metaphors " (*Herrick !*); and, among the later select ones, a whole regiment of obscure versifiers, like the military *supers* of the theatre, march past indistinguishably dull. One particular piece gains an accidental interest as showing how tolerant a true poet like Campbell could be of the most frigid and stilted conventionality of diction. In one of his letters to Scott [1] he calls 'The Field of Battle,' by Thomas Penrose, "one of the very finest poems in the English language;" and it has its place accordingly in the 'Specimens.' It begins—

> " Faintly bray'd the battle's roar
>   Distant down the hollow wind;
> Panting terror fled before,
>   Wounds and death were left behind."—

goes on—

> " O'er the sad scene of dreariest view,
>   Abandon'd all to horrors wild,
> With frantic step Maria flew,
>   Maria, Sorrow's early child."

and ends—

> " Her ghastly hope was well-nigh fled—
>   When late pale Edgar's form she found,
> Half buried with the hostile dead,
>   And gored with many a grisly wound.
>
> She knew—she sunk—the night-bird scream'd,—
>   The moon withdrew her troubled light,
> And left the fair, though fall'n she seem'd,
>   To worse than death, and deepest night."

This ballad, in fourteen stanzas, no doubt made its impression on the poet's mind in very juvenile days (battle-subjects always took hold of him) and suggested his own ' Wounded Hussar;' but it is curious that in the maturity of his judgment he could include it—and fifty still worse productions, in a collection of the choicest specimens.

[1] Life, 256.

The introductory Essay included a defence of Pope against some strictures of an editor of that poet, (Pope has certainly been rather unlucky in his editors!) the Rev. William Lisle Bowles, who gave as one reason for placing Pope in a lower rank among poets than that usually assigned to him, that his images are drawn from art rather than from nature. Campbell in defending Pope, said the greatest poets had drawn some of their noblest imagery from artificial objects, and also instanced the launching of a ship of the line as one of " the sublime objects of artificial life." The passage is an example of his best prose writing. " Of that spectacle I can never forget the impression, and of having witnessed it reflected from the faces of ten thousand spectators. They seem yet before me, I sympathise with their deep and silent expectation, and with their final burst of enthusiasm. It was not a vulgar joy, but an affecting national solemnity. When the vast bulwark sprang from her cradle, the calm water on which she swung majestically round, gave the imagination a contrast of the stormy element on which she was soon to ride. All the days of battle and nights of danger which she had to encounter, all the ends of the earth which she had to visit, and all that she had to do and to suffer for her country rose in awful presentiment before the mind; and when the heart gave her a benediction, it was like one pronounced on a living being." An admired and elegant passage—yet not satisfactory; felt to be itself somewhat artificial both in substance and in style; in plain truth, *depth* there is nowhere in Campbell's writing, whether prose or verse. Mr. Bowles rejoined; and argued that the new ship owed her poetry chiefly to the water and wind and sunshine, and the associated ideas of

voyaging to distant lands, tempests to be encoun-
tered, &c. Lord Byron took up the cudgels on
Campbell's side of the controversy, and laid about
him with scornful vigour, and other combatants
joined the fray, which made a good deal of noise
in the world of letters.

Campbell had said in his Essay, " There are
exclusionists in taste, who think that they cannot speak with sufficient disparagement of the
English poets of the first part of the eighteenth
century; and they are armed with a noble pro-
vocative to English contempt, when they have it
to say that those poets belong to a French school.
Indeed, Dryden himself is generally included in
that school; though more genuine English is to
be found in no man's pages. But in poetry ' there
are many mansions.'" Curious to observe once
more (for it is no rare experience) how a critic
who was thus broad in doctrine retrospectively,
showed himself extremely narrow in sympathy
when he turned to contemporary literature.
Things may be too near us to be properly seen.

In 1820 Campbell revisited Germany (the Rhine,
Vienna, &c.) and stayed away from May till No-
vember. Before starting, he signed an agreement
with Mr. Colburn the publisher, to take the edi-
torship of the ' New Monthly Magazine' for three
years, annual salary £500, and the publisher pro-
viding a sub-editor. Campbell had recently been
delivering a revised and improved series of lectures
on poetry at the Royal Institution; which lectures
he agreed to publish in the magazine, and also to
supply six contributions in verse. Thus his three
years' share in the writing was easily enough provided for; and as to the editing, he managed that
by the method of doing as little as possible, leaving
it almost entirely, except the vaguest sort of super-

vision, to his sub-editor, Mr. Cyrus Redding. His name, however, proved to be a good signboard; the magazine for some time flourished; the agreement between editor and publisher was renewed, and Campbell held his post—always acting consistently on the minimum-of-work principle—for ten years in all. In 1824 he published 'Theodric, a Domestic Tale,' which though quiet and unromantic, he expected, he wrote to his sister,[1] would "attain a steady popularity." But this expectation was never fulfilled. It was found tame, and had no one line or phrase that passed into currency. It has the merit, however, of a subdued harmony of tone; and the pathos (see, near the end, the last five lines of Constance's letter) is conveyed in simpler and more touching language than in 'Gertrude.'

We must touch more hastily on the prominent incidents of his middle and later life. Those who desire a closer acquaintance will consult the biography of the poet by his steadfast and affectionate old friend, Dr. Beattie. He gave up his little house at Sydenham after comparatively peaceful years, and moved into town; living first in Margaret Street, then for some years in Seymour Street West. Here his good wife, whose health had long been feeble, died (May 9, 1828) and left his hearth desolate. His son, his only living child, had shown at an early age symptoms of mental disorder, and had some years before this been placed in a private asylum. It was a sad state now, that of Campbell; the evening of life drawing in, and he lonely in the world. His health had never been strong, and henceforward alternate nervous irritability and melancholia in-

---

[1] Life, ii. 434.

creased upon him, from which he sometimes sought temporary relief in too much wine. All the rest of his life, he unhappily kept chopping and changing his residence, was for ever furnishing and unfurnishing, his books and papers in admired disorder, and his whole condition almost one of chronic *flitting.* Many journeys, too, he made hither and thither, often suddenly and to no adequate purpose, and finding, it is to be feared, in change of place no change of pain. Of various literary enterprises in which he engaged at the instance of publishers—'Life of Petrarch,' 'Life and Times of Frederick the Great,' little need be said. It was job-work, which he did reluctantly and lazily; his name was advertised, his fee paid, and so many volumes were added to the waste paper of the world. The 'Life of Mrs. Siddons' had a more promising origin, in his admiration and friendship for the actress, but he flagged in the execution, and it also is but a poor piece of work.

Viewed less closely, however, his life would have seemed far from unprosperous. The newspaper reader of the day would have heard of Thomas Campbell, Esq., the celebrated poet, lecturing with great applause, speaking at public dinners, founding an 'Association of the Friends of Poland,' chosen Lord Rector of the University of Glasgow, twice Lord Rector, nay, *thrice,*—a rare, if not unprecedented honour. All these—whether we reckon them as important as they might seem to the newspaper reader of the day, and perhaps did to Campbell himself—or count them to be in the main wasteful futilities (for out of his threefold Rectorship sprung a plentiful crop of correspondence, journeys, speeches, banquets, &c. &c.)—took up a very large part of Campbell's time and filled it with feverish unrest.   Unwholesome as that was, he perhaps welcomed it as an alternative to dark and torpid despondency; for the hearth-fire of his domestic joy, as we have seen, was quite gone out; his body, never strong, troubled him more and more, and he exasperated its evils by frequent neglect of regimen.   His local surroundings were seldom comfortable, and disturbed by the frequent changes of residence ; and his financial management was so bad that it was a miracle how he escaped without any serious crisis.   Not that, after early days, he was ever really bare of money. He had his pension, his legacy, his editor's salary, his author's profits, his subscription editions; his friend Telford left him £1000, and another friend £200. His money difficulties, trivial and perpetual, not dangerous, and resulting in loss to nobody, all came from mismanagement.   He never knew how his accounts stood; used to leave his purse at home on starting on a journey, and come back for it perhaps a hundred miles.   One summer, being in Germany, he wrote to Dr. Beattie saying he had locked up a parcel of bank-notes in his bedroom press in Victoria Square, Westminster (where he had at this time taken a small house), and requesting him to find the money and send him £50.   The doctor, accompanied by his solicitor, searched the press, but found no bank-notes ; searched every repository in the room, and in every room of the house, drawers, desks, canisters, coatpockets, &c., all in vain.   Again they tried the bedroom, again without result, till, in shutting a wardrobe door, Dr. Beattie found the point of an embroidered slipper in the way and pushed it aside; it felt hard, he picked it up, and behold, it was stuffed full of little rolls of white paper, like spills to light caudles with, which, in short, were Bank of England notes. The other slipper proved equally rich, and the pair yielded a sum of more than £300.

The Polish Society was established in rooms in Duke Street, St. James's Square, and Campbell appointed 'Perpetual Chairman;' and in meetings, subscriptions, correspondence, interviews, dinners, &c. &c., connected with the cause of Poland, he spent a vast deal of time, exertion, and money. Another undertaking in which he was prime mover was 'The Literary Club,' intended to be the most choicely intellectual and superior of all possible clubs, and started with splendid names and high hope; but which, after it had cost him much trouble and vexation, and probably some money, fell insolvent, and was shut up. He was more successful in the project for the London University, of which he was in his own opinion the originator—was certainly a chief and active promoter; which project was launched before the public by Brougham in 1825, and has grown into what we see.

We have spoken of Campbell's frequent journeyings, short and long, often undertaken on a sudden impulse. In 1834, being in Paris, he was seized with a desire to visit Algeria, did so, and stayed in that country the winter and spring; returning to London " in improved health, looking, as every one observed, some years younger than when he set forth on his travels." And indeed, some years later, when he had passed his *grand climacteric*, we find him rejoicing in an easier state of body than usual during the greater part of his life. Soon after this, however, a change for the worse set in, and he rapidly turned into an old man. He published an account of his visit to

Algeria in the 'Metropolitan Magazine,' and afterwards in book form, under the title of 'Letters from the South.'

In 1842 (age sixty-four) he published 'The Pilgrim of Glencoe, with other Poems,' but this volume found even less favour than 'Theodric.' 'The Pilgrim,' written a good deal in the style of Crabbe, had scarce more substance than would have sufficed for a ballad. New and brilliant lights were rising on the poetic horizon. The volume had no chance of success; and the expected fountain of "profits" stood dry and dusty; whereupon Campbell, always not only a bad financier but a liberal giver to those who claimed his help, began to find his purse low and to fear the pinch of straitened means.

The latest of many removals, to 8, Victoria Square, had not given him the comfort expected from it, and the house now seemed too expensive to keep up. He resolved to dispose of it, and to quit London altogether, and even England, for some cheap and pleasant spot on the Continent. After no little questioning, he fixed on Boulogne for his future abode; discovering, as usual, prospectively, a number of advantages, most of which experience, as usual, proved to be imaginary. July 13th, 1843, found the poet, with a niece who now lived with him, in the French seaport; and while summer and autumn lasted, the place pleased him well: but with winter came freezing weather, loneliness, home-sickness, and, worst of all, increase of the symptoms of disease (liver); continual chilliness among them, with languor and debility. He gradually dropped all personal intercourse with acquaintances, and would see no visitors; but reading was still a pleasure, and music. "He was always fond of music, particularly those airs with which he had been familiar in early life. His great favourite was the Marseillaise hymn, which he first heard at Ratisbon, in 1800; and he now listened with evident satisfaction while Miss Campbell played it to him."[1] When he did converse or write a rare letter to Dr. Beattie, he still preserved a cheerful tone and an interest in his usual subjects of thought.

Spring brought some flush of improvement to the invalid; but a transient one, soon followed by increase of bad symptoms and decay of strength. Receiving ever worse accounts, the good Dr. Beattie, in the beginning of June, crossed the Channel, accompanied by his wife, and repaired to the poet's bedside. "The arrival of old friends seemed to revive him; his words were, as he held my hand—'Visit of angels from heaven.' ... He spoke to each with a faint smile, but in few words, and with that peculiar lightning of the eye which gave forcible expression to all he said."[2] Ten days the friends took their turns, day and night, at the dying man's bed. After much restlessness, quiet hours came on. It was a Saturday afternoon, June the 15th, 1844; the mild sea-breeze flowed into the open window of the room in the Upper Town; the face, turned on its left side and propped with pillows, was silently watched by loving eyes, that found it now sharper and more defined than they knew it, but perfectly serene, save for a slight convulsive twitch at times. At two o'clock he opened his eyes, then closed them again. "At a quarter past four (wrote Dr. Beattie in his journal) our beloved poet, Thomas Campbell, expired, without a struggle. His niece, Dr. Allott, and myself were standing by his bedside. The

---

[1] Life, iii. 362.   [2] Life, iii. 367.

last sound he uttered was a short faint shriek—
such as a person utters at the sudden appearance
of a friend, expressive of pleasure and surprise.
This may seem fanciful, but I know of nothing
else that it might be said to resemble."[1]

Two days after, casts of the head and right
hand were taken. "The head is remarkable in
shape, the natural form was quite concealed by
the peruke which he wore for more than forty
years." One would have liked more particulars
therefore. Where is the cast? It would be of
rather more interest than Sir Thomas Lawrence's
dandified picture, or Mr. Marshall's theatrical
statue.

Was his grave to be in Glasgow Cemetery or in
Westminster Abbey? In the abbey, it was decided; the Dean and Chapter agreeing, and the
fee (over £70) being duly paid. On July the 3rd
was the funeral; present, among many other men
of distinction, Sir Robert Peel, then premier, Lord
Brougham, Mr. Benjamin Disraeli, Mr. Macaulay,
Mr. Thackeray; there were also numerous Poles,
and a guard of Polish nobles. The grave is in
the aisle of Poet's Corner; and the name upon the
stone, I may add, is already beginning to be ob-
literated: but not so from our selection-books
and memories, the 'Soldier's Dream,' 'Lord
Ullin's Daughter,' 'Hohenlinden,' and the rest.

Campbell was lucky in the launch of his first
venture. Edinburgh was small enough to be
occupied with the appearance of a new poem, by
a Scotchman to boot; and important enough to
stamp it with a recommendation. He wrote in
the taste of the time, yet with recognizable ori-
ginality, and he handled topics of immediate,

---

[1] Life, iii. 377. Dr. Beattie himself, while we write
(March, 1875), has also passed out of this world.

though not ephemeral interest. His battle-pieces, too, on names and subjects known to all, had the true popular ring, a bold tramp of metre. When closely examined, perhaps nothing great can be found in his work. A poet is apt to be more or less like the mountain to which "distance lends enchantment;" standing a blue jewel on the horizon, a beacon and landmark to many valleys, the climber finds much of it to be rough, dull and barren, and its geologic structure forces itself on his attention. But neither is the microscopic view of the mountain the true one. Little matters, how Campbell managed to produce 'Ye Mariners of England,' the 'Soldier's Dream,' tho 'Battle of the Baltic,' the fine passages of the 'Pleasures of Hope,' 'Gertrude,' and 'O'Connor's Child,' Indeed, *how*, exactly, no critical acumen could by any possibility find out. He had *the touch*; that is what is certain. Numberless English verses were written during his career by men and women all over the globe, but it so happened, and passing time has made it clearer, that in particular qualities he excelled all others, even of the good artists, of his school; which school was not, however, the highest. In art, nothing succeeds *but* success; a man can only prove the possibility of doing a thing by actually doing it. How many hundred English landscape painters (for an illustration) have for a century gone on painting how many thousand landscapes : then, after slow process of elimination, we begin to find the handiwork of a Crome, a Cotman, a Mason, placed by general consent in the choicest places of private and public galleries, while ninety per cent. of their contemporaries are forgotten or hung in garrets.

The 'Exile of Erin' is a somewhat artificial production ; we are afflicted with a sense of unreality in "the bold anthem of Erin-go-bragh," and the harp covered with "wild-woven flowers :" neither actual Ireland (which the poet by the bye never saw at any time of his life), nor an actual Irish exile, are hinted to our imagination. But the metre, as usual with Campbell, carries one forward like the springy movement of a good horse,—

> " ' Sad is my fate !' said the heart-broken stranger :
>   ' The wild deer and wolf to a covert can flee,
>   But I have no refuge from famine and danger,
>   A home and a country remain not to me.'

As faults of detail I must reckon the awkwardness of

> " One dying wish my lone bosom can draw ;"

the rhyme (both common and licentious), of " wild wood" and " childhood"; and in particular, the scenery of the first stanza. " Twilight" at once suggests *evening* twilight, the natural time for such musings, and we are startled and confused to find in the next line but one that *morning* twilight is meant, and that the " day-star" is rising. That the Exile in his thin robe should be wandering by the wind-beaten hill at such an hour, struck me when I first read the poem in my boyhood, and equally strikes me now, not as pathetic but absurd; nor is it easy to conceive how the sun could rise o'er his own native isle of the ocean. Certainly it never could if the exile were at Hamburgh, or any point of the European continent; and if we place him in America, the geographical interval is so great, as much to damage, if not to destroy, the naturalness of the thought. Anthony McCann, straying sad one evening on the bank of the Elbe, has been so much ' idealized,' that his own mother would hardly know him.   In fact, Campbell himself tells us he saw Anthony on a hillside above the Elbe, watching the day-star *set* over his beloved Erin—in that direction at all events; and why the poet did not simply write 'set' instead of 'rose' in the song is to me a dark enigma.[1]

'Glenara' shows great skill in the difficult feat of compression.   A dramatic story is put before us in thirty-two lines; and the solemn scene of the funeral on the moorland comes out with a few strong touches.   Perhaps there is a little blur of obscurity at one or two points which might have been cleared away.   The last stanza unluckily is the worst:—

> "In dust, low the traitor has knelt to the ground,
> And the desert reveal'd where his lady was found;
> From a rock of the ocean that beauty is borne—
> Now joy to the house of fair Ellen of Lorn."

It needs reflection to discover the simple meaning of the second line.   'And revealed the hid place,' or 'disclosed the hid place,' would be better, though not good.   This poem is founded on a traditionary, perhaps true story; and a small, rocky island, between Mull and the mainland, is shown as that on which the chieftain placed his wife in durance, giving out that she was dead.   The scene of the still finer ballad,

---

[1] "Hamburgh, Sept. 14, 1825.   I found my Exile of Erin as glad to see me as if we had but parted a quarter of a year instead of a quarter of a century.   Tony and I repaired to the spot where we had often walked when the day-star was setting in the west over our country.   It is now a tea-garden on a hill that overlooks a long course of the Elbe, and the prospect from it is compared by the natives to the view from Richmond Hill."   Letter of Campbell, Life, ii. 444.

'Lord Ullin's Daughter,' is also in the West Highlands, Loch Gyle, a branch of Loch Long. If we were required to crown the finest of modern narrative ballads, it would not be an easy thing to find any competitors fit to enter the lists against 'Lord Ullin's Daughter.' The subject is simple and interesting, the situation dramatic, the scenery grand, the crisis pathetic; we pity all— the lovers, the father, and, not least, the brave ferryman. The treatment is broad, concise, direct; the language at once natural and vigorous, the rhythm and rhyme are as far from forcing as from commonplace. In repeating the magnificent stanza,—

> " By this the storm grew loud apace,
>   The water-wraith was shrieking;
>   And in the scowl of heaven each face
>   Grew dark as they were speaking,"—

I have always striven hard to retain my first impression that the water-wraith was some kind of sea-bird, though it must, I fear, be acknowledged that the poet meant a ghost. He had a weakness for supernatural articles, and could produce them at unfortunate times, witness that absurd singing mermaid in 'The Battle of the Baltic.' I do not say but the shriek of the " water - wraith " might have been effectively brought into the ballad; as it stands it is incongruous and disturbing, a touch of wrong colour; the only defect, I think, in a priceless little work of art. One even finer is 'The Soldier's Dream.' The subject is of universal interest, and so obvious that one wonders how it had escaped being used a thousand times. It is here presented with such union of conciseness and completeness, easy vigour of language and metre, justness of proportions and harmony of colouring, as make up a result that looks natural and simple as daisy in green field; but how rare and precious, those best know who best know and love the lyric muse. The true dream-like transition, sudden yet not startling, in the third stanza, "'Twas Autumn," &c., is most admirable. 'Ye Mariners of England' is very much a bit of good luck, springing, as it does, directly and avowedly, both as to subject and form, from the old song of Martyn Parker:—

> " Ye Gentlemen of England,
>   That live at home at ease,
> Ah ! little do you think upon
>   The dangers of the seas.
> Give ear unto the mariners,
>   And they will plainly show
> All the cares and the fears
>   When the stormy winds do blow.

> " If enemies oppose us,
>   When England is at war
> With any foreign nation,
>   We fear not wound or scar;
> Our roaring guns shall teach 'em
>   Our valour for to know,
> Whilst they reel on the keel,
>   And the stormy winds do blow," &c.

But luck is only luck to him that can use it; and there was but one man living from whom the variation on the old strain could have come in such a form as,—

> " Britannia needs no bulwarks,
>   No towers along the steep;
> Her march is o'er the mountain-waves,
>   Her home is on the deep."

The rushing vigour and sonority of its lines will long keep the battle sketch, 'Hohenlinden,' in our selection books. In 'Lochiel's Warning' Campbell had chosen a strong and pathetic subject, and used his favourite galloping metre with great

skill and effect, giving us some of his happiest
lines :—

> " O weep ! but thy tears cannot number the dead."

> " And like reapers descend to the harvest of death."

> " When her bonneted chieftains to victory crowd,
>   Clanronald the dauntless, and Moray the proud,
>   All plaided and plumed in their tartan array."

> " And coming events cast their shadows before."

But the wave of eloquence surges at times into
bombast, and the whole impression left is theatrical rather than solemn and heroic. I must count
among bad faults of execution, the use of "Lochiel"
as a trisyllable ; and it is an awkward line,
" A field of the dead rushes red on my sight."
" 'Tis the sunset of life gives me mystical lore"
seems a clever rather than an admirable thought,
an exercise of the fancy, a line made to fit its
famous fellow (of " the coming events"), which
latter is said to have suddenly occurred to the
poet in the watches of the night ; he started up,
lit a candle, and secured it in black on white.
Neither can I like those images of

> " The red eye of battle is closed in despair,"

and

> " Say, mounts he to ocean wave, banish'd, forlorn,
>   Like a limb from his country cast bleeding and torn."

There is already a superabundance of blood in
the picture. No one but Campbell could have
written 'Lochiel,' but he has also written things
better in style. The 'Battle of the Baltic'
shows his special powers in war-business ; the
stanzas are like salvoes of artillery,—

> " Spread a death-shade round the ships
>   Like the hurricane eclipse
>   Of the sun ;"

and other passages, are unsurpassable in their kind. Some faults there may be; "their bulwarks on the brine" must sound odd to a sailor's ear, since 'bulwarks,' here put for ships, means nautically a part of a ship, and a part which is never "on the brine," save in a wreck. "Now joy, Old England, *raise!*" is not a happy expedient for getting a rhyme to "blaze." And the last stanza we could almost wish to expunge bodily :—

> " Soft sigh the winds of Heaven o'er their grave !
> While the billow mournful rolls "—

is not in any keeping with the fine close of the preceding stanza,—

> " Let us think of them that sleep
> Full many a fathom deep,
> By thy wild and stormy steep,
> Elsinore !"

and the ' mermaid,' whose

> " Song condoles,
> Singing glory to the souls
> Of the brave !"

is indeed a strange monster.

In the second rank, among Campbell's lyrics, might be reckoned ' Field Flowers,' ' Ode to Winter,' ' The Beechtree's Petition,' ' On visiting a Scene in Argyleshire;' and a piece, produced in his later period, which perhaps may stand with these, is the ' Lines on the Camp Hill, near Hastings.' But many of his other short poems have the unmistakable stamp of our artist upon them. Compared as lyrical writers, Campbell seems to me to have a finer touch than Scott or Byron, the former of whom is apt to be rough, the latter turgid. Among predecessors, Cowper, in his lines on ' The Loss of the Royal George,' most reminds us of Campbell.

But in whatever rank one or another reader may place the poetry of Thomas Campbell, all will agree that he has made genuine additions to English literature ; we could not afford to lose them ; and he who has done this has done no small thing.

Glasgow, while we write, is planning a statue to her poet. It is easier to raise a monument to poet or prophet than to lay up his teaching in our hearts. Glasgow is not likely to choose for inscription on the pedestal of her Campbell, those strong and heartfelt lines of his, ' On Revisiting a Scottish River,'[1] albeit they are of more intimate concern to Glasgow than all else he has ever written.

[1] Page 178 of this book.

THE PLEASURES OF HOPE.

IN TWO PARTS.

ANALYSIS OF PART I.

The poem opens with a comparison between the beauty of remote objects in a landscape, and those ideal scenes of felicity which the imagination delights to contemplate—the influence of anticipation upon the other passions is next delineated—an allusion is made to the well-known fiction in Pagan tradition, that, when all the guardian deities of mankind abandoned the world, Hope alone was left behind —the consolations of this passion in situations of danger and distress —the seaman on his watch—the soldier marching into battle— allusion to the interesting adventures of Byron.

The inspiration of Hope, as it actuates the efforts of genius, whether in the department of science, or of taste—domestic felicity, how intimately connected with views of future happiness—picture of a mother watching her infant when asleep—pictures of the prisoner, the maniac, and the wanderer.

From the consolations of individual misery a transition is made to prospects of political improvement in the future state of society—the wide field that is yet open for the progress of humanizing arts among uncivilized nations—from these views of amelioration of society, and the extension of liberty and truth over despotic and barbarous countries, by a melancholy contrast of ideas, we are led to reflect upon the hard fate of a brave people recently conspicuous in their struggles for independence—description of the capture of Warsaw, of the last contest of the oppressors and the oppressed, and the massacre of the Polish patriots at the bridge of Prague—apostrophe to the self-interested enemies of human improvement—the wrongs of Africa— the barbarous policy of Europeans in India—prophecy in the Hindoo mythology of the expected descent of the Deity to redress the miseries of their race, and to take vengeance on the violators of justice and mercy.

PART I.

AT summer eve, when Heaven's ethereal bow
    Spans with bright arch the glittering hills below,
Why to yon mountain turns the musing eye,

Whose sunbright summit mingles with the sky?
Why do those cliffs of shadowy tint appear
More sweet than all the landscape smiling near?—
'Tis distance lends enchantment to the view,
And robes the mountain in its azure hue.
Thus, with delight, we linger to survey
The promised joys of life's unmeasured way;
Thus, from afar, each dim-discover'd scene
More pleasing seems than all the past hath been,
And every form, that Fancy can repair
From dark oblivion, glows divinely there.
   What potent spirit guides the raptured eye
To pierce the shades of dim futurity?
Can Wisdom lend, with all her heavenly power,
The pledge of Joy's anticipated hour?
Ah, no! she darkly sees the fate of man—
Her dim horizon bounded to a span;
Or, if she hold an image to the view,
'Tis Nature pictured too severely true.
With thee, sweet Hope! resides the heavenly light,
That pours remotest rapture on the sight:
Thine is the charm of life's bewilder'd way,
That calls each slumbering passion into play.
Waked by thy touch, I see the sister-band,
On tiptoe watching, start at thy command,
And fly where'er thy mandate bids them steer,
To Pleasure's path, or Glory's bright career.
   Primeval Hope, the Aönian Muses say,
When Man and Nature mourn'd their first decay;
When every form of death, and every woe,
Shot from malignant stars to earth below;
When Murder bared her arm, and rampant War
Yoked the red dragons of her iron car;
When Peace and Mercy, banish'd from the plain,
Sprung on the viewless winds to Heaven again;
All, all forsook the friendless, guilty mind,
But Hope, the charmer, linger'd still behind.

Thus, while Elijah's burning wheels prepare
From Carmel's heights to sweep the fields of air,
The prophet's mantle, ere his flight began,
Dropt on the world—a sacred gift to man.
Auspicious Hope ! in thy sweet garden grow
Wreaths for each toil, a charm for every woe;
Won by their sweets, in Nature's languid hour,
The way-worn pilgrim seeks thy summer bower;
There, as the wild bee murmurs on the wing,
What peaceful dreams thy handmaid spirits bring !
What viewless forms th' Æolian organ play,
And sweep the furrow'd lines of anxious thought
  away.
Angel of life ! thy glittering wings explore
Earth's loneliest bounds, and Ocean's wildest
  shore.
Lo ! to the wintry winds the pilot yields
His bark careering o'er unfathom'd fields;
Now on Atlantic waves he rides afar,
Where Andes, giant of the western star,
With meteor-standard to the winds unfurl'd,
Looks from his throne of clouds o'er half the world !
  Now far he sweeps, where scarce a summer
  smiles,
On Behring's rocks, or Greenland's naked isles:
Cold on his midnight watch the breezes blow,
From wastes that slumber in eternal snow;
And waft, across the waves' tumultuous roar,
The wolf's long howl from Oonalaska's shore.
Poor child of danger, nursling of the storm,
Sad are the woes that wreck thy manly form !
Rocks, waves, and winds, the shatter'd bark delay;
Thy heart is sad, thy home is far away.
But Hope can here her moonlight vigils keep,
And sing to charm the spirit of the deep:
Swift as yon streamer lights the starry pole,
Her visions warm the watchman's pensive soul ;

His native hills that rise in happier climes,
The grot that heard his song of other times,
His cottage home, his bark of slender sail,
His glassy lake, and broomwood-blossom'd vale,
Rush on his thought; he sweeps before the wind,
Treads the loved shore he sigh'd to leave behind;
Meets at each step a friend's familiar face,
And flies at last to Helen's long embrace;
Wipes from her cheek the rapture-speaking tear!
And clasps, with many a sigh, his children dear!
While, long neglected, but at length caress'd,
His faithful dog salutes the smiling guest,
Points to the master's eyes (where'er they roam)
His wistful face, and whines a welcome home.

Friend of the brave! in peril's darkest hour,
Intrepid Virtue looks to thee for power;
To thee the heart its trembling homage yields,
On stormy floods, and carnage-cover'd fields,
When front to front the banner'd hosts combine,
Halt ere they close, and form the dreadful line.
When all is still on Death's devoted soil,
The march-worn soldier mingles for the toil;
As rings his glittering tube, he lifts on high
The dauntless brow, and spirit-speaking eye,
Hails in his heart the triumph yet to come,
And hears thy stormy music in the drum!

And such thy strength-inspiring aid that bore
The hardy Byron to his native shore—
In horrid climes, where Chiloe's tempests sweep
Tumultuous murmurs o'er the troubled deep,
'Twas his to mourn Misfortune's rudest shock,
Scourged by the winds, and cradled on the rock,
To wake each joyless morn and search again
The famish'd haunts of solitary men;
Whose race, unyielding as their native storm,
Know not a trace of Nature but the form;
Yet, at thy call, the hardy tar pursued,

Pale, but intrepid, sad, but unsubdued,
Pierced the deep woods, and hailing from afar
The moon's pale planet and the northern star,
Paused at each dreary cry unheard before,
Hyænas in the wild, and mermaids on the shore;
Till, led by thee o'er many a cliff sublime,
He found a warmer world, a milder clime,
A home to rest, a shelter to defend,
Peace and repose, a Briton and a friend!
  Congenial Hope! thy passion-kindling power,
How bright, how strong, in youth's untroubled
      hour!
On yon proud height, with Genius hand-in-hand,
I see thee light, and wave thy golden wand.
    "Go, child of Heaven! (thy winged words pro-
      claim)
'Tis thine to search the boundless fields of fame!
Lo! Newton, priest of Nature, shines afar,
Scans the wide world, and numbers every star!
Wilt thou, with him, mysterious rites apply,
And watch the shrine with wonder-beaming eye!
Yes, thou shalt mark, with magic art profound,
The speed of light, the circling march of sound;
With Franklin grasp the lightning's fiery wing,
Or yield the lyre of Heaven another string.
  "The Swedish sage admires, in yonder bowers,
His winged insects, and his rosy flowers;
Calls from their woodland haunts the savage train,
With sounding horn, and counts them on the
      plain—
So once, at Heaven's command, the wanderers came
To Eden's shade, and heard their various name.
  " Far from the world, in yon sequester'd clime,
Slow pass the sons of Wisdom, more sublime;
Calm as the fields of Heaven, his sapient eye
The loved Athenian lifts to realms on high,
Admiring Plato, on his spotless page,

Stamps the bright dictates of the Father sage :
' Shall Nature bound to Earth's diurnal span
The fire of God, th' immortal soul of man ? '
  " Turn, child of Heaven, thy rapture-lighten'd
     eye
To Wisdom's walks, the sacred Nine are nigh :
Hark ! from bright spires that gild the Delphian
     height,
From streams that wander in eternal light,
Ranged on their hill, Harmonia's daughters swell
The mingling tones of horn, and harp, and shell ;
Deep from his vaults the Loxian murmurs flow,
And Pythia's awful organ peals below.
  " Beloved of Heaven ! the smiling Muse shall
     shed
Her moonlight halo on thy beauteous head ;
Shall swell thy heart to rapture unconfined,
And breathe a holy madness o'er thy mind.
I see thee roam her guardian power beneath,
And talk with spirits on the midnight heath ;
Enquire of guilty wanderers whence they came,
And ask each blood-stain'd form his earthly name ;
Then weave in rapid verse the deeds they tell,
And read the trembling world the tales of hell.
  " When Venus, throned in clouds of rosy hue,
Flings from her golden urn the vesper dew,
And bids fond man her glimmering noon employ,
Sacred to love, and walks of tender joy ;
A milder mood the goddess shall recall,
And soft as dew thy tones of music fall ;
While Beauty's deeply-pictured smiles impart
A pang more dear than pleasure to the heart—
Warm as thy sighs shall flow the Lesbian strain,
And plead in Beauty's ear, nor plead in vain.
  " Or wilt thou Orphean hymns more sacred deem,
And steep thy song in Mercy's mellow stream ;
To pensive drops the radiant eye beguile—

For Beauty's tears are lovelier than her smile;—
On Nature's throbbing anguish pour relief,
And teach impassion'd souls the joy of grief?
  "Yes; to thy tongue shall seraph words be given,
And power on earth to plead the cause of Heaven;
The proud, the cold untroubled heart of stone,
That never mused on sorrow but its own,
Unlocks a generous store at thy command,
Like Horeb's rocks beneath the prophet's hand.
The living lumber of his kindred earth,
Charm'd into soul, receives a second birth,
Feels thy dread power another heart afford,
Whose passion-touch'd harmonious strings accord
True as the circling spheres to Nature's plan;
And man, the brother, lives the friend of man.
  "Bright as the pillar rose at Heaven's command,
When Israel march'd along the desert land,
Blazed through the night on lonely wilds afar,
And told the path,—a never-setting star:
So, Heavenly Genius, in thy course divine,
Hope is thy star, her light is ever thine."
  Propitious Power! when rankling cares annoy
The sacred home of Hymenean joy;
When doom'd to Poverty's sequester'd dell,
The wedded pair of love and virtue dwell,
Unpitied by the world, unknown to fame,
Their woes, their wishes, and their hearts the
        same—
Oh, there, prophetic Hope! thy smile bestow,
And chase the pangs that worth should never
        know—
There, as the parent deals his scanty store
To friendless babes, and weeps to give no more,
Tell, that his manly race shall yet assuage
Their father's wrongs, and shield his latter age.
What though for him no Hybla sweets distil,
Nor bloomy vines wave purple on the hill;

Tell, that when silent years have pass'd away,
That when his eye grows dim, his tresses grey,
These busy hands a lovelier cot shall build,
And deck with fairer flowers his little field,
And call from Heaven propitious dews to breathe
Arcadian beauty on the barren heath;
Tell, that while Love's spontaneous smile endears
The days of peace, the sabbath of his years,
Health shall prolong to many a festive hour
The social pleasures of his humble bower.
  Lo! at the couch where infant beauty sleeps,
Her silent watch the mournful mother keeps;
She, while the lovely babe unconscious lies,
Smiles on her slumbering child with pensive eyes,
And weaves a song of melancholy joy—
" Sleep, image of thy father, sleep, my boy;
No lingering hour of sorrow shall be thine;
No sigh that rends thy father's heart and mine;
Bright as his manly sire the son shall be
In form and soul; but, ah! more blest than he!
Thy fame, thy worth, thy filial love at last,
Shall soothe his aching heart for all the past—
With many a smile my solitude repay,
And chase the world's ungenerous scorn away.
  " And say, when summon'd from the world and
        thee,
I lay my head beneath the willow tree,
Wilt *thou*, sweet mourner! at my stone appear,
And soothe my parted spirit lingering near?
Oh, wilt thou come at evening hour to shed
The tears of Memory o'er my narrow bed;
With aching temples on thy hand reclined,
Muse on the last farewell I leave behind,
Breathe a deep sigh to winds that murmur low,
And think on all my love, and all my woe?"
  So speaks Affection, ere the infant eye
Can look regard, or brighten in reply;

But when the cherub lip hath learnt to claim
A mother's ear by that endearing name ;
Soon as the playful innocent can prove
A tear of pity, or a smile of love,
Or cons his murmuring task beneath her care,
Or lisps with holy look his evening prayer,
Or gazing, mutely pensive sits to hear
The mournful ballad warbled in his ear ;
How fondly looks admiring Hope the while,
At every artless tear, and every smile ;
How glows the joyous parent to descry
A guileless bosom, true to sympathy !
    Where is the troubled heart consign'd to share
Tumultuous toils, or solitary care,
Unblest by visionary thoughts that stray
To count the joys of Fortune's better day !
Lo ! nature, life, and liberty relume
The dim-eyed tenant of the dungeon gloom,
A long-lost friend, or hapless child restored,
Smiles at his blazing hearth and social board ;
Warm from his heart the tears of rapture flow,
And virtue triumphs o'er remember'd woe.
    Chide not his peace, proud Reason ! nor destroy
The shadowy forms of uncreated joy,
That urge the lingering tide of life, and pour
Spontaneous slumber on his midnight hour.
Hark ! the wild maniac sings, to chide the gale
That wafts so slow her lover's distant sail ;
She, sad spectatress, on the wintry shore,
Watch'd the rude surge his shroudless corse that
      bore,
Knew the pale form, and shrieking, in amaze,
Clasp'd her cold hands, and fix'd her maddening
      gaze :
Poor widow'd wretch ; 'twas there she wept in vain,
Till Memory fled her agonizing brain ;—
But Mercy gave to charm the sense of woe,

Ideal peace, that truth could ne'er bestow ;
Warm on her heart the joys of Fancy beam,
And aimless Hope delights her darkest dream.
    Oft when yon moon has climb'd the midnight
        sky,
And the lone sea-bird wakes its wildest cry,
Piled on the steep, her blazing faggots burn
To hail the bark that never can return ;
And still she waits, but scarce forbears to weep
That constant love can linger on the deep.
    And, mark the wretch, whose wanderings never
        knew
The world's regard, that soothes, though half un-
        true;
Whose erring heart the lash of sorrow bore,
But found not pity when it err'd no more.
Yon friendless man, at whose dejected eye
Th' unfeeling proud one looks—and passes by,
Condemn'd on Penury's barren path to roam,
Scorn'd by the world, and left without a home—
Even he at evening, should he chance to stray
Down by the hamlet's hawthorn-scented way,
Where, round the cot's romantic glade, are seen
The blossom'd bean-field, and the sloping green,
Leans o'er its humble gate, and thinks the while—
Oh ! that for me some home like this would smile,
Some hamlet shade, to yield my sickly form
Health in the breeze, and shelter in the storm !
There should my hand no stinted boon assign
To wretched hearts with sorrow such as mine !—
That generous wish can soothe unpitied care,
And Hope half mingles with the poor man's prayer.
    Hope ! when I mourn, with sympathizing mind,
The wrongs of fate, the woes of human kind,
Thy blissful omens bid my spirit see
The boundless fields of rapture yet to be ;
I watch the wheels of Nature's mazy plan,

And learn the future by the past of man.
    Come, bright Improvement! on the car of Time,
And rule the spacious world from clime to clime !
Thy handmaid arts shall every wild explore,
Trace every wave, and culture every shore.
On Erie's banks, where tigers steal along,
And the dread Indian chants a dismal song,
Where human fiends on midnight errands walk,
And bathe in brains the murderous tomahawk,
There shall the flocks on thymy pasture stray,
And shepherds dance at Summer's opening day ;
Each wandering genius of the lonely glen
Shall start to view the glittering haunts of men,
And silent watch on woodland heights around,
The village curfew as it tolls profound.
    In Libyan groves, where damned rites are done,
That bathe the rocks in blood, and veil the sun,
Truth shall arrest the murderous arm profane,
Wild Obi flies—the veil is rent in twain.
    Where barbarous hordes on Scythian mountains
        roam,
Truth, Mercy, Freedom, yet shall find a home ;
Where'er degraded Nature bleeds and pines,
From Guinea's coast to Sibir's dreary mines,
Truth shall pervade th'unfathom'd darkness there,
And light the dreadful features of despair.—
Hark ! the stern captive spurns his heavy load,
And asks the image back that Heaven bestow'd !
Fierce in his eye the fire of valour burns,
And as the slave departs, the man returns.
    Oh ! sacred Truth ! thy triumph ceased awhile,
And Hope, thy sister, ceased with thee to smile,
When leagued Oppression pour'd to Northern wars
Her whisker'd pandoors and her fierce hussars,
Waved her dread standard to the breeze of morn,
Peal'd her loud drum, and twang'd her trumpet
        horn,

Tumultuous horror brooded o'er her van,
Presaging wrath to Poland—and to man !
  Warsaw's last champion from her height sur-
      vey'd,
Wide o'er the fields, a waste of ruin laid,—
"O Heaven !" he cried, "my bleeding country
      save !—
Is there no hand on high to shield the brave ?
Yet, though destruction sweep those lovely plains,
Rise, fellow-men ! our country yet remains !
By that dread name, we wave the sword on high !
And swear for her to live !—with her to die !"
  He said, and on the rampart-heights array'd
His trusty warriors, few, but undismay'd ;
Firm-paced and slow, a horrid front they form,
Still as the breeze, but dreadful as the storm ;
Low murmuring sounds along their banners fly,
Revenge, or death,—the watchword and reply ;
Then peal'd the notes, omnipotent to charm,
And the loud tocsin toll'd their last alarm !—
  In vain, alas ! in vain, ye gallant few !
From rank to rank your volley'd thunder flew :—
Oh, bloodiest picture in the book of Time, ·
Sarmatia fell, unwept, without a crime ;
Found not a generous friend, a pitying foe,
Strength in her arms, nor mercy in her woe !
Dropp'd from her nerveless grasp the shatter'd
      spear,
Closed her bright eye, and curb'd her high career ;—
Hope, for a season, bade the world farewell,
And Freedom shriek'd—as Kosciusko fell !
  The sun went down, nor ceased the carnage there,
Tumultuous Murder shook the midnight air—
On Prague's proud arch the fires of ruin glow,
His blood-dyed waters murmuring far below ;
The storm prevails, the rampart yields a way,
Bursts the wild cry of horror and dismay !

Hark, as the smouldering piles with thunder fall,
A thousand shrieks for hopeless mercy call!
Earth shook—red meteors flash'd along the sky,
And conscious Nature shudder'd at the cry!
   Oh! righteous Heaven; ere Freedom found a
      grave,
Why slept the sword omnipotent to save?
Where was thine arm, O Vengeance! where thy
      rod,
That smote the foes of Zion and of God;
That crush'd proud Ammon, when his iron car
Was yoked in wrath, and thunder'd from afar?
Where was the storm that slumber'd till the host
Of blood-stain'd Pharaoh left their trembling coast:
Then bade the deep in wild commotion flow,
And heaved an ocean on their march below?
   Departed spirits of the mighty dead!
Ye that at Marathon and Leuctra bled!
Friends of the world! restore your swords to man,
Fight in his sacred cause, and lead the van!
Yet for Sarmatia's tears of blood atone,
And make her arm puissant as your own!
Oh! once again to Freedom's cause return
The patriot Tell—the Bruce of Bannockburn!
   Yes! thy proud lords, unpitied land! shall see
That man hath yet a soul—and dare be free!
A little while, along thy saddening plains,
The starless night of Desolation reigns;
Truth shall restore the light by Nature given,
And, like Prometheus, bring the fire of Heaven!
Prone to the dust Oppression shall be hurl'd,
Her name, her nature, wither'd from the world!
   Ye that the rising morn invidious mark,
And hate the light—because your deeds are dark;
Ye that expanding truth invidious view,
And think, or wish, the song of Hope untrue;
Perhaps your little hands presume to span

The march of Genius and the powers of man ;
Perhaps ye watch, at Pride's unhallow'd shrine,
Her victims, newly slain, and thus divine :—
" Here shall thy triumph, Genius, cease,—and here
Truth, Science, Virtue, close your short career."
　　Tyrants ! in vain ye trace the wizard ring ;
In vain ye limit Mind's unwearied spring :
What ! can ye lull the winged winds asleep,
Arrest the rolling world, or chain the deep ?
No !—the wild wave contemns your sceptred hand :
It roll'd not back when Canute gave command !
　　Man ! can thy doom no brighter soul allow ?
Still must thou live a blot on Nature's brow ?
Shall War's polluted banner ne'er be furl'd ?
Shall crimes and tyrants cease but with the world ?
What ! are thy triumphs, sacred Truth, belied ?
Why then hath Plato lived—or Sidney died ?—
　　Ye fond adorers of departed fame,
Who warm at Scipio's worth, or Tully's name !
Ye that in fancied vision, can admire
The sword of Brutus, and the Theban lyre !
Rapt in historic ardour, who adore
Each classic haunt, and well-remember'd shore,
Where Valour tuned, amidst her chosen throng,
The Thracian trumpet, and the Spartan song;
Or, wandering thence, behold the later charms
Of England's glory, and Helvetia's arms !
See Roman fire in Hampden's bosom swell,
And fate and freedom in the shaft of Tell !
Say, ye fond zealots to the worth of yore,
Hath valour left the world—to live no more ?
No more shall Brutus bid a tyrant die,
And sternly smile with vengeance in his eye ?
Hampden no more, when suffering Freedom calls,
Encounter Fate, and triumph as he falls ?
Nor Tell disclose, through peril and alarm,
The might that slumbers in a peasant's arm ?

Yes! in that generous cause, for ever strong,
The patriot's virtue and the poet's song,
Still, as the tide of ages rolls away,
Shall charm the world, unconscious of decay!
  Yes! there are hearts, prophetic Hope may trust,
That slumber yet in uncreated dust,
Ordain'd to fire th' adoring sons of earth
With every charm of wisdom and of worth;
Ordain'd to light, with intellectual day,
The mazy wheels of Nature as they play,
Or, warm with Fancy's energy, to glow,
And rival all but Shakspeare's name below.
  And say, supernal Powers! who deeply scan
Heaven's dark decrees, unfathom'd yet by man,
When shall the world call down, to cleanse her
          shame,
That embryo spirit, yet without a name,—
That friend of Nature, whose avenging hands
Shall burst the Libyan's adamantine bands ?
Who, sternly marking on his native soil
The blood, the tears, the anguish, and the toil,
Shall bid each righteous heart exult to see
Peace to the slave, and vengeance on the free !
  Yet, yet, degraded men, th' expected day
That breaks your bitter cup, is far away;
Trade, wealth, and fashion, ask you still to bleed,
And holy men give Scripture for the deed;
Scourged, and debased, no Briton stoops to save
A wretch, a coward ; yes, because a slave !—
  Eternal Nature ! when thy giant hand
Had heaved the floods, and fix'd the trembling land,
When life sprang startling at thy plastic call,
Endless her forms, and man the lord of all !—
Say, was that lordly form inspired by thee,
To wear eternal chains and bow the knee ?
Was man ordain'd the slave of man to toil,
Yoked with the brutes, and fetter'd to the soil;

Weigh'd in a tyrant's balance with his gold?
No!—Nature stamp'd us in a heavenly mould!
She bade no wretch his thankless labour urge,
Nor, trembling, take the pittance and the scourge!
No homeless Libyan, on the stormy deep,
To call upon his country's name, and weep!—
    Lo! once in triumph, on his boundless plain,
The quiver'd chief of Congo loved to reign;
With fires proportion'd to his native sky,
Strength in his arm, and lightning in his eye;
Scour'd with wild feet his sun-illumined zone,
The spear, the lion, and the woods, his own!
Or led the combat, bold without a plan,
An artless savage, but a fearless man!
    The plunderer came!—alas! no glory smiles
For Congo's chief, on yonder Indian isles;
For ever fall'n! no son of Nature now,
With freedom charter'd on his manly brow;
Faint, bleeding, bound, he weeps the night away,
And when the sea-wind wafts the dewless day,
Starts, with a bursting heart, for evermore
To curse the sun that lights their guilty shore!
    The shrill horn blew; at that alarum knell
His guardian angel took a last farewell!
That funeral dirge to darkness hath resign'd
The fiery grandeur of a generous mind!
Poor fetter'd man! I hear thee whispering low
Unhallow'd vows to Guilt, the child of Woe,
Friendless thy heart; and canst thou harbour there
A wish but death—a passion but despair?
    The widow'd Indian, when her lord expires,
Mounts the dread pile, and braves the funeral fires!
So falls the heart at Thraldom's bitter sigh!
So Virtue dies, the spouse of Liberty!
    But not to Libya's barren climes alone,
To Chili, or the wild Siberian zone,
Belong the wretched heart and haggard eye,

Degraded worth, and poor misfortune's sigh !—
Ye orient realms, where Ganges' waters run !
Prolific fields ! dominions of the sun !
How long your tribes have trembled and obey'd !
How long was Timour's iron sceptre sway'd,
Whose marshall'd hosts, the lions of the plain,
From Scythia's northern mountains to the main,
Raged o'er your plunder'd shrines and altars bare,
With blazing torch and gory scimitar,—
Stunn'd with the cries of death each gentle gale,
And bathed in blood the verdure of the vale !
Yet could no pangs the immortal spirit tame,
When Brama's children perish'd for his name ;
The martyr smiled beneath avenging power,
And braved the tyrant in his torturing hour !
    When Europe sought your subject realms to
        gain,
And stretch'd her giant sceptre o'er the main ;
Taught her proud barks the winding way to shape,
And braved the stormy Spirit of the Cape ;
Children of Brama ! then was Mercy nigh
To wash the stain of blood's eternal dye ?
Did Peace descend to triumph and to save,
When freeborn Britons cross'd the Indian wave ?
Ah, no ! to more than Rome's ambition true,
The Nurse of Freedom gave it not to you !
She the bold route of Europe's guilt began,
And, in the march of nations, led the van !
    Rich in the gems of India's gaudy zone,
And plunder piled from kingdoms not their own,
Degenerate trade ! thy minions could despise
The heart-born anguish of a thousand cries ;
Could lock, with impious hands, their teeming
        store,
While famish'd nations died along the shore :
Could mock the groans of fellow-men, and bear
The curse of kingdoms peopled with despair ;

Could stamp disgrace on man's polluted name,
And barter, with their gold, eternal shame!
   But hark! as bow'd to earth the Bramin
        kneels,
From heavenly climes propitious thunder peals!
Of India's fate her guardian spirits tell,
Prophetic murmurs breathing on the shell,
And solemn sounds that awe the listening mind,
Roll on the azure paths of every wind.
   " Foes of mankind!" (her guardian spirits say,)
" Revolving ages bring the bitter day,
When Heaven's unerring arm shall fall on you,
And blood for blood these Indian plains bedew;
Nine times have Brama's wheels of lightning
        hurl'd
His awful presence o'er the alarmed world;
Nine times hath Guilt, through all his giant .
        frame,
Convulsive trembled, as the Mighty came;
Nine times hath suffering Mercy spared in vain—
But Heaven shall burst her starry gates again!
He comes! dread Brama shakes the sunless sky
With murmuring wrath, and thunders from on
        high;
Heaven's fiery horse, beneath his warrior form,
Paws the light clouds and gallops on the storm!
Wide waves his flick'ring sword; his bright arms
        glow
Like summer suns, and light the world below!
Earth, and her trembling isles in Ocean's bed,
Are shook; and Nature rocks beneath his tread!
   " To pour redress on India's injured realm,
The oppressor to dethrone, the proud to whelm;
To chase destruction from her plunder'd shore
With hearts and arms that triumph'd once before,
The tenth Avatar comes! at Heaven's command
Shall Seriswattee wave her hallow'd wand!

And Camdeo bright, and Ganesa sublime,
Shall bless with joy their own propitious clime !—
Come, Heavenly Powers ! primeval peace restore !
Love !—Mercy !—Wisdom !—rule for evermore !"

ANALYSIS OF PART II.

APOSTROPHE to the power of Love—its intimate connection with
generous and social Sensibility—allusion to that beautiful passage in
the beginning of the book of Genesis, which represents the happiness
of Paradise itself incomplete, till love was superadded to its other
blessings—the dreams of future felicity which a lively imagination is
apt to cherish, when Hope is animated by refined attachment—this
disposition to combine, in one imaginary scene of residence, all that
is pleasing in our estimate of happiness, compared to the skill of the
great artist who personified perfect beauty, in the picture of Venus,
by an assemblage of the most beautiful features he could find—a
summer and winter evening described, as they may be supposed to
arise in the mind of one who wishes, with enthusiasm, for the union
of friendship and retirement.

Hope and Imagination inseparable agents—even in those contemplative moments when our imagination wanders beyond the boundaries
of this world, our minds are not unattended with an impression that
we shall some day have a wider and more distinct prospect of the
universe, instead of the partial glimpse we now enjoy.

The last and most sublime influence of Hope is the concluding topic
of the poem—the predominance of a belief in a future state over the
terrors attendant on dissolution—the baneful influence of that
sceptical philosophy which bars us from such comforts—allusion to
the fate of a suicide—episode of Conrad and Ellenore—conclusion.

PART II.

IN joyous youth, what soul hath never
            known
      Thought, feeling, taste, harmonious to
            its own ?
Who hath not paused while Beauty's pensive eye
Ask'd from his heart the homage of a sigh ?
Who hath not own'd, with rapture-smitten frame,
The power of grace, the magic of a name !
      There be, perhaps, who barren hearts avow,
Cold as the rocks on Torneo's hoary brow ;

There be, whose loveless wisdom never fail'd,
In self-adoring pride securely mail'd :—
But triumph not, ye peace-enamour'd few !
Fire, Nature, Genius, never dwelt with you !
For you no fancy consecrates the scene
Where rapture utter'd vows, and wept between ;
'Tis yours, unmoved, to sever and to meet ;
No pledge is sacred, and no home is sweet !
   Who that would ask a heart to dulness wed,
The waveless calm, the slumber of the dead ?
No ; the wild bliss of Nature needs alloy,
And fear and sorrow fan the fire of joy !
And say, without our hopes, without our fears,
Without the home that plighted love endears,
Without the smile from partial beauty won,
Oh ! what were man ?—a world without a sun.
   Till Hymen brought his love-delighted hour,
There dwelt no joy in Eden's rosy bower !
In vain the viewless seraph lingering there,
At starry midnight charm'd the silent air ;
In vain the wild bird caroll'd on the steep,
To hail the sun, slow wheeling from the deep ;
In vain, to soothe the solitary shade,
Aërial notes in mingling measure play'd ;
The summer wind that shook the spangled tree,
The whispering wave, the murmur of the bee ;—
Still slowly pass'd the melancholy day,
And still the stranger wist not where to stray.
The world was sad !—the garden was a wild !
And man, the hermit, sigh'd—till woman smiled !
   True, the sad power to generous hearts may
     bring
Delirious anguish on his fiery wing ;
Barr'd from delight by Fate's untimely hand,
By wealthless lot or pitiless command ;
Or doom'd to gaze on beauties that adorn
The smile of triumph or the frown of scorn ;

While Memory watches o'er the sad review
Of joys that faded like the morning dew;
Peace may depart—and life and nature seem
A barren path, a wildness, and a dream!
But can the noble mind for ever brood,
The willing victim of a weary mood,
On heartless cares that squander life away,
And cloud young Genius brightening into day?—
Shame to the coward thought that e'er betray'd
The noon of manhood to a myrtle shade!—
If Hope's creative spirit cannot raise
One trophy sacred to thy future days,
Scorn the dull crowd that haunt the gloomy shrine,
Of hopeless love to murmur and repine!
But, should a sigh of milder mood express
Thy heart-warm wishes, true to happiness,
Should Heaven's fair harbinger delight to pour
Her blissful visions on thy pensive hour,
No tear to blot thy memory's pictured page,
No fears but such as fancy can assuage;
Though thy wild heart some hapless hour may miss
The peaceful tenor of unvaried bliss
(For love pursues an ever-devious race,
True to the winding lineaments of grace),
Yet still may Hope her talisman employ
To snatch from Heaven anticipated joy,
And all her kindred energies impart
That burn the brightest in the purest heart.
When first the Rhodian's mimic art array'd
The Queen of Beauty in her Cyprian shade,
The happy master mingled on his piece
Each look that charm'd him in the fair of Greece.
To faultless Nature true, he stole a grace
From every finer form and sweeter face;
And as he sojourn'd on the Ægean isles,
Woo'd all their love, and treasured all their smiles;
Then glow'd the tints, pure, precious, and refined,

And mortal charms seem'd heavenly when com-
      bined !
Love on the picture smiled ! Expression pour'd
Her mingling spirit there—and Greece adored !
    So thy fair hand, enamour'd Fancy ! gleans
The treasured pictures of a thousand scenes ;
Thy pencil traces on the lover's thought
Some cottage-home, from towns and toil remote,
Where love and lore may claim alternate hours,
With Peace embosom'd in Idalian bowers !
Remote from busy Life's bewilder'd way,
O'er all his heart shall Taste and Beauty sway !
Free on the sunny slope, or winding shore,
With hermit steps to wander and adore !
There shall he love, when genial morn appears,
Like pensive Beauty smiling in her tears,
To watch the brightening roses of the sky,
And muse on Nature with a poet's eye !—
And when the sun's last splendour lights the deep,
The woods and waves, and murmuring winds
      asleep,
When fairy harps th' Hesperian planet hail,
And the lone cuckoo sighs along the vale,
His path shall be where streamy mountains swell
Their shadowy grandeur o'er the narrow dell,
Where mouldering piles and forests intervene,
Mingling with darker tints the living green ;
No circling hills his ravish'd eye to bound,
Heaven, Earth, and Ocean, blazing all around.
    The moon is up—the watch-tower dimly burns—
And down the vale his sober step returns ;
But pauses oft, as winding rocks convey
The still sweet fall of music far away ;
And oft he lingers from his home awhile
To watch the dying notes !—and start, and smile !
    Let Winter come ! let polar spirits sweep
The darkening world, and tempest-troubled deep !

Though boundless snows the wither'd heath de-
    form,
And the dim sun scarce wanders through the storm,
Yet shall the smile of social love repay,
With mental light, the melancholy day !
And, when its short and sullen noon is o'er,
The ice-chain'd waters slumbering on the shore,
How bright the faggots in his little hall
Blaze on the hearth, and warm the pictured wall !

How blest he names, in Love's familiar tone,
The kind fair friend, by nature mark'd his own ;
And, in the waveless mirror of his mind,
Views the fleet years of pleasure left behind,
Since when her empire o'er his heart began !
Since first he call'd her his before the holy man !

Trim the gay taper in his rustic dome,
And light the wintry paradise of home ;
And let the half-uncurtain'd window hail
Some way-worn man benighted in the vale !
Now, while the moaning night-wind rages high,
As sweep the shot-stars down the troubled sky,
While fiery hosts in Heaven's wide circle play,
And bathe in lurid light the milky-way,
Safe from the storm, the meteor, and the shower,
Some pleasing page shall charm the solemn hour—
With pathos shall command, with wit beguile,
A generous tear of anguish, or a smile—
Thy woes, Arion ! and thy simple tale,
O'er all the heart shall triumph and prevail !
Charm'd as they read the verse too sadly true,
How gallant Albert, and his weary crew,
Heaved o'er their guns, their foundering bark to
    save,
And toil'd—and shriek'd—and perish'd on the
    wave !

Yes, at the dead of night, by Lonna's steep,
The seaman's cry was heard along the deep;

There on his funeral waters, dark and wild,
The dying father bless'd his darling child!
Oh! Mercy, shield her innocence, he cried,
Spent on the prayer his bursting heart, and died!
    Or they will learn how generous worth sublimes
The robber Moor, and pleads for all his crimes!
How poor Amelia kiss'd, with many a tear,
His hand, blood-stain'd, but ever, ever dear!
Hung on the tortured bosom of her lord,
And wept and pray'd perdition from his sword!
Nor sought in vain! at that heart-piercing cry
The strings of Nature crack'd with agony!
He, with delirious laugh, the dagger hurl'd,
And burst the ties that bound him to the world!
Turn from his dying words, that smite with steel
The shuddering thoughts, or wind them on the
            wheel—
Turn to the gentler melodies that suit
Thalia's harp, or Pan's Arcadian lute;
Or, down the stream of Truth's historic page,
From clime to clime descend, from age to age!
    Yet there, perhaps, may darker scenes obtrude
Than Fancy fashions in her wildest mood;
There shall he pause with horrent brow, to rate
What millions died—that Cæsar might be great!
Or learn the fate that bleeding thousands bore,
March'd by their Charles to Dnieper's swampy
            shore;
Faint in his wounds, and shivering in the blast,
The Swedish soldier sunk—and groan'd his last!
File after file the stormy showers benumb,
Freeze every standard-sheet, and hush the drum;
Horseman and horse confess'd the bitter pang,
And arms and warriors fell with hollow clang!
Yet, ere he sunk in Nature's last repose,
Ere life's warm torrent to the fountain froze,
The dying man to Sweden turn'd his eye,

Thought of his home, and closed it with a sigh!
Imperial Pride look'd sullen on his plight,
And Charles beheld—nor shudder'd at the sight!
  Above, below, in Ocean, Earth, and Sky,
Thy fairy worlds, Imagination, lie;
And Hope attends, companion of the way,
Thy dream by night, thy visions of the day!
In yonder pensile orb, and every sphere
That gems the starry girdle of the year;
In those unmeasured worlds, she bids thee tell,
Pure from their God, created millions dwell,
Whose names and natures, unreveal'd below,
We yet shall learn, and wonder as we know;
For, as Iona's saint, a giant form,
Throned on her towers, conversing with the storm,
(When o'er each Runic altar, weed-entwined,
The vesper clock tolls mournful to the wind,)
Counts every wave-worn isle, and mountain hoar,
From Kilda to the green Ierne's shore;
So, when thy pure and renovated mind
This perishable dust hath left behind,
Thy seraph eye shall count the starry train,
Like distant isles embosom'd in the main;
Rapt to the shrine where motion first began,
And light and life in mingling torrent ran;
From whence each bright rotundity was hurl'd,
The throne of God,—the centre of the world!
  Oh! vainly wise, the moral Muse hath sung
That suasive Hope hath but a Syren tongue!
True; she may sport with life's untutor'd day,
Nor heed the solace of its last decay,
The guileless heart her happy mansion spurn,
And part, like Ajut—never to return!
  But yet, methinks, when Wisdom shall assuage
The grief and passions of our greener age,
Though dull the close of life, and far away
Each flower that hail'd the dawning of the day;

Yet o'er her lovely hopes, that once were dear,
The time-taught spirit, pensive, not severe,
With milder griefs her aged eye shall fill,
And weep their falsehood, though she loves them
      still!
   Thus, with forgiving tears, and reconciled,
The king of Judah mourn'd his rebel child!
Musing on days, when yet the guiltless boy
Smiled on his sire, and fill'd his heart with joy!
My Absalom! the voice of Nature cried,
Oh! that for thee thy father could have died!
For bloody was the deed, and rashly done,
That slew my Absalom!—my son! my son!

   Unfading Hope! when life's last embers burn,
When soul to soul, and dust to dust return!
Heaven to thy charge resigns the awful hour!
Oh! then, thy kingdom comes! Immortal Power!
What though each spark of earth-born rapture fly
The quivering lip, pale cheek, and closing eye!
Bright to the soul thy seraph hands convey
The morning dream of life's eternal day—
Then, then, the triumph and the trance begin,
And all the phœnix spirit burns within!

   Oh! deep-enchanting prelude to repose,
The dawn of bliss, the twilight of our woes!
Yet half I hear the panting spirit sigh,
It is a dread and awful thing to die!
Mysterious worlds, untravell'd by the sun!
Where Time's far-wandering tide has never run,
From your unfathom'd shades, and viewless
      spheres,
A warning comes, unheard by other ears.
'Tis Heaven's commanding trumpet, long and loud,
Like Sinai's thunder, pealing from the cloud!
While Nature hears, with terror-mingled trust,
The shock that hurls her fabric to the dust;
And, like the trembling Hebrew, when he trod

The roaring waves, and call'd upon his God,
With mortal terrors clouds immortal bliss,
And shrieks, and hovers o'er the dark abyss!
  Daughter of Faith, awake, arise, illume
The dread unknown, the chaos of the tomb;
Melt, and dispel, ye spectre-doubts, that roll
Cimmerian darkness o'er the parting soul!
Fly, like the moon-eyed herald of Dismay,
Chased on his night-steed by the star of day!
The strife is o'er—the pangs of Nature close,
And life's last rapture triumphs o'er her woes.
Hark! as the spirit eyes, with eagle gaze,
The noon of Heaven undazzled by the blaze,
On heavenly winds that waft her to the sky,
Float the sweet tones of star-born melody;
Wild as that hallow'd anthem sent to hail
Bethlehem's shepherds in the lonely vale,
When Jordan hush'd his waves, and midnight still
Watch'd on the holy towers of Zion's hill!
  Soul of the just! companion of the dead!
Where is thy home, and whither art thou fled?
Back to its heavenly source thy being goes,
Swift as the comet wheels to whence he rose;
Doom'd on his airy path awhile to burn,
And doom'd, like thee, to travel and return.—
Hark! from the world's exploding centre driven,
With sounds that shook the firmament of Heaven,
Careers the fiery giant, fast and far,
On bickering wheels, and adamantine car;
From planet whirl'd to planet more remote,
He visits realms beyond the reach of thought;
But wheeling homeward, when his course is run,
Curbs the red yoke, and mingles with the sun!
So hath the traveller of earth unfurl'd
Her trembling wings, emerging from the world;
And o'er the path by mortal never trod,
Sprung to her source, the bosom of her God!

Oh! lives there, Heaven! beneath thy dread
        expanse,
One hopeless, dark idolater of Chance,
Content to feed, with pleasures unrefined,
The lukewarm passions of a lowly mind;
Who, mouldering earthward, 'reft of every trust,
In joyless union wedded to the dust,
Could all his parting energy dismiss,
And call this barren world sufficient bliss?—
There live, alas! of heaven-directed mien,
Of cultured soul, and sapient eye serene,
Who hail thee, Man! the pilgrim of a day,
Spouse of the worm, and brother of the clay,
Frail as the leaf in Autumn's yellow bower,
Dust in the wind, or dew upon the flower;
A friendless slave, a child without a sire,
Whose mortal life and momentary fire,
Light to the grave his chance-created form,
As ocean-wrecks illuminate the storm;
And, when the gun's tremendous flash is o'er,
To night and silence sink for evermore!

Are these the pompous tidings ye proclaim,
Lights of the world, and demi-gods of Fame?
Is this your triumph—this your proud applause,
Children of Truth, and champions of her cause?
For this hath Science search'd on weary wing,
By shore and sea—each mute and living thing!
Launch'd with Iberia's pilot from the steep,
To worlds unknown, and isles beyond the deep?
Or round the cope her living chariot driven,
And wheel'd in triumph through the signs of
        Heaven!
Oh! star-eyed Science, hast thou wander'd there,
To waft us home the message of despair?
Then bind the palm, thy sage's brow to suit,
Of blasted leaf, and death-distilling fruit?
Ah me! the laurell'd wreath that Murder rears,

Blood-nursed, and water'd by the widow's tears,
Seems not so foul, so tainted, and so dread,
As waves the nightshade round the sceptic head.
What is the bigot's torch, the tyrant's chain?
I smile on death, if Heaven-ward Hope remain!
But, if the warring winds of Nature's strife
Be all the faithless charter of my life,
If Chance awaked, inexorable power,
This frail and feverish being of an hour;
Doom'd o'er the world's precarious scene to sweep
Swift as the tempest travels on the deep,
To know Delight but by her parting smile,
And toil, and wish, and weep a little while;
Then melt, ye elements that form'd in vain
This troubled pulse, and visionary brain!
Fade, ye wild flowers, memorials of my doom,
And sink, ye stars, that light me to the tomb!
Truth, ever lovely,—since the world began,
The foe of tyrants, and the friend of man,—
How can thy words from balmy slumber start
Reposing Virtue, pillow'd on the heart!
Yet, if thy voice the note of thunder roll'd,
And that were true which Nature never told,
Let Wisdom smile not on her conquer'd field;
No rapture dawns, no treasure is reveal'd!
Oh! let her read, nor loudly, nor elate,
The doom that bars us from a better fate;
But, sad as angels for the good man's sin,
Weep to record, and blush to give it in!

And well may Doubt, the mother of Dismay,
Pause at her martyr's tomb, and read the lay.
Down by the wilds of yon deserted vale,
It darkly hints a melancholy tale!
There as the homeless madman sits alone,
In hollow winds he hears a spirit moan!
And there, they say, a wizard orgie crowds,
When the Moon lights her watch-tower in the
        clouds.

Poor lost Alonzo! Fate's neglected child!
Mild be the doom of Heaven—as thou wert mild!
For oh! thy heart in holy mould was cast,
And all thy deeds were blameless, but the last.
Poor lost Alonzo! still I seem to hear
The clod that struck thy hollow-sounding bier!
When Friendship paid, in speechless sorrow
    drown'd,
Thy midnight rites, but not on hallow'd ground!
  Cease, every joy, to glimmer on my mind,
But leave—oh! leave the light of Hope behind!
What though my winged hours of bliss have been,
Like angel-visits, few and far between,
Her musing mood shall every pang appease,
And charm—when pleasures lose the power to
    please!
Yes; let each rapture, dear to Nature, flee:
Close not the light of Fortune's stormy sea—
Mirth, Music, Friendship, Love's propitious smile,
Chase every care, and charm a little while,
Ecstatic throbs the fluttering heart employ,
And all her strings are harmonized to joy!—
But why so short is Love's delighted hour?
Why fades the dew on Beauty's sweetest flower?
Why can no hymned charm of music heal
The sleepless woes impassion'd spirits feel?
Can Fancy's fairy hands no veil create,
To hide the sad realities of fate?—
  No! not the quaint remark, the sapient rule,
Nor all the pride of Wisdom's worldly school,
Have power to soothe, unaided and alone,
The heart that vibrates to a feeling tone!
When stepdame Nature every bliss recalls,
Fleet as the meteor o'er the desert falls;
When, 'reft of all, yon widow'd sire appears
A lonely hermit in the vale of years;
Say, can the world one joyous thought bestow

To Friendship, weeping at the couch of Woe ?
No ! but a brighter soothes the last adieu,—
Souls of impassion'd mould, she speaks to you !
Weep not, she says, at Nature's transient pain,
Congenial spirits part to meet again !
  What plaintive sobs thy filial spirit drew,
What sorrow choked thy long and last adieu !
Daughter of Conrad ! when he heard his knell,
And bade his country and his child farewell !
Doom'd the long isles of Sydney-cove to see,
The martyr of his crimes, but true to thee ?
Thrice the sad father tore thee from his heart,
And thrice return'd, to bless thee, and to part ;
Thrice from his trembling lips he murmur'd low
The plaint that own'd unutterable woe ;
Till Faith, prevailing o'er his sullen doom,
As bursts the morn on night's unfathom'd gloom,
Lured his dim eye to deathless hopes sublime,
Beyond the realms of Nature and of Time !
  "And weep not thus," he cried, "young Ellenore,
My bosom bleeds, but soon shall bleed no more !
Short shall this half-extinguish'd spirit burn,
And soon these limbs to kindred dust return !
But not, my child, with life's precarious fire,
The immortal ties of Nature shall expire ;
These shall resist the triumph of decay,
When time is o'er, and worlds have pass'd away !
Cold in the dust this perish'd heart may lie,
But that which warm'd it once shall never die !
That spark, unburied in its mortal frame,
With living light, eternal, and the same,
Shall beam on Joy's interminable years,
Unveil'd by darkness—unassuaged by tears !
  " Yet, on the barren shore and stormy deep,
One tedious watch is Conrad doom'd to weep ;
But when I gain the home without a friend,
And press the uneasy couch where none attend,

This last embrace, still cherish'd in my heart,
Shall calm the struggling spirit ere it part!
Thy darling form shall seem to hover nigh,
And hush the groan of life's last agony!
 " Farewell! when strangers lift thy father's bier,
And place my nameless stone without a tear;
When each returning pledge hath told my child
That Conrad's tomb is on the desert piled;
And when the dream of troubled Fancy sees
Its lonely rank grass waving in the breeze;
Who then will soothe thy grief, when mine is o'er
Who will protect thee, helpless Ellenore?
Shall secret scenes thy filial sorrows hide,
Scorn'd by the world, to factious guilt allied?
Ah, no! methinks the generous and the good
Will woo thee from the shades of solitude!
O'er friendless grief Compassion shall awake,
And smile on Innocence for Mercy's sake!"
 Inspiring thought of rapture yet to be,
The tears of Love were hopeless, but for thee!
If in that frame no deathless spirit dwell,
If that faint murmur be the last farewell,
If Fate unite the faithful but to part,
Why is their memory sacred to the heart?
Why does the brother of my childhood seem
Restored a while in every pleasing dream?
Why do I joy the lonely spot to view,
By artless friendship bless'd when life was new?
 Eternal Hope! when yonder spheres sublime
Peal'd their first notes to sound the march of Time,
Thy joyous youth began—but not to fade.—
When all the sister planets have decay'd;
When wrapt in fire the realms of ether glow,
And Heaven's last thunder shakes the world
          below;
Thou, undismay'd, shalt o'er the ruins smile,
And light thy torch at Nature's funeral pile.

THEODRIC.

A DOMESTIC TALE

'TWAS sunset, and the Ranz des Vaches
          was sung,
     And lights were o'er th' Helvetian
          mountains flung,
That gave the glacier tops their richest glow,
And tinged the lakes like molten gold below:
Warmth flush'd the wonted regions of the storm,
Where, phœnix-like, you saw the eagle's form,
That high in Heaven's vermilion wheel'd and
          soar'd,
Woods nearer frown'd, and cataracts dash'd and
          roar'd
From heights browsed by the bounding bouquetin;
Herds tinkling roam'd the long-drawn vales
          between,
And hamlets glitter'd white, and gardens flourish'd
          green:
'Twas transport to inhale the bright sweet air!
The mountain-bee was revelling in its glare,
And roving with his minstrelsy across
The scented wild weeds, and enamell'd moss.
Earth's features so harmoniously were link'd,
She seem'd one great glad form, with life instinct,
That felt Heaven's ardent breath, and smiled
          below
Its flush of love, with consentaneous glow.
     A Gothic church was near; the spot around
Was beautiful, ev'n though sepulchral ground;
For there nor yew nor cypress spread their gloom,
But roses blossom'd by each rustic tomb.
Amidst them one of spotless marble shone—

A maiden's grave—and 'twas inscribed thereon,
That young and loved she died whose dust was
      there :
  " Yes," said my comrade, "young she died and
      fair !
Grace form'd her, and the soul of gladness play'd
Once in the blue eyes of that mountain-maid :
Her fingers witch'd the chords they pass'd along,
And her lips seem'd to kiss the soul in song :
Yet woo'd, and worshipp'd as she was, till few
Aspired to hope, 'twas sadly, strangely true,
That heart, the martyr of its fondness, burn'd
And died of love that could not be return'd.
  Her father dwelt where yonder Castle shines
O'er clustering trees and terrace-mantling vines :
As gay as ever, the laburnum's pride
Waves o'er each walk where she was wont to
      glide,—
And still the garden whence she graced her brow,
As lovely blooms, though trode by strangers now.
How oft, from yonder window o'er the lake,
Her song of wild Helvetian swell and shake
Has made the rudest fisher bend his ear,
And rest enchanted on his oar to hear !
Thus bright, accomplish'd, spirited, and bland,
Well-born, and wealthy for that simple land,
Why had no gallant native youth the art
To win so warm—so exquisite a heart ?
She, 'midst these rocks inspired with feelings
     strong
By mountain-freedom—music—fancy—song,
Herself descended from the brave in arms,
And conscious of romance-inspiring charms,
Dreamt of Heroic beings ; hoped to find
Some extant spirit of chivalric kind ;
And scorning wealth, look'd cold ev'n on the claim
Of manly worth, that lack'd the wreath of fame.

Her younger brother, sixteen summers old,
And much her likeness both in mind and mould,
Had gone, poor boy ! in soldiership to shine,
And bore an Austrian banner on the Rhine.
'Twas when, alas ! our Empire's evil star
Shed all the plagues, without the pride, of war;
When patriots bled, and bitterer anguish cross'd
Our brave, to die in battles foully lost.
The youth wrote home the rout of many a day
Yet still he said, and still with truth could say
One corps had ever made a valiant stand,—
The corps in which he served,—Theodric's band.
His fame, forgotten chief ! is now gone by,
Eclipsed by brighter orbs in Glory's sky;
Yet once it shone, and veterans, when they show
Our fields of battle twenty years ago,
Will tell you feats his small brigade perform'd
In charges nobly faced and trenches storm'd.
Time was, when songs were chanted to his fame,
And soldiers loved the march that bore his name:
The zeal of martial hearts was at his call,
And that Helvetian's, Udolph's, most of all.
'Twas touching, when the storm of war blew wild,
To see a blooming boy,—almost a child,—
Spur fearless at his leader's words and signs,
Brave death in reconnoitring hostile lines,
And speed each task, and tell each message clear,
In scenes where war-train'd men were stunn'd
    with fear.
Theodric praised him, and they wept for joy
In yonder house,—when letters from the boy
Thank'd Heaven for life, and more, to use his
    phrase,
Than twenty lives—his own Commander's praise.
Then follow'd glowing pages, blazoning forth
The fancied image of his leader's worth,
With such hyperbolés of youthful style

As made his parents dry their tears and smile:
But differently far his words impress'd
A wondering sister's well-believing breast ;—
She caught th' illusion, bless'd Theodric's name
And wildly magnified his worth and fame ;
Rejoicing life's reality contain'd
One, heretofore, her fancy had but feign'd,
Whose love could make her proud !—and time and
          chance
To passion raised that day-dream of Romance.
    Once, when with hasty charge of horse and man
Our arrière-guard had check'd the Gallic van,
Theodric, visiting the outposts, found
His Udolph wounded, weltering on the ground :
Sore crush'd,—half-swooning, half-upraised he lay
And bent his brow, fair boy ! and grasp'd the clay
His fate moved ev'n the common soldier's ruth—
Theodric succour'd him ; nor left the youth
To vulgar hands, but brought him to his tent,
And lent what aid a brother would have lent.
    Meanwhile, to save his kindred half the smart
The war-gazette's dread blood-roll might impart,
He wrote th' event to them ; and soon could tell
Of pains assuaged and symptoms auguring well ;
And last of all, prognosticating cure,
Enclosed the leech's vouching signature.
    Their answers, on whose pages you might note
That tears had fall'n, whilst trembling fingers
          wrote,
Gave boundless thanks for benefits conferr'd,
Of which the boy, in secret, sent them word,
Whose memory Time, they said, would never blot ;
But which the giver had himself forgot.
    In time, the stripling, vigorous and heal'd,
Resumed his barb and banner in the field,
And bore himself right soldier-like, till now
The third campaign had manlier bronzed his brow,

When peace, though but a scanty pause for
    breath,—
A curtain-drop between the acts of death,—
A check in frantic war's unfinish'd game,
Yet dearly bought, and direly welcome, came.
The camp broke up, and Udolph left his chief
As with a son's or younger brother's grief:
But journeying home, how rapt his spirits rose!
How light his footsteps crush'd St. Gothard's
    snows;
How dear seem'd ev'n the waste and wild Shreck-
    horn,
Though wrapt in clouds, and frowning as in scorn
Upon a downward world of pastoral charms;
Where, by the very smell of dairy-farms,
And fragrance from the mountain-herbage blown,
Blindfold his native hills he could have known!
    His coming down yon lake,—his boat in view
Of windows where love's fluttering kerchief flew,—
The arms spread out for him—the tears that burst,—
('Twas Julia's, 'twas his sister's, met him first:)
Their pride to see war's medal at his breast,
And all their rapture's greeting, may be guess'd.
    Ere long, his bosom triumph'd to unfold
A gift he meant their gayest room to hold,—
The picture of a friend in warlike dress;
And who it was he first bade Julia guess.
'Yes,' she replied, ''twas he methought in sleep,
When you were wounded, told me not to weep.'
The painting long in that sweet mansion drew
Regards its living semblance little knew.
    Meanwhile Theodric, who had years before
Learnt England's tongue, and loved her classic lore,
A glad enthusiast now explored the land
Where Nature, Freedom, Art, smile hand in hand
Her women fair; her men robust for toil;
Her vigorous souls, high-cultured as her soil;

Her towns, where civic independence flings
The gauntlet down to senates, courts, and kings;
Her works of art, resembling magic's powers;
Her mighty fleets, and learning's beauteous
          bowers,—
These he had visited, with wonder's smile,
And scarce endured to quit so fair an isle.
But how our fates from unmomentous things
May rise, like rivers out of little springs!
A trivial chance postponed his parting day,
And public tidings caused, in that delay,
An English Jubilee.   'Twas a glorious sight!
At eve stupendous London, clad in light,
Pour'd out triumphant multitudes to gaze;
Youth, age, wealth, penury, smiling in the blaze;
Th' illumined atmosphere was warm and bland,
And Beauty's groups, the fairest of the land,
Conspicuous, as in some wide festive room,
In open chariots pass'd with pearl and plume.
Amidst them he remark'd a lovelier mien
Than e'er his thoughts had shaped, or eyes had
          seen;
The throng detain'd her till he rein'd his steed,
And, ere the beauty pass'd, had time to read
The motto and the arms her carriage bore.
Led by that clue, he left not England's shore
Till he had known her; and to know her well
Prolong'd, exalted, bound, enchantment's spell;
For with affections warm, intense, refined,
She mix'd such calm and holy strength of mind,
That, like Heaven's image in the smiling brook,
Celestial peace was pictured in her look.
Hers was the brow, in trials unperplex'd,
That cheer'd the sad, and tranquillized the vex'd;
She studied not the meanest to eclipse,
And yet the wisest listen'd to her lips;
She sang not, knew not Music's magic skill,

But yet her voice had tones that sway'd the will.
He sought—he won her—and resolved to make
His future home in England for her sake.
    Yet, ere they wedded, matters of concern
To Cæsar's Court commanded his return,
A season's space,—and on his Alpine way,
He reach'd those bowers, that rang with joy that
        day :
The boy was half beside himself,—the sire,
All frankness, honour, and Helvetian fire,
Of speedy parting would not hear him speak;
And tears bedew'd and brighten'd Julia's cheek.
    Thus, loth to wound their hospitable pride,
A month he promised with them to abide ;
As blithe he trod the mountain-sward as they,
And felt his joy make ev'n the young more gay.
How jocund was their breakfast-parlour, fann'd
By yon blue water's breath,—their walks how
        bland !
Fair Julia seem'd her brother's soften'd sprite—
A gem reflecting Nature's purest light,—
And with her graceful wit there was inwrought
A wildly sweet unworldliness of thought,
That almost child-like to his kindness drew,
And twin with Udolph in his friendship grew.
But did his thoughts to love one moment range ?—
No ! he who had loved Constance could not
        change !
Besides, till grief betray'd her undesign'd,
Th' unlikely thought could scarcely reach his mind,
That eyes so young on years like his should beam
Unwoo'd devotion back for pure esteem.
    True she sang to his very soul, and brought
Those trains before him of luxuriant thought,
Which only Music's heaven-born art can bring,
To sweep across the mind with angel wing.
Once, as he smiled amidst that waking trance,

She paused o'ercome: he thought it might be
    chance,
And, when his first suspicions dimly stole,
Rebuked them back like phantoms from his soul.
But when he saw his caution gave her pain,
And kindness brought suspense's rack again,
Faith, honour, friendship, bound him to unmask
Truths which her timid fondness fear'd to ask.
    And yet with gracefully ingenuous power
Her spirit met th' explanatory hour;
Ev'n conscious beauty brighten'd in her eyes,
That told she knew their love no vulgar prize;
And pride like that of one more woman-grown,
Enlarged her mien, enrich'd her voice's tone.
'Twas then she struck the keys, and music made
That mock'd all skill her hand had e'er display'd.
Inspired and warbling, rapt from things around,
She look'd the very Muse of magic sound,
Painting in sound the forms of joy and woe,
Until the mind's eye saw them melt and glow.
Her closing strain composed and calm she play'd,
And sang no words to give its pathos aid;
But grief seem'd lingering in its lengthen'd swell,
And like so many tears the trickling touches fell.
Of Constance then she heard Theodric speak,
And stedfast smoothness still possess'd her cheek.
But when he told her how he oft had plann'd
Of old a journey to their mountain-land,
That might have brought him hither years before,
' Ah! then,' she cried, ' you knew not England's
    shore
And had you come,—and wherefore did you not?'
' Yes,' he replied, ' it would have changed our lot!'
Then burst her tears through pride's restraining
    bands,
And with her handkerchief, and both her hands,
She hid her face and wept.—Contrition stung

Theodric for the tears his words had wrung.
' But no,' she cried, ' unsay not what you've said,
Nor grudge one prop on which my pride is stay'd;
To think I could have merited your faith
Shall be my solace even unto death!'
' Julia,' Theodric said, with purposed look
Of firmness, ' my reply deserved rebuke;
But by your pure and sacred peace of mind,
And by the dignity of womankind,
Swear that when I am gone you'll do your best
To chase this dream of fondness from your breast.'

Th' abrupt appeal electrified her thought;—
She look'd to Heaven as if its aid she sought,
Dried hastily the tear-drops from her cheek,
And signified the vow she could not speak.

Ere long he communed with her mother mild:
' Alas!' she said, ' I warn'd—conjured my child,
And grieved for this affection from the first,
But like fatality it has been nursed;
For when her fill'd eyes on your picture fix'd,
And when your name in all she spoke was mix'd,
'Twas hard to chide an over-grateful mind!
Then each attempt a likelier choice to find
Made only fresh-rejected suitors grieve,
And Udolph's pride—perhaps her own—believe
That, could she meet, she might enchant ev'n you.
You came.—I augur'd the event, 'tis true,
But how was Udolph's mother to exclude
The guest that claim'd our boundless gratitude?
And that unconscious you had cast a spell
On Julia's peace, my pride refused to tell:
Yet in my child's illusion I have seen,
Believe me well, how blameless you have been:
Nor can it cancel, howsoe'er it end,
Our debt of friendship to our boy's best friend.'
At night he parted with the aged pair;
At early morn rose Julia to prepare

The last repast her hands for him should make :
And Udolph to convoy him o'er the lake.
The parting was to her such bitter grief,
That of her own accord she made it brief ;
But, lingering at her window, long survey'd
His boat's last glimpses melting into shade.
   Theodric sped to Austria, and achieved
His journey's object. Much was he relieved
When Udolph's letters told that Julia's mind
Had borne his loss firm, tranquil, and resign'd.
He took the Rhenish route to England, high
Elate with hopes, fulfill'd their ecstasy,
And interchanged with Constance's own breath
The sweet eternal vows that bound their faith.
   To paint that being to a grovelling mind
Were like portraying pictures to the blind.
'Twas needful ev'n infectiously to feel
Her temper's fond and firm and gladsome zeal,
To share existence with her, and to gain
Sparks from her love's electrifying chain
Of that pure pride, which, lessening to her breast
Life's ills, gave all its joys a treble zest,
Before the mind completely understood
That mighty truth—how happy are the good !
   Ev'n when her light forsook him, it bequeath'd
Ennobling sorrow ; and her memory breathed
A sweetness that survived her living days,
As odorous scents outlast the censer's blaze.
   Or, if a trouble dimm'd their golden joy,
'Twas outward dross, and not infused alloy :
Their home knew but affection's looks and speech—
A little Heaven, above dissension's reach.
But midst her kindred there was strife and gall ;
Save one congenial sister, they were all
Such foils to her bright intellect and grace,
As if she had engross'd the virtue of her race.
Her nature strove th' unnatural feuds to heal,

Her wisdom made the weak to her appeal;
And, tho' the wounds she cured were soon unclosed,
Unwearied still her kindness interposed.
    Oft on those errands though she went in vain,
And home, a blank without her, gave him pain,
He bore her absence for its pious end.—
But public grief his spirit came to bend;
For war laid waste his native land once more,
And German honour bled at every pore.
Oh! were he there, he thought, to rally back
One broken band, or perish in the wrack!
Nor think that Constance sought to move and melt
His purpose: like herself she spoke and felt:—
' Your fame is mine, and I will bear all woe
Except its loss!—but with you let me go
To arm you for, to embrace you from, the fight;
Harm will not reach me—hazards will delight!'
He knew those hazards better; one campaign
In England he conjured her to remain,
And she express'd assent, altho' her heart
In secret had resolved *they* should not part.
    How oft the wisest on misfortune's shelves
Are wreck'd by errors most unlike themselves!
That little fault, *that* fraud of love's romance,
That plan's concealment, wrought their whole
        mischance.
He knew it not preparing to embark,
But felt extinct his comfort's latest spark,
When, 'midst those number'd days, she made repair
Again to kindred worthless of her care.
'Tis true, she said the tidings she would write
Would make her absence on his heart sit light;
But, haplessly, reveal'd not yet her plan,
And left him in his home a lonely man.
    Thus damp'd in thoughts, he mused upon the
        past:
'Twas long since he had heard from Udolph last,

And deep misgivings on his spirit fell
That all with Udolph's household was not well.
'Twas that too-true prophetic mood of fear
That augurs griefs inevitably near,
Yet makes them not less startling to the mind
When come.   Least look'd-for then of humankind,
His Udolph ('twas, he thought at first, his sprite,)
With mournful joy that morn surprised his sight.
How changed was Udolph ! Scarce Theodric durst
Inquire his tidings,—he reveal'd the worst.
' At first,' he said, 'as Julia bade me tell,
She bore her fate high-mindedly and well,
Resolved from common eyes her grief to hide,
And from the world's compassion saved our pride ;
But still her health gave way to secret woe,
And long she pined—for broken hearts die slow !
Her reason went, but came returning, like
The warning of her death-hour—soon to strike ;
And all for which she now, poor sufferer ! sighs,
Is once to see Theodric ere she dies.
Why should I come to tell you this caprice ?
Forgive me ! for my mind has lost its peace.
I blame myself, and ne'er shall cease to blame,
That my insane ambition for the name
Of brother to Theodric founded all
Those high-built hopes that crush'd her by their
       fall.
I made her slight her mother's counsel sage,
But now my parents droop with grief and age :
And, though my sister's eyes mean no rebuke,
They overwhelm me with their dying look.
The journey's long, but you are full of ruth ;
And she who shares your heart, and knows its truth,
Has faith in your affection, far above
The fear of a poor dying object's love.'—
' She has, my Udolph,' he replied, ' 'tis true :
And oft we talk of Julia—oft of you.'

Their converse came abruptly to a close;
For scarce could each his troubled looks compose,
When visitants, to Constance near akin,
(In all but traits of soul,) were usher'd in.
They brought not her, nor 'midst their kindred band
The sister who alone, like her, was bland;
But said—and smiled to see it gave him pain—
That Constance would a fortnight yet remain.
Vex'd by their tidings, and the haughty view
They cast on Udolph as the youth withdrew,
Theodric blamed his Constance's intent.—
The demons went, and left him as they went
To read, when they were gone beyond recall,
A note from her loved hand explaining all.
She said, that with their house she only staid
That parting peace might with them all be made;
But pray'd for love to share his foreign life,
And shun all future chance of kindred strife.
He wrote with speed, his soul's consent to say:
The letter miss'd her on her homeward way.
In six hours Constance was within his arms:
Moved, flush'd, unlike her wonted calm of charms,
And breathless—with uplifted hands outspread—
Burst into tears upon his neck, and said,—
' I knew that those who brought your message
          laugh'd,
With poison of their own to point the shaft;
And this my one kind sister thought, yet loth
Confess'd she fear'd 'twas true you had been wroth.
But here you are, and smile on me: my pain
Is gone, and Constance is herself again.'
His ecstasy, it may be guess'd, was much:
Yet pain's extreme and pleasure's seem'd to touch.
What pride! embracing beauty's perfect mould;
What terror! lest his few rash words mistold,
Had agonized her pulse to fever's heat:
But calm'd again so soon it healthful beat,

And such sweet tones were in her voice's sound,
Composed herself, she breathed composure round.
    Fair being ! with what sympathetic grace
She heard, bewail'd, and pleaded Julia's case ;
Implored he would her dying wish attend,
' And go,' she said, ' to-morrow with your friend;
I'll wait for your return on England's shore,
And then we'll cross the deep, and part no more.'
    To-morrow both his soul's compassion drew
To Julia's call, and Constance urged anew
That not to heed her now would be to bind
A load of pain for life upon his mind.
He went with Udolph—from his Constance went—
Stifling, alas ! a dark presentiment
Some ailment lurk'd, ev'n whilst she smiled, to
        mock
His fears of harm from yester-morning's shock.
Meanwhile a faithful page he singled out,
To watch at home, and follow straight his route,
If aught of threaten'd change her health should
        show.
—With Udolph then he reach'd the house of woe.
    That winter's eve, how darkly Nature's brow
Scowl'd on the scenes it lights so lovely now !
The tempest, raging o'er the realms of ice,
Shook fragments from the rifted precipice ;
And, whilst their falling echoed to the wind,
The wolf's long howl in dismal discord join'd.
While white yon water's foam was raised in clouds
That whirl'd like spirits wailing in their shrouds :
Without was Nature's elemental din—
And beauty died, and friendship wept, within !
    Sweet Julia, though her fate was finish'd half,
Still knew him—smiled on him with feeble laugh—
And bless'd him, till she drew her latest sigh !
But lo ! while Udolph's bursts of agony,
And age's tremulous wailings, round him rose,

What accents pierced him deeper yet than those!
'Twas tidings, by his English messenger,
Of Constance—brief and terrible they were.
She still was living when the page set out
From home, but whether now was left in doubt.
Poor Julia! saw he then thy death's relief—
Stunn'd into stupor more than wrung with grief?
It was not strange; for in the human breast
Two master-passions cannot co-exist,
And that alarm which now usurp'd his brain
Shut out not only peace, but other pain.
'Twas fancying Constance underneath the shroud
That cover'd Julia made him first weep loud,
And tear himself away from them that wept.
Fast hurrying homeward, night nor day he slept,
Till, launch'd at sea, he dreamt that his soul's saint
Clung to him on a bridge of ice, pale, faint,
O'er cataracts of blood.   Awake, he bless'd
The shore; nor hope left utterly his breast,
Till reaching home, terrific omen! there
The straw-laid street preluded his despair—
The servant's look—the table that reveal'd
His letter sent to Constance last, still seal'd—
Though speech and hearing left him, told too clear
That he had now to suffer—not to fear.
He felt as if he ne'er should cease to feel—
A wretch live-broken on misfortune's wheel;
Her death's cause—he might make his peace with
          Heaven,
Absolved from guilt, but never self-forgiven.
   The ocean has its ebbings—so has grief;
'Twas vent to anguish, if 'twas not relief,
To lay his brow ev'n on her death-cold cheek.
Then first he heard her one kind sister speak:
She bade him, in the name of Heaven, forbear
With self-reproach to deepen his despair:
   ' 'Twas blame,' she said, ' I shudder to relate,

But none of yours, that caused our darling's fate;
Her mother (must I call her such ?) foresaw,
Should Constance leave the land, she would with-
				draw
Our House's charm against the world's neglect—
The only gem that drew it some respect.
Hence, when you went, she came and vainly spoke
To change her purpose—grew incensed, and broke
With execrations from her kneeling child.
Start not ! your angel from her knee rose mild,
Fear'd that she should not long the scene outlive,
Yet bade ev'n you th' unnatural one forgive.
Till then her ailment had been slight, or none :
But fast she droop'd, and fatal pains came on :
Foreseeing their event, she dictated
And sign'd these words for you.'	The letter said—
	' Theodric, this is destiny above
Our power to baffle ; bear it then, my love !
Rave not to learn the usage I have borne,
For one true sister left me not forlorn ;
And though you're absent in another land,
Sent from me by my own well-meant command,
Your soul, I know, as firm is knit to mine
As these clasp'd hands in blessing you now join :
Shape not imagined horrors in my fate—
Ev'n now my sufferings are not very great ;
And when your grief's first transports shall sub-
				side,
I call upon your strength of soul and pride
To pay my memory, if 'tis worth the debt,
Love's glorying tribute—not forlorn regret :
I charge my name with power to conjure up
Reflection's balmy, not its bitter cup.
My pardoning angel, at the gates of Heaven,
Shall look not more regard than you have given
To me ; and our life's union has been clad
In smiles of bliss as sweet as life e'er had.

Shall gloom be from such bright remembrance cast
Shall bitterness outflow from sweetness past?
No! imaged in the sanctuary of your breast,
There let me smile, amidst high thoughts at rest;
And let contentment on your spirit shine,
As if its peace were still a part of mine:
For if you war not proudly with your pain,
For you I shall have worse than lived in vain.
But I conjure your manliness to bear
My loss with noble spirit—not despair;
I ask you by our love to promise this,
And kiss these words, where I have left a kiss,—
The latest from my living lips for yours.'—
　　Words that will solace him while life endures:
For though his spirit from affliction's surge
Could ne'er to life, as life had been, emerge,
Yet still that mind whose harmony elate
Rang sweetness, ev'n beneath the crush of fate,—
That mind in whose regard all things were placed
In views that soften'd them, or lights that graced,
That soul's example could not but dispense
A portion of its own bless'd influence;
Invoking him to peace and that self-sway
Which Fortune cannot give, nor take away:
And though he mourn'd her long, 'twas with such
　　　　woe
As if her spirit watch'd him still below."

TRANSLATIONS.

MARTIAL ELEGY.

FROM THE GREEK OF TYRTÆUS.

OW glorious fall the valiant, sword in
      hand,
  In front of battle for their native land!
  But oh! what ills await the wretch that
      yields,
A recreant outcast from hisc ountry's fields;
The mother whom he loves shall quit her home,
An aged father at his side shall roam;
His little ones shall weeping with him go,
And a young wife participate his woe;
While scorn'd and scowl'd upon by every face,
They pine for food, and beg from place to place.

Stain of his breed! dishonouring manhood's form,
All ills shall cleave to him:—Affliction's storm
Shall blind him wandering in the vale of years,
Till, lost to all but ignominious fears,
He shall not blush to leave a recreant's name,
And children, like himself, inured to shame.

But we will combat for our fathers' land,
And we will drain the life-blood where we stand,
To save our children:—fight ye side by side,
And serried close, ye men of youthful pride,
Disdaining fear, and deeming light the cost
Of life itself in glorious battle lost.

Leave not our sires to stem the unequal fight,
Whose limbs are nerved no more with buoyant
      might;

Nor, lagging backward, let the younger breast
Permit the man of age (a sight unbless'd)
To welter in the combat's foremost thrust,
His hoary head dishevell'd in the dust,
And venerable bosom bleeding bare.

But youth's fair form, though fallen, is ever fair,
And beautiful in death the boy appears,
The hero boy, that dies in blooming years :
In man's regret he lives, and woman's tears ;
More sacred than in life, and lovelier far,
For having perish'd in the front of war.

SONG OF HYBRIAS THE CRETAN.

MY wealth's a burly spear and brand,
     And a right good shield of hides un-
          tann'd,
     Which on my arm I buckle :
With these I plough, I reap, I sow,
With these I make the sweet vintage flow,
     And all around me truckle.

But your wights that take no pride to wield
A massy spear and well-made shield,
     Nor joy to draw the sword :
Oh, I bring those heartless, hapless drones,
Down in a trice on their marrow-bones,
     To call me King and Lord.

FRAGMENT.

FROM THE GREEK OF ALCMAN.

THE mountain summits sleep: glens,
  cliffs, and caves
    Are silent—all the black earth's
    reptile brood—
The bees—the wild beasts of the mountain
  wood :
In depths beneath the dark red ocean's waves
  Its monsters rest, whilst wrapt in bower and
    spray
Each bird is hush'd that stretch'd its pinions to
  the day.

SPECIMENS OF TRANSLATIONS

FROM MEDEA.

Σκαιοὺς δὲ λέγων, κοὐδέν τι σοφοὺς,
Τοὺς πρόσθε βροτοὺς, οὐκ ἂν ἁμάρτοις.
Medea, v. 194, p. 33, Glasg. edit.

TELL me, ye bards, whose skill sublime
  First charm'd the ear of youthful Time,
  With numbers wrapt in heavenly fire,
  Who bade delighted Echo swell
The trembling transports of the lyre,
The murmur of the shell—
Why to the burst of joy alone
Accords sweet Music's soothing tone?
Why can no bard, with magic strain,
In slumbers steep the heart of pain ?
While varied tones obey your sweep,
The mild, the plaintive, and the deep,

Bends not despairing Grief to hear
Your golden lute with ravish'd ear?
Has all your art no power to bind
The fiercer pangs that shake the mind,
And lull the wrath at whose command
Murder bares her gory hand?
When flush'd with joy, the rosy throng
Weave the light dance, ye swell the song!
Cease, ye vain warblers! cease to charm!
The breast with other raptures warm!
Cease! till your hand with magic strain
In slumbers steep the heart of pain!

SPEECH OF THE CHORUS,

IN THE SAME TRAGEDY,

To Dissuade Medea from her Purpose of Putting her Children
to Death, and Flying for Protection to Athens.

HAGGARD queen! to Athens dost
thou guide
Thy glowing chariot, steep'd in kin-
dred gore;
Or seek to hide thy foul infanticide
Where Peace and Mercy dwell for evermore?

The land where Truth, pure, precious, and sublime,
Woos the deep silence of sequester'd bowers,
And warriors, matchless since the first of time,
Rear their bright banners o'er unconquer'd
towers!

Where joyous youth, to Music's mellow strain,
Twines in the dance with nymphs for ever fair,
While Spring eternal on the lilied plain,
Waves amber radiance through the fields of air!

The tuneful Nine (so sacred legends tell)
   First waked their heavenly lyre these scenes
      among ;
Still in your greenwood bowers they love to dwell ;
   Still in your vales they swell the choral song !

But there the tuneful, chaste, Pierian fair,
   The guardian nymphs of green Parnassus, now
Sprung from Harmonia, while her graceful hair
   Waved in high auburn o'er her polish'd brow !

ANTISTROPHE I.

Where silent vales, and glades of green array,
   The murmuring wreaths of cool Cephisus lave,
There, as the muse hath sung, at noon of day,
   The Queen of Beauty bow'd to taste the wave;

And bless'd the stream, and breathed across the
      land
   The soft sweet gale that fans yon summer
      bowers ;
And there the sister Loves, a smiling band,
   Crown'd with the fragrant wreaths of rosy
      flowers !

" And go," she cries, " in yonder valleys rove,
   With Beauty's torch the solemn scenes illume ;
Wake in each eye the radiant light of Love,
   Breathe on each cheek young Passion's tender
      bloom !

Entwine, with myrtle chains, your soft controul,
   To sway the hearts of Freedom's darling kind !
With glowing charms enrapture Wisdom's soul,
   And mould to grace ethereal Virtue's mind."

STROPHE II.

The land where Heaven's own hallow'd waters
    play,
  Where friendship binds the generous and the
    good,
Say, shall it hail thee from thy frantic way,
  Unholy woman! with thy hands embrued

In thine own children's gore! Oh! ere they bleed,
  Let Nature's voice thy ruthless heart appal!
Pause at the bold, irrevocable deed—
  The mother strikes—the guiltless babes shall
    fall!

Think what remorse thy maddening thoughts shall
    sting,
  When dying pangs their gentle bosoms tear!
Where shalt thou sink, when lingering echoes ring
  The screams of horror in thy tortured ear?

No! let thy bosom melt to Pity's cry,—
  In dust we kneel—by sacred Heaven implore—
O! stop thy lifted arm, ere yet they die,
  Nor dip thy horrid hands in infant gore!

ANTISTROPHE II.

Say, how shalt thou that barbarous soul assume,
  Undamp'd by horror at the daring plan?
Hast thou a heart to work thy children's doom?
  Or hands to finish what thy wrath began?

When o'er each babe you look a last adieu,
  And gaze on Innocence that smiles asleep,
Shall no fond feeling beat to Nature true,
  Charm thee to pensive thought—and bid thee
    weep?

When the young suppliants clasp their parent dear,
  Heave the deep sob, and pour the artless prayer—
Ay! thou shalt melt;—and many a heart-shed tear
  Gush o'er the harden'd features of despair!

Nature shall throb in every tender string,—
  Thy trembling heart the ruffian's task deny;—
Thy horror-smitten hands afar shall fling
  The blade, undrench'd in blood's eternal dye.

CHORUS.

  Hallow'd Earth! with indignation
    Mark, oh mark, the murderous deed!
  Radiant eye of wide creation,
    Watch th' accurs'd infanticide!

  Yet, ere Colchia's rugged daughter
    Perpetrate the dire design,
  And consign to kindred slaughter
    Children of thy golden line!

  Shall mortal hand, with murder gory,
    Cause immortal blood to flow?
  Sun of Heaven!—array'd in glory
    Rise, forbid, avert the blow!

  In the vales of placid gladness
    Let no rueful maniac range;
  Chase afar the fiend of Madness,
    Wrest the dagger from Revenge!

  Say, hast thou, with kind protection,
    Rear'd thy smiling race in vain;
  Fostering Nature's fond affection,
    Tender cares, and pleasing pain?

  Hast thou, on the troubled ocean,
    Braved the tempest loud and strong,
  Where the waves, in wild commotion,
    Roar Cyanean rocks among?

Didst thou roam the paths of danger,
   Hymenean joys to prove?
Spare, O sanguinary stranger,
   Pledges of thy sacred love!

Ask not Heaven's commiseration,
   After thou hast done the deed:
Mercy, pardon, expiation,
   Perish when thy victims bleed.

O'CONNOR'S CHILD;

OR, " THE FLOWER OF LOVE LIES BLEEDING."

I.

H! once the harp of Innisfail
   Was strung full high to notes of glad-
      ness;
   But yet it often told a tale
Of more prevailing sadness.
Sad was the note, and wild its fall,
As winds that moan at night forlorn
Along the isles of Fion-Gall,
When, for O'Connor's child to mourn,
The harper told, how lone, how far
From any mansion's twinkling star,
From any path of social men,
Or voice, but from the fox's den,
The lady in the desert dwelt;
And yet no wrongs, no fears she felt:
Say, why should dwell in place so wild,
O'Connor's pale and lovely child?

II.

Sweet lady! she no more inspires
Green Erin's hearts with beauty's power,

As, iu the palace of her sires,
She bloom'd a peerless flower.
Gone from her hand aud bosom, gone,
The royal brooch, the jewell'd ring,
That o'er her dazzling whiteness shone,
Like dews on lilies of the spring.
Yet why, though fall'n her brothers' kerne
Beneath De Bourgo's battle stern,
While yet in Leinster uuexplored,
Her friends survive the English sword ;
Why lingers she from Erin's host,
So far on Galway's shipwreck'd coast ;
Why wanders she a huntress wild—
O'Connor's pale and lovely child ?

III.

And fix'd on empty space, why burn
Her eyes with momentary wildness;
And wherefore do they then return
To more than woman's mildness ?
Dishevell'd are her raveu locks ;
On Connocht Moran's name she calls ;
And oft amidst the lonely rocks
She sings sweet madrigals.
Placed 'midst the foxglove and the moss,
Behold a parted warrior's cross !
That is the spot where, evermore,
The lady, at her shieling door,
Enjoys that, in communion sweet,
The living and the dead can meet,
For, lo ! to love-lorn fantasy,
The hero of her heart is nigh.

IV.

Bright as the bow that spans the storm,
In Erin's yellow vesture clad,
A son of light—a lovely form,

He comes and makes her glad;
Now on the grass-green turf he sits,
His tassell'd horn beside him laid;
Now o'er the hills in chase he flits,
The hunter and the deer a shade!
Sweet mourner! these are shadows vain
That cross the twilight of her brain;
Yet she will tell you, she is blest,
Of Connocht Moran's tomb possess'd,
More richly than in Aghrim's bower,
When bards high praised her beauty's power,
And kneeling pages offer'd up
The mórat in a golden cup.

V.

" A hero's bride! this desert bower,
It ill befits thy gentle breeding:
And wherefore dost thou love this flower
To call—'My love lies bleeding?'"
" This purple flower my tears have nursed;
A hero's blood supplied its bloom:
I love it, for it was the first
That grew on Connocht Moran's tomb.
Oh! hearken, stranger, to my voice!
This desert mansion is my choice!
And blest, though fatal, be the star
That led me to its wilds afar:
For here these pathless mountains free
Gave shelter to my love and me;
And every rock and every stone
Bore witness that he was my own.

VI.

O'Connor's child, I was the bud
Of Erin's royal tree of glory;
But woe to them that wrapt in blood
The tissue of my story!

Still as I clasp my burning brain,
A death-scene rushes on my sight;
It rises o'er and o'er again,
The bloody feud—the fatal night,
When chafing Connocht Moran's scorn,
They call'd my hero basely-born;
And bade him choose a meaner bride
Than from O'Connor's house of pride.
Their tribe, they said, their high degree,
Was sung in Tara's psaltery;
Witness their Eath's victorious brand;
And Cathal of the bloody hand;
Glory (they said) and power and honour
Were in the mansion of O'Connor:
But he, my loved one, bore in field
A humbler crest, a meaner shield.

VII.

Ah, brothers! what did it avail,
That fiercely and triumphantly
Ye fought the English of the Pale,
And stemm'd De Bourgo's chivalry!
And what was it to love and me,
That barons by your standard rode;
Or beal-fires for your jubilee
Upon a hundred mountains glow'd?
What though the lords of tower and dome
From Shannon to the North-sea foam,—
Thought ye your iron hands of pride
Could break the knot that love had tied?
No:—let the eagle change his plume,
The leaf its hue, the flower its bloom;
But ties around this heart were spun,
That could not, would not, be undone!

VIII.

At bleating of the wild watch-fold

Thus sang my love—' Oh, come with me ;
Our bark is on the lake, behold
Our steeds are fasten'd to the tree.
Come far from Castle-Connor's clans :—
Come with thy belted forestere,
And I, beside the lake of swans,
Shall hunt for thee the fallow-deer ;
And build thy hut, and bring thee home
The wild fowl and the honey-comb ;
And berries from the wood provide,
And play my clarshech by thy side.
Then come, my love !'—How could I stay ?
Our nimble stag-hounds track'd the way,
And I pursued, by moonless skies,
The light of Connocht Moran's eyes.

IX.

And fast and far, before the star
Of day-spring, rush'd we through the glade,
And saw at dawn the lofty bawn
Of Castle-Connor fade.
Sweet was to us the hermitage
Of this unplough'd, untrodden shore ;
Like birds all joyous from the cage,
For man's neglect we loved it more,
And well he knew, my huntsman dear,
To search the game with hawk and spear ;
While I, his evening food to dress,
Would sing to him in happiness.
But, oh, that midnight of despair !
When I was doom'd to rend my hair :
The night, to me, of shrieking sorrow !
The night, to him, that had no morrow !

X.

When all was hush'd at even tide,
I heard the baying of their beagle :

Be hush'd ! my Connocht Moran cried,
'Tis but the screaming of the eagle.
Alas ! 'twas not the eyrie's sound;
Their bloody bands had track'd us out;
Up-listening starts our couchant hound—
And, hark ! again, that nearer shout
Brings faster on the murderers.
Spare—spare him—Brazil—Desmond fierce !
In vain—no voice the adder charms;
Their weapons cross'd my sheltering arms :
Another's sword has laid him low—
Another's and another's ;
And every hand that dealt the blow—
Ah me ! it was a brother's !
Yes, when his moanings died away,
Their iron hands had dug the clay,
And o'er his burial-turf they trod,
And I behold—oh God ! oh God !—
His life-blood oozing from the sod !

XI.

Warm in his death-wounds sepulchred,
Alas ! my warrior's spirit brave
Nor mass nor ulla-lulla heard,
Lamenting, soothe his grave.
Dragg'd to their hated mansion back,
How long in thraldom's grasp I lay
I knew not, for my soul was black,
And knew no change of night or day.
One night of horror round me grew ;
Or if I saw, or felt, or knew,
'Twas but when those grim visages,
The angry brothers of my race,
Glared on each eye-ball's aching throb,
And check'd my bosom's power to sob,
Or when my heart with pulses drear
Beat like a death-watch to my ear.

XII.

But Heaven, at last, my soul's eclipse
Did with a vision bright inspire;
I woke and felt upon my lips
A prophetess's fire.
Thrice in the east a war-drum beat,
I heard the Saxon's trumpet sound,
And ranged, as to the judgment-seat,
My guilty, trembling brothers round.
Clad in the helm and shield they came;
For now De Bourgo's sword and flame
Had ravaged Ulster's boundaries,
And lighted up the midnight skies.
The standard of O'Connor's sway
Was in the turret where I lay;
That standard, with so dire a look,
As ghastly shone the moon and pale,
I gave,—that every bosom shook
Beneath its iron mail.

XIII.

And go! (I cried) the combat seek,
Ye hearts that unappallèd bore
The anguish of a sister's shriek,
Go!—and return no more!
For sooner guilt the ordeal brand
Shall grasp unhurt, than ye shall hold
The banner with victorious hand
Beneath a sister's curse unroll'd.
O stranger! by my country's loss!
And by my love! and by the cross!
I swear I never could have spoke
The curse that sever'd nature's yoke,
But that a spirit o'er me stood,
And fired me with the wrathful mood;
And frenzy to my heart was given,
To speak the malison of heaven.

XIV.

They would have cross'd themselves, all mute;
They would have pray'd to burst the spell;
But at the stamping of my foot
Each hand down powerless fell!
And go to Athunree! (I cried)
High lift the banner of your pride!
But know that where its sheet unrolls,
The weight of blood is on your souls!
Go where the havoc of your kerne
Shall float as high as mountain fern!
Men shall no more your mansion know;
The nettles on your hearth shall grow!
Dead, as the green oblivious flood
That mantles by your walls, shall be
The glory of O'Connor's blood!
Away! away to Athunree!
Where, downward when the sun shall fall,
The raven's wing shall be your pall!
And not a vassal shall unlace
The vizor from your dying face!

XV.

A bolt that overhung our dome
Suspended till my curse was given,
Soon as it pass'd these lips of foam,
Peal'd in the blood-red heaven.
Dire was the look that o'er their backs
The angry parting brothers threw:
But now, behold! like cataracts,
Come down the hills in view
O'Connor's plumed partisans;
Thrice ten Kilnagorvian clans
Were marching to their doom:
A sudden storm their plumage toss'd,
A flash of lightning o'er them cross'd,
And all again was gloom!

XVI.

Stranger ! I fled the home of grief,
At Connocht Moran's tomb to fall ;
I found the helmet of my chief,
His bow still hanging on our wall,
And took it down, and vow'd to rove
This desert place a huntress bold ;
Nor would I change my buried love
For any heart of living mould.
No ! for I am a hero's child ;
I'll hunt my quarry in the wild ;
And still my home this mansion make,
Of all unheeded and unheeding,
And cherish, for my warrior's sake—
'The flower of love lies bleeding.' "

LOCHIEL'S WARNING.

WIZARD—LOCHIEL.

WIZARD.

LOCHIEL, Lochiel ! beware of the day
    When the Lowlands shall meet thee in
        battle array !
    For a field of the dead rushes red on
  my sight,
And the clans of Culloden are scatter'd in fight.
They rally, they bleed, for their kingdom and
        crown ;
Woe, woe to the riders that trample them down !
Proud Cumberland prances, insulting the slain,
And their hoof-beaten bosoms are trod to the plain.
But hark ! through the fast-flashing lightning of
        war,

What steed to the desert flies frantic and far?
'Tis thine, O Glenullin! whose bride shall await,
Like a love-lighted watch-fire, all night at the gate.
A steed comes at morning: no rider is there;
But its bridle is red with the sign of despair.
Weep, Albin! to death and captivity led!
Oh weep! but thy tears cannot number the dead:
For a merciless sword on Culloden shall wave,
Culloden! that reeks with the blood of the brave.

LOCHIEL.

Go, preach to the coward, thou death-telling seer!
Or, if gory Culloden so dreadful appear,
Draw, dotard, around thy old wavering sight,
This mantle, to cover the phantoms of fright.

WIZARD.

Ha! laugh'st thou, Lochiel, my vision to scorn?
Proud bird of the mountain, thy plume shall be
        torn!
Say, rush'd the bold eagle exultingly forth,
From his home, in the dark rolling clouds of the
        north?
Lo! the death-shot of foemen outspeeding, he rode
Companionless, bearing destruction abroad;
But down let him stoop from his havoc on high!
Ah! home let him speed,—for the spoiler is nigh!
Why flames the far summit? Why shoot to the
        blast
Those embers, like stars from the firmament cast?
'Tis the fire-shower of ruin, all dreadfully driven
From his eyrie, that beacons the darkness of heaven.
Oh, crested Lochiel! the peerless in might,
Whose banners arise on the battlements' height,
Heaven's fire is around thee, to blast and to burn;
Return to thy dwelling! all lonely return!

For the blackness of ashes shall mark where it
    stood,
And a wild mother scream o'er her famishing brood.

LOCHIEL.

False Wizard, avaunt ! I have marshall'd my clan,
Their swords are a thousand, their bosoms are one !
They are true to the last of their blood and their
    breath,
And like reapers descend to the harvest of death.
Then welcome be Cumberland's steed to the shock !
Let him dash his proud foam like a wave on the
    rock !
But woe to his kindred, and woe to his cause,
When Albin her claymore indignantly draws ;
When her bonneted chieftains to victory crowd,
Clanronald the dauntless, and Moray the proud,
All plaided and plumed in their tartan array—

WIZARD.

—Lochiel, Lochiel ! beware of the day :
For, dark and despairing, my sight I may seal,
But man cannot cover what God would reveal ;
'Tis the sunset of life gives me mystical lore,
And coming events cast their shadows before.
I tell thee, Culloden's dread echoes shall ring
With the bloodhounds that bark for thy fugitive
    king.
Lo ! anointed by Heaven with the vials of wrath,
Behold, where he flies on his desolate path !
Now in darkness and billows, he sweeps from my
    sight ;
Rise, rise ! ye wild tempests, and cover his flight !
'Tis finish'd. Their thunders are hush'd on the
    moors ;
Culloden is lost, and my country deplores.
But where is the iron-bound prisoner ? Where ?

For the red eye of battle is shut in despair.
Say, mounts he the ocean-wave, banish'd, forlorn,
Like a limb from his country cast bleeding and
     torn ?
Ah no ! for a darker departure is near ;
The war-drum is muffled, and black is the bier ;
His death-bell is tolling : oh ! mercy, dispel
Yon sight, that it freezes my spirit to tell !
Life flutters convulsed in his quivering limbs,
And his blood-streaming nostril in agony swims.
Accursed be the faggots, that blaze at his feet,
Where his heart shall be thrown, ere it ceases to
     beat,
With the smoke of its ashes to poison the gale—

LOCHIEL.

—Down, soothless insulter ! I trust not the tale :
For never shall Albin a destiny meet,
So black with dishonour, so foul with retreat.
Tho' my perishing ranks should be strew'd in
     their gore,
Like ocean-weeds heap'd on the surf-beaten shore,
Lochiel, untainted by flight or by chains,
While the kindling of life in his bosom remains,
Shall victor exult, or in death be laid low,
With his back to the field, and his feet to the foe !
And leaving in battle no blot on his name,
Look proudly to Heaven from the death-bed of
     fame.

BATTLE OF THE BALTIC.

I.

OF Nelson and the North,
Sing the glorious day's renown,
When to battle fierce came forth
All the might of Denmark's crown,
And her arms along the deep proudly shone;
By each gun the lighted brand,
In a bold determined hand,
And the Prince of all the land
Led them on.—

II.

Like leviathans afloat,
Lay their bulwarks on the brine;
While the sign of battle flew
On the lofty British line:
It was ten of April morn by the chime:
As they drifted on their path,
There was silence deep as death;
And the boldest held his breath,
For a time.—

III.

But the might of England flush'd
To anticipate the scene;
And her van the fleeter rush'd
O'er the deadly space between.
" Hearts of oak ! " our captains cried; when each
     gun
From its adamantine lips
Spread a death-shade round the ships,
Like the hurricane eclipse
Of the sun.

IV.

Again! again! again!
And the havoc did not slack,
Till a feeble cheer the Dane
To our cheering sent us back ;—
Their shots along the deep slowly boom :—
Then ceased—and all is wail,
As they strike the shatter'd sail ;
Or, in conflagration pale,
Light the gloom.—

V.

Out spoke the victor then,
As he hail'd them o'er the wave :
" Ye are brothers ! ye are men !
And we conquer but to save ;—
So peace instead of death let us bring;
But yield, proud foe, thy fleet,
With the crews, at England's feet,
And make submission meet
To our King."—

VI.

Then Denmark bless'd our chief,
That he gave her wounds repose ;
And the sounds of joy and grief
From her people wildly rose,
As death withdrew his shades from the day.
While the sun look'd smiling bright
O'er a wide and woeful sight,
Where the fires of funeral light
Died away.

VII.

Now joy, Old England, raise !
For the tidings of thy might,
By the festal cities' blaze,
Whilst the wine-cup shines in light ;

And yet amidst that joy and uproar,
Let us think of them that sleep,
Full many a fathom deep,
By thy wild and stormy steep,
Elsinore !

VIII.

Brave hearts ! to Britain's pride
Once so faithful and so true,
On the deck of fame that died;—
With the gallant good Riou ;[1]
Soft sigh the winds of Heaven o'er their grave !
While the billow mournful rolls
And the mermaid's song condoles,
Singing glory to the souls
Of the brave !—

YE MARINERS OF ENGLAND.

A NAVAL ODE.

I.

YE Mariners of England !
　　That guard our native seas ;
　　Whose flag has braved, a thousand
　　　　years,
　　The battle and the breeze !
　　Your glorious standard launch again
　　To match another foe !
　　And sweep through the deep,
　　While the stormy winds do blow ;
　　While the battle rages loud and long,
　　And the stormy winds do blow.

---

[1] Capt. Riou, styled by Lord Nelson the gallant and the good.

II.

The spirits of your fathers
Shall start from every wave!—
For the deck it was their field of fame,
And Ocean was their grave:
Where Blake and mighty Nelson fell,
Your manly hearts shall glow,
As ye sweep through the deep,
While the stormy winds do blow;
While the battle rages loud and long,
And the stormy winds do blow.

III.

Britannia needs no bulwarks,
No towers along the steep;
Her march is o'er the mountain-waves,
Her home is on the deep.
With thunders from her native oak,
She quells the floods below,—
As they roar on the shore,
When the stormy winds do blow;
When the battle rages loud and long,
And the stormy winds do blow.

IV.

The meteor flag of England
Shall yet terrific burn;
Till danger's troubled night depart,
And the star of peace return.
Then, then, ye ocean warriors!
Our song and feast shall flow
To the fame of your name,
When the storm has ceased to blow;
When the fiery fight is heard no more,
And the storm has ceased to blow.

HOHENLINDEN.

ON Linden, when the sun was low,
   All bloodless lay th' untrodden snow,
   And dark as winter was the flow
   Of Iser, rolling rapidly:

But Linden saw another sight,
When the drum beat at dead of night,
Commanding fires of death to light
The darkness of her scenery.

By torch and trumpet fast array'd,
Each horseman drew his battle-blade,
And furious every charger neigh'd,
To join the dreadful revelry.

Then shook the hills with thunder riven,
Then rush'd the steed to battle driven,
And louder than the bolts of heaven,
Far flash'd the red artillery.

But redder yet that light shall glow
On Linden's hills of stained snow,
And bloodier yet the torrent flow
Of Iser, rolling rapidly.

'Tis morn, but scarce yon level sun
Can pierce the war-clouds, rolling dun,
Where furious Frank, and fiery Hun,
Shout in their sulph'rous canopy.

The combat deepens.　On, ye brave,
Who rush to glory, or the grave!
Wave, Munich! all thy banners wave,
And charge with all thy chivalry!

Few, few, shall part where many meet!
The snow shall be their winding-sheet,
And every turf beneath their feet
Shall be a soldier's sepulchre.

GLENARA.

 HEARD ye yon pibroch sound sad in
　　　the gale,
　　Where a band cometh slowly with
　　　weeping and wail?
'Tis the chief of Glenara laments for his dear;
And her sire, and the people, are call'd to her bier.

Glenara came first with the mourners and shroud;
Her kinsmen they follow'd, but mourn'd not aloud:
Their plaids all their bosoms were folded around;
They march'd all in silence,—they look'd on the
　　　ground.

In silence they reach'd over mountain and moor,
To a heath, where the oak-tree grew lonely and
　　　hoar:
" Now here let us place the grey stone of her
　　　cairn:
Why speak ye no word ?"—said Glenara the stern.

"And tell me, I charge you ! ye clan of my spouse,
Why fold ye your mantles, why cloud ye your
　　　brows ?"
So spake the rude chieftain :—no answer is made,
But each mantle unfolding, a dagger display'd.

" I dreamt of my lady, I dreamt of her shroud,"
Cried a voice from the kinsmen, all wrathful and
　　　loud;

"And empty that shroud and that coffin did seem :
Glenara ! Glenara ! now read me my dream !"

O ! pale grew the cheek of that chieftain, I ween,
When the shroud was unclosed, and no lady was
　　　seen ;
When a voice from the kinsmen spoke louder in
　　　scorn,
'Twas the youth who had loved the fair Ellen of
　　　Lorn :

" I dreamt of my lady, I dreamt of her grief,
I dreamt that her lord was a barbarous chief :
On a rock of the ocean fair Ellen did seem :
Glenara ! Glenara ! now read me my dream !"

In dust, low the traitor has knelt to the ground,
And the desert reveal'd where his lady was found ;
From a rock of the ocean that beauty is borne—
Now joy to the house of fair Ellen of Lorn !

EXILE OF ERIN.

THERE came to the beach a poor exile of
　　　Erin,
　　　The dew on his thin robe was heavy
　　　and chill :
For his country he sigh'd, when at twilight re-
　　　pairing
　　To wander alone by the wind-beaten hill :
But the day-star attracted his eye's sad devotion,
For it rose o'er his own native isle of the ocean,
Where once, in the fire of his youthful emotion,
　　He sang the bold anthem of Erin go bragh.

Sad is my fate ! said the heart-broken stranger :
   The wild deer and wolf to a covert can flee,
But I have no refuge from famine and danger,
   A home and a country remain not to me.
Never again, in the green sunny bowers,
Where my forefathers lived, shall I spend the
      sweet hours,
Or cover my harp with the wild-woven flowers,
   And strike to the numbers of Erin go bragh !

Erin, my country ! though sad and forsaken,
   In dreams I revisit thy sea-beaten shore ;
But, alas ! in a far foreign land I awaken,
   And sigh for the friends who can meet me no
      more !
Oh cruel fate ! wilt thou never replace me
In a mansion of peace—where no perils can chase
      me ?
Never again shall my brothers embrace me ?
   They died to defend me, or live to deplore !

Where is my cabin-door, fast by the wild wood ?
   Sisters and sire ! did ye weep for its fall ?
Where is the mother that look'd on my childhood?
   And where is the bosom friend, dearer than
      all ?
Oh ! my sad heart ! long abandon'd by pleasure,
Why did it dote on a fast-fading treasure ?
Tears, like the rain-drop, may fall without measure,
   But rapture and beauty they cannot recall.

Yet all its sad recollections suppressing,
   One dying wish my lone bosom can draw :
Erin ! an exile bequeaths thee his blessing !
   Land of my forefathers ! Erin go bragh !
Buried and cold, when my heart stills her
      motion,

Green be thy fields,—sweetest isle of the ocean!
And thy harp-striking bards sing aloud with de-
    votion,—
Erin mavournin—Erin go bragh![1]

LORD ULLIN'S DAUGHTER.

 CHIEFTAIN, to the Highlands bound,
    Cries, " Boatman, do not tarry!
And I'll give thee a silver pound
    To row us o'er the ferry."—

" Now who be ye, would cross Lochgyle,
    This dark and stormy water?"
" O, I'm the chief of Ulva's isle,
    And this Lord Ullin's daughter.—

And fast before her father's men
    Three days we've fled together,
For should he find us in the glen,
    My blood would stain the heather.

His horsemen hard behind us ride;
    Should they our steps discover,
Then who will cheer my bonny bride
    When they have slain her lover?"—

Out spoke the hardy Highland wight,
    " I'll go, my chief—I'm ready:
It is not for your silver bright;
    But for your winsome lady:

And by my word! the bonny bird
    In danger shall not tarry:
So though the waves are raging white,
    I'll row you o'er the ferry."—

[1] Ireland my darling, Ireland for ever.

By this the storm grew loud apace,
    The water-wraith was shrieking;
And in the scowl of Heaven each face
    Grew dark as they were speaking.

But still as wilder blew the wind,
    And as the night grew drearer,
Adown the glen rode armed men,
    Their trampling sounded nearer.—

" O haste thee, haste !" the lady cries,
    " Though tempests round us gather;
I'll meet the raging of the skies,
    But not an angry father."—

The boat has left a stormy land,
    A stormy sea before her,—
When, oh ! too strong for human hand,
    The tempest gather'd o'er her.—

And still they row'd amidst the roar
    Of waters fast prevailing :
Lord Ullin reach'd that fatal shore,
    His wrath was changed to wailing.—

For sore dismay'd, through storm and shade,
    His child he did discover :—
One lovely hand she stretch'd for aid,
    And one was round her lover.

" Come back ! come back !" he cried in grief,
    " Across this stormy water :
And I'll forgive your Highland chief,
    My daughter !—oh, my daughter !"—

'Twas vain :—the loud waves lash'd the shore,
    Return or aid preventing :—
The waters wild went o'er his child,
    And he was left lamenting.

ODE TO THE MEMORY OF BURNS.

SOUL of the Poet ! wheresoe'er
    Reclaim'd from earth, thy genius
        plume
    Her wings of immortality :
Suspend thy harp in happier sphere,
And with thine influence illume
The gladness of our jubilee.

And fly like fiends from secret spell,
Discord and Strife, at Burns's name,
Exorcised by his memory ;
For he was chief of bards that swell
The heart with songs of social flame,
And high delicious revelry.

And Love's own strain to him was given,
To warble all its ecstasies
With Pythian words unsought, unwill'd,—
Love, the surviving gift of Heaven,
The choicest sweet of Paradise,
In life's else bitter cup distill'd.

Who that has melted o'er his lay
To Mary's soul, in Heaven above,
But pictured sees, in fancy strong,
The landscape and the livelong day
That smiled upon their mutual love ?
Who that has felt forgets the song ?

Nor skill'd one flame alone to fan :
His country's high-soul'd peasantry
What patriot-pride he taught !—how much
To weigh the inborn worth of man !
And rustic life and poverty
Grow beautiful beneath his touch.

Him in his clay-built cot, the Muse
Entranced, and show'd him all the forms,
Of fairy-light and wizard gloom,
(That only gifted Poet views,)
The Genii of the floods and storms,
And martial shades from Glory's tomb.

On Bannock-field what thoughts arouse
The swain whom Burns's song inspires!
Beat not his Caledonian veins,
As o'er the heroic turf he ploughs,
With all the spirit of his sires,
And all their scorn of death and chains?

And see the Scottish exile, tann'd
By many a far and foreign clime,
Bend o'er his home-born verse, and weep
In memory of his native land,
With love that scorns the lapse of time,
And ties that stretch beyond the deep.

Encamp'd by Indian rivers wild,
The soldier resting on his arms,
In Burns's carol sweet recalls
The scenes that bless'd him when a child,
And glows and gladdens at the charms
Of Scotia's woods and waterfalls.

O deem not, 'midst this worldly strife,
An idle art the Poet brings:
Let high Philosophy control,
And sages calm, the stream of life,
'Tis he refines its fountain-springs,
The nobler passions of the soul.

It is the muse that consecrates
The native banner of the brave,
Unfurling at the trumpet's breath,

Rose, thistle, harp; 'tis she elates
To sweep the field or ride the wave,
A sunburst in the storm of death.

And thou, young hero, when thy pall
Is cross'd with mournful sword and plume,
When public grief begins to fade,
And only tears of kindred fall,
Who but the Bard shall dress thy tomb,
And greet with fame thy gallant shade!

Such was the soldier—Burns, forgive
That sorrows of mine own intrude
In strains to thy great memory due.
In verse like thine, oh! could he live,
The friend I mourn'd—the brave—the good—
Edward that died at Waterloo![1]

Farewell, high chief of Scottish song!
That couldst alternately impart
Wisdom and rapture in thy page,
And brand each vice with satire strong,
Whose lines are mottoes of the heart,
Whose truths electrify the sage.

Farewell! and ne'er may Envy dare
To wring one baleful poison drop
From the crush'd laurels of thy bust:
But while the lark sings sweet in air,
Still may the grateful pilgrim stop,
To bless the spot that holds thy dust.

[1] Major Edward Hodge, of the 7th Hussars, who fell at the head
of his squadron, in the attack of the Polish Lancers.

LINES

WRITTEN ON VISITING A SCENE IN ARGYLESHIRE.

AT the silence of twilight's contemplative
      hour,
    I have mused in a sorrowful mood,
    On the wind-shaken weeds that em-
    bosom the bower,
Where the home of my forefathers stood.
All ruin'd and wild is their roofless abode,
    And lonely the dark raven's sheltering tree:
And travell'd by few is the grass-cover'd road,
Where the hunter of deer and the warrior trode,
    To his hills that encircle the sea.

Yet wandering, I found on my ruinous walk,
    By the dial-stone aged and green,
One rose of the wilderness left on its stalk,
    To mark where a garden had been :
Like a brotherless hermit, the last of its race,
    All wild in the silence of nature, it drew,
From each wandering sun-beam, a lonely embrace,
For the night-weed and thorn overshadow'd the
    place,
    Where the flower of my forefathers grew.

Sweet bud of the wilderness ! emblem of all
    That remains in this desolate heart !
The fabric of bliss to its centre may fall,
    But patience shall never depart !
Though the wilds of enchantment, all vernal and
    bright,
    In the days of delusion by fancy combined

With the vanishing phantoms of love and delight,
Abandon my soul, like a dream of the night,
  And leave but a desert behind.

Be hush'd, my dark spirit ! for wisdom condemns
  When the faint and the feeble deplore ;
Be strong as the rock of the ocean that stems
  A thousand wild waves on the shore !
Through the perils of chance, and the scowl of
    disdain,
  May thy front be unalter'd, thy courage elate !
Yea ! even the name I have worshipp'd in vain
Shall awake not the sigh of remembrance again :
  To bear is to conquer our fate.

THE SOLDIER'S DREAM.

UR bugles sang truce, for the night-
  cloud had lower'd,
    And the sentinel stars set their
    watch in the sky;
And thousands had sunk on the ground overpower'd,
  The weary to sleep and the wounded to die.

When reposing that night on my pallet of straw,
  By the wolf-scaring faggot that guarded the
    slain ;
At the dead of the night a sweet vision I saw,
  And thrice ere the morning I dreamt it again.

Methought from the battle-field's dreadful array,
  Far, far I had roam'd on a desolate track :
'Twas Autumn,—and sunshine arose on the way
  To the home of my fathers, that welcomed me
    back.

I flew to the pleasant fields traversed so oft
  In life's morning march, when my bosom was
      young;
I heard my own mountain-goats bleating aloft,
  And knew the sweet strain that the corn-reapers
      sung.

Then pledged we the wine-cup, and fondly I swore,
  From my home and my weeping friends never
      to part;
My little ones kiss'd me a thousand times o'er,
  And my wife sobb'd aloud in her fulness of heart,

Stay, stay with us,—rest, thou art weary and worn!
  And fain was their war-broken soldier to stay;—
But sorrow return'd with the dawning of morn,
  And the voice in my dreaming ear melted away.

TO THE RAINBOW.

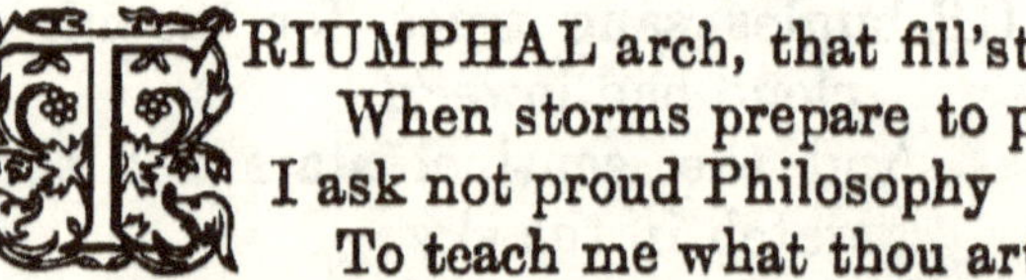

RIUMPHAL arch, that fill'st the sky,
  When storms prepare to part,
I ask not proud Philosophy
  To teach me what thou art—

Still seem, as to my childhood's sight,
  A midway station given
For happy spirits to alight
  Betwixt the earth and heaven.

Can all that optics teach, unfold
  Thy form to please me so,
As when I dreamt of gems and gold
  Hid in thy radiant bow?

When Science from Creation's face
  Enchantment's veil withdraws,
What lovely visions yield their place
  To cold material laws!

And yet, fair bow, no fabling dreams,
  But words of the Most High,
Have told why first thy robe of beams
  Was woven in the sky.

When o'er the green undeluged earth
  Heaven's covenant thou didst shine,
How came the world's grey fathers forth
  To watch thy sacred sign !

And when its yellow lustre smiled
  O'er mountains yet untrod,
Each mother held aloft her child
  To bless the bow of God.

Methinks thy jubilee to keep,
  The first-made anthem rang
On earth deliver'd from the deep,
  And the first poet sang.

Nor ever shall the Muse's eye
  Unraptured greet thy beam :
Theme of primeval prophecy,
  Be still the prophet's theme !

The earth to thee her incense yields,
  The lark thy welcome sings,
When glittering in the freshen'd fields
  The snowy mushroom springs.

How glorious is thy girdle, cast
  O'er mountain, tower, and town,
Or mirror'd in the ocean vast,
  A thousand fathoms down !

As fresh in yon horizon dark,
  As young thy beauties seem
As when the eagle from the ark
  First sported in thy beam :

For, faithful to its sacred page,
  Heaven still rebuilds thy span,
Nor lets the type grow pale with age
  That first spoke peace to man.

A DREAM.

WELL may sleep present us fictions,
  Since our waking moments teem
With such fanciful convictions
  As make life itself a dream.—
Half our daylight faith's a fable;
  Sleep disports with shadows too,
Seeming in their turn as stable
  As the world we wake to view.
Ne'er by day did Reason's mint
Give my thoughts a clearer print
Of assured reality,
Than was left by Phantasy
Stamp'd and colour'd on my sprite,
In a dream of yesternight.

In a bark, methought, lone steering,
  I was cast on Ocean's strife;
This, 'twas whisper'd in my hearing,
  Meant the sea of life.
Sad regrets from past existence
  Came, like gales of chilling breath,
Shadow'd in the forward distance,
  Lay the land of Death.
Now seeming more, now less remote,
On that dim-seen shore, methought,
I beheld two hands a space
Slow unshroud a spectre's face;
And my flesh's hair upstood,—
'Twas mine own similitude.—

But my soul revived at seeing
  Ocean, like an emerald spark,
Kindle, while an air-dropt being
  Smiling steer'd my bark.
Heaven-like—yet he look'd as human
  As supernal beauty can,
More compassionate than woman,
  Lordly more than man.
And as some sweet clarion's breath
Stirs the soldier's scorn of death—
So his accents bade me brook
The spectre's eyes of icy look,
Till it shut them—turn'd its head,
Like a beaten foe, and fled.

" Types not this," I said, " fair spirit!
  That my death-hour is not come ?
Say, what days shall I inherit ?—
  Tell my soul their sum."
" No," he said, " yon phantom's aspect,
  Trust me, would appal thee worse,
Held in clearly measured prospect :—
  Ask not for a curse!
Make not, for I overhear
Thine unspoken thoughts as clear
As thy mortal ear could catch
The close-brought tickings of a watch—
Make not the untold request
That's now revolving in thy breast.

'Tis to live again, remeasuring
  Youth's years, like a scene rehearsed,
In thy second life-time treasuring
  Knowledge from the first.
Hast thou felt, poor self-deceiver !
  Life's career so void of pain,
As to wish its fitful fever
  New begun again ?

Could experience, ten times thine,
Pain from Being disentwine—
Threads by Fate together spun?
Could thy flight Heaven's lightning shun?
No, nor could thy foresight's glance
'Scape the myriad shafts of Chance.

Wouldst thou bear again Love's trouble—
    Friendship's death-dissever'd ties;
Toil to grasp or miss the bubble
    Of Ambition's prize?
Say thy life's new guided action
    Flow'd from Virtue's fairest springs—
Still would Envy and Detraction
Double not their stings?
Worth itself is but a charter
To be mankind's distinguish'd martyr."
—I caught the moral, and cried, " Hail!
Spirit! let us onward sail,
Envying, fearing, hating none—
Guardian Spirit, steer me on!"

THE LAST MAN.

ALL worldly shapes shall melt in gloom,
    The Sun himself must die,
Before this mortal shall assume
    Its immortality!
I saw a vision in my sleep,
That gave my spirit strength to sweep
    Adown the gulf of Time!
I saw the last of human mould
That shall Creation's death behold,
    As Adam saw her prime!

THE LAST MAN.

The Sun's eye had a sickly glare,
   The Earth with age was wan,
The skeletons of nations were
   Around that lonely man !
Some had expired in fight,—the brands
Still rusted in their bony hands ;
   In plague and famine some !
Earth's cities had no sound nor tread ;
And ships were drifting with the dead
   To shores where all was dumb !

Yet, prophet-like, that lone one stood
   With dauntless words and high,
That shook the sere leaves from the wood
   As if a storm pass'd by,
Saying, We are twins in death, proud Sun !
Thy face is cold, thy race is run,
   'Tis Mercy bids thee go ;
For thou ten thousand thousand years
Hast seen the tide of human tears,
   That shall no longer flow.

What though beneath thee man put forth
   His pomp, his pride, his skill ;
And arts that made fire, flood, and earth,
   The vassals of his will ?—
Yet mourn I not thy parted sway,
Thou dim discrowned king of day :
   For all those trophied arts
And triumphs that beneath thee sprang,
Heal'd not a passion or a pang
   Entail'd on human hearts.

Go, let oblivion's curtain fall
   Upon the stage of men,
Nor with thy rising beams recall
   Life's tragedy again :

Its piteous pageants bring not back,
Nor waken flesh, upon the rack
 Of pain anew to writhe;
Stretch'd in disease's shapes abhorr'd
Or mown in battle by the sword,
 Like grass beneath the scythe.

Ev'n I am weary in yon skies
 To watch thy fading fire;
Test of all sumless agonies,
 Behold not me expire.
My lips that speak thy dirge of death—
Their rounded gasp and gurgling breath
 To see thou shalt not boast.
The eclipse of Nature spreads my pall,—
The majesty of darkness shall
 Receive my parting ghost!

This spirit shall return to Him
 Who gave its heavenly spark;
Yet think not, Sun, it shall be dim
 When thou thyself art dark!
No! it shall live again, and shine
In bliss unknown to beams of thine,
 By Him recall'd to breath,
Who captive led captivity,
Who robb'd the grave of Victory,—
 And took the sting from Death!

Go, Sun, while Mercy holds me up
 On Nature's awful waste
To drink this last and bitter cup
 Of grief that man shall taste—
Go, tell the night that hides thy face,
Thou saw'st the last of Adam's race,
 On Earth's sepulchral clod,
The darkening universe defy
To quench his Immortality,
 Or shake his trust in God!

VALEDICTORY STANZAS TO

J. P. KEMBLE, Esq.

COMPOSED FOR A PUBLIC MEETING HELD JUNE, 1817.

PRIDE of the British stage,
   A long and last adieu !
   Whose image brought th' heroic age
   Revived to Fancy's view.
Like fields refresh'd with dewy light
   When the sun smiles his last,
Thy parting presence makes more bright
   Our memory of the past;
And memory conjures feelings up
   That wine or music need not swell,
As high we lift the festal cup
   To Kemble—fare thee well !

His was the spell o'er hearts
   Which only Acting lends,—
The youngest of the sister Arts,
   Where all their beauty blends :
For ill can Poetry express
   Full many a tone of thought sublime,
And Painting, mute and motionless,
   Steals but a glance of time.
But by the mighty actor brought,
   Illusion's perfect triumphs come,—
Verse ceases to be airy thought,
   And Sculpture to be dumb.

Time may again revive,
   But ne'er eclipse the charm,
When Cato spoke in him alive,
   Or Hotspur kindled warm.

What soul was not resign'd entire
    To the deep sorrows of the Moor,—
What English heart was not on fire
    With him at Agincourt?
And yet a majesty possess'd
    His transport's most impetuous tone,
And to each passion of the breast
    The Graces gave their zone.

High were the task—too high,
    Ye conscious bosoms here!
In words to paint your memory
    Of Kemble and of Lear;
But who forgets that white discrowned head,
    Those bursts of Reason's half-extinguish'd glare;
Those tears upon Cordelia's bosom shed,
    In doubt more touching than despair,
        If 'twas reality he felt?
            Had Shakspeare's self amidst you been,
            Friends, he had seen you melt,
                And triumph'd to have seen!

And there was many an hour
    Of blended kindred fame,
When Siddons's auxiliar power
    And sister magic came.
Together at the Muse's side
    The tragic paragons had grown—
They were the children of her pride,
    The columns of her throne;
And undivided favour ran
    From heart to heart in their applause,
Save for the gallantry of man
    In lovelier woman's cause.

Fair as some classic dome,
    Robust and richly graced,

Your Kemble's spirit was the home
   Of genius and of taste;
Taste, like the silent dial's power,
   That when supernal light is given,
Can measure inspiration's hour,
   And tell its height in heaven.
At once ennobled and correct,
   His mind survey'd the tragic page,
And what the actor could effect,
   The scholar could presage.

These were his traits of worth :—
   And must we lose them now!
And shall the scene no more show forth
   His sternly-pleasing brow!
Alas, the moral brings a tear!—
   'Tis all a transient hour below;
And we that would detain thee here,
   Ourselves as fleetly go!
Yet shall our latest age
   This parting scene review :—
Pride of the British stage,
   A long and last adieu!

GERTRUDE OF WYOMING.

IN THREE PARTS.

ADVERTISEMENT.

Most of the popular histories of England, as well as of the American war, give an authentic account of the desolation of Wyoming, in Pennsylvania, which took place in 1778, by an incursion of the Indians. The Scenery and Incidents of the following Poem are connected with that event. The testimonies of historians and travellers concur in describing the infant colony as one of the happiest spots of human existence, for the hospitable and innocent manners of the inhabitants, the beauty of the country, and the luxuriant fertility of the soil and climate. In an evil hour, the junction of European with Indian arms converted this terrestrial paradise into a frightful waste. Mr. Isaac Weld informs us, that the ruins of many of the villages, perforated with balls, and bearing marks of conflagration, were still preserved by the recent inhabitants, when he travelled through America in 1796.

Part I.

I.

ON Susquehanna's side, fair Wyoming !
 Although the wild-flower on thy ruin'd
  wall,
 And roofless homes, a sad remem-
  brance bring
Of what thy gentle people did befall ;
Yet thou wert once the loveliest land of all
That see the Atlantic wave their morn restore.
Sweet land ! may I thy lost delights recall,
And paint thy Gertrude in her bowers of yore,
Whose beauty was the love of Pennsylvania's
  shore !

II.

Delightful Wyoming ! beneath thy skies,
The happy shepherd swains had nought to do
But feed their flocks on green declivities,
Or skim perchance thy lake with light canoe,

From morn till evening's sweeter pastime grew,
With timbrel, when beneath the forests brown,
Thy lovely maidens would the dance renew ;
And aye those sunny mountains half-way down
Would echo flagelet from some romantic town.

III.

Then, where of Indian hills the daylight takes
His leave, how might you the flamingo see
Disporting like a meteor on the lakes—
And playful squirrel on his nut-grown tree :
And every sound of life was full of glee,
From merry mock-bird's song, or hum of men ; ·
While heark'ning, fearing nought their revelry,
The wild deer arch'd his neck from glades, and then,
Unhunted, sought his woods and wilderness again.

IV.

And scarce had Wyoming of war or crime
Heard, but in transatlantic story rung,
For here the exile met from every clime,
And spoke in friendship every distant tongue :
Men from the blood of warring Europe sprung
Were but divided by the running brook ;
And happy where no Rhenish trumpet sung,
On plains no sieging mine's volcano shook,
The blue-eyed German changed his sword to
    pruning-hook.

V.

Nor far some Andalusian saraband
Would sound to many a native roundelay—
But who is he that yet a dearer land
Remembers, over hills and far away ?
Green Albin ![1] what though he no more survey

[1] Scotland.

Thy ships at anchor on the quiet shore,
Thy pellochs[1] rolling from the mountain bay,
Thy lone sepulchral cairn upon the moor,
And distant isles that hear the loud Corbrechtan[2]
     roar !

VI.

Alas ! poor Caledonia's mountaineer,
That want's stern edict e'er, and feudal grief,
Had forced him from a home he loved so dear !
Yet found he here a home and glad relief,
And plied the beverage from his own fair sheaf,
That fired his Highland blood with mickle glee :
And England sent her men, of men the chief,
Who taught those sires of Empire yet to be,
To plant the tree of life,—to plant fair Freedom's
     tree !

VII.

Here was not mingled in the city's pomp
Of life's extremes the grandeur and the gloom ;
Judgment awoke not here her dismal tromp,
Nor seal'd in blood a fellow-creature's doom,
Nor mourn'd the captive in a living tomb.
One venerable man, beloved of all,
Sufficed, where innocence was yet in bloom,
To sway the strife, that seldom might befall :
And Albert was their judge, in patriarchal hall.

VIII.

How reverend was the look, serenely aged,
He bore, this gentle Pennsylvanian sire,
Where all but kindly fervours were assuaged,
Undimm'd by weakness' shade, or turbid ire !
And though, amidst the calm of thought entire,

    [1] The Gaelic appellation for the porpoise.
    [2] The great whirlpool of the Western Hebrides.

Some high and haughty features might betray
A soul impetuous once, 'twas earthly fire
That fled composure's intellectual ray,
As Ætna's fires grow dim before the rising day.

IX.

I boast no song in magic wonders rife,
But yet, oh Nature ! is there nought to prize,
Familiar in thy bosom scenes of life ?
And dwells in day-light truth's salubrious skies
No form with which the soul may sympathize ?—
Young, innocent, on whose sweet forehead mild
The parted ringlet shone in simplest guise,
An inmate in the home of Albert smiled,
Or blest his noonday-walk—she was his only child.

X.

The rose of England bloom'd on Gertrude's cheek—
What though these shades had seen her birth, her
    sire
A Briton's independence taught to seek
Far western worlds ; and there his household fire
The light of social love did long inspire,
And many a halcyon day he lived to see
Unbroken but by one misfortune dire,
When fate had reft his mutual heart—but she
Was gone—and Gertrude climb'd a widow'd father's
    knee.

XI.

A loved bequest,—and I may half impart—
To them that feel the strong paternal tie,
How like a new existence to his heart
That living flower uprose beneath his eye,
Dear as she was from cherub infancy,

From hours when she would round his garden play,
To time when as the ripening years went by,
Her lovely mind could culture well repay,
And more engaging grew, from pleasing day to day.

XII.

I may not paint those thousand infant charms;
(Unconscious fascination, undesign'd!)
The orison repeated in his arms,
For God to bless her sire and all mankind;
The book, the bosom on his knee reclined,
Or how sweet fairy-lore he heard her con,
(The playmate ere the teacher of her mind:)
All uncompanion'd else her heart had gone
Till now, in Gertrude's eyes, their ninth blue
        summer shone.

XIII.

And summer was the tide, and sweet the hour,
When sire and daughter saw, with fleet descent,
An Indian from his bark approach their bower,
Of buskin'd limb, and swarthy lineament;
The red wild feathers on his brow were blent,
And bracelets bound the arm that help'd to light
A boy, who seem'd, as he beside him went,
Of Christian vesture, and complexion bright,
Led by his dusky guide, like morning brought by
        night.

XIV.

Yet pensive seem'd the boy for one so young—
The dimple from his polish'd cheek had fled;
When, leaning on his forest-bow unstrung,
Th' Oneyda warrior to the planter said,
And laid his hand upon the stripling's head,
" Peace be to thee! my words this belt approve
The paths of peace my steps have hither led:

This little nursling, take him to thy love,
And shield the bird unfledged, since gone the
    parent dove.

XV.

Christian! I am the foeman of thy foe;
Our wampum league thy brethren did embrace:
Upon the Michigan, three moons ago,
We launch'd our pirogues for the bison chase,
And with the Hurons planted for a space,
With true and faithful hands, the olive-stalk;
But snakes are in the bosoms of their race,
And though they held with us a friendly talk,
The hollow peace-tree fell beneath their tomahawk!

XVI.

It was encamping on the lake's far port,
A cry of Areouski[1] broke our sleep,
Where storm'd an ambush'd foe thy nation's fort,
And rapid, rapid whoops came o'er the deep;
But long thy country's war-sign on the steep
Appear'd through ghastly intervals of light,
And deathfully their thunders seem'd to sweep,
Till utter darkness swallow'd up the sight,
As if a shower of blood had quench'd the fiery
    fight!

XVII.

It slept—it rose again—on high their tower
Sprung upwards like a torch to light the skies,
Then down again it rain'd an ember shower,
And louder lamentations heard we rise:
As when the evil Manitou that dries
Th' Ohio woods, consumes them in his ire,
In vain the desolated panther flies,

[1] The Indian God of War.

And howls amidst his wilderness of fire :
Alas ! too late, we reach'd and smote those Hurons
          dire !

XVIII.

But as the fox beneath the nobler hound,
So died their warriors by our battle brand;
And from the tree we, with her child, unbound
A lonely mother of the Christian land:—
Her lord—the captain of the British band—
Amidst the slaughter of his soldiers lay.
Scarce knew the widow our delivering hand;
Upon her child she sobb'd and swoon'd away,
Or shriek'd unto the God to whom the Christians
          pray.

XIX.

Our virgins fed her with their kindly bowls
Of fever-balm and sweet sagamité :
But she was journeying to the land of souls,
And lifted up her dying head to pray
That we should bid an ancient friend convey
Her orphan to his home of England's shore ;
And take, she said, this token far away,
To one that will remember us of yore,
When he beholds the ring that Waldegrave's
          Julia wore.

XX.

And I, the eagle of my tribe, have rush'd
With this lorn dove."—A sage's self-command
Had quell'd the tears from Albert's heart that
          gush'd ;
But yet his cheek—his agitated hand—
That shower'd upon the stranger of the land
No common boon, in grief but ill beguiled
A soul that was not wont to be unmann'd ;

" And stay," he cried, " dear pilgrim of the wild,
Preserver of my old, my boon companion's child !—

XXI.

Child of a race whose name my bosom warms,
On earth's remotest bounds how welcome here !
Whose mother oft, a child, has fill'd these arms,
Young as thyself, and innocently dear,
Whose grandsire was my early life's compeer.
Ah, happiest home of England's happy clime !
How beautiful ev'n now thy scenes appear,
As in the noon and sunshine of my prime !
How gone like yesterday these thrice ten years of
            time !

XXII.

And Julia ! when thou wert like Gertrude now,
Can I forget thee, favourite child of yore ?
Or thought I, in thy father's house, when thou
Wert lightest-hearted on his festive floor,
And first of all his hospitable door
To meet and kiss me at my journey's end ?
But where was I when Waldegrave was no more ?
And thou didst pale thy gentle head extend
In woes, that ev'n the tribe of deserts was thy
            friend !"

XXIII.

He said—and strain'd unto his heart the boy ;—
Far differently, the mute Oneyda took
His calumet of peace, and cup of joy ;
As monumental bronze unchanged his look ;
A soul that pity touch'd but never shook ;
Train'd from his tree-rock'd cradle to his bier
The fierce extreme of good and ill to brook
Impassive—fearing but the shame of fear—
A stoic of the woods—a man without a tear.

XXIV.

Yet deem not goodness on the savage stock
Of Outalissi's heart disdain'd to grow ;
As lives the oak unwither'd on the rock
By storms above, and barrenness below ;
He scorn'd his own, who felt another's woe :
And ere the wolf-skin on his back he flung,
Or laced his mocassins, in act to go,
A song of parting to the boy he sung,
Who slept on Albert's couch, nor heard his friendly
       tongue.

XXV.

" Sleep, wearied one ! and in the dreaming land
Shouldst thou to-morrow with thy mother meet,
Oh ! tell her spirit that the white man's hand
Hath pluck'd the thorns of sorrow from thy feet ;
While I in lonely wilderness shall greet
Thy little foot-prints—or by traces know
The fountain, where at noon I thought it sweet
To feed thee with the quarry of my bow,
And pour'd the lotus-horn, or slew the mountain
       roe.

XXVI.

Adieu ! sweet scion of the rising sun !
But should affliction's storms thy blossom mock,
Then come again—my own adopted one !
And I will graft thee on a noble stock :
The crocodile, the condor of the rock,
Shall be the pastime of thy sylvan wars ;
And I will teach thee in the battle's shock
To pay with Huron blood thy father's scars,
And gratulate his soul rejoicing in the stars !"

XXVII.

So finish'd he the rhyme (howe'er uncouth)
That true to nature's fervid feelings ran ;

(And song is but the eloquence of truth:)
Then forth uprose that lone wayfaring man;
But dauntless he, nor chart, nor journey's plan
In woods required, whose trained eye was keen,
As eagle of the wilderness, to scan
His path by mountain, swamp, or deep ravine,
Or ken far friendly huts on good savannas green.

XXVIII.

Old Albert saw him from the valley's side—
His pirogue launch'd—his pilgrimage begun—
Far, like the red-bird's wing he seem'd to glide;
Then dived, and vanish'd in the woodlands dun.
Oft, to that spot by tender memory won,
Would Albert climb the promontory's height,
If but a dim sail glimmer'd in the sun;
But never more to bless his longing sight,
Was Outalissi hail'd, with bark and plumage bright.

PART II.

I.

 VALLEY from the river shore with
　　　drawn
　　Was Albert's home, two quiet woods
　　　between,
Whose lofty verdure overlook'd his lawn;
And waters to their resting-place serene
Came freshening, and reflecting all the scene:
(A mirror in the depth of flowery shelves;)
So sweet a spot of earth, you might (I ween)
Have guess'd some congregation of the elves,
To sport by summer moons, had shaped it for
　　　themselves.

II.

Yet wanted not the eye far scope to muse,
Nor vistas open'd by the wandering stream ;
Both where at evening Alleghany views,
Through ridges burning in her western beam,
Lake after lake interminably gleam :
And past those settlers' haunts the eye might roam
Where earth's unliving silence all would seem ;
Save where on rocks the beaver built his dome,
Or buffalo remote low'd far from human home.

III.

But silent not that adverse eastern path,
Which saw Aurora's hills th' horizon crown ;
There was the river heard, in bed of wrath,
(A precipice of foam from mountains brown,)
Like tumults heard from some far distant town ;
But softening in approach he left his gloom,
And murmur'd pleasantly, and laid him down
To kiss those easy curving banks of bloom,
That lent the windward air an exquisite perfume.

IV.

It seem'd as if those scenes sweet influence had
On Gertrude's soul, and kindness like their own
Inspired those eyes affectionate and glad,
That seem'd to love whate'er they look'd upon ;
Whether with Hebe's mirth her features shone,
Or if a shade more pleasing them o'ercast,
(As if for heavenly musing meant alone ;)
Yet so becomingly th' expression past,
That each succeeding look was lovelier than the
        last.

V.

Nor guess I, was that Pennsylvanian home,
With all its picturesque and balmy grace,

And fields that were a luxury to roam,
Lost on the soul that look'd from such a face!
Enthusiast of the woods! when years apace
Had bound thy lovely waist with woman's zone,
The sunrise path, at morn, I see thee trace
To hills with high magnolia overgrown,
And joy to breathe the groves, romantic and alone.

VI.

The sunrise drew her thoughts to Europe forth,
That thus apostrophized its viewless scene:
" Land of my father's love, my mother's birth!
The home of kindred I have never seen!
We know not other—oceans are between:
Yet say, far friendly hearts! from whence we came,
Of us does oft remembrance intervene?
My mother sure—my sire a thought may claim;—
But Gertrude is to you an unregarded name.

VII.

And yet, loved England! when thy name I trace
In many a pilgrim's tale and poet's song,
How can I choose but wish for one embrace
Of them, the dear unknown, to whom belong
My mother's looks,—perhaps her likeness strong?
Oh, parent! with what reverential awe,
From features of thine own related throng,
An image of thy face my soul could draw!
And see thee once again whom I too shortly saw!"

VIII.

Yet deem not Gertrude sigh'd for foreign joy;
To soothe a father's couch her only care,
And keep his reverend head from all annoy;
For this, methinks, her homeward steps repair,
Soon as the morning wreath had bound her hair;

While yet the wild deer trod in spangling dew,
While boatmen carol'd to the fresh-blown air,
And woods a horizontal shadow threw,
And early fox appear'd in momentary view.

IX.

Apart there was a deep untrodden grot,
Where oft the reading hours sweet Gertrude wore;
Tradition had not named its lonely spot;
But here (methinks) might India's sons explore
Their fathers' dust, or lift, perchance of yore,
Their voice to the great Spirit :—rocks sublime
To human art a sportive semblance bore,
And yellow lichens colour'd all the clime,
Like moonlight battlements, and towers decay'd
        by time.

X.

But high in amphitheatre above,
Gay tinted woods their massy foliage threw :
Breathed but an air of heaven, and all the grove
As if instinct with living spirit grew,
Rolling its verdant gulfs of every hue;
And now suspended was the pleasing din,
Now from a murmur faint it swell'd anew,
Like the first note of organ heard within
Cathedral aisles,—ere yet its symphony begin.

XI.

It was in this lone valley she would charm
The lingering noon, where flowers a couch had
        strown ;
Her cheek reclining, and her snowy arm
On hillock by the pine-tree half o'ergrown :
And aye that volume on her lap is thrown,
Which every heart of human mould endears ;
With Shakspeare's self she speaks and smiles alone,

And no intruding visitation fears,
To shame the unconscious laugh, or stop her
          sweetest tears.

XII.

And nought within the grove was seen or heard
But stock-doves plaining through its gloom pro-
          found,
Or winglet of the fairy humming-bird,
Like atoms of the rainbow fluttering round ;
When, lo ! there enter'd to its inmost ground
A youth, the stranger of a distant land ;
He was, to weet, for eastern mountains bound ;
But late th' equator suns his cheek had tann'd,
And California's gales his roving bosom fann'd.

XIII.

A steed, whose rein hung loosely o'er his arm,
IIe led dismounted ; ere his leisure pace,
Amid the brown leaves, could her ear alarm,
Close he had come, and worshipp'd for a space
Those downcast features :—she her lovely face
Uplift on one, whose lineaments and frame
Wore youth and manhood's intermingled grace :
Iberian seem'd his boot—his robe the same,
And well the Spanish plume his lofty looks became.

XIV.

For Albert's home he sought—her finger fair
Has pointed where the father's mansion stood.
Returning from the copse he soon was there ;
And soon has Gertrude hied from dark greenwood ;
Nor joyless, by the converse, understood
Between the man of age and pilgrim young,
That gay congeniality of mood,
And early liking from acquaintance sprung ;
Full fluently conversed their guest in England's
          tongue.

XV.

And well could he his pilgrimage of taste
Unfold,—and much they loved his fervid strain,
While he each fair variety retraced
Of climes, and manners, o'er the eastern main.
Now happy Switzer's hills,—romantic Spain,—
Gay lilied fields of France,—or, more refined,
The soft Ausonia's monumental reign ;
Nor less each rural image he design'd
Than all the city's pomp and home of humankind.

XVI.

Anon some wilder portraiture he draws ;
Of Nature's savage glories he would speak,—
The loneliness of earth that overawes,—
Where, resting by some tomb of old Cacique,
The lama-driver on Peruvia's peak
Nor living voice nor motion marks around ;
But storks that to the boundless forest shriek,
Or wild-cane arch high flung o'er gulf profound,
That fluctuates when the storms of El Dorado
  sound.

XVII.

Pleased with his guest, the good man still would
  ply
Each earnest question, and his converse court ;
But Gertrude, as she eyed him, knew not why
A strange and troubling wonder stopt her short.
" In England thou hast been,—and, by report,
An orphan's name (quoth Albert) may'st have
  known.
Sad tale !—when latest fell our frontier fort,—
One innocent—one soldier's child—alone
Was spared, and brought to me, who loved him as
  my own.

XVIII.

Young Henry Waldegrave! three delightful years
These very walls his infant sports did see,
But most I loved him when his parting tears
Alternately bedew'd my child and me:
His sorest parting, Gertrude, was from thee;
Nor half its grief his little heart could hold;
By kindred he was sent for o'er the sea,
They tore him from us when but twelve years old,
And scarcely for his loss have I been yet consoled!"

XIX.

His face the wanderer hid—but could not hide
A tear, a smile, upon his cheek that dwelt;
" And speak! mysterious stranger!" (Gertrude
        cried)
" It is!—it is!—I knew—I knew him well;
'Tis Waldegrave's self, of Waldegrave come to tell!"
A burst of joy the father's lips declare!
But Gertrude speechless on his bosom fell;
At once his open arms embraced the pair,
Was never group more blest in this wide world of
        care.

XX.

" And will ye pardon then (replied the youth)
Your Waldegrave's feigned name, and false attire?
I durst not in the neighbourhood, in truth,
The very fortunes of your house inquire;
Lest one that knew me might some tidings dire
Impart, and I my weakness all betray,
For had I lost my Gertrude and my sire,
I meant but o'er your tombs to weep a day,
Unknown I meant to weep, unknown to pass away.

XXI.

But here ye live, ye bloom,—in each dear face,
The changing hand of time I may not blame;

For there, it hath but shed more reverend grace,
And here, of beauty perfected the frame:
And well I know your hearts are still the same—
They could not change—ye look the very way,
As when an orphan first to you I came.
And have ye heard of my poor guide, I pray?
Nay, wherefore weep ye, friends, on such a joyous
      day?"

XXII.

"And art thou here? or is it but a dream?
And wilt thou, Waldegrave, wilt thou, leave us
      more?"
"No, never! thou that yet dost lovelier seem
Than aught on earth—than ev'n thyself of yore—
I will not part thee from thy father's shore;
But we shall cherish him with mutual arms,
And hand in hand again the path explore
Which every ray of young remembrance warms,
While thou shalt be my own, with all thy truth and
      charms!"

XXIII.

At morn, as if beneath a galaxy
Of over-arching groves in blossoms white,
Where all was odorous scent and harmony,
And gladness to the heart, nerve, ear, and sight:
There, if, O gentle Love! I read aright
The utterance that seal'd thy sacred bond,
'Twas listening to these accents of delight,
She hid upon his breast those eyes, beyond
Expression's power to paint, all languishingly
      fond—

XXIV.

"Flower of my life, so lovely and so lone!
Whom I would rather in this desert meet,

Scorning, and scorn'd by fortune's power, than own
Her pomp and splendours lavish'd at my feet !
Turn not from me thy breath, more exquisite
Than odours cast on heaven's own shrine—to
        please—
Give me thy love, than luxury more sweet,
And more than all the wealth that loads the breeze,
When Coromandel's ships return from Indian
        seas."

XXV.

Then would that home admit them—happier far
Than grandeur's most magnificent saloon,
While, here and there, a solitary star
Flush'd in the darkening firmament of June ;
And silence brought the soul-felt hour, full soon.
Ineffable, which I may not portray ;
For never did the hymenean moon
A paradise of hearts more sacred sway,
In all that slept beneath her soft voluptuous ray.

Part III.

I.

LOVE ! in such a wilderness as this,
    Where transport and security entwine,
    Here is the empire of thy perfect bliss,
And here thou art a god indeed divine.
Here shall no forms abridge, no hours confine,
The views, the walks, that boundless joy inspire !
Roll on, ye days of raptured influence, shine !
Nor, blind with ecstasy's celestial fire,
Shall love behold the spark of earth-born time expire

II.

Three little moons, how short! amidst the grove
And pastoral savannas they consume!
While she, beside her buskin'd youth to rove,
Delights, in fancifully wild costume,
Her lovely brow to shade with Indian plume;
And forth in hunter-seeming vest they fare;
But not to chase the deer in forest gloom,
'Tis but the breath of heaven—the blessed air—
And interchange of hearts unknown, unseen to
       share.

III.

What though the sportive dog oft round them note,
Or fawn, or wild bird bursting on the wing;
Yet who, in Love's own presence, would devote
To death those gentle throats that wake the spring,
Or writhing from the brook its victim bring?
No!—nor let fear one little warbler rouse;
But, fed by Gertrude's hand, still let them sing,
Acquaintance of her path, amidst the boughs,
That shade ev'n now her love, and witness'd first
       her vows.

IV.

Now labyrinths, which but themselves can pierce,
Methinks, conduct them to some pleasant ground,
Where welcome hills shut out the universe,
And pines their lawny walk encompass round;
There, if a pause delicious converse found.
'Twas but when o'er each heart th' idea stole,
(Perchance a while in joy's oblivion drown'd)
That come what may, while life's glad pulses roll,
Indissolubly thus should soul be knit to soul.

V.

And in the visions of romantic youth,
What years of endless bliss are yet to flow!

But mortal pleasure, what art thou in truth?
The torrent's smoothness, ere it dash below!
And must I change my song? and must I show,
Sweet Wyoming! the day when thou wert doom'd,
Guiltless, to mourn thy loveliest bowers laid low!
When where of yesterday a garden bloom'd,
Death overspread his pall, and blackening ashes
    gloom'd?

VI.

Sad was the year, by proud oppression driven,
When Transatlantic Liberty arose,
Not in the sunshine and the smile of heaven,
But wrapt in whirlwinds, and begirt with woes,
Amidst the strife of fratricidal foes;
Her birth-star was the light of burning plains;[1]
Her baptism is the weight of blood that flows
From kindred hearts—the blood of British veins—
And famine tracks her steps, and pestilential pains.

VII.

Yet, ere the storm of death had raged remote,
Or siege unseen in heaven reflects its beams,
Who now each dreadful circumstance shall note,
That fills pale Gertrude's thoughts, and nightly
    dreams?
Dismal to her the forge of battle gleams
Portentous light! and music's voice is dumb;
Save where the fife its shrill réveillé screams,
Or midnight streets re-echo to the drum,
That speaks of maddening strife, and blood-stained
    fields to come.

VIII.

It was in truth a momentary pang;
Yet how comprising myriad shapes of woe!

[1] Alluding to the miseries that attended the American civil war.

I

First when in Gertrude's ear the summons rang,
A husband to the battle doom'd to go !
" Nay meet not thou (she cried) thy kindred foe !
But peaceful let us seek fair England's strand !"
" Ah, Gertrude, thy beloved heart, I know,
Would feel like mine the stigmatising brand !
Could I forsake the cause of Freedom's holy band !

IX.

But shame—but flight—a recreant's name to prove,
To hide in exile ignominious fears ;
Say, ev'n if this I brook'd, the public love
Thy father's bosom to his home endears :
And how could I his few remaining years,
My Gertrude, sever from so dear a child ?"
So, day by day, her boding heart he cheers :
At last that heart to hope is half beguiled,
And, pale through tears suppress'd, the mournful
    beauty smiled.

X.

Night came,—and in their lighted bower, full late,
The joy of converse had endured—when, hark !
Abrupt and loud, a summons shook their gate ;
And heedless of the dog's obstrep'rous bark,
A form had rush'd amidst them from the dark,
And spread his arms,—and fell upon the floor :
Of aged strength his limbs retain'd the mark ;
But desolate he look'd, and famish'd poor,
As ever shipwreck'd wretch lone left on desert
    shore.

XI.

Uprisen, each wond'ring brow is knit and arch'd:
A spirit from the dead they deem him first :
To speak he tries ; but quivering, pale, and parch'd,
From lips, as by some powerless dream accursed,

Emotions unintelligible burst ;
And long his filmed eye is red and dim ;
At length the pity-proffer'd cup his thirst
Had half assuaged, and nerved his shuddering limb,
When Albert's hand he grasp'd ; but Albert knew
      not him—

XII.

" And hast thou then forgot," (he cried forlorn,
And eyed the group with half indignant air,)
" Oh ! hast thou, Christian chief, forgot the morn
When I with thee the cup of peace did share ?
Then stately was this head, and dark this hair,
That now is white as Appalachia's snow ;
But, if the weight of fifteen years' despair,
And age hath bow'd me, and the torturing foe,
Bring me my boy—and he will his deliverer
      know ! "—

XIII.

It was not long, with eyes and heart of flame,
Ere Henry to his loved Oneyda flew :
" Bless thee, my guide !"—but backward, as he
      came,
The chief his old bewilder'd head withdrew,
And grasp'd his arm, and look'd and look'd him
      through.
'Twas strange—nor could the group a smile
      control—
The long, the doubtful scrutiny to view :
At last delight o'er all his features stole,
" It is—my own," he cried, and clasp'd him to his
      soul.

XIV.

" Yes ! thou recall'st my pride of years, for then
The bowstring of my spirit was not slack,

When, spite of woods, and floods, and ambush'd
        men,
I bore thee like the quiver on my back,
Fleet as the whirlwind hurries on the rack;
Nor foeman then, nor cougar's crouch I fear'd,[1]
For I was strong as mountain cataract:
And dost thou not remember how we cheer'd,
Upon the last hill-top, when white men's huts
        appear'd ?

XV.

Then welcome be my death-song, and my death !
Since I have seen thee, and again embraced."
And longer had he spent his toil-worn breath:
But with affectionate and eager haste,
Was every arm outstretch'd around their guest,
To welcome and to bless his aged head.
Soon was the hospitable banquet placed;
And Gertrude's lovely hands a balsam shed
On wounds with fever'd joy that more profusely
        bled.

XVI.

" But this is not a time,"—he started up,
And smote his breast with woe-denouncing hand—
" This is no time to fill the joyous cup,
The Mammoth comes,—the foe,—the Monster
        Brandt,—
With all his howling desolating band;
These eyes have seen their blade and burning pine
Awake at once, and silence half your land.
Red is the cup they drink; but not with wine:
Awake, and watch to-night, or see no morning
        shine !

Cougar, the American tiger.

XVII.

Scorning to wield the hatchet for his bribe,
'Gainst Brandt himself I went to battle forth :
Accursed Brandt ! he left of all my tribe
Nor man, nor child, nor thing of living birth :
No ! not the dog that watch'd my household hearth,
Escaped that night of blood, upon our plains !
All perish'd !—I alone am left on earth !
To whom nor relative nor blood remains,
No !—not a kindred drop that runs in human veins !

XVIII.

But go !—and rouse your warriors, for, if right
These old bewilder'd eyes could guess, by signs
Of striped, and starred banners, on yon height
Of eastern cedars, o'er the creek of pines—
Some fort embattled by your country shines :
Deep roars th' innavigable gulf below
Its squared rock, and palisaded lines.
Go! seek the light its warlike beacons show ;
Whilst I in ambush wait, for vengeance, and the
          foe !"

XIX.

Scarce had he utter'd—when Heaven's verge ex-
          treme
Reverberates the bomb's descending star,
And sounds that mingled laugh,—and shout,—and
          scream,—
To freeze the blood in one discordant jar
Rung to the pealing thunderbolts of war.
Whoop after whoop with rack the ear assail'd ;
As if unearthly fiends had burst their bar ;
While rapidly the marksman's shot prevail'd :—
And aye, as if for death, some lonely trumpet wail'd.

XX.

Then look'd they to the hills, where fire o'erhung
The bandit groups, in one Vesuvian glare;
Or swept, far seen, the tower, whose clock unrung
Told legible that midnight of despair.
She faints,—she falters not,—th' heroic fair,—
As he the sword and plume in haste array'd.
One short embrace—he clasp'd his dearest care—
But hark! what nearer war-drum shakes the glade?
Joy, joy! Columbia's friends are trampling through
       the shade.

XXI.

Then came of every race the mingled swarm,
Far rung the groves and gleam'd the midnight
       grass,
With flambeau, javelin, and naked arm;
As warriors wheel'd their culverins of brass,
Sprung from the woods, a bold athletic mass,
Whom virtue fires, and liberty combines:
And first the wild Moravian yagers pass,
His plumed host the dark Iberian joins—
And Scotia's sword beneath the Highland thistle
       shines.

XXII.

And in, the buskin'd hunters of the deer,
To Albert's home, with shout and cymbal throng—
Roused by their warlike pomp, and mirth, and
       cheer,
Old Outalissi woke his battle-song,
And, beating with his war-club cadence strong,
Tells how his deep-stung indignation smarts,
Of them that wrapt his house in flames, ere long,
To whet a dagger on their stony hearts,
And smile aveng'd ere yet his eagle spirit parts.—

XXIII.

Calm, opposite the Christian father rose,
Pale on his venerable brow its rays
Of martyr light the conflagration throws ;
One hand upon his lovely child he lays,
And one th' uncover'd crowd to silence sways ;
While, though the battle-flash is faster driven,—
Unaw'd, with eye unstartled by the blaze,
He for his bleeding country prays to Heaven,—
Prays that the men of blood themselves may be for-
    giv'n.

XXIV.

Short time is now for gratulating speech :
And yet, beloved Gertrude, ere began
Thy country's flight, yon distant towers to reach,
Look'd not on thee the rudest partisan
With brow relax'd to love? And murmurs ran,
As round and round their willing ranks they drew
From beauty's sight to shield the hostile van.
Grateful on them a placid look she threw,
Nor wept, but as she bade her mother's grave adieu.

XXV.

Past was the flight, and welcome seem'd the tower,
That like a giant standard-bearer frown'd
Defiance on the roving Indian power,
Beneath, each bold and promontory mound
With embrasure emboss'd, and armour crown'd,
And arrowy frize, and wedg'd ravelin,
Wove like a diadem its tracery round
The lofty summit of that mountain green ;
Here stood secure the group, and ey'd a distant
    scene.—

XXVI.

A scene of death ! where fires beneath the sun,
And blended arms, and white pavilions glow ;

And for the business of destruction done,
Its requiem the war-horn seem'd to blow:
There, sad spectatress of her country's woe!
The lovely Gertrude, safe from present hárm,
Had laid her cheek, and clasp'd her hands of snow
On Waldegrave's shoulder, half within his arm
Enclosed, that felt her heart, and hush'd its wild
      alarm!

XXVII.

But short that contemplation—sad and short
The pause to bid each much-loved scene adieu!
Beneath the very shadow of the fort,
Where friendly swords were drawn, and banners
      flew.
Ah! who could deem that foot of Indian crew
Was near?—yet there, with lust of murd'rous deeds,
Gleam'd like a basilisk, from woods in view,
The ambush'd foeman's eye—his volley speeds,
And Albert—Albert falls! the dear old father
      bleeds!

XXVIII.

And tranced in giddy horror Gertrude swoon'd;
Yet, while she clasps him lifeless to her zone,
Say, burst they, borrow'd from her father's wound,
These drops?—Oh, God! the life-blood is her own!
And faltering, on her Waldegrave's bosom thrown;
" Weep not, O Love!"—she cries, " to see me bleed;
Thee, Gertrude's sad survivor, thee alone
Heaven's peace commiserate; for scarce I heed
These wounds;—yet thee to leave is death, is death
      indeed!

XXIX.

Clasp me a little longer on the brink
Of fate! while I can feel thy dear caress;

Aud when this heart hath ceased to beat—oh!
        thiuk,
And let it mitigate thy woe's excess,
That thou hast been to me all tenderness,
And friend to more than human friendship just.
Oh! by that retrospect of happiness,
And by the hopes of an immortal trust,
God shall assuage thy pangs—when I am laid in
        dust!

XXX.

Go, Henry, go not back, wheu I depart,
The scene thy bursting tears too deep will move,
Where my dear father took thee to his heart,
And Gertrude thought it ecstasy to rove
With thee, as with an angel, through the grove
Of peace, imagining her lot was cast
In heaven; for ours was not like earthly love.
And must this parting be our very last?
No! I shall love thee still, when death itself is
        past.—

XXXI.

Half could I bear, methinks, to leave this earth,—
And thee, more lov'd than aught beneath the suu,
If I had lived to smile but on the birth
Of one dear pledge;—but shall there then be none,
In future times—no gentle little one,
To clasp thy ueck, and look, resembling me?
Yet seems it, ev'n while life's last pulses run,
A sweetness in the cup of death to be,
Lord of my bosom's love! to die beholding thee!'

XXXII.

Hush'd were his Gertrude's lips! but still their
        bland
And beautiful expression seem'd to melt
With love that could not die! and still his hand

She presses to the heart no more that felt.
Ah, heart ! where once each fond affection dwelt,
And features yet that spoke a soul more fair.
Mute, gazing, agonising as he knelt,—
Of them that stood encircling his despair,
He heard some friendly words ;—but knew not what
      they were.

XXXIII.

For now, to mourn their judge and child, arrives
A faithful band.   With solemn rites between
'Twas sung, how they were lovely in their lives,
And in their deaths had not divided been.
Touch'd by the music, and the melting scene,
Was scarce one tearless eye amidst the crowd :—
Stern warriors, resting on their swords, were seen
To veil their eyes, as pass'd each much-loved shroud,
While woman's softer soul in woe dissolv'd aloud.

XXXIV.

Then mournfully the parting bugle bid
Its farewell, o'er the grave of worth and truth ;
Prone to the dust, afflicted Waldegrave hid
His face on earth ;—him watch'd, in gloomy ruth,
His woodland guide ; but words had none to soothe
The grief that knew not consolation's name ;
Casting his Indian mantle o'er the youth,
He watch'd, beneath its folds, each burst that came
Convulsive, ague-like, across his shuddering frame !

XXXV.

  " And I could weep ;"—th' Oneyda chief
His descant wildly thus begun :
  " But that I may not stain with grief
The death-song of my father's son,
  Or bow this head in woe !
For by my wrongs, and by my wrath !

To-morrow Areouski's breath,
(That fires yon heaven with storms of death,)
Shall light us to the foe :
And we shall share, my Christian boy !
The foeman's blood, the avenger's joy !

XXXVI.

But thee, my flower, whose breath was given
By milder genii o'er the deep,
The spirits of the white man's heaven
Forbid not thee to weep :—
Nor will the Christian host,
Nor will thy father's spirit grieve,
To see thee, on the battle's eve,
Lamenting take a mournful leave
Of her who loved thee most :
She was the rainbow to thy sight!
Thy sun—thy heaven—of lost delight.

XXXVII.

To-morrow let us do or die !
But when the bolt of death is hurl'd,
Ah ! whither then with thee to fly,
Shall Outalissi roam the world?
Seek we thy once-loved home ?
The hand is gone that cropt its flowers :
Unheard their clock repeats its hours !
Cold is the hearth within their bowers !
And should we thither roam,
Its echoes, and its empty tread,
Would sound like voices from the dead !

XXXVIII.

Or shall we cross yon mountains blue,
Whose streams my kindred nation quaff'd,
And by my side, in battle true,
A thousand warriors drew the shaft ?
Ah ! there, in desolation cold,

The desert serpent dwells alone,
Where grass o'ergrows each mouldering bone,
And stones themselves to ruin grown,
Like me are death-like old.
Then seek we not their camp,—for there—
The silence dwells of my despair!

XXXIX.

But hark, the trump!—to-morrow thou
In glory's fires shalt dry thy tears:
Ev'n from the land of shadows now
My father's awful ghost appears,
Amidst the clouds that round us roll;
He bids my soul for battle thirst—
He bids me dry the last—the first—
The only tears that ever burst
From Outalissi's soul;
Because I may not stain with grief
The death-song of an Indian chief!"

LINES

WRITTEN AT THE REQUEST OF THE HIGHLAND SOCIETY IN
LONDON, WHEN MET TO COMMEMORATE THE 21ST OF
MARCH, THE DAY OF VICTORY IN EGYPT.

PLEDGE to the much-loved land that
　　　gave us birth!
　　　Invincible romantic Scotia's shore!
　　　Pledge to the memory of her parted
worth!
And first, amidst the brave, remember Moore!

And be it deem'd not wrong that name to give,
    In festive hours, which prompts the patriot's
        sigh!
Who would not envy such as Moore to live?
    And died he not as heroes wish to die?

Yes, though too soon attaining glory's goal,
    To us his bright career too short was given;
Yet in a mighty cause his phœnix soul
    Rose on the flames of victory to Heaven!

How oft (if beats in subjugated Spain
    One patriot heart) in secret shall it mourn
For him!—How oft on far Corunna's plain
    Shall British exiles weep upon his urn!

Peace to the mighty dead!—our bosom thanks
    In sprightlier strains the living may inspire!
Joy to the chiefs that lead old Scotia's ranks,
    Of Roman garb and more than Roman fire!

Triumphant be the thistle still unfurl'd,
    Dear symbol wild! on Freedom's hills it grows,
Where Fingal stemm'd the tyrants of the world,
    And Roman eagles found unconquer'd foes.

Joy to the band[1] this day on Egypt's coast,
    Whose valour tamed proud France's tricolor,
And wrench'd the banner from her bravest host,
    Baptised Invincible in Austria's gore!

Joy for the day on red Vimeira's strand,
    When, bayonet to bayonet opposed,
First of Britannia's host her Highland band
    Gave but the death-shot once, and foremost
        closed!

The 42nd Regiment.

Is there a son of generous England here,
    Or fervid Erin?—he with us shall join,
To pray that in eternal union dear,
    The rose, the shamrock, and the thistle twine!

Types of a race who shall th' invader scorn,
    As rocks resist the billows round their shore;
Types of a race who shall to time unborn
    Their country leave unconquer'd as of yore!

STANZAS

TO THE MEMORY OF THE SPANISH PATRIOTS LATEST KILLED IN RESISTING THE REGENCY AND THE DUKE OF ANGOULEME.

BRAVE men who at the Trocadero fell—
    Beside your cannons conquer'd not, though slain,
    There is a victory in dying well
For Freedom,—and ye have not died in vain;
For come what may, there shall be hearts in Spain
To honour, ay, embrace your martyr'd lot,
Cursing the Bigot's and the Bourbon's chain,
And looking on your graves, though trophied not,
As holier hallow'd ground than priests could make the spot!

What though your cause be baffled—freemen cast
In dungeons—dragg'd to death, or forced to flee?
Hope is not wither'd in affliction's blast—
The patriot's blood's the seed of Freedom's tree;
And short your orgies of revenge shall be,
Cowl'd Demons of the Inquisitorial cell!
Earth shudders at your victory,—for ye

Are worse than common fiends from Heaven that
      fell,
The baser, ranker sprung *Autochthones* of Hell!

Go to your bloody rites again—bring back
The hall of horrors and the assessor's pen,
Recording answers shriek'd upon the rack;
Smile o'er the gaspings of spine-broken men ;—
Preach, perpetrate damnation in your den ;—
Then let your altars, ye blasphemers! peal
With thanks to Heaven, that let you loose again,
To practise deeds with torturing fire and steel
No eye may search—no tongue may challenge or
      reveal !

Yet laugh not in your carnival of crime
Too proudly, ye oppressors !—Spain was free,
Her soil has felt the foot-prints, and her clime
Been winnow'd by the wings of Liberty ;
And these even parting scatter as they flee
Thoughts—influences, to live in hearts unborn,
Opinions that shall wrench the prison-key
From Persecution—show her mask off-torn,
And tramp her bloated head beneath the foot of
      Scorn.

Glory to them that die in this great cause ;
Kings, Bigots, can inflict no brand of shame,
Or shape of death, to shroud them from applause:—
No !—manglers of the martyr's earthly frame !
Your hangmen fingers cannot touch his fame.
Still in your prostrate land there shall be some
Proud hearts, the shrines of Freedom's vestal flame.
Long trains of ill may pass unheeded, dumb,
But Vengeance is behind, and Justice is to come.

SONG OF THE GREEKS.

AGAIN to the battle, Achaians!
Our hearts bid the tyrants defiance;
Our land, the first garden of Liberty's
tree—
It has been, and shall yet be, the land of the free.
For the cross of our faith is replanted,
The pale dying crescent is daunted,
And we march that the foot-prints of Mahomet's
slaves
May be wash'd out in blood from our forefather's
graves.
Their spirits are hovering o'er us,
And the sword shall to glory restore us.

Ah! what though no succour advances,
Nor Christendom's chivalrous lances
Are stretch'd in our aid—be the combat our own!
And we'll perish or conquer more proudly alone;
For we've sworn by our Country's assaulters,
By the virgins they've dragged from our altars,
By our massacred patriots, our children in chains,
By our heroes of old, and their blood in our veins,
That, living, we shall be victorious,
Or that, dying, our deaths shall be glorious.

A breath of submission we breathe not;
The sword that we've drawn we will sheathe
not!
Its scabbard is left where our martyrs are laid,
And the vengeance of ages has whetted its blade.
Earth may hide—waves engulf—fire consume us,
But they shall not to slavery doom us:

If they rule, it shall be o'er our ashes and graves;
But we've smote them already with fire on the
     waves,
And new triumphs on land are before us,
To the charge !—Heaven's banner is o'er us.

This day shall ye blush for its story,
Or brighten your lives with its glory.
Our women, oh say, shall they shriek in despair,
Or embrace us from conquest with wreaths in their
     hair?
Accursed may his memory blacken,
If a coward there be that would slacken
Till we've trampled the turban, and shown our-
     selves worth
Being sprung from and named for the godlike of
     earth.
Strike home, and the world shall revere us
As heroes descended from heroes.

Old Greece lightens up with emotion
Her inlands, her isles of the Ocean;
Fanes rebuilt and fair towns shall with jubilee ring,
And the Nine shall new-hallow their Helicon's
     spring :
Our hearths shall be kindled in gladness,
That were cold and extinguish'd in sadness;
Whilst our maidens shall dance with their white-
     waving arms,
Singing joy to the brave that deliver'd their charms,
When the blood of yon Mussulman cravens
Shall have purpled the beaks of our ravens.

ODE TO WINTER.

WHEN first the fiery-mantled sun
   His heavenly race began to run ;
   Round the earth and ocean blue,
   His children four the Seasons flew.
First, in green apparel dancing,
   The young Spring smil'd with angel grace ;
Rosy Summer next advancing,
   Rush'd into her sire's embrace :—
Her bright-hair'd sire who bade her keep
   For ever nearest to his smiles,
On Calpe's olive-shaded steep,
   On India's citron-cover'd isles :
More remote and buxom-brown,
   The Queen of vintage bow'd before his throne ;
A rich pomegranate gemm'd her crown,
   A ripe sheaf bound her zone.

But howling Winter fled afar,
To hills that prop the polar star,
And loves on deer-borne car to ride
With barren darkness by his side,
Round the shore where loud Lofoden
   Whirls to death the roaring whale,
Round the hall where Runic Odin
   Howls his war-song to the gale ;
Save when adown the ravaged globe
   He travels on his native storm,
Deflowering Nature's grassy robe,
   And trampling on her faded form :—
Till light's returning lord assume
   The shaft that drives him to his polar field,
Of power to pierce his raven plume
   And crystal-cover'd shield.

Oh, sire of storms! whose savage ear
The Lapland drum delights to hear,
When Frenzy with her blood-shot eye
Implores thy dreadful deity,
Archangel! power of desolation!
   Fast descending as thou art,
Say, hath mortal invocation
   Spells to touch thy stony heart?
Then, sullen Winter, hear my prayer,
And gently rule the ruin'd year;
Nor chill the wanderer's bosom bare,
Nor freeze the wretch's falling tear;
To shuddering Want's unmantled bed
Thy horror-breathing agues cease to lead,
And gently on the orphan head
Of innocence descend.—

But chiefly spare, O king of clouds!
The sailor on his airy shrouds;
When wrecks and beacons strew the steep,
And spectres walk along the deep.
Milder yet thy snowy breezes
   Pour on yonder tented shores,
Where the Rhine's broad billow freezes,
   Or the dark-brown Danube roars.
Oh, winds of Winter! list ye there
   To many a deep and dying groan;
Or start, ye demons of the midnight air,
   At shrieks and thunders louder than your own.
Alas! ev'n your unhallow'd breath
   May spare the victim fallen low;
But man will ask no truce to death,—
   No bounds to human woe.[1]

[1] This ode was written in Germany, at the close of 1800, before the conclusion of hostilities.

LINES

SPOKEN BY MRS. BARTLEY AT DRURY-LANE THEATRE, ON THE
FIRST OPENING OF THE HOUSE AFTER THE DEATH
OF THE PRINCESS CHARLOTTE, 1817.

BRITONS ! although our task is but to
    show
    The scenes and passions of fictitious
    woe,
Think not we come this night without a part
In that deep sorrow of the public heart,
Which like a shade hath darken'd every place,
And moisten'd with a tear the manliest face !
The bell is scarcely hush'd in Windsor's piles,
That toll'd a requiem from the solemn aisles,
For her, the royal flower, low laid in dust,
That was your fairest hope, your fondest trust.
Unconscious of the doom, we dreamt, alas !
That ev'n these walls, ere many months should
    pass,
Which but return sad accents for her now,
Perhaps had witness'd her benignant brow,
Cheer'd by the voice you would have raised on
    high,
In bursts of British love and loyalty.
But, Britain ! now thy chief, thy people mourn,
And Claremont's home of love is left forlorn :—
There, where the happiest of the happy dwelt,
The 'scutcheon glooms, and royalty hath felt
A wound that every bosom feels its own,—
The blessing of a father's heart o'erthrown—
The most beloved and most devoted bride
Torn from an agonised husband's side,

Who " long as Memory holds her seat " shall view
That speechless, more than spoken last adieu,
When the fix'd eye long look'd connubial faith,
And beam'd affection in the trance of death.
Sad was the pomp that yesternight beheld,
As with the mourner's heart the anthem swell'd;
While torch succeeding torch illumed each high
And banner'd arch of England's chivalry.
The rich-plumed canopy, the gorgeous pall,
The sacred march, and sable-vested wall,—
These were not rites of inexpressive show,
But hallow'd as the types of real woe!
Daughter of England! for a nation's sighs,
A nation's heart went with thine obsequies!—
And oft shall time revert a look of grief
On thine existence, beautiful and brief.
Fair spirit! send thy blessing from above
On realms where thou art canonised by love!
Give to a father's, husband's bleeding mind,
The peace that angels lend to human kind;
To us who in thy loved remembrance feel
A sorrowing, but a soul-ennobling zeal—
A loyalty that touches all the best
And loftiest principles of England's breast!
Still may thy name speak concord from the tomb—
Still in the Muse's breath thy memory bloom!
They shall describe thy life—thy form portray
But all the love that mourns thee swept away,
'Tis not in language or expressive arts
To paint—ye feel it, Britons, in your hearts!

REULLURA.[1]

STAR of the morn and eve,
   Reullura shone like thee,
And well for her might Aodh grieve,
   The dark-attired Culdee.
Peace to their shades! the pure Culdees
   Were Albyn's earliest priests of God,
Ere yet an island of her seas
   By foot of Saxon monk was trod,
Long ere her churchmen by bigotry
Were barr'd from wedlock's holy tie.
'Twas then that Aodh, famed afar,
   In Iona preach'd the word with power,
And Reullura, beauty's star,
   Was the partner of his bower.

But, Aodh, the roof lies low,
   And the thistle-down waves bleaching,
And the bat flits to and fro
   Where the Gaël once heard thy preaching;
And fallen is each column'd aisle
   Where the chiefs and the people knelt.
'Twas near that temple's goodly pile
   That honour'd of men they dwelt.
For Aodh was wise in the sacred law,
And bright Reullura's eyes oft saw
   The veil of fate uplifted.
Alas, with what visions of awe
   Her soul in that hour was gifted—
When pale in the temple and faint,
   With Aodh she stood alone
By the statue of an aged Saint!

---

[1] Reullura, in Gaëlic, signifies " beautiful star."

Fair sculptured was the stone,
It bore a crucifix;
  Fame said it once had graced
A Christian temple, which the Picts
  In the Briton's land laid waste:
The Pictish men, by St. Columb taught,
  Had hither the holy relic brought.
Reullura eyed the statue's face,
  And cried, " It is, he shall come,
Even he, in this very place,
  To avenge my martyrdom.

For, woe to the Gaël people!
  Ulvfagre is on the main,
And Iona shall look from tower and steeple
  On the coming ships of the Dane;
And, dames and daughters, shall all your locks
  With the spoiler's grasp entwine?
No! some shall have shelter in caves and rocks,
  And the deep sea shall be mine.
Baffled by me shall the Dane return,
And here shall his torch in the temple burn,
Until that holy man shall plough
  The waves from Innisfail.
His sail is on the deep e'en now,
  And swells to the southern gale."

" Ah! knowest thou not, my bride,"
  The holy Aodh said,
" That the Saint whose form we stand beside
  Has for ages slept with the dead?"
" He liveth, he liveth," she said again,
  " For the span of his life tenfold extends
Beyond the wonted years of men.
  He sits by the graves of well-loved friends
That died ere thy grandsire's grandsire's birth;
The oak is decay'd with age on earth,

Whose acorn-seed had been planted by him ;
  And his parents remember the day of dread
When the sun on the cross look'd dim,
  And the graves gave up their dead.
Yet preaching from clime to clime,
  He hath roam'd the earth for ages,
And hither he shall come in time
  When the wrath of the heathen rages,
In time a remnant from the sword—
  Ah ! but a remnant to deliver ;
Yet, blest be the name of the Lord ;
  His Martyrs shall go into bliss for ever.
Lochlin,[1] appall'd, shall put up her steel,
And thou shalt embark on the bounding keel ;
Safe shalt thou pass through her hundred ships,
  With the Saint and a remnant of the Gaël,
And the Lord will instruct thy lips
  To preach in Innisfail !"[2]

The sun, now about to set,
  Was burning o'er Tiree,
And no gathering cry rose yet
  O'er the isles of Albyn's sea,
Whilst Reullura saw far rowers dip
  Their oars beneath the sun,
And the phantom of many a Danish ship,
  Where ship there yet was none.
And the shield of alarm was dumb,
Nor did their warning till midnight come,
When watch-fires burst from across the main,
  From Rona, and Uist, and Skye,
To tell that the ships of the Dane
  And the red-hair'd slayers were nigh.
Our islemen arose from slumbers,
  And buckled on their arms ;

[1] Denmark.   [2] Ireland.

But few, alas! were their numbers
  To Lochlin's mailed swarms.
And the blade of the bloody Norse
  Has fill'd the shores of the Gaël
With many a floating corse,
  And with many a woman's wail.
They have lighted the islands with ruin's torch,
And the holy men of Iona's church
In the temple of God lay slain ;
  All but Aodh, the last Culdee,
But bound with many an iron chain,
  Bound in that church was he.
And where is Aodh's bride ?
  Rocks of the ocean flood !
Plunged she not from your heights in pride,
  And mock'd the men of blood ?

  Then Ulvfagre and his bands
  In the temple lighted their banquet up,
And the print of their blood-red hands
  Was left on the altar cup.
'Twas then that the Norseman to Aodh said,
" Tell where thy church's treasure's laid,
  Or I'll hew thee limb from limb."
    As he spoke the bell struck three,
  And every torch grew dim
    That lighted their revelry.

But the torches again burn'd bright,
  And brighter than before,
When an aged man of majestic height
  Enter'd the temple door.
Hush'd was the revellers' sound,
  They were struck as mute as the dead,
And their hearts were appall'd by the very sound
  Of his footsteps' measured tread.
Nor word was spoken by one beholder,

Whilst he flung his white robe back o'er his
     shoulder,
And stretching his arms—as eath
   Unriveted Aodh's bands,
As if the gyves had been a wreath
   Of willows in his hands.

All saw the stranger's similitude
   To the ancient statue's form;
The Saint before his own image stood,
   And grasp'd Ulvfagre's arm.
Then up rose the Danes at last to deliver
   Their chief, and shouting with one accord,
They drew the shaft from its rattling quiver,
   They lifted the spear and sword,
And levell'd their spears in rows ;
But down went axes and spears and bows,
When the Saint with his crosier sign'd,
   The archer's hand on the string was stopp'd,
And down, like reeds laid flat by the wind,
   Their lifted weapons dropp'd.
The Saint then gave a signal mute,
   And though Ulvfagre will'd it not,
He came and stood at the statue's foot,
   Spell-riveted to the spot,
Till hands invisible shook the wall,
   And the tottering image was dash'd
Down from its lofty pedestal.
   On Ulvfagre's helm it crash'd—
Helmet, and skull, and flesh, and brain,
It crush'd as millstones crush the grain.
Then spoke the Saint, whilst all and each
   Of the heathen trembled round,
And the pauses amidst his speech
   Were as awful as the sound :
" Go back, ye wolves ! to your dens," (he cried,)
   " And tell the nations abroad,

How the fiercest of your herd has died
  That slaughter'd the flock of God.
Gather him bone by bone,
  And take with you o'er the flood
The fragments of that avenging stone
  That drank his heathen blood.
These are the spoils from Iona's sack,
The only spoils ye shall carry back;
For the hand that uplifteth spear or sword
  Shall be wither'd by palsy's shock,
And I come in the name of the Lord
  To deliver a remnant of his flock."

A remnant was call'd together,
  A doleful remnant of the Gaël,
And the Saint in the ship that had brought him
      hither
  Took the mourners to Innisfail.
Unscathed they left Iona's strand,
  When the opal morn first flush'd the sky,
For the Norse dropp'd spear, and bow, and brand,
  And look'd on them silently;
Safe from their hiding-places came
Orphans and mothers, child and dame:
But, alas! when the search for Reullura spread,
  No answering voice was given,
For the sea had gone o'er her lovely head,
  And her spirit was in heaven.

THE TURKISH LADY.

'TWAS the hour when rites unholy
      Call'd each Paynim voice to prayer,
  And the star that faded slowly
      Left to dews the freshen'd air.

Day her sultry fires had wasted,
   Calm and sweet the moonlight rose ;
Ev'n a captive spirit tasted
   Half oblivion of his woes.

Then 'twas from an Emir's palace
   Came an Eastern lady bright :
She, in spite of tyrants jealous,
   Saw and loved an English knight.

" Tell me, captive, why in anguish
   Foes have dragg'd thee here to dwell,
Where poor Christians as they languish
   Hear no sound of Sabbath bell ?"—

" 'Twas on Transylvania's Bannat,
   When the Crescent shone afar,
Like a pale disastrous planet
   O'er the purple tide of war—

In that day of desolation,
   Lady, I was captive made ;
Bleeding for my Christian nation
   By the walls of high Belgrade."

" Captive ! could the brightest jewel
   From my turban set thee free ?"
" Lady, no !—the gift were cruel,
   Ransom'd, yet if reft of thee.

Say, fair princess ! would it grieve thee
   Christian climes should we behold ?"—
" Nay, bold knight ! I would not leave thee
   Were thy ransom paid in gold."

Now in heaven's blue expansion
   Rose the midnight star to view,
When to quit her father's mansion
   Thrice she wept, and bade adieu !

" Fly we then, while none discover !
    Tyrant barks, in vain ye ride !"—
Soon at Rhodes the British lover
    Clasp'd his blooming Eastern bride.

THE BRAVE ROLAND.

THE brave Roland!—the brave Roland !—
    False tidings reach'd the Rhenish
        strand
    That he had fallen in fight ;
And thy faithful bosom swoon'd with pain,
O loveliest maiden of Allémayne !
    For the loss of thine own true knight.

But why so rash has she ta'en the veil,
In yon Nonnenwerder's cloisters pale ?
    For her vow had scarce been sworn,
And the fatal mantle o'er her flung,
When the Drachenfels to a trumpet rung—
    'Twas her own dear warrior's horn !

Woe ! woe ! each heart shall bleed—shall break !
She would have hung upon his neck,
    Had he come but yester-even ;
And he had clasp'd those peerless charms
That shall never, never fill his arms,
    Or meet him but in heaven.

Yet Roland the brave—Roland the true—
He could not bid that spot adieu ;
    It was dear still 'midst his woes,
For he loved to breathe the neighbouring air,
And to think she bless'd him in her prayer,
    When the Halleluiah rose.

There's yet one window of that pile,
Which he built above the Nun's green isle ;
　　　Thence sad and oft look'd he
(When the chant and organ sounded slow)
On the mansion of his love below,
　　　For herself he might not see.

She died !—He sought the battle-plain !
Her image fill'd his dying brain,
　　　When he fell and wish'd to fall :
And her name was in his latest sigh,
When Roland, the flower of chivalry,
　　　Expired at Roncevall.

LINES ON THE GRAVE OF A SUICIDE.

BY strangers left upon a lonely shore,
　　　Unknown, unhonour'd, was the
　　　friendless dead ;
　　　For child to weep, or widow to deplore,
There never came to his unburied head :—
All from his dreary habitation fled.
Nor will the lantern'd fisherman at eve
　Launch on that water by the witches' tower,
Where hellebore and hemlock seem to weave
　Round its dark vaults a melancholy bower
　For spirits of the dead at night's enchanted hour.

They dread to meet thee, poor unfortunate !
　Whose crime it was, on Life's unfinish'd road,
To feel the step-dame buffetings of fate,
　And render back thy being's heavy load.
　Ah ! once, perhaps, the social passions glow'd

In thy devoted bosom—and the hand
  That smote its kindred heart, might yet be
    prone
To deeds of mercy.   Who may understand
  Thy many woes, poor suicide, unknown ?—
  He who thy being gave shall judge of thee alone.

THE SPECTRE BOAT.

A BALLAD.

LIGHT rued false Ferdinand to leave a
    lovely maid forlorn,
  Who broke her heart and died to hide
    her blushing cheek from scorn.
One night he dreamt he woo'd her in their wonted
  bower of love,
Where the flowers sprang thick around them, and
  the birds sang sweet above.

But the scene was swiftly changed into a church-
  yard's dismal view,
And her lips grew black beneath his kiss, from
  love's delicious hue.
What more he dreamt, he told to none ; but shuddering, pale, and dumb,
Look'd out upon the waves, like one that knew
  his hour was come.

Twas now the dead watch of the night—the helm
  was lash'd a-lee,
And the ship rode where Mount Ætna lights the
  deep Levantine sea ;

When beneath its glare a boat came, row'd by a
  woman in her shroud,
Who, with eyes that made our blood run cold, stood
  up and spoke aloud :—

" Come, Traitor, down, for whom my ghost still
  wanders unforgiven !
Come down, false Ferdinand, for whom I broke
  my peace with heaven !"—
It was vain to hold the victim, for he plunged to
  meet her call,
Like the bird that shrieks and flutters in the
  gazing serpent's thrall.

You may guess the boldest mariner shrunk daunted
  from the sight,
For the Spectre and her winding-sheet shone blue
  with hideous light ;
Like a fiery wheel the boat spun with the waving
  of her hand,
And round they went, and down they went, as
  the cock crew from the land.

THE LOVER TO HIS MISTRESS.

ON HER BIRTHDAY.

IF any white-wing'd Power above
    My joys and griefs survey,
  The day when thou wert born, my
      love—
He surely bless'd that day.

  I laugh'd (till taught by thee) when told
    Of Beauty's magic powers,
  That ripen'd life's dull ore to gold,
    And changed its weeds to flowers.

My mind had lovely shapes portray'd;
  But thought I earth had one
Could make even Fancy's visions fade
  Like stars before the sun?

I gazed and felt upon my lips
  The unfinish'd accents hang:
One moment's bliss, one burning kiss,
  To rapture changed each pang.

And though as swift as lightning's flash
  Those tranced moments flew,
Not all the waves of time shall wash
  Their memory from my view.

But duly shall my raptured song,
  And gladly shall my eyes
Still bless this day's return, as long
  As thou shalt see it rise.

SONG.

    H, how hard it is to find
      The one just suited to our mind!
        And if that one should be
      False, unkind, or found too late,
What can we do but sigh at fate,
  And sing, "Woe's me—Woe's me?"

Love's a boundless burning waste,
Where Bliss's stream we seldom taste,
  And still more seldom flee
Suspense's thorns, Suspicion's stings;
Yet somehow Love a something brings
  That's sweet—even when we sigh "Woe's me!"

LINES

ON RECEIVING A SEAL WITH THE CAMPBELL CREST,

FROM K. M——, BEFORE HER MARRIAGE.

THIS wax returns not back more fair
    Th' impression of the gift you send,
Than stamp'd upon my thoughts I bear
    The image of your worth, my
friend !—

We are not friends of yesterday ;—
    But poet's fancies are a little
Disposed to heat and cool, (they say,)—
    By turns impressible and brittle.

Well ! should its frailty e'er condemn
    My heart to prize or please you less,
Your type is still the sealing gem,
    And *mine* the waxen brittleness.

What transcripts of my weal and woe
    This little signet yet may lock,—
What utterances to friend or foe,
    In reason's calm or passion's shock !

What scenes of life's yet curtain'd stage
    May own its confidential die,
Whose stamp awaits th' unwritten page,
    And feelings of futurity !—

Yet wheresoe'er my pen I lift
    To date the epistolary sheet,
The blest occasion of the gift
    Shall make its recollection sweet;

Sent when the star that rules your fates
    Hath reach'd its influence most benign—

When every heart congratulates
  And none more cordially than mine.

So speed my song—mark'd with the crest
  That erst the advent'rous Norman wore,
Who won the Lady of the West,
  The daughter of Macaillan Mor.

Crest of my sires ! whose blood it seal'd
  With glory in the strife of swords,
Ne'er may the scroll that bears it yield
  Degenerate thoughts or faithless words !

Yet little might I prize the stone,
  If it but typed the feudal tree
From whence, a scatter'd leaf, I'm blown
  In Fortune's mutability.

No !—but it tells me of a heart
  Allied by friendship's living tie ;
A prize beyond the herald's art—
  Our soul-sprung consanguinity !

Kath'rine ! to many an hour of mine
  Light wings and sunshine you have lent ;
And so adieu, and still be thine
  The all-in-all of life—Content !

ADELGITHA.

THE ordeal's fatal trumpet sounded,
  And sad pale Adelgitha came,
When forth a valiant champion bounded,
  And slew the slanderer of her fame.

She wept, deliver'd from her danger ;
    But when he knelt to claim her glove—
" Seek not," she cried, " oh ! gallant stranger,
    For hapless Adelgitha's love.

For he is in a foreign far land
    Whose arms should now have set me free ;
And I must wear the willow garland
    For him that's dead or false to me."

" Nay ! say not that his faith is tainted ! "
    He raised his vizor—At the sight
She fell into his arms and fainted ;
    It was indeed her own true knight !

THE RITTER BANN.

THE Ritter Bann from Hungary
    Came back, renown'd in arms,
But scorning jousts of chivalry,
    And love and ladies' charms.

While other knights held revels, he
    Was wrapp'd in thoughts of gloom,
And in Vienna's hostelrie
    Slow paced his lonely room.

There enter'd one whose face he knew,—
    Whose voice, he was aware,
He oft at mass had listen'd to
    In the holy house of prayer.

'Twas the Abbot of St. James's monks,
    A fresh and fair old man :
His reverend air arrested even
    The gloomy Ritter Bann.

But seeing with him an ancient dame
  Come clad in Scotch attire,
The Ritter's colour went and came,
  And loud he spoke in ire:

" Ha! nurse of her that was my bane,
  Name not her name to me;
I wish it blotted from my brain:
  Art poor?—take alms, and flee."

" Sir Knight," the abbot interposed,
  " This case your ear demands;"
And the crone cried, with a cross enclosed
  In both her trembling hands:—

" Remember, each his sentence waits;
  And he that shall rebut
Sweet Mercy's suit, on him the gates
  Of Mercy shall be shut.

You wedded, undispensed by Church,
  Your cousin Jane in Spring;
In Autumn, when you went to search
  For churchmen's pardoning,

Her house denounced your marriage-band,
  Betrothed her to De Grey,
And the ring you put upon her hand
  Was wrench'd by force away.

Then wept your Jane upon my neck,
  Crying, ' Help me, nurse, to flee
To my Howel Bann's Glamorgan hills;'
  But word arrived—ah me!—

You were not there; and 'twas their threat,
  By foul means or by fair,
To-morrow morning was to set
  The seal on her despair.

I had a son, a sea-boy, in
    A ship at Hartland Bay ;
By his aid from her cruel kin
    I bore my bird away.

To Scotland from the Devon's
    Green myrtle shores we fled ;
And the Hand that sent the ravens
    To Elijah, gave us bread.

She wrote you by my son, but he
    From England sent us word
You had gone into some far countrie,
    In grief and gloom, he heard.

For they that wrong'd you, to elude
    Your wrath, defamed my child ;
And you—ay, blush, Sir, as you should—
    Believed, and were beguiled.

To die but at your feet, she vow'd
    To roam the world; and we
Would both have sped and begg'd our bread,
    But so it might not be.

For when the snow-storm beat our roof,
    She bore a boy, Sir Bann,
Who grew as fair your likeness proof
    As child e'er grew like man.

'Twas smiling on that babe one morn
    While heath bloom'd on the moor,
Her beauty struck young Lord Kinghorn
    As he hunted past our door.

She shunn'd him, but he raved of Jane,
    And roused his mother's pride :
Who came to us in high disdain,—
    ' And where's the face,' she cried,

' Has witch'd my boy to wish for one
    So wretched for his wife ?—
Dost love thy husband ?   Know, my son
    Has sworn to seek his life.

Her anger sore dismay'd us,
    For our mite was wearing scant,
And, unless that dame would aid us,
    There was none to aid our want.

So I told her, weeping bitterly,
    What all our woes had been ;
And, though she was a stern ladie,
    The tears stood in her een.

And she housed us both, when, cheerfully,
    My child to her had sworn,
That even if made a widow, she
    Would never wed Kinghorn."—

Here paused the nurse, and then began
    The abbot, standing by :—
" Three months ago a wounded man
    To our abbey came to die.

He heard me long, with ghastly eyes
    And hand obdurate clench'd,
Speak of the worm that never dies,
    And the fire that is not quench'd.

At last by what this scroll attests
    He left atonement brief,
For years of anguish to the breasts
    His guilt had wrung with grief.

' There lived,' he said, ' a fair young dame
    Beneath my mother's roof;
I loved her, but against my flame
    Her purity was proof.

.I feign'd repentance, friendship pure;
    That mood she did not check,
But let her husband's miniature
    Be copied from her neck,

As means to search him; my deceit
    Took care to him was borne
Nought but his picture's counterfeit,
    And Jane's reported scorn.

The treachery took : she waited wild;
    My slave came back and lied
Whate'er I wish'd; she clasp'd her child,
    And swoon'd, and all but died.

I felt her tears for years and years
    Quench not my flame, but stir;
The very hate I bore her mate
    Increased my love for her.

Fame told us of his glory, while
    Joy flush'd the face of Jane :
And while she bless'd his name, her smile
    Struck fire into my brain.

No fears could damp; I reach'd the camp,
    Sought out its champion;
And if my broad-sword fail'd at last,
    'Twas long and well laid on.

This wound 's my meed, my name's Kinghorn,
    My foe 's the Ritter Bann.'—
The wafer to his lips was borne,
    And we shrived the dying man.

He died not till you went to fight
    The Turks at Warradein;
But I see my tale has changed you pale."—
    The abbot went for wine;

And brought a little page who pour'd ·
  It out, and knelt and smiled;
The stunn'd knight saw himself restored
  To childhood in his child;

And stoop'd and caught him to his breast,
  Laugh'd loud and wept anon,
And with a shower of kisses press'd
  The darling little one.

"And where went Jane?"—"To a nunnery, Sir—
  Look not again so pale—
Kinghorn's old dame grew harsh to her."—
  " And has she ta'en the veil?"—

" Sit down, Sir," said the priest, "I bar
  Rash words."—They sat all three,
And the boy play'd with the knight's broad star,
  As he kept him on his knee.

" Think ere you ask her dwelling-place,"
  The abbot further said;
" Time draws a veil o'er beauty's face
  More deep than cloister's shade.

Grief may have made her what you can
  Scarce love perhaps for life."
" Hush, abbot," cried the Ritter Bann,
  " Or tell me where's my wife."

The priest undid two doors that hid
  The inn's adjacent room,
And there a lovely woman stood,
  Tears bathed her beauty's bloom.

One moment may with bliss repay
  Unnumber'd hours of pain;
Such was the throb and mutual sob
  Of the Knight embracing Jane.

GILDEROY.

 THE last, the fatal hour is come
That bears my love from me :
I hear the dead note of the drum,
I mark the gallows-tree !

The bell has toll'd ; it shakes my heart ;
The trumpet speaks thy name ;
And must my Gilderoy depart
To bear a death of shame ?

No bosom trembles for thy doom ;
No mourner wipes a tear ;
The gallows' foot is all thy tomb,
The sledge is all thy bier.

Oh, Gilderoy ! bethought we then
So soon, so sad to part,
When first in Roslin's lovely glen
You triumph'd o'er my heart ?

Your locks they glitter'd to the sheen,
Your hunter garb was trim ;
And graceful was the ribbon green
That bound your manly limb !

Ah ! little thought I to deplore
Those limbs in fetters bound ;
Or hear upon the scaffold floor,
The midnight hammer sound.

Ye cruel, cruel, that combined
The guiltless to pursue ;
My Gilderoy was ever kind,
He could not injure you !

A long adieu ! but where shall fly
  Thy widow all forlorn,
When every mean and cruel eye
  Regards my woe with scorn ?

Yes ! they will mock thy widow's tears,
  And hate thine orphan boy ;
Alas ! his infant beauty wears
  The form of Gilderoy.

Then will I seek the dreary mound
  That wraps thy mouldering clay,
And weep and linger on the ground,
  And sigh my heart away.

STANZAS ON THE THREATENED
INVASION.   1803.

OUR bosoms we'll bare for the glorious
      strife,
    And our oath is recorded on high,
  To prevail in the cause that is dearer
    than life,
Or crush'd in its ruins to die !
Then rise, fellow freemen, and stretch the right
      hand,
And swear to prevail in your dear native land !

'Tis the home we hold sacred is laid to our trust—
  God bless the green Isle of the brave !
Should a conqueror tread on our forefathers' dust,
  It would rouse the old dead from their grave !
Then rise, fellow freemen, and stretch the right
      hand,
And swear to prevail in your dear native land !

In a Briton's sweet home shall a spoiler abide,
  Profaning its loves and its charms?
Shall a Frenchman insult the loved fair at our
    side?
  To arms! oh, my Country, to arms!
Then rise, fellow freemen, and stretch the right
    hand,
And swear to prevail in your dear native land!

Shall a tyrant enslave us, my countrymen?—No!
  His head to the sword shall be given—
A death-bed repentance be taught the proud foe,
  And his blood be an offering to Heaven!
Then rise, fellow freemen, and stretch the right
    hand,
And swear to prevail in your dear native land!

SONG.

"MEN OF ENGLAND."

MEN of England! who inherit
  Rights that cost your sires their
    blood!
Men whose undegenerate spirit
Has been proved on field and flood:—

By the foes you've fought uncounted,
  By the glorious deeds ye've done,
Trophies captured—breaches mounted,
  Navies conquer'd—kingdoms won!

Yet, remember, England gathers
  Hence but fruitless wreaths of fame,
If the freedom of your fathers
  Glow not in your hearts the same.

What are monuments of bravery,
   Where no public virtues bloom ?
What avail in lands of slavery,
   Trophied temples, arch, and tomb ?

Pageants !—Let the world revere us
   For our people's rights and laws,
And the breasts of civic heroes
   Bared in Freedom's holy cause.

Yours are Hampden's, Russell's glory,
   Sidney's matchless shade is yours,—
Martyrs in heroic story,
   Worth a hundred Agincourts !

We're the sons of sires that baffled
   Crown'd and mitred tyranny ;—
They defied the field and scaffold
   For their birthrights—so will we !

THE HARPER.

ON the green banks of Shannon when
   Sheelah was nigh,
No blithe Irish lad was so happy as I ;
No harp like my own could so cheerily
   play,
And wherever I went was my poor dog Tray.

When at last I was forced from my Sheelah to
   part,
She said, (while the sorrow was big at her heart,)
Oh ! remember your Sheelah, when far, far away :
And be kind, my dear Pat, to our poor dog Tray.

Poor dog! he was faithful and kind, to be sure,
And he constantly loved me although I was poor;
When the sour-looking folks sent me heartless
    away,
I had always a friend in my poor dog Tray.

When the road was so dark, and the night was so
    cold,
And Pat and his dog were grown weary and old,
How snugly we slept in my old coat of grey,
And he lick'd me for kindness—my poor dog Tray.

Though my wallet was scant, I remember'd his
    case,
Nor refused my last crust to his pitiful face;
But he died at my feet on a cold winter day,
And I play'd a sad lament for my poor dog Tray.

Where now shall I go, poor, forsaken, and blind?
Can I find one to guide me, so faithful and kind?
To my sweet native village, so far, far away,
I can never more return with my poor dog Tray.

THE WOUNDED HUSSAR.

ALONE to the banks of the dark-rolling
    Danube
Fair Adelaide hied when the battle
    was o'er:—
"Oh whither," she cried, "hast thou wander'd, my
    lover,
  Or here dost thou welter and bleed on the shore?

What voice did I hear? 'twas my Henry that
        sigh'd !"
All mournful she hasten'd; nor wander'd she far,
When bleeding, and low, on the heath she descried,
    By the light of the moon, her poor wounded
        Hussar !

From his bosom that heaved the last torrent was
        streaming,
    And pale was his visage deep mark'd with a scar!
And dim was that eye, once expressively beaming,
    That melted in love and that kindled in war !

How smit was poor Adelaide's heart at the sight !
    How bitter she wept o'er the victim of war !
"Hast thou come, my fond Love, this last sorrowful
        night,
    To cheer the lone heart of your wounded Hussar?"

" Thou shalt live," she replied, " Heaven's mercy
        relieving
    Each anguishing wound shall forbid me to
        mourn !"
" Ah no ! the last pang of my bosom is heaving !
    No light of the morn shall to Henry return !

Thou charmer of life, ever tender and true !
    Ye babes of my love, that await me afar !"
His faltering tongue scarce could murmur adieu,
    When he sunk in her arms—the poor wounded
        Hussar !

LOVE AND MADNESS.

AN ELEGY.

WRITTEN IN 1795.

ARK! from the battlements of yonder
      tower[1]
The solemn bell has toll'd the midnight
      hour!
Roused from drear visions of distemper'd sleep,
Poor B——k wakes—in solitude to weep!

" Cease, Memory, cease (the friendless mourner
      cried)
To probe the bosom too severely tried!
Oh! ever cease, my pensive thoughts, to stray
Through the bright fields of Fortune's better day,
When youthful Hope, the music of the mind,
Tuned all its charms, and E——n was kind!

Yet, can I cease, while glows this trembling
      frame,
In sighs to speak thy melancholy name!
I hear thy spirit wail in every storm!
In midnight shades I view thy passing form!
Pale as in that sad hour when doom'd to feel,
Deep in thy perjured heart, the bloody steel!

Demons of Vengeance! ye at whose command
I grasp'd the sword with more than woman's hand,
Say ye, did Pity's trembling voice control,
Or horror damp the purpose of my soul?
No! my wild heart sat smiling o'er the plan,
Till Hate fulfill'd what baffled Love began!

[1] Warwick Castle.

Yes; let the clay-cold breast that never knew
One tender pang to generous Nature true,
Half-mingling pity with the gall of scorn,
Condemn this heart, that bled in love forlorn!

And ye, proud fair, whose soul no gladness warms,
Save Rapture's homage to your conscious charms!
Delighted idols of a gaudy train,
Ill can your blunter feelings guess the pain,
When the fond faithful heart, inspired to prove
Friendship refined, the calm delight of Love,
Feels all its tender strings with anguish torn,
And bleeds at perjured Pride's inhuman scorn.

Say, then, did pitying Heaven condemn the deed,
When Vengeance bade thee, faithless lover! bleed?
Long had I watch'd thy dark foreboding brow,
What time thy bosom scorn'd its dearest vow!
Sad, though I wept the friend, the lover changed,
Still thy cold look was scornful and estranged,
Till from thy pity, love, and shelter thrown,
I wander'd hopeless, friendless, and alone!

Oh! righteous Heaven! 'twas then my tortured
    soul
First gave to wrath unlimited control!
Adieu the silent look! the streaming eye!
The murmur'd plaint! the deep heart-heaving sigh!
Long-slumbering Vengeance wakes to better deeds;
He shrieks, he falls, the perjured lover bleeds!
Now the last laugh of agony is o'er,
And pale in blood he sleeps, to wake no more!

'Tis done! the flame of hate no longer burns:
Nature relents, but, ah! too late returns!
Why does my soul this gush of fondness feel?
Trembling and faint I drop the guilty steel!

M

Cold on my heart the hand of terror lies,
And shades of horror close my languid eyes!
Oh! 'twas a deed of murder's deepest grain!
Could B——k's soul so true to wrath remain?
A friend long true, a once fond lover fell!—
Where love was foster'd could not Pity dwell?

Unhappy youth! while yon pale crescent glows
To watch on silent Nature's deep repose,
Thy sleepless spirit, breathing from the tomb,
Foretells my fate, and summons me to come!
Once more I see thy sheeted spectre stand,
Roll the dim eye, and wave the paly hand!

Soon may this fluttering spark of vital flame
Forsake its languid melancholy frame!
Soon may these eyes their trembling lustre close,
Welcome the dreamless night of long repose!
Soon may this woe-worn spirit seek the bourne
Where, lull'd to slumber, Grief forgets to mourn!"

HALLOWED GROUND.

WHAT'S hallow'd ground? Has earth a
        clod
        Its Maker meant not should be trod
        By man, the image of his God
    Erect and free,
Unscourged by Superstition's rod
        To bow the knee?

That's hallow'd ground—where, mourn'd and
        miss'd,
The lips repose our love has kiss'd;—

But where 's their memory's mansion ? Is't
    Yon churchyard's bowers?
No ! in ourselves their souls exist,
    A part of ours.

A kiss can consecrate the ground
Where mated hearts are mutual bound :
The spot where love's first links were wound,
    That ne'er are riven,
Is hallow'd down to earth's profound,
    And up to heaven !

For time makes all but true love old ;
The burning thoughts that then were told
Run molten still in memory's mould ;
    And will not cool,
Until the heart itself be cold
    In Lethe's pool.

What hallows ground where heroes sleep ?
'Tis not the sculptured piles you heap !
In dews that heavens far distant weep
    Their turf may bloom ;
Or Genii twine beneath the deep
    Their coral tomb :

But strew his ashes to the wind
Whose sword or voice has served mankind—
And is he dead, whose glorious mind
    Lifts thine on high ?—
To live in hearts we leave behind,
    Is not to die.

Is't death to fall for Freedom's right ?
He 's dead alone that lacks her light !
And murder sullies in Heaven's sight
    The sword he draws :—
What can alone ennoble fight ?
    A noble cause !

Give that! and welcome War to brace
Her drums! and rend Heaven's reeking space!
The colours planted face to face,
    The charging cheer,
Though death's pale horse lead on the chase,
    Shall still be dear.

And place our trophies where men kneel
To Heaven! but Heaven rebukes my zeal.
The cause of Truth and human weal,
    O God above!
Transfer it from the sword's appeal
    To Peace and Love.

Peace, Love! the cherubim, that join
Their spread wings o'er Devotion's shrine,
Prayers sound in vain, and temples shine,
    Where they are not—
The heart alone can make divine
    Religion's spot.

To incantations dost thou trust,
And pompous rites in domes august?
See mouldering stones and metal's rust
    Belie the vaunt,
That men can bless one pile of dust
    With chime or chaunt.

The ticking wood-worm mocks thee, man!
Thy temples—creeds themselves grow wan!
But there's a dome of nobler span,
    A temple given
Thy faith, that bigots dare not ban—
    Its space is Heaven!

Its roof star-pictured Nature's ceiling,
Where trancing the rapt spirit's feeling,
And God himself to man revealing,

The harmonious spheres
Make music, though unheard their pealing
By mortal ears.

Fair stars! are not your beings pure?
Can sin, can death your worlds obscure?
Else why so swell the thoughts at your
Aspect above?
Ye must be Heavens that make us sure
Of heavenly love!

And in your harmony sublime
I read the doom of distant time;
That man's regenerate soul from crime
Shall yet be drawn,
And reason on his mortal clime
Immortal dawn.

What's hallow'd ground?   'Tis what gives birth
To sacred thoughts in souls of worth!—
Peace! Independence! Truth! go forth
Earth's compass round;
And your high-priesthood shall make earth
All hallow'd ground.

SONG.

WITHDRAW not yet those lips and
fingers,
Whose touch to mine is rapture's
spell;
Life's joy for us a moment lingers,
And death seems in the word—Farewell.
The hour that bids us part and go,
It sounds not yet,—oh! no, no, no!

Time, whilst I gaze upon thy sweetness,
    Flies like a courser nigh the goal ;
To-morrow where shall be his fleetness,
    When thou art parted from my soul ?
Our hearts shall beat, our tears shall flow,
But not together—no, no, no !

CAROLINE.

PART I.

'LL bid the hyacinth to blow,
    I'll teach my grotto green to be ;
And sing my true love, all below
    The holly bower and myrtle tree.

There all his wild-wood sweets to bring,
    The sweet South wind shall wander by,
And with the music of his wing
    Delight my rustling canopy.

Come to my close and clustering bower,
    Thou spirit of a milder clime,
Fresh with the dews of fruit and flower,
    Of mountain heath, and moory thyme.

With all thy rural echoes come,
    Sweet comrade of the rosy day,
Wafting the wild bee's gentle hum,
    Or cuckoo's plaintive roundelay.

Where'er thy morning breath has play'd,
    Whatever isles of ocean fann'd,
Come to my blossom-woven shade,
    Thou wandering wind of fairy-land.

For sure from some enchanted isle,
   Where Heaven and Love their sabbath hold,
Where pure and happy spirits smile,
   Of beauty's fairest, brightest mould:

From some green Eden of the deep,
   Where Pleasure's sigh alone is heaved,
Where tears of rapture lovers weep,
   Endear'd, undoubting, undeceived:

From some sweet paradise afar,
   Thy music wanders, distant, lost—
Where Nature lights her leading star,
   And love is never, never cross'd.

Oh, gentle gale of Eden bowers,
   If back thy rosy feet should roam,
To revel with the cloudless Hours
   In Nature's more propitious home,

Name to thy loved Elysian groves,
   That o'er enchanted spirits twine,
A fairer form than Cherub loves,
   And let the name be CAROLINE.

CAROLINE.

PART II.

TO THE EVENING STAR.

GEM of the crimson-colour'd Even,
   Companion of retiring day,
Why at the closing gates of heaven,
   Beloved star, dost thou delay?

So fair thy pensile beauty burns,
  When soft the tear of twilight flows,
So due thy plighted love returns,
  To chambers brighter than the rose:

To Peace, to Pleasure, and to Love,
  So kind a star thou seem'st to be,
Sure some enamour'd orb above
  Descends and burns to meet with thee.

Thine is the breathing, blushing hour
  When all unheavenly passions fly,
Chased by the soul-subduing power
  Of Love's delicious witchery.

O ! sacred to the fall of day,
  Queen of propitious stars, appear,
And early rise, and long delay,
  When Caroline herself is here !

Shine on her chosen green resort,
  Whose trees the sunward summit crown,
And wanton flowers, that well may court
  An angel's feet to tread them down.

Shine on her sweetly scented road,
  Thou star of evening's purple dome,
That lead'st the nightingale abroad,
  And guid'st the pilgrim to his home.

Shine where my charmer's sweeter breath
  Embalms the soft exhaling dew,
Where dying winds a sigh bequeath
  To kiss the cheek of rosy hue.

Where, winnow'd by the gentle air,
  Her silken tresses darkly flow
And fall upon her brow so fair,
  Like shadows on the mountain snow.

Thus, ever thus, at day's decline,
  In converse sweet, to wander far,
O bring with thee my Caroline,
  And thou shalt be my Ruling Star!

SONG.

DRINK ye to her that each loves best,
  And if you nurse a flame
That 's told but to her mutual breast,
  We will not ask her name.

Enough, while memory tranced and glad
  Paints silently the fair,
That each should dream of joys he 's had,
  Or yet may hope to share.

Yet far, far hence, be jest or boast
  From hallow'd thoughts so dear;
But drink to her that each loves most,
  As she would love to hear.

THE BEECH-TREE'S PETITION.

O LEAVE this barren spot to me!
  Spare, woodman, spare the beechen
    tree!
Though bush or floweret never grow
My dark unwarming shade below;
Nor summer bud perfume the dew
Of rosy blush, or yellow hue!
Nor fruits of autumn, blossom born,
My green and glossy leaves adorn;

Nor murmuring tribes from me derive
Th' ambrosial amber of the hive;
Yet leave this barren spot to me:
Spare, woodman, spare the beechen tree!

Thrice twenty summers I have seen
The sky grow bright, the forest green;
And many a wintry wind have stood
In bloomless, fruitless solitude,
Since childhood in my pleasant bower
First spent its sweet and sportive hour;
Since youthful lovers in my shade
Their vows of truth and rapture made,
And on my trunk's surviving frame
Carved many a long-forgotten name.
Oh! by the sighs of gentle sound,
First breathed upon this sacred ground;
By all that Love has whisper'd here,
Or beauty heard with ravish'd ear;
As Love's own altar honour me:
Spare, woodman, spare the beechen tree!

FIELD FLOWERS.

YE field flowers! the gardens eclipse you,
        'tis true,
        Yet, wildings of Nature, I dote upon
        you,
    For ye waft me to summers of old,
When the earth teem'd around me with fairy
        delight,
And when daisies and buttercups gladden'd my
        sight,
    Like treasures of silver and gold.

I love you for lulling me back into dreams
Of the blue Highland mountains and echoing
    streams,
    And of birchen glades breathing their balm,
While the deer was seen glancing in sunshine
    remote,
And the deep mellow crush of the wood-pigeon's
    note
    Made music that sweeten'd the calm.

Not a pastoral song has a pleasanter tune
Than ye speak to my heart, little wildings of June :
    Of old ruinous castles ye tell,
Where I thought it delightful your beauties to find,
When the magic of Nature first breathed on my
    mind,
    And your blossoms were part of her spell.

Even now what affections the violet awakes !
What loved little islands, twice seen in their lakes,
    Can the wild water-lily restore !
What landscapes I read in the primrose's looks,
And what pictures of pebbled and minnowy brooks,
    In the vetches that tangled their shore.

Earth's cultureless buds, to my heart ye were dear,
Ere the fever of passion, or ague of fear,
    Had scathed my existence's bloom ;
Once I welcome you more, in life's passionless
    stage,
With the visions of youth to revisit my age,
    And I wish you to grow on my tomb.

SONG.

STAR that bringest home the bee,
　And sett'st the weary labourer free!
If any star shed peace, 'tis thou,
　That send'st it from above,
Appearing when Heaven's breath and brow
　Are sweet as hers we love.

Come to the luxuriant skies,
Whilst the landscape's odours rise,
Whilst far-off lowing herds are heard,
　And songs when toil is done,
From cottages whose smoke unstirr'd
　Curls yellow in the sun.

Star of love's soft interviews,
Parted lovers on thee muse;
Their remembrancer in Heaven
　Of thrilling vows thou art,
Too delicious to be riven
　By absence from the heart.

STANZAS TO PAINTING.

THOU by whose expressive art
　Her perfect image Nature sees
In union with the Graces start,
　And sweeter by reflection please!

In whose creative hand the hues
　Fresh from yon orient rainbow shine;
I bless thee, Promethéan Muse!
　And call thee brightest of the Nine!

Possessing more than vocal power,
   Persuasive more than poet's tongue;
Whose lineage, in a raptured hour,
   From Love, the Sire of Nature, sprung;

Does Hope her high possession meet?
   Is joy triumphant, sorrow flown?
Sweet is the trance, the tremor sweet,
   When all we love is all our own.

But oh! thou pulse of pleasure dear,
   Slow throbbing, cold, I feel thee part;
Lone absence plants a pang severe,
   Or death inflicts a keener dart.

Then for a beam of joy to light
   In memory's sad and wakeful eye;
Or banish from the noon of night
   Her dreams of deeper agony.

Shall Song its witching cadence roll?
   Yea, even the tenderest air repeat,
That breathed when soul was knit to soul,
   And heart to heart responsive beat?

What visions rise! to charm, to melt!
   The lost, the loved, the dead, are near!
Oh, hush that strain too deeply felt!
   And cease that solace too severe!

But thou, serenely silent art!
   By heaven and love wast taught to lend
A milder solace to the heart,
   The sacred image of a friend.

All is not lost! if, yet possest,
   To me that sweet memorial shine :—
If close and closer to my breast
   I hold that idol all divine.

Or, gazing through luxurious tears,
   Melt o'er the loved departed form,
Till death's cold bosom half appears
   With life, and speech, and spirit warm.

She looks! she lives! this trancèd hour,
   Her bright eye seems a purer gem
Than sparkles on the throne of power,
   Or glory's wealthy diadem.

Yes, Genius, yes! thy mimic aid
   A treasure to my soul has given,
Where beauty's canonisèd shade
   Smiles in the sainted hues of heaven.

No spectre forms of pleasure fled,
   Thy softening, sweetening, tints restore;
For thou canst give us back the dead,
   E'en in the loveliest looks they wore.

Then blest be Nature's guardian Muse,
   Whose hand her perish'd grace redeems;
Whose tablet of a thousand hues
   The mirror of creation seems.

From Love began thy high descent;
   And lovers, charm'd by gifts of thine,
Shall bless thee mutely eloquent;
   And call thee brightest of the Nine!

THE MAID'S REMONSTRANCE.

NEVER wedding, ever wooing!
   Still a love-lorn heart pursuing,
   Read you not the wrong you're doing
     In my cheek's pale hue?
All my life with sorrow strewing,
   Wed, or cease to woo.

Rivals banish'd, bosoms plighted,
Still our days are disunited;
Now the lamp of hope is lighted,
   Now half quench'd appears,
Damp'd, and wavering, and benighted,
   'Midst my sighs and tears.

Charms you call your dearest blessing,
Lips that thrill at your caressing,
Eyes a mutual soul confessing,
   Soon you'll make them grow
Dim, and worthless your possessing,
   Not with age, but woe!

.LINES

INSCRIBED ON THE MONUMENT LATELY FINISHED

BY MR. CHANTREY,

Which has been erected by the Widow of Admiral Sir G. Campbell,
K. C. B., to the memory of her husband.

TO him, whose loyal, brave, and gentle
    heart,
   Fulfill'd the hero's and the patriot's
    part,—
Whose charity, like that which Paul enjoin'd,
Was warm, beneficent, and unconfined,—
This stone is rear'd : to public duty true,
The seaman's friend, the father of his crew—
Mild in reproof, sagacious in command,
He spread fraternal zeal throughout his band,
And led each arm to act, each heart to feel,
What British valour owes to Britain's weal.
These were his public virtues :—but to trace
His private life's fair purity and grace,

To paint the traits that drew affection strong
From friends, an ample and an ardent throng,
And, more, to speak his memory's grateful claim
On her who mourns him most, and bears his
       name—
O'ercomes the trembling hand of widow'd grief,
O'ercomes the heart, unconscious of relief,
Save in religion's high and holy trust,
Whilst placing their memorial o'er his dust.

STANZAS

ON THE BATTLE OF NAVARINO.

HEARTS of oak that have bravely de-
       liver'd the brave,
    And uplifted old Greece from the brink
       of the grave,
'Twas the helpless to help, and the hopeless to
       save,
    That your thunderbolts swept o'er the brine :
And as long as yon sun shall look down on the
       wave,
    The light of your glory shall shine.

For the guerdon ye sought with your bloodshed
       and toil,
Was it slaves, or dominion, or rapine, or spoil ?
No ! your lofty emprise was to fetter and foil
    The uprooter of Greece's domain !
When he tore the last remnant of food from her
       soil
    Till her famish'd sank pale as the slain !

Yet, Navarin's heroes ! does Christendom breed
The base hearts that will question the fame of your
    deed !
Are they men ?—let ineffable scorn be their meed,
    And oblivion shadow their graves !—
Are they women ?—to Turkish serails let them
    speed ;
    And be mothers of Mussulman slaves.

Abettors of massacre ! dare ye deplore
That the death-shriek is silenced on Hellas's shore ?
That the mother aghast sees her offspring no more
    By the hand of Infanticide grasp'd ?
And that stretch'd on yon billows distain'd by
    their gore
    Missolonghi's assassins have gasp'd ?

Prouder scene never hallow'd war's pomp to the
    mind,
Than when Christendom's pennons woo'd social
    the wind,
And the flower of her brave for the combat
    combined,
    Their watch-word, humanity's vow ;
Not a sea-boy that fought in that cause, but man-
    kind
    Owes a garland to honour his brow !

Nor grudge, by our side, that to conquer or fall,
Came the hardy rude Russ, and the high-mettled
    Gaul ;
For whose was the genius, that plann'd at its call,
    Where the whirlwind of battle should roll ?
All were brave ! but the star of success over all
    Was the light of our Codrington's soul.

That star of thy day-spring, regenerate Greek !
Dimm'd the Saracen's moon, and struck pallid his
    cheek :   N

In its fast flushing morning thy Muses shall speak
    When their lore and their lutes they reclaim :
And the first of their songs from Parnassus's peak
    Shall be " *Glory to Codrington's name !*"

LINES

ON REVISITING A SCOTTISH RIVER.

AND call they this Improvement?—to have changed,
    My native Clyde, thy once romantic shore,
Where Nature's face is banish'd and estranged,
And Heaven reflected in thy wave no more ;
Whose banks, that sweeten'd May-day's breath before,
Lie sere and leafless now in summer's beam,
With sooty exhalations cover'd o'er ;
And for the daisied green-sward, down thy stream
Unsightly brick-lanes smoke, and clanking engines gleam.

Speak not to me of swarms the scene sustains ;
One heart free tasting Nature's breath and bloom
Is worth a thousand slaves to Mammon's gains.
But whither goes that wealth, and gladdening whom ?
See, left but life enough and breathing-room
The hunger and the hope of life to feel,
Yon pale Mechanic bending o'er his loom,
And Childhood's self as at Ixion's wheel,
From morn till midnight task'd to earn its little meal.

Is this Improvement?—where the human breed
Degenerates as they swarm and overflow,
Till toil grows cheaper than the trodden weed,
And man competes with man, like foe with foe,
Till Death, that thins them scarce seems public
      woe?
Improvement!—smiles it in the poor man's eyes,
Or blooms it on the cheek of Labour?—No—
To gorge a few with Trade's precarious prize,
We banish rural life, and breathe unwholesome
      skies.

Nor call that evil slight; God has not given
This passion to the heart of man in vain,
For Earth's green face, th' untainted air of Heaven,
And all the bliss of Nature's rustic reign.
For not alone our frame imbibes a stain
From fetid skies; the spirit's healthy pride
Fades in their gloom—And therefore I complain,
That thou no more through pastoral scenes shouldst
      glide,
My Wallace's own stream, and once romantic
      Clyde!

THE "NAME UNKNOWN."

IN IMITATION OF KLOPSTOCK.

PROPHETIC pencil! wilt thou trace
    A faithful image of the face,
      Or wilt thou write the "Name Un-
      known,"
    Ordain'd to bless my charmed soul,
    And all my future fate control,
      Unrivall'd and alone?

Delicious Idol of my thought!
Though sylph or spirit hath not taught
　　My boding heart thy precious name;
Yet musing on my distant fate,
To charms unseen I consecrate
　　A visionary flame.

Thy rosy blush, thy meaning eye,
Thy virgin voice of melody,
　　Are ever present to my heart;
Thy murmur'd vows shall yet be mine,
My thrilling hand shall meet with thine,
　　And never, never part!

Then fly, my days, on rapid wing,
Till Love the viewless treasure bring:
　　While I, like conscious Athens, own
A power in mystic silence seal'd,
A guardian angel unreveal'd,
　　And bless the " Name Unknown !"

LINES

ON THE CAMP HILL, NEAR HASTINGS.

ON the deep blue of eve,
　　Ere the twinkling of stars had begun,
　　Or the lark took his leave
Of the skies and the sweet setting sun.

I climb'd to yon heights,
Where the Norman encamp'd him of old,
　　With his bowmen and knights,
And his banner all burnish'd with gold.

At the Conqueror's side
There his minstrelsy sat harp in hand,
In pavilion wide:
And they chanted the deeds of Roland.

Still the ramparted ground
With a vision my fancy inspires,
And I hear the trump sound,
As it marshall'd our Chivalry's sires.

On each turf of that mead
Stood the captors of England's domains,
That ennobled her breed
And high-mettled the blood of her veins,

Over hauberk and helm
As the sun's setting splendour was thrown,
Thence they look'd o'er a realm—
And to-morrow beheld it their own.

FAREWELL TO LOVE.

I HAD a heart that doted once in passion's boundless pain,
And though the tyrant I abjured, I could not break his chain;
But now that Fancy's fire is quench'd, and ne'er can burn anew,
I've bid to Love, for all my life, adieu! adieu! adieu!

I've known, if ever mortal knew, the spells of Beauty's thrall,
And if my song has told them not, my soul has felt them all;

But Passion robs my peace no more, and Beauty's
    witching sway
Is now to me a star that's fallen—a dream that's
    pass'd away.

Hail ! welcome tide of life, when no tumultuous
    billows roll,
How wondrous to myself appears this halcyon
    calm of soul !
The wearied bird blown o'er the deep would sooner
    quit its shore,
Than I would cross the gulf again that time has
    brought me o'er.

Why say they Angels feel the flame ?—Oh, spirits
    of the skies !
Can love like ours, that dotes on dust, in heavenly
    bosoms rise ?—
Ah no ! the hearts that best have felt its power,
    the best can tell,
That peace on earth itself begins when Love has
    bid farewell.

SONG.

OW delicious is the winning
  Of a kiss at Love's beginning,
  When two mutual hearts are sighing
  For the knot there's no untying !

Yet remember, 'midst your wooing,
Love has bliss, but Love has ruing ;
Other smiles may make you fickle,
Tears for other charms may trickle.

Love he comes, and Love he tarries,
Just as fate or fancy carries ;

Longest stays, when sorest chidden ;
Laughs and flies, when press'd and bidden.

Bind the sea to slumber stilly,
Bind its odour to the lily,
Bind the aspen ne'er to quiver,
Then bind Love to last for ever !

Love's a fire that needs renewal
Of fresh beauty for its fuel :
Love's wing moults when caged and captured,
Only free, he soars enraptured.

Can you keep the bee from ranging,
Or the ringdove's neck from changing?
No ! nor fetter'd Love from dying
In the knot there's no untying.

LINES ON POLAND.

AND have I lived to see thee sword in
hand
Uprise again, immortal Polish Land !—
Whose flag brings more than chivalry
to mind,
And leaves the tri-color in shade behind ;
A theme for uninspired lips too strong !
That swells my heart beyond the power of song :—
Majestic men, whose deeds have dazzled faith,
Ah ! yet your fate's suspense arrests my breath ;
Whilst envying bosoms bared to shot and steel,
I feel the more that fruitlessly I feel.

Poles ! with what indignation I endure
Th' half-pitying servile mouths that call you poor ;

Poor! is it England mocks you with her grief,
Who hates, but dares not chide, th' *Imperial Thief?*
France with her soul beneath a Bourbon's thrall,
And Germany that has no soul at all,—
States, quailing at the giant overgrown,
Whom dauntless Poland grapples with alone!
No, ye are rich in fame e'en whilst ye bleed :
We cannot aid you—*we* are poor indeed!
In fate's defiance—in the world's great eye,
Poland has won her immortality;
The Butcher, should he reach her bosom now,
Could not tear Glory's garland from her brow;
Wreath'd, filleted, the victim falls renown'd,
And all her ashes will be holy ground!
But turn, my soul, from presages so dark :
Great Poland's spirit is a deathless spark
That's fann'd by Heaven to mock the Tyrant's
          rage :
She, like the eagle, will renew her age,
And fresh historic plumes of Fame put on,
Another Athens after Marathon,—
Where eloquence shall fulmine, arts refine,
Bright as her arms that now in battle shine.
Come—should the heavenly shock my life destroy,
And shut its flood-gates with excess of joy!
Come but the day when Poland's fight is won—
And on my grave-stone shine the morrow's sun—
The day that sees Warsaw's cathedral glow
With endless ensigns ravish'd from the foe,—
Her women lifting their fair hands with thanks,
Her pious warriors kneeling in their ranks,
The scutcheon'd walls of high heraldic boast,
The odorous altars' elevated host,
The organ sounding through the aisle's long glooms,
The mighty dead seen sculptured o'er their tombs;
(John, Europe's saviour—Poniatowski's fair
Resemblance—Kosciusko's shall be there ;)

The taper'd pomp—the hallelujah's swell,
Shall o'er the soul's devotion cast a spell,
Till visions cross the rapt enthusiast's glance,
And all the scene becomes a waking trance.
Should Fate put far—far off that glorious scene,
And gulfs of havoc interpose between,
Imagine not, ye men of every clime,
Who act, or by your sufferance share, the crime—
Your brother Abel's blood shall vainly plead
Against the " *deep damnation* " of the deed.
Germans, ye view its horror and disgrace
With cold phosphoric eyes and phlegm of face.
Is Allemagne profound in science, lore,
And minstrel art ?—her shame is but the more
To doze and dream by governments oppress'd,
The spirit of a book-worm in each breast.
Well can ye mouth fair Freedom's classic line
And talk of Constitutions o'er your wine :
But all your vows to break the tyrant's yoke
Expire in Bacchanalian song and smoke ;
Heavens ! can no ray of foresight pierce the leads
And mystic metaphysics of your heads,
To show the self-same grave, Oppression delves
For Poland's rights, is yawning for yourselves ?

See, whilst the Pole, the vanguard aid of France,
Has vaulted on his barb and couch'd the lance,
France turns from her abandon'd friends afresh,
And soothes the Bear that prowls for patriot flesh ;
Buys, ignominious purchase ! short repose,
With dying curses, and the groans of those
That served, and loved, and put in her their trust.
Frenchmen ! the dead accuse you from the dust—
Brows laurell'd—bosoms mark'd with many a scar
For France—that wore her Legion's noblest star,
Cast dumb reproaches from the field of Death
On Gallic honour : and this broken faith

Has robb'd you more of Fame—the life of life—
Than twenty battles lost in glorious strife!
And what of England?—is she steep'd so low
In poverty, crest-fallen, and palsied so,
That we must sit much wroth, but timorous more,
With Murder knocking at our neighbour's door!—
Not Murder mask'd and cloak'd with hidden knife,
Whose owner owes the gallows life for life ;
But *Public Murder !*—that with pomp and gaud,
And royal scorn of Justice, walks abroad
To wring more tears and blood than e'er were
            wrung
By all the culprits Justice ever hung!
We read the diadem'd Assassin's vaunt,
And wince, and wish we had not hearts to pant
With useless indignation—sigh, and frown,
But have not hearts to throw the gauntlet down.

If but a doubt hung o'er the grounds of fray,
Or trivial rapine stopp'd the world's highway;
Were this some common strife of States em-
            broil'd;—
Britannia on the spoiler and the spoil'd
Might calmly look, and, asking time to breathe,
Still honourably wear her olive wreath.
But this is Darkness combating with Light ;
Earth's adverse Principles for empire fight:
Oppression, that has belted half the globe,
Far as his knout could reach or dagger probe,
Holds reeking o'er our brother-freemen slain
That dagger—shakes it at us in disdain ;
Talks big to Freedom's states of Poland's thrall,
And, trampling one, contemns them one and all.

My country ! colours not thy once proud brow
At this affront !—Hast thou not fleets enow
With Glory's streamer, lofty as the lark,

Gay fluttering o'er each thunder-bearing bark,
To warm the insulter's seas with barbarous blood,
And interdict his flag from Ocean's flood ?
Ev'n now far off the sea-cliff, where I sing,
I see, my Country and my Patriot king !
Your ensign glad the deep.   Becalm'd and slow
A war-ship rides ; while Heaven's prismatic bow
Uprisen behind her on th' horizon's base,
Shines flushing through the tackle, shrouds, and
        stays,
And wraps her giant form in one majestic blaze.
My soul accepts the omen ; Fancy's eye
Has sometimes a veracious augury :
The Rainbow types Heaven's promise to my sight ;
The Ship, Britannia's interposing Might !
But if there should be none to aid you, Poles,
Ye'll but to prouder pitch wind up your souls,
Above example, pity, praise, or blame,
To sow and reap a boundless field of Fame.
Ask aid no more from Nations that forget
Your championship—old Europe's mighty debt.
Though Poland, Lazarus-like, has burst the gloom,
She rises not a beggar from the tomb :
In Fortune's frown, on Danger's giddiest brink,
Despair and Poland's name must never link.
All ills have bounds—plague, whirlwind, fire, and
        flood :
Ev'n Power can spill but bounded sums of blood.
States caring not what Freedom's price may be,
May late or soon, but must at last be free ;
For body-killing tyrants cannot kill
The public soul—the hereditary will
That downward, as from sire to son it goes,
By shifting bosoms more intensely glows :
Its heir-loom is the heart, and slaughter'd men
Fight fiercer in their orphans o'er again.
Poland recasts—though rich in heroes old—

Her men in more and more heroic mould :
Her eagle ensign best among mankind
Becomes, and types her eagle-strength of mind :
Her praise upon my faltering lips expires :
Resume it, younger bards, and nobler lyres !

THE POWER OF RUSSIA.

SO all this gallant blood has gush'd in
      vain ;
  And Poland, by the Northern Condor's
      beak
And talons torn, lies prostrated again !
O British patriots, that were wont to speak
Once loudly on this theme, now hush'd or meek !
O heartless men of Europe—Goth and Gaul,
Cold, adder-deaf to Poland's dying shriek ;—
That saw the world's last land of heroes fall—
The brand of burning shame is on you all—all—
    all !

But this is not the drama's closing act !
Its tragic curtain must uprise anew.
Nations, mute accessories to the fact !
That Upas-tree of power, whose fostering dew
Was Polish blood, has yet to cast o'er you
The lengthening shadow of its head elate—
A deadly shadow, darkening Nature's hue.
To all that's hallow'd, righteous, pure and great,
Wo ! wo ! when they are reach'd by Russia's
    withering hate.

Russia, that on his throne of adamant,
Consults what nation's breast shall next be
    gored :
He on Polonia's Golgotha will plant

His standard fresh ; and horde succeeding horde,
On patriot tombstones he will whet the sword,
For more stupendous slaughters of the free.
Then Europe's realms, when their best blood is
    pour'd,
Shall miss thee, Poland ! as they bend the knee,
All—all in grief, but none in glory, likening thee.

Why smote ye not the Giant whilst he reel'd ?
O fair occasion, gone for ever by !
To have lock'd his lances in their northern field,
Innocuous as the phantom chivalry
That flames and hurtles from yon boreal sky !
Now wave thy pennon, Russia, o'er the land
Once Poland ; build thy bristling castles high ;
Dig dungeons deep ; for Poland's wrested brand
Is now a weapon new to widen thy command—

An awful width ! Norwegian woods shall build
His fleets ; the Swede his vassal, and the Dane ;
The glebe of fifty kingdoms shall be till'd
To feed his dazzling, desolating train,
Camp'd sumless, 'twixt the Black and Baltic
    main :
Brute hosts, I own ; but Sparta could not write,
And Rome, half-barbarous, bound Achaia's
    chain :
So Russia's spirit, 'midst Sclavonic night,
Burns with a fire more dread than all your polish'd
    light.

But Russia's limbs (so blinded statesmen speak)
Are crude, and too colossal to cohere.
O, lamentable weakness ! reckoning weak
The stripling Titan, strengthening year by year.
What implement lacks he for war's career,
That grows on earth, or in its floods and mines,
(Eighth sharer of the inhabitable sphere)

Whom Persia bows to, China ill confines,
And India's homage waits, when Albion's star
    declines ?

But time will teach the Russ, ev'n conquering
    War
Has handmaid arts: ay, ay, the Russ will woo
All sciences that speed Bellona's car,
All murder's tactic arts, and win them too;
But never holier Muses shall imbue
His breast, that's made of nature's basest clay;
The sabre, knout, and dungeon's vapour blue
His laws and ethics; far from him away
Are all the lovely Nine, that breathe but Free-
    dom's day.

Say, ev'n his serfs, half-humanized, should learn
Their human rights,—will Mars put out his
    flame
In Russian bosoms ? no, he'll bid them burn
A thousand years for nought but martial fame,
Like Romans:—yet forgive me, Roman name !
Rome could impart what Russia never can;
Proud civic rights to salve submission's shame.
Our strife is coming; but in freedom's van
The Polish eagle's fall is big with fate to man.

Proud bird of old ! Mohammed's moon recoil'd
Before thy swoop: had we been timely bold,
That swoop, still free, had stunn'd the Russ, and
    foil'd
Earth's new oppressors, as it foil'd her old.
Now thy majestic eyes are shut and cold:
And colder still Polonia's children find
The sympathetic hands, that we outhold.
But, Poles, when we are gone, the world will
    mind,
Ye bore the brunt of fate, and bled for human-
    kind.

So hallow'dly have ye fulfill'd your part,
My pride repudiates ev'n the sigh that blends
With Poland's name—name written on my heart.
My heroes, my grief-consecrated friends !
Your sorrow, in nobility, transcends
Your conqueror's joy : his cheek may blush ; but
    shame
Can tinge not yours, though exile's tear de-
    scends ;
Nor would ye change your conscience, cause, and
    name,
For his, with all his wealth, and all his felon fame.

Thee, Niemciewitz, whose song of stirring power
The Czar forbids to sound in Polish lands ;
Thee, Czartoryski, in thy banish'd bower,
The patricide, who in thy palace stands,
May envy ; proudly may Polonia's bands
Throw down their swords at Europe's feet in
    scorn,
Saying—" Russia from the metal of these brands
Shall forge the fetters of your sons unborn ;
Our setting star is your misfortunes' rising morn."

MARGARET AND DORA.

MARGARET'S beauteous—Grecian arts
    Ne'er drew form completer,
    Yet why, in my heart of hearts,
    Hold I Dora's sweeter ?

    Dora's eyes of heavenly blue
    Pass all painting's reach,
    Ringdoves' notes are discord
    The music of her speech.

Artists ! Margaret's smile receive,
And on canvas show it ;
But for perfect worship leave
Dora to her poet.

LINES

ADIEU the woods and waters' side,
    Imperial Danube's rich domain !
Adieu the grotto, wild and wide,
    The rocks abrupt, and grassy plain !
For pallid Autumn once again
Hath swell'd each torrent of the hill ;
    Her clouds collect, her shadows sail,
    And watery winds that sweep the vale,
Grow loud and louder still.

But not the storm, dethroning fast
    Yon monarch oak of massy pile ;
Nor river roaring to the blast
    Around its dark and desert isle ;
    Nor church-bell tolling to beguile
The cloud-born thunder passing by,
    Can sound in discord to my soul :
    Roll on, ye mighty waters, roll !
And rage, thou darken'd sky !

Thy blossoms now no longer bright ;
    Thy wither'd woods no longer green ;
Yet, Eldurn shore, with dark delight
    I visit thy unlovely scene !
    For many a sunset hour serene

My steps have trod thy mellow dew;
  When his green light the glow-worm gave,
  When Cynthia from the distant wave
Her twilight anchor drew,

And plough'd as with a swelling sail,
  The billowy clouds and starry sea;
Then while thy hermit nightingale
  Sang on his fragrant apple-tree,—
  Romantic, solitary, free,
The visitant of Eldurn's shore,
  On such a moonlight mountain stray'd,
  As echo'd to the music made
By Druid harps of yore.

Around thy savage hills of oak,
  Around thy waters bright and blue,
No hunter's horn the silence broke,
  No dying shriek thine echo knew;
  But safe, sweet Eldurn woods, to you
The wounded wild deer ever ran,
  Whose myrtle bound their grassy cave,
  Whose very rocks a shelter gave
From blood-pursuing man.

Oh! heart effusions, that arose
  From nightly wanderings cherish'd here;
To him who flies from many woes,
  Even homeless deserts can be dear!
  The last and solitary cheer
Of those that own no earthly home,
  Say—is it not, ye banish'd race,
  In such a loved and lonely place
Companionless to roam?

Yes! I have loved thy wild abode,
  Unknown, unplough'd, untrodden shore;

Where scarce the woodman finds a road,
　　And scarce the fisher plies an oar;
　　For man's neglect I love thee more;
That art nor avarice intrude
　　To tame thy torrent's thunder-shock,
　　Or prune thy vintage of the rock
Magnificently rude.

Unheeded spreads thy blossom'd bud
　　Its milky bosom to the bee;
Unheeded falls along the flood
　　Thy desolate and aged tree.
　　Forsaken scene, how like to thee
The fate of unbefriended Worth!
　　Like thine her fruit dishonour'd falls;
　　Like thee in solitude she calls
A thousand treasures forth.

Oh! silent spirit of the place,
　　If, lingering with the ruin'd year,
Thy hoary form and awful face
　　I yet might watch and worship here!
　　Thy storm were music to mine ear,
Thy wildest walk a shelter given
　　Sublimer thoughts on earth to find,
　　And share, with no unhallow'd mind,
The majesty of heaven.

What though the bosom friends of Fate,—
　　Prosperity's unweaned brood,—
Thy consolations cannot rate,
　　O self-dependent Solitude!
　　Yet with a spirit unsubdued,
Though darken'd by the clouds of Care,
　　To worship thy congenial gloom,
　　A pilgrim to the Prophet's tomb
The Friendless shall repair.

On him the world hath never smiled
   Or look'd but with accusing eye;—
All-silent goddess of the wild,
   To thee that misanthrope shall fly!
   I hear his deep soliloquy,
I mark his proud but ravaged form,
   As stern he wraps his mantle round,
   And bids, on winter's bleakest ground,
Defiance to the storm.

Peace to his banish'd heart, at last,
   In thy dominions shall descend,
And, strong as beechwood in the blast,
   His spirit shall refuse to bend;
   Enduring life without a friend,
The world and falsehood left behind,
   Thy votary shall bear elate,
   (Triumphant o'er opposing Fate)
His dark inspired mind.

But dost thou, Folly, mock the Muse
   A wanderer's mountain walk to sing,
Who shuns a warring world, nor woos
   The vulture cover of its wing?
   Then fly, thou cowering, shivering thing,
Back to the fostering world beguiled,
   To waste in self-consuming strife
   The loveless brotherhood of life,
Reviling and reviled !

Away, thou lover of the race
   That hither chased yon weeping deer !
If Nature's all majestic face
   More pitiless than man's appear;
   Or if the wild winds seem more drear
Than man's cold charities below,
   Behold around his peopled plains,
   Where'er the social savage reigns,
Exuberance of woe !

His art and honours would'st thou seek
   Emboss'd on grandeur's giant walls?
Or hear his moral thunders speak
   Where senates light their airy halls,
   Where man his brother man enthrals;
Or sends his whirlwind warrant forth
   To rouse the slumbering fiends of war,
   To dye the blood-warm waves afar,
And desolate the earth?

From clime to clime pursue the scene,
   And mark in all thy spacious way,
Where'er the tyrant man has been,
   There Peace, the cherub, cannot stay;
   In wilds and woodlands far away
She builds her solitary bower,
   Where only anchorites have trod,
   Or friendless men, to worship God,
Have wander'd for an hour.

In such a far forsaken vale,—
   And such, sweet Eldurn vale, is thine,—
Afflicted nature shall inhale
   Heaven-borrow'd thoughts and joys divine;
   No longer wish, no more repine
For man's neglect or woman's scorn;—
   Then wed thee to an exile's lot,
   For if the world hath loved thee not,
Its absence may be borne.

THE DEATH-BOAT OF HELIGOLAND.

CAN restlessness reach the cold sepul-
    chred head ?—
  Ay, the quick have their sleep-walkers,
    so have the dead.
There are brains, though they moulder, that dream
  in the tomb,
And that maddening forehear the last trumpet of
  doom,
Till their corses start sheeted to revel on earth,
Making horror more deep by the semblance of
    mirth :
By the glare of new-lighted volcanoes they dance,
Or at mid-sea appal the chill'd mariner's glance.
Such, I wot, was the band of cadaverous smile
Seen ploughing the night-surge of Heligo's isle.

The foam of the Baltic had sparkled like fire,
And the red moon look'd down with an aspect of
    ire ;
But her beams on a sudden grew sick-like and grey,
And the mews that had slept clang'd and shriek'd
    far away—
And the buoys and the beacons extinguish'd their
    light,
As the boat of the stony-eyed dead came in sight,
High bounding from billow to billow; each form
Had its shroud like a plaid flying loose to the
    storm ;
With an oar in each pulseless and icy-cold hand,
Fast they plough'd by the lee-shore of Heligoland,
Such breakers as boat of the living ne'er cross'd ;
Now surf-sunk for minutes again they uptoss'd,
And with livid lips shouted reply o'er the flood

To the challenging watchman, that curdled his
        blood—
" We are dead—we are bound from our graves in
        the west,
First to Hecla, and then to—" Unmeet was the
        rest
For man's ear.   The old abbey bell thunder'd its
        clang,
And their eyes gleam'd with phosphorous light as
        it rang :
Ere they vanish'd, they stopp'd, and gazed silently
        grim,
Till the eye could define them, garb, feature, and
        limb.

Now who were those roamers ?—of gallows or
        wheel
Bore they marks, or the mangling anatomist's steel ?
No, by magistrates' chains 'mid their grave-clothes
        you saw
They were felons too proud to have perish'd by law :
But a ribbon that hung where a rope should have
        been,
'Twas the badge of their faction, its hue was not
        green,
Show'd them men who had trampled and tortured
        and driven
To rebellion the fairest Isle breath'd on by
        Heaven,—
Men whose heirs would yet finish the tyrannous
        task,
If the Truth and the Time had not dragg'd off their
        mask.
They parted—but not till the sight might discern
A scutcheon distinct at their pinnace's stern,
Where letters emblazon'd in blood-colour'd flame,
Named their faction—I blot not my page with its
        name.

A THOUGHT SUGGESTED BY THE
NEW YEAR.

THE more we live, more brief appear
　　Our life's succeeding stages :
A day to childhood seems a year,
　　And years like passing ages.

The gladsome current of our youth,
　　Ere passion yet disorders,
Steals, lingering like a river smooth
　　Along its grassy borders.

But as the care-worn cheek grows wan,
　　And sorrow's shafts fly thicker,
Ye stars, that measure life to man,
　　Why seem your courses quicker ?

When joys have lost their bloom and breath,
　　And life itself is vapid,
Why, as we reach the Falls of death,
　　Feel we its tide more rapid ?

It may be strange—yet who would change
　　Time's course to slower speeding ;
When one by one our friends have gone,
　　And left our bosoms bleeding ?

Heaven gives our years of fading strength
　　Indemnifying fleetness ;
And those of youth, a *seeming length*,
　　Proportion'd to their sweetness.

ABSENCE.

'TIS not the loss of love's assurance,
　　It is not doubting what thou art,
But 'tis the too, too long endurance
　　Of absence, that afflicts my heart.

The fondest thoughts two hearts can cherish,
　　When each is lonely doom'd to weep,
Are fruits on desert isles that perish,
　　Or riches buried in the deep.

What though, untouch'd by jealous madness,
　　Our bosom's peace may fall to wreck;
Th' undoubting heart that breaks with sadness,
　　Is but more slowly doom'd to break.

Absence! is not the soul torn by it
　　From more than light, or life, or breath?
'Tis Lethe's gloom, but not its quiet,—
　　The pain, without the peace of death!

SONG.

WHEN Love came first to earth, the
　　　　Spring
　　Spread rose-beds to receive him,
　　And back he vow'd his flight he'd wing
To Heaven, if she should leave him.

But Spring departing, saw his faith
　　Pledged to the next new-comer—
He revell'd in the warmer breath
　　And richer bowers of Summer.

Then sportive Autumn claim'd by rights
  An Archer for her lover,
And even in Winter's dark cold nights
  A charm he could discover.

Her routs and balls, and fireside joy,
  For this time were his reasons—
In short, Young Love 's a gallant boy,
  That likes all times and seasons.

SONG.

EARL March look'd on his dying child,
  And smit with grief to view her—
The youth, he cried, whom I exiled,
  Shall be restored to woo her.

She 's at the window many an hour
  His coming to discover:
And *he* look'd up to Ellen's bower,
  And *she* look'd on her lover—

But ah! so pale, he knew her not,
  Though her smile on him was dwelling.
And am I then forgot—forgot?
  It broke the heart of Ellen.

In vain he weeps, in vain he sighs,
  Her cheek is cold as ashes;
Nor love's own kiss shall wake those eyes
  To lift their silken lashes.

SONG.

 HEN Napoleon was flying
        From the field of Waterloo,
A British soldier dying
        To his brother bade adieu.

" And take," he said, " this token
        To the maid that owns my faith,
With the words that I have spoken
        In affection's latest breath."

Sore mourn'd the brother's heart,
        When the youth beside him fell;
But the trumpet warn'd to part,
        And they took a sad farewell.

There was many a friend to lose him,
        For that gallant soldier sigh'd;
But the maiden of his bosom,
        Wept when all their tears were dried.

LINES TO JULIA M——.

SENT WITH A COPY OF THE AUTHOR'S POEMS.

INCE there is magic in your look,
        And in your voice a witching charm,
        As all our hearts consenting tell,
        Enchantress, smile upon my book,
And guard its lays from hate and harm
By beauty's most resistless spell.
The sunny dew-drop of thy praise,
Young day-star of the rising time,
Shall with its odoriferous morn

Refresh my sere and wither'd bays.
Smile, and I will believe my rhyme
Shall please the beautiful unborn.
Go forth, my pictured thoughts, and rise
In traits and tints of sweeter tone,
When Julia's glance is o'er ye flung;
Glow, gladden, linger in her eyes,
And catch a magic not your own,
Read by the music of her tongue.

LINES

ON THE DEPARTURE OF EMIGRANTS FOR NEW

SOUTH WALES.

ON England's shore I saw a pensive band,
  With sails unfurl'd for earth's remotest
    strand,
  Like children parting from a mother,
  shed
Tears for the home that could not yield them bread;
Grief mark'd each face receding from the view,
'Twas grief to nature honourably true.
And long, poor wanderers o'er th' ecliptic deep,
The song that names but home shall make you
    weep;
Oft shall ye fold your flocks by stars above
In that far world, and miss the stars ye love!
Oft when its tuneless birds scream round forlorn,
Regret the lark that gladdens England's morn,
And, giving England's names to distant scenes,
Lament that earth's extension intervenes.

But cloud not yet too long, industrious train,
Your solid good with sorrow nursed in vain:

For has the heart no interest yet as bland
As that which binds us to our native land?
The deep-drawn wish, when children crown our
      hearth,
To hear the cherub-chorus of their mirth,
Undamp'd by dread that want may e'er unhouse,
Or servile misery knit those smiling brows :
The pride to rear an independent shed,
And give the lips we love unborrow'd bread :
To see a world, from shadowy forests won,
In youthful beauty wedded to the sun ;
To skirt our home with harvests widely sown,
And call the blooming landscape all our own,
Our children's heritage, in prospect long,
These are the hopes, high-minded hopes, and
      strong,
That beckon England's wanderers o'er the brine,
To realms where foreign constellations shine;
Where streams from undiscover'd fountains roll,
And winds shall fan them from th' Antarctic pole.
And what though doom'd to shores so far apart
From England's home, that ev'n the home-sick
      heart
Quails, thinking, ere that gulf can be recross'd,
How large a space of fleeting life is lost :
Yet there, by time, their bosoms shall be changed,
And strangers once shall cease to sigh estranged,
But jocund in the year's long sunshine roam,
That yields their sickle twice its harvest-home.

There, marking o'er his farm's expanding ring
New fleeces whiten and new fruits upspring,
The grey-hair'd swain, his grandchild sporting
      round,
Shall walk at eve his little empire's bound,
Emblazed with ruby vintage, ripening corn,
And verdant rampart of acacian thorn,

While, mingling with the scent his pipe exhales,
The orange-grove's and fig-tree's breath prevails ;
Survey with pride beyond a monarch's spoil,
His honest arm's own subjugated soil ;
And summing all the blessings God has given,
Put up his patriarchal prayer to Heaven,
That when his bones shall here repose in peace,
The scions of his love may still increase,
And o'er a land where life has ample room,
In health and plenty innocently bloom.

Delightful land, in wildness ev'n benign,
The glorious past is ours, the future thine !
As in a cradled Hercules, we trace
The lines of empire in thine infant face.
What nations in thy wide horizon's span
Shall teem on tracts untrodden yet by man !
What spacious cities with their spires shall gleam,
Where now the panther laps a lonely stream,
And all but brute or reptile life is dumb !
Land of the free ! thy kingdom is to come,
Of states, with laws from Gothic bondage burst,
And creeds by charter'd priesthoods unaccurst :
Of navies, hoisting their emblazon'd flags,
Where shipless seas now wash unbeacon'd crags :
Of hosts review'd in dazzling files and squares,
Their pennon'd trumpets breathing native airs,—
For minstrels thou shalt have of native fire,
And maids to sing the songs themselves inspire :—
Our very speech, methinks, in after time,
Shall catch th' Ionian blandness of thy clime ;
And whilst the light and luxury of thy skies
Give brighter smiles to beauteous woman's eyes,
The Arts, whose soul is love, shall all spontaneous
        rise.

Untrack'd in deserts lies the marble mine,
Undug the ore that 'midst thy roofs shall shine ;

Unborn the hands—but born they are to be—
Fair Australasia, that shall give to thee
Proud temple domes, with galleries winding high,
So vast in space, so just in symmetry,
They widen to the contemplating eye,
With colonnaded aisles in long array,
And windows that enrich the flood of day
O'er tesselated pavements, pictures fair,
And nichèd statues breathing golden air.
Nor there, whilst all that's seen bids Fancy swell,
Shall Music's voice refuse to seal the spell;
But choral hymns shall wake enchantment round,
And organs yield their tempests of sweet sound.

Meanwhile, ere Arts triumphant reach their goal,
How blest the years of pastoral life shall roll!
Ev'n should some wayward hour the settler's
        mind
Brood sad on scenes for ever left behind,
Yet not a pang that England's name imparts
Shall touch a fibre of his children's hearts;
Bound to that native land by nature's bond,
Full little shall their wishes rove beyond
Its mountains blue, and melon-skirted streams,
Since childhood loved and dreamt of in their
        dreams.
How many a name, to us uncouthly wild,
Shall thrill that region's patriotic child,
And bring as sweet thoughts o'er his bosom's
        chords,
As aught that's named in song to us affords!
Dear shall that river's margin be to him,
Where sportive first he bathed his boyish limb,
Or petted birds, still brighter than their bowers,
Or twined his tame young kangaroo with flowers.
But more magnetic yet to memory
Shall be the sacred spot, still blooming nigh,

The bower of love, where first his bosom burn'd,
And smiling passion saw its smile return'd.

Go forth and prosper then, emprising band:
May He, who in the hollow of his hand
The ocean holds, and rules the whirlwind's sweep,
Assuage its wrath, and guide you on the deep!

THE CHERUBS.

SUGGESTED BY AN APOLOGUE IN THE WORKS
OF FRANKLIN.

TWO spirits reach'd this world of ours:
　　The lightning's locomotive powers
　　　Were slow to their agility:
　　In broad day-light they moved incog.,
Enjoying, without mist or fog,
　　Entire invisibility.

The one, a simple cherub lad,
Much interest in our planet had,
　　Its face was so romantic;
He couldn't persuade himself that man
Was such as heavenly rumours ran,
　　A being base and frantic.

The elder spirit, wise and cool,
Brought down the youth as to a school;
　　But strictly on condition,
Whatever they should see or hear,
With mortals not to interfere;
　　'Twas not in their commission.

They reach'd a sovereign city proud,
Whose emperor pray'd to God aloud,
　　With all his people kneeling,

And priests perform'd religious rites:
" Come," said the younger of the sprites,
" This shows a pious feeling."

YOUNG SPIRIT.

" Ar'n't these a decent godly race?"

OLD SPIRIT.

" The dirtiest thieves on Nature's face."

YOUNG SPIRIT.

" But hark, what cheers they 're giving
Their emperor!—And is he a thief?"

OLD SPIRIT.

" Ay, and a cut-throat too;—in brief,
THE GREATEST SCOUNDREL LIVING."

YOUNG SPIRIT.

" But say, what were they praying for,
This people and their emperor?"

OLD SPIRIT.

"—Why, but for God's assistance
To help their army, late sent out:
And what that army is about,
You 'll see at no great distance."

On wings outspeeding mail or post,
Our sprites o'ertook the Imperial host,
In massacres it wallow'd:
A noble nation met its hordes,
But broken fell their cause and swords,
Unfortunate, though hallow'd.

They saw a late bombarded town,
Its streets still warm with blood ran down;
Still smoked each burning rafter;

And hideously, 'midst rape and sack,
The murderer's laughter answer'd back
   His prey's convulsive laughter.

They saw the captive eye the dead,
With envy of his gory bed,—
   Death's quick reward of bravery:
They heard the clank of chains, and then
Saw thirty thousand bleeding men
   Dragg'd manacled to slavery.

" Fie! fie!" the younger heavenly spark
Exclaim'd:—" we must have miss'd our mark,
   And enter'd hell's own portals:
Earth can't be stain'd with crimes so black;
Nay, sure, we've got among a pack
   Of fiends, and not of mortals."

" No," said the elder; "no such thing:
Fiends are not fools enough to wring
   The necks of one another:—
They know their interests too well:
Men fight; but every devil in hell
   Lives friendly with his brother.

And I could point you out some fellows,
On this ill-fated planet Tellus,
   In royal power that revel;
Who, at the opening of the book
Of judgment, may have cause to look
   With envy at the devil."

Name but the devil, and he'll appear.
Old Satan in a trice was near,
   With smutty face and figure:
But spotless spirits of the skies,
Unseen to e'en his saucer eyes,
   Could watch the fiendish nigger.

" Halloo !" he cried, " I smell a trick :
A mortal supersedes Old Nick,
　　The scourge of earth appointed :
He robs me of my trade, outrants
The blasphemy of Hell, and vaunts
　　Himself the Lord's anointed !

Folks make a fuss about my mischief :
D——d fools ! they tamely suffer this chief
　　To play his pranks unbounded."
The cherubs flew ; but saw from high,
At human inhumanity,
　　The devil himself astounded.

DRINKING SONG OF MUNICH.

SWEET Iser ! were thy sunny realm
　　And flowery gardens mine,
　Thy waters I would shade with elm
　　To prop the tender vine ;
My golden flagons I would fill
With rosy draughts from every hill ;
　And under every myrtle bower
My gay companions should prolong
The laugh, the revel, and the song,
　　To many an idle hour.

　Like rivers crimson'd with the beam
　　Of yonder planet bright,
　Our balmy cups should ever stream
　　Profusion of delight ;
　No care should touch the mellow heart,
　And sad or sober none depart ;

For wine can triumph over woe,
And Love and Bacchus, brother powers,
Could build in Iser's sunny bowers
A paradise below.

LINES ON REVISITING CATHCART.

H ! scenes of my childhood, and dear to
my heart,
Ye green waving woods on the margin
of Cart,
How blest in the morning of life I have stray'd
By the stream of the vale and the grass-cover'd
glade !

Then, then every rapture was young and sincere,
Ere the sunshine of bliss was bedimm'd by a tear,
And a sweeter delight every scene seem'd to lend,
That the mansion of peace was the home of a friend.

Now the scenes of my childhood and dear to my
heart
All pensive I visit, and sigh to depart ;
Their flowers seem to languish, their beauty to
cease,
For a *stranger* inhabits the mansion of peace.

But hush'd be the sigh that untimely complains,
While Friendship and all its enchantment remains,
While it blooms like the flower of a winterless clime,
Untainted by chance, unabated by time.

TO SIR FRANCIS BURDETT,

ON HIS SPEECH DELIVERED IN PARLIAMENT, AUGUST 7, 1832,

RESPECTING THE FOREIGN POLICY OF GREAT BRITAIN.

BURDETT, enjoy thy justly foremost
    fame,
    Through good and ill report—through
      calm and storm—
For forty years the pilot of reform !
But that which shall afresh entwine thy name
    With patriot laurels never to be sere,
Is that thou hast come nobly forth to chide
Our slumbering statesmen for their lack of pride—
    Their flattery of Oppressors, and their fear—
When Britain's lifted finger, and her frown,
Might call the nations up, and cast their tyrants
    down !

Invoke the scorn—Alas ! too few inherit
    The scorn for despots cherish'd by our sires,
    That baffled Europe's persecuting fires,
And shelter'd helpless states !—Recall that spirit,
    And conjure back Old England's haughty
      mind—
Convert the men who waver now, and pause
    Between their love of self and humankind ;
And move, Amphion-like, those hearts of stone—
The hearts that have been deaf to Poland's dying
    groan !

Tell them, we hold the Rights of Man too dear,
    To bless ourselves with lonely freedom blest ;
    But could we hope, with sole and selfish breast,
To breathe untroubled Freedom's atmosphere ?—

Suppose we wish'd it ? England could not stand
A lone oasis in the desert ground
Of Europe's slavery ; from the waste around
    Oppression's fiery blast and whirling sand
Would reach and scathe us ! No ; it may not be :
Britannia and the world conjointly must be free!

Burdett, demand why Britons send abroad
    Soft greetings to th' infanticidal Czar,
    The Bear on Poland's babes that wages war.
Once, we are told, a mother's shriek o'eraw'd
    A lion, and he dropt her lifted child :
But Nicholas, whom neither God nor law,
Nor Poland's shrieking mothers overawe,
Outholds to us his friendship's gory clutch ;
Shrink, Britain—shrink, my king and country,
        from the touch !

He prays to Heaven for England's king, he says—
    And dares he to the God of mercy kneel,
    Besmear'd with massacres from head to heel ?
No ; Moloch is his god—to him he prays ;
    And if his weird-like prayers had power to bring
An influence, their power would be to curse.
His hate is baleful, but his love is worse—
    A serpent's slaver deadlier than its sting !
Oh, feeble statesmen—ignominious times,
That lick the tyrant's feet, and smile upon his
        crimes.

ODE TO THE GERMANS.

THE spirit of Britannia
    Invokes, across the main,
Her sister Allemannia
    To burst the Tyrant's chain:
By our kindred blood, she cries,
Rise, Allemannians, rise,
    And hallow'd thrice the band
Of our kindred hearts shall be,
    When your land shall be the land
        Of the free—of the free!

With Freedom's lion-banner
    Britannia rules the waves;
Whilst your broad stone of honour[1]
    Is still the camp of slaves.
For shame, for glory's sake,
Wake, Allemannians, wake,
    And thy tyrants now that whelm
Half the world shall quail and flee,
    When your realm shall be the realm
        Of the free—of the free!

Mars owes to you his thunder[2]
    That shakes the battle-field,
Yet to break your bonds asunder
    No martial bolt has peal'd.
Shall the laurell'd land of art
Wear shackles on her heart?

---

[1] Ehrenbreitstein signifies, in German, *"the broad stone of honour."*
[2] Germany invented gunpowder, clock-making, and printing.

No ! the clock ye framed to tell
By its sound, the march of time ;
  Let it clang oppression's knell
        O'er your clime—o'er your clime !

The press's magic letters,
  That blessing ye brought forth,—
Behold ! it lies in fetters
  On the soil that gave it birth :
But the trumpet must be heard,
And the charger must be spurr'd ;
  For your father Armin's Sprite
Calls down from heaven, that ye
  Shall gird you for the fight,
        And be free !—and be free !

LINES

ON THE VIEW FROM ST. LEONARDS.

AIL to thy face and odours, glorious
        Sea !
    'Twere thanklessness in me to bless
        thee not,
Great beauteous Being ! in whose breath and smile
My heart beats calmer, and my very mind
Inhales salubrious thoughts.   How welcomer
Thy murmurs than the murmurs of the world !
Though like the world thou fluctuatest, thy din
To me is peace, thy restlessness repose.
Ev'n gladly I exchange yon spring-green lanes
With all the darling field-flowers in their prime,
And gardens haunted by the nightingale's
Long trills and gushing ecstacies of song,
For these wild headlands, and the sea-mew's
    clang—

With thee beneath my windows, pleasant Sea,
I long not to o'erlook earth's fairest glades
And green savannahs—Earth has not a plain
So boundless or so beautiful as thine;
The eagle's vision cannot take it in :
The lightning's wing, too weak to sweep its space,
Sinks half-way o'er it like a wearied bird :
It is the mirror of the stars, where all
Their hosts within the concave firmament,
Gay marching to the music of the spheres,
Can see themselves at once.
                                  Nor on the stage
Of rural landscape are there lights and shades
Of more harmonious dance and play than thine.
How vividly this moment brightens forth,
Between grey parallel and leaden breadths,
A belt of hues that stripes thee many a league,
Flush'd like the rainbow, or the ringdove's neck,
And giving to the glancing sea-bird's wing
The semblance of a meteor.
                                  Mighty Sea !
 Cameleon-like thou changest, but there's love
In all thy change, and constant sympathy
With yonder Sky—thy mistress; from her brow
Thou tak'st thy moods and wear'st her colours on
Thy faithful bosom; morning's milky white,
Noon's sapphire, or the saffron glow of eve ;
And all thy balmier hours, fair Element,
Have such divine complexion—crisped smiles,
Luxuriant heavings, and sweet whisperings,
That little is the wonder Love's own Queen
From thee of old was fabled to have sprung—
Creation's common ! which no human power
Can parcel or inclose; the lordliest floods
And cataracts that the tiny hands of man
Can tame, conduct, or bound, are drops of dew
To thee that couldst subdue the Earth itself,

And brook'st commandment from the heavens
    alone
For marshalling thy waves.
                    Yet, potent Sea!
How placidly thy moist lips speak ev'n now
Along yon sparkling shingles.   Who can be
So fanciless as to feel no gratitude
That power and grandeur can be so serene,
Soothing the home-bound navy's peaceful way,
And rocking ev'n the fisher's little bark
As gently as a mother rocks her child ?—

    The inhabitants of other worlds behold
Our orb more lucid for thy spacious share
On earth's rotundity; and is he not
A blind worm in the dust, great Deep, the man
Who sees not or who seeing has no joy
In thy magnificence?   What though thou art
Unconscious and material, thou canst reach
The inmost immaterial mind's recess,
And with thy tints and motion stir its chords
To music, like the light on Memnon's lyre!

    The Spirit of the Universe in thee
Is visible; thou hast in thee the life—
The eternal, graceful, and majestic life
Of nature, and the natural human heart
Is therefore bound to thee with holy love.

    Earth has her gorgeous towns; the earth-circling
    sea
Has spires and mansions more amusive still—
Men's volant homes that measure liquid space
On wheel or wing.   The chariot of the land
With pain'd and panting steeds and clouds of dust
Has no sight-gladdening motion like these fair
Careerers with the foam beneath their bows,
Whose streaming ensigns charm the waves by day,

Whose carols and whose watch-bells cheer the night,
Moor'd as they cast the shadows of their masts
In long array, or hither flit and yond
Mysteriously with slow and crossing lights,
Like spirits on the darkness of the deep.

There is a magnet-like attraction in
These waters to the imaginative power
That links the viewless with the visible,
And pictures things unseen.   To realms beyond
Yon highway of the world my fancy flies,
When by her tall and triple mast we know
Some noble voyager that has to woo
The trade-winds and to stem th' ecliptic surge.
The coral groves—the shores of conch and pearl,
Where she will cast her anchor and reflect
Her cabin-window lights on warmer waves,
And under planets brighter than our own :
The nights of palmy isles, that she will see
Lit boundless by the fire-fly—all the smells
Of tropic fruits that will regale her—all
The pomp of nature, and th' inspiriting
Varieties of life she has to greet,
Come swarming o'er the meditative mind.

True, to the dream of Fancy, Ocean has
His darker tints ; but where's the element
That chequers not its usefulness to man
With casual terror ? Scathes not Earth sometimes
Her children with Tartarean fires, or shakes
Their shrieking cities, and, with one last clang
Of bells for their own ruin, strews them flat
As riddled ashes—silent as the grave ?
Walks not Contagion on the Air itself ?
I should—old Ocean's Saturnalian days
And roaring nights of revelry and sport
With wreck and human woe—be loth to sing ;

For they are few and all their ills weigh light
Against his sacred usefulness, that bids
Our pensile globe revolve in purer air.
Here Morn and Eve with blushing thanks receive
Their freshening dews, gay fluttering breezes cool
Their wings to fan the brow of fever'd climes,
And here the Spring dips down her emerald urn
For showers to glad the earth.

                                    Old Ocean was
Infinity of ages ere we breathed
Existence—and he will be beautiful
When all the living world that sees him now
Shall roll unconscious dust around the sun.
Quelling from age to age the vital throb
In human hearts, Death shall not subjugate
The pulse that swells in *his* stupendous breast,
Or interdict his minstrelsy to sound
In thundering concert with the quiring winds;
But long as Man to parent Nature owns
Instinctive homage, and in times beyond
The power of thought to reach, bard after bard
Shall sing thy glory, beatific Sea.

SENEX'S SOLILOQUY ON HIS
YOUTHFUL IDOL.

PLATONIC friendship at your years,
    Says Conscience, should content ye:
Nay, name not fondness to her ears,
    The darling's scarcely twenty.

Yes, and she'll loathe me unforgiven,
    To dote thus out of season;
But beauty is a beam from heaven,
    That dazzles blind our reason.

I'll challenge Plato from the skies,
   Yes, from his spheres harmonic,
To look in M——y C————'s eyes,
   And try to be Platonic.

THE DEAD EAGLE.

WRITTEN AT ORAN.

FALL'N as he is, this king of birds still
     seems'
  Like royalty in ruins. Though his eyes
  Are shut, that look undazzled on the
sun,
He was the sultan of the sky, and earth
Paid tribute to his eyry. It was perch'd
Higher than human conqueror ever built
His banner'd fort. Where Atlas' top looks o'er
Zahara's desert to the equator's line:
From thence the winged despot mark'd his prey,
Above th' encampments of the Bedouins, ere
Their watchfires were extinct, or camels knelt
To take their loads, or horsemen scour'd the plain,
And there he dried his feathers in the dawn,
Whilst yet th' unwaken'd world was dark below.

  There's such a charm in natural strength and
     power,
That human fancy has for ever paid
Poetic homage to the bird of Jove.
Hence, 'neath his image, Rome array'd her turms
And cohorts for the conquest of the world.
And figuring his flight, the mind is fill'd
With thoughts that mock the pride of wingless
     man.

True the carr'd aeronaut can mount as high;
But what's the triumph of his volant art ?
A rash intrusion on the realms of air.
His helmless vehicle, a silken toy,
A bubble bursting in the thunder-cloud;
His course has no volition, and he drifts
The passive plaything of the winds.   Not such
Was this proud bird : he clove the adverse storm,
And cuff'd it with his wings.   He stopp'd his flight
As easily as the Arab reins his steed,
And stood at pleasure 'neath heaven's zenith, like
A lamp suspended from its azure dome,
Whilst underneath him the world's mountains lay
Like molehills, and her streams like lucid threads.
Then downward, faster than a falling star,
He near'd the earth, until his shape distinct
Was blackly shadow'd on the sunny ground;
And deeper terror hush'd the wilderness,
To hear his nearer whoop.   Then, up again
He soar'd and wheel'd. There was an air of scorn
In all his movements, whether he threw round
His crested head to look behind him; or
Lay vertical and sportively display'd
The inside whiteness of his wing declined,
In gyres and undulations full of grace,
An object beautifying heaven itself.

     He—reckless who was victor, and above
The hearing of their guns—saw fleets engaged
In flaming combat.   It was nought to him
What carnage, Moor or Christian, strew'd their
          decks.
But if his intellect had match'd his wings,
Methinks he would have scorn'd man's vaunted
          power
To plough the deep; his pinions bore him down
To Algiers the warlike, or the coral groves,

That blush beneath the green of Bona's waves ;
And traversed in an hour a wider space
Than yonder gallant ship, with all her sails
Wooing the winds, can cross from morn till eve.
His bright eyes were his compass, earth his chart,
His talons anchor'd on the stormiest cliff,
And on the very lighthouse rock he perch'd,
When winds churn'd white the waves.

                        The earthquake's self
Disturb'd not him that memorable day,
When o'er yon table-land, where Spain had built
Cathedrals, cannon'd forts, and palaces,
A palsy-stroke of Nature shook Oran,
Turning her city to a sepulchre,
And strewing into rubbish all her homes ;
Amidst whose traceable foundations now,
Of streets and squares, the hyæna hides himself.
That hour beheld him fly as careless o'er
The stifled shrieks of thousands buried quick,
As lately when he pounced the speckled snake,
Coil'd in yon mallows and wide nettle fields
That mantle o'er the dead old Spanish town.

Strange is the imagination's dread delight
In objects link'd with danger, death, and pain !
Fresh from the luxuries of polish'd life,
The echo of these wilds enchanted me ;
And my heart beat with joy when first I heard
A lion's roar come down the Libyan wind,
Across yon long, wide, lonely inland lake,
Where boat ne'er sails from homeless shore to
      shore.

And yet Numidia's landscape has its spots
Of pastoral pleasantness—though far between,
The village planted near the Maraboot's
Round roof has aye its feathery palm trees

Pair'd, for in solitude they bear no fruits.
Here nature's hues all harmonize—fields white
With alasum, or blue with bugloss—banks
Of glossy fennel, blent with tulips wild,
And sunflowers, like a garment prankt with gold;
Acres and miles of opal asphodel,
Where sports and couches the black-eyed gazelle.
Here, too, the air's harmonious—deep-toned doves
Coo to the fife-like carol of the lark ;
And when they cease, the holy nightingale
Winds up his long, long shakes of ecstasy,
With notes that seem but the protracted sounds
Of glassy runnels bubbling over rocks.

SONG.

TO Love in my heart, I exclaim'd t'other
    morning,
    Thou hast dwelt here too long, little
      lodger, take warning ;
Thou shalt tempt me no more from my life's sober
    duty,
To go gadding, bewitch'd by the young eyes of
    beauty.
   For weary's the wooing, ah ! weary,
When an old man will have a young dearie !

The god left my heart, at its surly reflections,
But came back on pretext of some sweet recol-
    lections,
And he made me forget what I ought to remember
That the rose-bud of June cannot bloom in
    November.
   Ah ! Tom, 'tis all o'er with thy gay days—
Write psalms, and not songs for the ladies.

But time's been so far from my wisdom enriching,
That the longer I live, beauty seems more be-
          witching;
And the only new lore my experience traces,
Is to find fresh enchantment in magical faces.
    How weary is wisdom, how weary!
When one sits by a smiling young dearie!

And should she be wroth that my homage pursues
          her,
I will turn and retort on my lovely accuser;
Who's to blame, that my heart by your image is
          haunted?—
It is you, the enchantress—not I, the enchanted.
    Would you have me behave more discreetly,
Beauty, look not so killingly sweetly.

LINES ON A PICTURE OF A GIRL IN

THE ATTITUDE OF PRAYER,

BY THE ARTIST GRUSE, IN THE POSSESSION OF

LADY STEPNEY.

WAS man e'er doom'd that beauty made
    By mimic art should haunt him;
Like Orpheus, I adore a shade,
    And dote upon a phantom.

Thou maid, that in my inmost thought
    Art fancifully sainted,
Why liv'st thou not—why art thou nought
    But canvas sweetly painted?

Whose looks seem lifted to the skies,
    Too pure for love of mortals—

As if they drew angelic eyes
　To greet thee at heaven's portals.

Yet loveliness has here no grace,
　Abstracted or ideal—
Art ne'er but from a living face
　Drew looks so seeming real.

What wert thou, maid?—thy life—thy name
　Oblivion hides in mystery;
Though from thy face my heart could frame
　A long romantic history.

Transported to thy time I seem,
　Though dust thy coffin covers—
And hear the songs, in fancy's dream,
　Of thy devoted lovers.

How witching must have been thy breath—
　How sweet the living charmer—
Whose every semblance after death
　Can make the heart grow warmer!

Adieu, the charms that vainly move
　My soul in their possession—
That prompt my lips to speak of love,
　Yet rob them of expression.

Yet thee, dear picture, to have praised
　Was but a poet's duty;
And shame to him that ever gazed
　Impassive on thy beauty.

LINES

WRITTEN IN A BLANK LEAF OF LA PEROUSE'S
VOYAGES.

OVED Voyager! his pages had a zest
More sweet than fiction to my wonder-
ing breast,
When, rapt in fancy, many a boyish day
track'd his wanderings o'er the watery way,
Roam'd round the Aleutian isles in waking dreams,
Or pluck'd the *fleur-de-lys* by Jesso's streams—
Or gladly leap'd on that far Tartar strand,
Where Europe's anchor ne'er had bit the sand,
Where scarce a roving wild tribe cross'd the plain,
Or human voice broke nature's silent reign ;
But vast and grassy deserts feed the bear,
And sweeping deer-herds dread no hunter's snare.
Such young delight his real records brought,
His truth so touch'd romantic springs of thought,
That all my after-life—his fate and fame
Entwined romance with La Perouse's name.—
Fair were his ships, expert his gallant crews,
And glorious was th' emprise of La Perouse,—
Humanely glorious ! Men will weep for him,
When many a guilty martial fame is dim :
He plough'd the deep to bind no captive's chain—
Pursued no rapine—strew'd no wreck with slain ;
And, save that in the deep themselves lie low,
His heroes pluck'd no wreath from human woe.
'Twas his the earth's remotest bound to scan,
Conciliating with gifts barbaric man—
Enrich the world's contemporaneous mind,
And amplify the picture of mankind.
Far on the vast Pacific—'midst those isles,
O'er which the earliest morn of Asia smiles,

He sounded and gave charts to many a shore
And gulf of Ocean new to nautic lore;
Yet he that led Discovery o'er the wave,
Still fills himself an undiscover'd grave.
He came not back,—Conjecture's cheek grew pale,
Year after year—in no propitious gale,
His lilied banner held its homeward way,
And Science sadden'd at her martyr's stay.
An age elapsed—no wreck told where or when
The chief went down with all his gallant men,
Or whether by the storm and wild sea flood
He perish'd, or by wilder men of blood—
The shuddering Fancy only guess'd his doom,
And Doubt to Sorrow gave but deeper gloom.
An age elapsed—when men were dead or grey,
Whose hearts had mourn'd him in their youthful
        day;
Fame traced on Mannicolo's shore at last,
The boiling surge had mounted o'er his mast.
The islesmen told of some surviving men,
But Christian eyes beheld them ne'er again.
Sad bourne of all his toils—with all his band—
To sleep, wreck'd, shroudless, on a savage strand!
Yet what is all that fires a hero's scorn
Of death?—the hope to live in hearts unborn:
Life to the brave is not its fleeting breath,
But worth—foretasting fame, that follows death.
That worth had La Perouse—that meed he won:
He sleeps—his life's long stormy watch is done.
In the great deep, whose boundaries and space
He measured, Fate ordain'd his resting-place;
But bade his fame, like th' Ocean rolling o'er
His relics—visit every earthly shore.
Fair Science on that Ocean's azure robe,
Still writes his name in picturing the globe,
And paints—(what fairer wreath could glory
        twine?)
His watery course—a world-encircling line.

TO

WILLIAM BEATTIE, M.D.,

IN REMEMBRANCE OF LONG-SUBSISTING AND MUTUAL FRIENDSHIP,

THE POEM " GLENCOE "

AND THE OTHER PIECES THAT FOLLOW IN THIS VOLUME,

ARE INSCRIBED BY

THE AUTHOR.

LONDON, *December*, 1842.

THE PILGRIM OF GLENCOE.

[I RECEIVED the substance of the tradition on which this Poem is
founded, in the first instance, from a friend in London, who wrote
to Matthew N. Macdonald, Esq., of Edinburgh. He had the kindness to send me a circumstantial account of the tradition; and that
gentleman's knowledge of the Highlands, as well as his particular
acquaintance with the district of Glencoe, leave me no doubt of the
incident having really happened. I have not departed from the
main facts of the tradition as reported to me by Mr. Macdonald;
only I have endeavoured to colour the personages of the story, and
to make them as distinctive as possible.]

THE sunset sheds a horizontal smile
O'er Highland frith and Hebridean isle,
While, gay with gambols of its finny
    shoals,
The glancing wave rejoices as it rolls
With streamer'd busses, that distinctly shine
All downward, pictured in the glassy brine;
Whose crews, with faces brightening in the sun,
Keep measure with their oars, and all in one
Strike up th' old Gaelic song.—Sweep, rowers,
    sweep!
The fisher's glorious spoils are in the deep.

Day sinks—but twilight owes the traveller soon,
To reach his bourne, a round unclouded moon,
Bespeaking long undarken'd hours of time;
False hope—the Scots are stedfast—not their
    clime.
A war-worn soldier from the western land
Seeks Cona's vale by Ballihoula's strand;
The vale, by eagle-haunted cliffs o'erhung,
Where Fingal fought and Ossian's harp was
    strung—
Our veteran's forehead, bronzed on sultry plains,
Had stood the brunt of thirty fought campaigns;
He well could vouch the sad romance of wars,
And count the dates of battles by his scars;
For he had served where o'er and o'er again
Britannia's oriflamb had lit the plain
Of glory—and victorious stamp'd her name
On Oudenarde's and Blenheim's fields of fame.
Nine times in battle-field his blood had stream'd,
Yet vivid still his veteran blue eye gleam'd;
Full well he bore his knapsack—unoppress'd,
And march'd with soldier-like erected crest:
Nor sign of ev'n loquacious age he wore,
Save when he told his life's adventures o'er;
Some tired of these; for terms to him were dear
Too tactical by far for vulgar ear;
As when he talk'd of rampart and ravine,
And trenches fenced with gabion and fascine—
But when his theme possess'd him all and whole,
He scorn'd proud puzzling words and warm'd the
    soul;
Hush'd groups hung on his lips with fond surprise,
That sketch'd old scenes—like pictures to their
    eyes:—
The wide war-plain, with banners glowing bright,
And bayonets to the furthest stretch of sight;
The pause, more dreadful than the peal to come

From volleys blazing at the beat of drum—
Till all the field of thundering lines became
Two level and confronted sheets of flame.
Then to the charge, when Marlbro's hot pursuit
Trod France's gilded lilies underfoot;
He came and kindled—and with martial lung
Would chant the very march their trumpets sung.—

Th' old soldier hoped, ere evening's light should
    fail,
To reach a home, south-east of Cona's vale;
But looking at Bennevis, capp'd with snow,
He saw its mists come curling down below,
And spread white darkness o'er the sunset glow;—
Fast rolling like tempestuous Ocean's spray,
Or clouds from troops in battle's fiery day—
So dense, his quarry 'scaped the falcon's sight,
The owl alone exulted, hating light.

Benighted thus our pilgrim groped his ground,
Half 'twixt the river's and the cataract's sound.
At last a sheep-dog's bark inform'd his ear
Some human habitation might be near;
Anon sheep-bleatings rose from rock to rock,—
'Twas Luath hounding to their fold the flock.
Ere long the cock's obstreperous clarion rang,
And next, a maid's sweet voice, that spinning
    sang:
At last amidst the greensward (gladsome sight!)
A cottage stood, with straw-roof golden bright.

He knock'd, was welcomed in; none ask'd his
    name,
Nor whither he was bound nor whence he came;
But he was beckon'd to the stranger's seat,
Right side the chimney fire of blazing peat.
Blest Hospitality makes not her home
In wallèd parks and castellated dome;

She flies the city's needy greedy crowd,
And shuns still more the mansions of the proud ;—
The balm of savage or of simple life,
A wild flower cut by culture's polish'd knife !

The house, no common sordid shieling cot,
Spoke inmates of a comfortable lot.
The Jacobite white rose festoon'd their door ;
The windows sash'd and glazed, the oaken floor,
The chimney graced with antlers of the deer,
The rafters hung with meat for winter cheer,
And all the mansion, indicated plain
Its master a superior shepherd swain.

Their supper came—the table soon was spread
With eggs and milk and cheese and barley bread.
The family were three—a father hoar,
Whose age you'd guess at seventy years or more,
His son look'd fifty—cheerful like her lord,
His comely wife presided at the board ;
All three had that peculiar courteous grace
Which marks the meanest of the Highland race ;
Warm hearts that burn alike in weal and woe,
As if the north-wind fann'd their bosoms' glow !
But wide unlike their souls: old Norman's eye
Was proudly savage ev'n in courtesy.
His sinewy shoulders—each, though aged and lean,
Broad as the curl'd Herculean head between,—
His scornful lip, his eyes of yellow fire,
And nostrils that dilated quick with ire,
With ever downward-slanting shaggy brows,
Mark'd the old lion you would dread to rouse.

Norman, in truth, had led his earlier life
In raids of red revenge and feudal strife ;
Religious duty in revenge he saw,
Proud Honour's right and Nature's honest law ;
First in the charge and foremost in pursuit,

Long-breath'd, deep-chested, and in speed of foot
A match for stags—still fleeter when the prey
Was man, in persecution's evil day;
Cheer'd to that chase by brutal bold Dundee,
No Highland hound had lapp'd more blood than he.
Oft had he changed the covenanter's breath
From strains of psalmody to howls of death;
And though long bound to peace, it irk'd him still
His dirk had ne'er one hated foe to kill.

Yet Norman had fierce virtues, that would mock
Cold-blooded tories of the modern stock,
Who starve the breadless poor with fraud and cant;
He slew and saved them from the pangs of want.
Nor was his solitary lawless charm
Mere dauntlessness of soul and strength of arm;
He had his moods of kindness now and then,
And feasted ev'n well-manner'd lowland men,
Who blew not up his Jacobitish flame,
Nor prefaced with " pretender " Charles's name.
Fierce, but by sense and kindness not unwon,
He loved, respected ev'n, his wiser son ;
And brook'd from him expostulations sage,
When all advisers else were spurn'd with rage

Far happier times had moulded Ronald's mind,
By nature too of more sagacious kind.
His breadth of brow, and Roman shape of chin,
Squared well with the firm man that reign'd within.
Contemning strife as childishness, he stood
With neighbours on kind terms of neighbourhood,
And whilst his father's anger nought avail'd,
His rational remonstrance never fail'd.
Full skilfully he managed farm and fold,
Wrote, cipher'd, profitably bought and sold ;
And, bless'd with pastoral leisure, deeply took
Delight to be inform'd, by speech or book,

Of that wide world beyond his mountain home,
Where oft his curious fancy loved to roam.
Oft while his faithful dog ran round his flock,
He read long hours when summer warm'd the rock:
Guests who could tell him aught were welcomed
        warm,
Ev'n pedlars' news had to his mind a charm;
That like an intellectual magnet-stone
Drew truth from judgments simpler than his own.

His soul's proud instinct sought not to enjoy
Romantic fictions, like a minstrel boy;
Truth, standing on her solid square, from youth
He worshipp'd—stern uncompromising truth.
His goddess kindlier smiled on him, to find
A votary of her light in land so blind;
She bade majestic History unroll
Broad views of public welfare to his soul,
Until he look'd on clannish feuds and foes
With scorn, as on the wars of kites and crows;
Whilst doubts assail'd him o'er and o'er again,
If men were made for kings or kings for men.
At last, to Norman's horror and dismay,
He flat denied the Stuarts' right to sway.
No blow-pipe ever whiten'd furnace fire,
Quick as these words lit up his father's ire;
Who envied even old Abraham for his faith,
Ordain'd to put his only son to death.
He started up—in such a mood of soul
The white bear bites his showman's stirring pole;
He danced too, and brought out, with snarl and
        howl,
" O Dia! Dia!" and, " Dioul! Dioul!" [1]
But sense foils fury—as the blowing whale
Spouts, bleeds, and dyes the waves without avail—
Wears out the cable's length that makes him fast,

[1] God and the devil—a favourite ejaculation of Highland saints.

But, worn himself, comes up harpoon'd at last—
E'en so, devoid of sense, succumbs at length
Mere strength of zeal to intellectual strength.
His son's close logic so perplex'd his pate,
Th' old hero rather shunn'd than sought debate;
Exhausting his vocabulary's store
Of oaths and nick-names, he could say no more,
But tapp'd his mull,[1] roll'd mutely in his chair,
Or only whistled Killiecrankie's air.

    Witch-legends Ronald scorn'd—ghost, kelpie,
        wraith,
And all the trumpery of vulgar faith;
Grave matrons ev'n were shock'd to hear him slight
Authenticated facts of second-sight—
Yet never flinch'd his mockery to confound
The brutal superstition reigning round.

    Reserved himself, still Ronald loved to scan
Men's natures—and he liked the old hearty man;
So did the partner of his heart and life—
Who pleased her Ronald, ne'er displeased his wife.
His sense, 'tis true, compared with Norman's son,
Was common-place—his tales too long outspun:
Yet Allan Campbell's sympathizing mind
Had held large intercourse with human kind;
Seen much and gaily graphically drew
The men of every country, clime, and hue;
Nor ever stoop'd though soldier-like his strain,
To ribaldry of mirth or oath profane.
All went harmonious till the guest began
To talk about his kindred, chief and clan,
And, with his own biography engross'd,
Mark'd not the changed demeanour of each host;
Nor how old choleric Norman's cheek became
Flush'd at the Campbell and Breadalbane name.

           [1] Snuff-horn.

Assigning, heedless of impending harm,
Their steadfast silence to his story's charm,
He touch'd a subject perilous to touch—
Saying, " Midst this well-known vale I wonder'd
    much
To lose my way.   In boyhood, long ago,
I roam'd, and loved each pathway of Glencoe:
Trapp'd leverets, pluck'd wild berries on its braes,
And fish'd along its banks long summer days.
But times grew stormy—bitter feuds arose,
Our clan was merciless to prostrate foes.
I never palliated my chieftain's blame,
But mourn'd the sin, and redden'd for the shame
Of that foul morn (Heaven blot it from the year !)
Whose shapes and shrieks still haunt my dream-
    ing ear.
What could I do ? a serf—Glenlyon's page,
A soldier sworn at nineteen years of age ;
T' have breathed one grieved remonstrance to our
    chief,
The pit or gallows[1] would have cured my grief.
Forced, passive as the musket in my hand,
I march'd—when, feigning royalty's command,
Against the clan Macdonald, Stair's lord
Sent forth exterminating fire and sword ;
And troops at midnight through the vale defiled,
Enjoin'd to slaughter woman, man, and child.
My clansmen many a year had cause to dread
The curse that day entail'd upon their head ;
Glenlyon's self confess'd th' avenging spell—
I saw it light on him.
                " It so befell :—
A soldier from our ranks to death was brought,
By sentence deem'd too dreadful for his fault ;

---

[1] To hang their vassals, or starve them to death in a dungeon,
was a privilege of the Highland chiefs who had hereditary jurisdictions.

All was prepared—the coffin and the cart
Stood near twelve muskets, levell'd at his heart.
The chief, whose breast for ruth had still some room,
Obtain'd reprieve a day before his doom ;—
But of the awarded boon surmised no breath.
The sufferer knelt, blindfolded, waiting death,—
And met it. Though Glenlyon had desired
The musketeers to watch before they fired ;
If from his pocket they should see he drew
A handkerchief—their volley should ensue ;
But if he held a paper in its place,
It should be hail'd the sign of pardoning grace :—
He, in a fatal moment's absent fit,
Drew forth the handkerchief, and not the writ ;
Wept o'er the corpse, and wrung his hands in woe
Crying, ' Here's thy curse again—Glencoe !
   Glencoe !' "

 Though thus his guest spoke feelings just and
  clear,
The cabin's patriarch lent impatient ear ;
Wroth that, beneath his roof, a living man
Should boast the swine-blood of the Campbell clan :
He hasten'd to the door—call'd out his son
To follow ; walk'd a space and thus begun :—
" You have not, Ronald, at this day to learn
The oath I took beside my father's cairn,
When you were but a babe a twelvemonth born ;
Sworn on my dirk—by all that's sacred, sworn
To be revenged for blood that cries to Heaven—
Blood unforgiveable, and unforgiven :
But never power, *since then*, have I possess'd
To plant my dagger in a Campbell's breast.
Now, here's a self-accusing partisan,
Steep'd in the slaughter of Macdonald's clan ;
I scorn his civil speech and sweet-lipp'd show
Of pity—he is still our house's foe :

I'll perjure not myself—but sacrifice
The caitiff ere to-morrow's sun arise.
Stand ! hear me—you're my son, the deed is just,
And if I say it must be done—it must :
A debt of honour which my clansmen crave,
Their very dead demand it from the grave."
Conjuring then their ghosts, he humbly pray'd
Their patience till the blood-debt should be paid.
But Ronald stopp'd him.—" Sir, sir, do not dim
Your honour by a moment's angry whim ;
Your soul's too just and generous, were you cool,
To act at once th' assassin and the fool.
Bring me the men on whom revenge is due,
And I will dirk them willingly as you !
But all the real authors of that black
Old deed are gone—you cannot bring them back.
And this poor guest, 'tis palpable to judge,
In all his life ne'er bore our clan a grudge ;
Dragg'd when a boy against his will to share
That massacre, he loath'd the foul affair.
Think, if your harden'd heart be conscience-proof,
To stab a stranger underneath your roof !
One who has broken bread within your gate—
Reflect—before reflection comes too late,—
Such ugly consequences there may be
As judge and jury, rope and gallows-tree.
The days of dirking snugly are gone by,
Where could you hide the body privily,
When search is made for't ?"
                                " Plunge it in yon flood,
That Campbells crimson'd with our kindred blood."
" Ay, but the corpse may float—"
                                     " Pshaw ! dead men tell
No tales—nor will it float if leaded well.
I am determined !"—What could Ronald do ?
No house within ear-reach of his halloo,
Though that would but have publish'd household
       shame,

He temporized with wrath he could not tame,
And said, " Come in, till night put off the deed,
And ask a few more questions ere he bleed."
They enter'd ; Norman with portentous air
Strode to a nook behind the stranger's chair,
And, speaking nought, sat grimly in the shade,
With dagger in his clutch beneath his plaid.
His son's own plaid, should Norman pounce his
        prey,
Was coil'd thick round his arm, to turn away
Or blunt the dirk.   He purposed leaving free
The door, and giving Allan time to flee,
Whilst he should wrestle with, (no safe emprise,)
His father's maniac strength and giant size.
Meanwhile he could nowise communicate
The impending peril to his anxious mate ;
But she, convinced no trifling matter now
Disturb'd the wonted calm of Ronald's brow,
Divined too well the cause of gloom that lower'd,
And sat with speechless terror overpower'd.
Her face was pale, so lately blithe and bland,
The stocking knitting-wire shook in her hand.
But Ronald and the guest resumed their thread
Of converse, still its theme that day of dread.
" Much," said the veteran, " much as I bemoan
That deed, when half a hundred years have flown,
Still on one circumstance I can reflect
That mitigates the dreadful retrospect :
A mother with her child before us flew,
I had the hideous mandate to pursue ;
But swift of foot, outspeeding bloodier men,
I chased, o'ertook her in the winding glen,
And show'd her palpitating, where to save
Herself and infant in a secret cave ;
Nor left them till I saw that they could mock
Pursuit and search within that sheltering rock."
" Heavens !" Ronald cried, in accents gladly wild,

" That woman was my mother—I the child!
Of you unknown by name she late and air [1]
Spoke, wept, and ever bless'd you in her prayer,
Ev'n to her death; describing you withal
A well-look'd florid youth, blue-eyed and tall."
They rose, exchanged embrace: the old lion then
Upstarted, metamorphosed, from his den;
Saying, " Come and make thy home with us for
          life,
Heaven-sent preserver of my child and wife.
I fear thou'rt poor, that Hanoverian thing
Rewards his soldiers ill."—" God save the King!"
With hand upon his heart, old Allan said,
" I wear his uniform, I eat his bread,
And whilst I've tooth to bite a cartridge, all
For him and Britain's fame I'll stand or fall."
" Bravo!" cried Ronald.   " I commend your zeal,"
Quoth Norman, " and I see your heart is leal;
But I have pray'd my soul may never thrive
If thou should'st leave this house of ours alive.
Nor shalt thou; in this home protract thy breath
Of easy life, nor leave it till thy death."

The following morn arose serene as glass,
And red Bennevis shone like molten brass;
While sunrise open'd flowers with gentle force,
The guest and Ronald walk'd in long discourse.
" Words fail me," Allan said, " to thank aright
Your father's kindness shown me yesternight;
Yet scarce I'd wish my latest days to spend
A fireside fixture with the dearest friend:
Besides, I've but a fortnight's furlough now,
To reach Macallin More,[2] beyond Lochawe.

---

[1] Scotch for late and early.		[2] The Duke of Argyle.

I'd fain memorialise the powers that be,
To deign remembrance of my wounds and me;
My life-long service never bore the brand
Of sentence—lash—disgrace or reprimand.
And so I've written, though in meagre style,
A long petition to his grace Argyle;
I mean, on reaching Innerara's shore,
To leave it safe within his castle door."
" Nay," Ronald said, " the letter that you bear
Entrust it to no lying varlet's care;
But say a soldier of King George demands
Access, to leave it in the Duke's own hands.
But show me, first, the epistle to your chief,
'Tis nought, unless succinctly clear and brief;
Great men have no great patience when they read,
And long petitions spoil the cause they plead."

That day saw Ronald from the field full soon
Return; and when they all had dined at noon,
He conn'd the old man's memorial—lopp'd its
        length,
And gave it style, simplicity, and strength;
'Twas finish'd in an hour—and in the next
Transcribed by Allan in perspicuous text.
At evening, he and Ronald shared once more
A long and pleasant walk by Cona's shore.
" I'd press you," quoth his host—(" I need not say
How warmly, ever more with us to stay;
But Charles intends, 'tis said, in these same parts
To try the fealty of our Highland hearts.
'Tis my belief, that he and all his line
Have—saving to be hang'd—no right divine;
From whose mad enterprise can only flow
To thousands slaughter, and to myriads woe.
Yet have they stirr'd my father's spirit sore,
He flints his pistols—whets his old claymore—
And longs as ardently to join the fray
As boy to dance who hears the bagpipe play.

Though calm one day, the next, disdaining rule,
He'd gore your red coat like an angry bull :
I told him, and he own'd it might be so,
Your tempers never could in concert flow.
But ' Mark,' he added, ' Ronald ! from our door
Let not this guest depart forlorn and poor ;
Let not your souls the niggardness evince
Of lowland pedlar, or of German prince ;
He gave you life—then feed him as you'd feed
Your very father were he cast in need.'
He gave—you'll find it by your bed to-night,
A leathern purse of crowns, all sterling bright :
You see I do you kindness not by stealth.'
My wife—no advocate of squandering wealth—
Vows that it would be parricide, or worse,
Should we neglect you—here's a silken purse,
Some golden pieces through the network shine,
'Tis proffer'd to you from her heart and mine.
But come ! no foolish delicacy, no !
We own, but cannot cancel what we owe—
This sum shall duly reach you once a year."
Poor Allan's furrow'd face and flowing tear
Confess'd sensations which he could not speak.
Old Norman bade him farewell kindly meek.

At morn, the smiling dame rejoiced to pack
With viands full the old soldier's havresack.
He fear'd not hungry grass[1] with such a load,
And Ronald saw him miles upon his road.
A march of three days brought him to Lochfyne.
Argyle, struck with his manly look benign,
And feeling interest in the veteran's lot,
Created him a sergeant on the spot—
An invalid, to serve not—but with pay

---

[1] When the hospitable Highlanders load a parting guest with provisions, they tell him he will need them, as he has to go over a great deal of *hungry grass.*

(A mighty sum to him), twelvepence a day.
"But have you heard not," said Macallin More,
" Charles Stuart's landed on Eriska's shore,
And Jacobites are arming?"—"What! indeed!
Arrived! then I'm no more an invalid;
My new-got halbert I must straight employ
In battle."—"As you please, old gallant boy:
Your grey hairs well might plead excuse, 'tis true
But now's the time we want such men as you."
In brief, at Innerara Allan staid,
And join'd the banners of Argyle's brigade.

Meanwhile, the old choleric shepherd of Glencoe
Spurn'd all advice, and girt himself to go.
What was't to him that foes would poind their fold,
Their lease, their very beds beneath them sold!
And firmly to his text he would have kept,
Though Ronald argued and his daughter wept.
But midst the impotence of tears and prayer,
Chance snatch'd them from proscription and
        despair.
Old Norman's blood was headward wont to mount
Too rapid from his heart's impetuous fount;
And one day, whilst the German rats he cursed,
An artery in his wise sensorium burst.
The lancet saved him: but how changed, alas,
From him who fought at Killiecrankie's pass!
Tame as a spaniel, timid as a child,
He mutter'd incoherent words and smiled;
He wept at kindness, roll'd a vacant eye,
And laugh'd full often when he meant to cry.
Poor man! whilst in this lamentable state,
Came Allan back one morning to his gate,
Hale and unburden'd by the woes of eild,
And fresh with credit from Culloden's field.
'Twas fear'd at first, the sight of him might touch
The old Macdonald's morbid mind too much;

But no ! though Norman knew him and disclosed
Ev'n rallying memory, he was still composed;
Ask'd all particulars of the fatal fight,
And only heaved a sigh for Charles's flight;
Then said, with but one moment's pride of air,
It might not have been so had I been there!
Few days elapsed till he reposed beneath
His grey cairn, on the wild and lonely heath;
Son, friends, and kindred of his dust took leave,
And Allan, with the crape bound round his sleeve.

Old Allan now hung up his sergeant's sword,
And sat, a guest for life, at Ronald's board.
He waked no longer at the barrack's drum,
Yet still you'd see, when peep of day was come,
Th' erect tall red-coat, walking pastures round,
Or delving with his spade the garden ground.
Of cheerful temper, habits strict and sage,
He reach'd, enjoy'd, a patriarchal age—
Loved to the last by the Macdonalds.   Near
Their house, his stone was placed with many a tear;
And Ronald's self, in stoic virtue brave,
Scorn'd not to weep at Allan Campbell's grave.

NAPOLEON AND THE BRITISH
SAILOR.[1]

LOVE contemplating—apart
From all his homicidal glory,
The traits that soften to our heart
Napoleon's story !

[1] This anecdote has been published in several public journals, both
French and British.   My belief in its authenticity was confirmed by
an Englishman long resident at Boulogne lately telling me, that he
remembered the circumstance to have been generally talked of in the
place.

'Twas when his banners at Boulogne
  Arm'd in our island every freeman,
His navy chanced to capture one
  Poor British seaman.

They suffer'd him—I know not how,
  Unprison'd on the shore to roam;
And aye was bent his longing brow
  On England's home.

His eye, methinks, pursued the flight
  Of birds to Britain half-way over:
With envy *they* could reach the white,
  Dear cliffs of Dover.

A stormy midnight watch, he thought,
  Than this sojourn would have been dearer,
If but the storm his vessel brought
  To England nearer.

At last, when care had banish'd sleep,
  He saw one morning—dreaming—doting,
An empty hogshead from the deep
  Come shoreward floating;

He hid it in a cave, and wrought
  The live-long day laborious; lurking
Until he launch'd a tiny boat
  By mighty working.

Heaven help us! 'twas a thing beyond
  Description wretched: such a wherry
Perhaps ne'er ventured on a pond,
  Or cross'd a ferry.

For ploughing in the salt-sea field,
  It would have made the boldest shudder
Untarr'd, uncompass'd, and unkeel'd,
  No sail—no rudder.

From neighb'ring woods he interlaced .
  His sorry skiff with wattled willows ;
And thus equipp'd he would have pass'd
  The foaming billows—

But Frenchmen caught him on the beach,
  His little Argo sorely jeering ;
Till tidings of him chanced to reach
  Napoleon's hearing.

With folded arms Napoleon stood,
  Serene alike in peace and danger ;
And, in his wonted attitude,
  Address'd the stranger :—

" Rash man, that wouldst yon Channel pass
  On twigs and staves so rudely fashion'd ;
Thy heart with some sweet British lass
  Must be impassion'd."

" I have no sweetheart," said the lad ;
  " But—absent long from one another—
Great was the longing that I had
  To see my mother."

" And so thou shalt," Napoleon said,
  " Ye 've both my favour fairly won ;
A noble mother must have bred
  So brave a son."

He gave the tar a piece of gold,
  And, with a flag of truce, commanded
He should be shipp'd to England Old,
  And safely landed.

Our sailor oft could scantly shift
  To find a dinner, plain and hearty ;
But *never* changed the coin and gift
  Of Bonaparté.

BENLOMOND.

HADST thou a genius on thy peak,
    What tales, white-headed Ben,
Could'st thou of ancient ages speak,
    That mock th' historian's pen !

Thy long duration makes our lives
    Seem but so many hours ;
And likens, to the bees' frail hives,
    Our most stupendous towers.

Temples and towers thou'st seen begun ;
    New creeds, new conquerors' sway,
And, like their shadows in the sun,
    Hast seen them swept away.

Thy stedfast summit, heaven-allied
    (Unlike life's little span),
Looks down, a Mentor, on the pride
    Of perishable man.

THE CHILD AND HIND.

[I wish I had preserved a copy of the Wiesbaden newspaper in which this anecdote of the "Child and Hind" is recorded ; but I have unfortunately lost it. The story, however, is a matter of fact ; it took place in 1838 : every circumstance mentioned in the following ballad literally happened. I was in Wiesbaden eight months ago, and was shown the very tree under which the boy was found sleeping with a bunch of flowers in his little hand. A similar occurrence is told by tradition, of Queen Genoveva's child being preserved by being suckled by a female deer, when that Princess—an early Christian —and now a Saint in the Romish calendar, was chased to the desert by her heathen enemies. The spot assigned to the traditionary event is not a hundred miles from Wiesbaden, where a chapel still stands to her memory.

I could not ascertain whether the Hind that watched my hero

" Wilhelm," suckled him or not ; but it was generally believed that
she had no milk to give him, and that the boy must have been for
two days and a-half entirely without food, unless it might be grass
or leaves. If this was the case, the circumstance of the Wiesbaden
deer watching the child, was a still more wonderful token of instinctive fondness than that of the deer in the Genoveva tradition, who
was naturally anxious to be relieved of her milk.]

OME, maids and matrons, to caress
   Wiesbaden's gentle hind ;
And smiling, deck its glossy neck
   With forest flowers entwined.

Your forest flowers are fair to show,
   And landscapes to enjoy ;
But fairer is your friendly doe
   That watch'd the sleeping boy.

'Twas after church—on Ascension day—
   When organs ceased to sound,
Wiesbaden's people crowded gay
   The deer-park's pleasant ground.

There, where Elysian meadows smile,
   And noble trees upshoot,
The wild thyme and the camomile
   Smell sweetly at their root ;

The aspen quivers nervously,
   The oak stands stilly bold—
And climbing bindweed hangs on high
   His bells of beaten gold.[1]

Nor stops the eye till mountains shine
   That bound a spacious view,
Beyond the lordly, lovely Rhine,
   In visionary blue.

[1] There is only one kind of bindweed that is yellow, and that is the
flower here mentioned, the Paniculatus Convolvulus.

There, monuments of ages dark
Awaken thoughts sublime;
Till, swifter than the steaming bark,
We mount the stream of time.

The ivy there old castles shades
That speak traditions high
Of minstrels—tournaments—crusades,
And mail-clad chivalry.

Here came a twelve years' married pair—
And with them wander'd free
Seven sons and daughters, blooming fair,
A gladsome sight to see.

Their Wilhelm, little innocent,
The youngest of the seven,
Was beautiful as painters paint
The cherubim of Heaven.

By turns he gave his hand, so dear,
To parent, sister, brother;
And each, that he was safe and near,
Confided in the other.

But Wilhelm loved the field-flowers bright,
With love beyond all measure;
And cull'd them with as keen delight
As misers gather treasure.

Unnoticed, he contrived to glide
Adown a greenwood alley,
By lilies lured—that grew beside
A streamlet in the valley;

And there, where under beech and birch
The rivulet meander'd,
He stray'd, till neither shout nor search
Could track where he had wander'd.

Still louder, with increasing dread,
They call'd his darling name;
But 'twas like speaking to the dead—
An echo only came.

Hours pass'd till evening's beetle roams,
And blackbirds' songs begin;
Then all went back to happy homes,
Save Wilhelm's kith and kin.

The night came on—all others slept
Their cares away till morn;
But sleepless, all night watch'd and wept
That family forlorn.

Betimes the town-crier had been sent
With loud bell, up and down;
And told th' afflicting accident
Throughout Wiesbaden's town:

The father, too, ere morning smiled,
Had all his wealth uncoffer'd;
And to the wight would bring his child,
A thousand crowns had offer'd.

Dear friends, who would have blush'd to take
That guerdon from his hand,
Soon join'd in groups—for pity's sake,
The child-exploring band.

The news reach'd Nassau's Duke: ere earth
Was gladden'd by the lark,
He sent a hundred soldiers forth
To ransack all his park.

Their side-arms glitter'd through the wood,
With bugle-horns to sound;
Would that on errand half so good
The soldier oft were found !

But though they roused up beast and bird
From many a nest and den,
No signal of success was heard
From all the hundred men.

A second morning's light expands,
Unfound the infant fair ;
And Wilhelm's household wring their hands
Abandon'd to despair.

But, haply, a poor artisan
Search'd ceaselessly, till he
Found safe asleep the little one,
Beneath a beechen tree.

His hand still grasp'd a bunch of flowers ;
And (true, though wondrous) near,
To sentry his reposing hours,
There stood a female deer—

Who dipp'd her horns at all that pass'd [1]
The spot where Wilhelm lay ;
Till force was had to hold her fast,
And bear the boy away.

Hail ! sacred love of childhood—hail !
How sweet it is to trace
Thine instinct in Creation's scale,
Ev'n 'neath the human race.

To this poor wanderer of the wild
Speech, reason were unknown—
And yet she watch'd a sleeping child
As if it were her own ;

[1] The female deer has no such antlers as the male, and sometimes
no horns at all ; but I have observed many with short ones suckling
their fawns.

And thou, Wiesbaden's artisan,
Restorer of the boy,
Was ever welcomed mortal man
With such a burst of joy ?

The father's ecstasy—the mother's
Hysteric bosom's swell ;
The sisters' sobs—the shout of brothers,
I have not power to tell.

The working man, with shoulders broad,
Took blithely to his wife
The thousand crowns ; a pleasant load,
That made him rich for life.

And Nassau's Duke the favourite took
Into his deer-park's centre,
To share a field with other pets
Where deer-slayer cannot enter.

There, whilst thou cropp'st thy flowery food,
Each hand shall pat thee kind ;
And man shall never spill thy blood—
Wiesbaden's gentle hind.

THE JILTED NYMPH.

A SONG, TO THE SCOTCH TUNE OF " WOO'D

AND MARRIED AND A'."

'M jilted, forsaken, outwitted ;
Yet think not I'll whimper or brawl—
The lass is alone to be pitied
Who ne'er has been courted at all ;

Never by great or small,
Woo'd or jilted at all ;
  Oh, how unhappy's the lass
Who has never been courted at all !

My brother call'd out the dear faithless,
  In fits I was ready to fall,
Till I found a policeman who, scatheless,
  Swore them both to the peace at Guildhall :
Seized them, seconds and all—
Pistols, powder and ball ;
  I wish'd him to die my devoted,
But not in a duel to sprawl.

What though at my heart he has tilted,
  What though I have met with a fall ?
Better be courted and jilted,
  Than never be courted at all.
Woo'd and jilted and all,
Still I will dance at the ball ;
  And waltz and quadrille
  With light heart and heel,
With proper young men, and tall.

But lately I've met with a suitor,
  Whose heart I have gotten in thrall,
And I hope soon to tell you in future
  That I'm woo'd, and married and all :
Woo'd and married and all,
What greater bliss can befall ?
  And you all shall partake
  Of my bridal cake,
When I'm woo'd and married, and all.

ON GETTING HOME THE PORTRAIT OF A
FEMALE CHILD, SIX YEARS OLD.

PAINTED BY EUGENIO LATILLA.

YPE of the Cherubim above,
  Come, live with me, and be my love!
  Smile from my wall, dear roguish sprite,
  By sunshine and by candle-light;
For both look sweetly on thy traits:
Or, were the Lady Moon to gaze,
She'd welcome thee with lustre bland,
Like some young fay from Fairyland.
Cast in simplicity's own mould,
How canst thou be so manifold
In sportively distracting charms?
Thy lips—thine eyes—thy little arms
That wrap thy shoulders and thy head,
In homeliest shawl of netted thread,
Brown woollen net-work; yet it seeks
Accordance with thy lovely cheeks,
And more becomes thy beauty's bloom
Than any shawl from Cashmere's loom.

Thou hast not, to adorn thee, girl,
Flower, link of gold, or gem or pearl—
I would not let a ruby speck
The peeping whiteness of thy neck:
Thou need'st no casket, witching elf,
No gawd—thy toilet is thyself;
Not ev'n a rose-bud from the bower,
Thyself a magnet—gem and flower.

My arch and playful little creature,
Thou hast a mind in every feature;

Thy brow, with its disparted locks,
Speaks language that translation mocks;
Thy lucid eyes so beam with soul,
They on the canvas seem to roll—
Instructing both my head and heart
To idolize the painter's art.

He marshals minds to Beauty's feast—
He is Humanity's high priest
Who proves, by heavenly forms on earth,
How much this world of ours is worth.
Inspire me, child, with visions fair!
For children, in Creation, are
The only things that could be given
Back, and alive—unchanged—to Heaven.

THE PARROT.

A DOMESTIC ANECDOTE.

[The following incident, so strongly illustrating the power of memory
and association in the lower animals, is not a fiction. I heard it many
years ago in the Island of Mull, from the family to whom the bird
belonged.]

THE deep affections of the breast,
　　That Heaven to living things imparts,
　Are not exclusively possess'd
　　By human hearts.

A parrot, from the Spanish Main,
　Full young, and early caged, came o'er
With bright wings, to the bleak domain
　Of Mulla's shore.

To spicy groves where he had won
　His plumage of resplendent hue,
His native fruits, and skies, and sun,
　He bade adieu.

For these he changed the smoke of turf,
  A heathery land and misty sky,
And turn'd on rocks and raging surf
  His golden eye.

But, petted, in our climate cold
  He lived and chatter'd many a day :
Until with age, from green and gold
  His wings grew grey.

At last, when blind and seeming dumb,
  He scolded, laugh'd, and spoke no more,
A Spanish stranger chanced to come
  To Mulla's shore;

He hail'd the bird in Spanish speech,
  The bird in Spanish speech replied,
Flapp'd round his cage with joyous screech,
  Dropt down, and died.

SONG OF THE COLONISTS DEPARTING
FOR NEW ZEALAND.

STEER, helmsman, till you steer our way,
  By stars beyond the line ;
We go to found a realm, one day,
  Like England's self to shine.

CHORUS.

Cheer up—cheer up—our course we'll keep,
  With dauntless heart and hand ;
And when we've plough'd the stormy deep,
  We'll plough a smiling land :—

A land, where beauties importune
    The Briton to its bowers,
To sow but plenteous seeds, and prune
    Luxuriant fruits and flowers.
        Chorus.—Cheer up—cheer up, &c.

There, tracts uncheer'd by human words,
    Seclusion's wildest holds,
Shall hear the lowing of our herds,
    And tinkling of our folds.
        Chorus.—Cheer up—cheer up, &c.

Like rubies set in gold, shall blush
    Our vineyards girt with corn ;
And wine, and oil, and gladness gush
    From Amalthea's horn.
        Chorus.—Cheer up—cheer up, &c.

Britannia's pride is in our hearts,
    Her blood is in our veins—
We'll girdle earth with British arts,
    Like Ariel's magic chains.

CHORUS.

Cheer up—cheer up—our course we'll keep
    With dauntless heart and hand ;
And when we've plough'd the stormy deep
    We'll plough a smiling land.

MOONLIGHT.

THE kiss that would make a maid's cheek
        flush
    Wroth, as if kissing were a sin
    Amidst the Argus eyes and din
And tell-tale glare of noon,
Brings but a murmur and a blush,
    Beneath the modest moon.

Ye days, gone—never to come back,
  When love return'd entranced me so,
  That still its pictures move and glow
    In the dark chamber of my heart;
Leave not my memory's future track—
  I will not let you part.

'Twas moonlight, when my earliest love
  First on my bosom dropt her head;
  A moment then concentrated
  The bliss of years, as if the spheres
    Their course had faster driven,
And carried, Enoch-like above,
  A living man to Heaven.

'Tis by the rolling moon we measure
  The date between our nuptial night
  And that blest hour which brings to light
    The pledge of faith—the fruit of bliss;
When we impress upon the treasure
  A father's earliest kiss.

The Moon's the Earth's enamour'd bride;
  True to him in her very changes,
  To other stars she never ranges:
    Though, cross'd by him, sometimes she dips
Her light, in short offended pride,
  And faints to an eclipse.

The fairies revel by her sheen;
  'Tis only when the Moon's above
  The fire-fly kindles into love,
    And flashes light to show it:
The nightingale salutes her Queen
  Of Heaven, her heav'nly poet.

Then ye that love—by moonlight gloom
  Meet at my grave, and plight regard.

Oh ! could I be the Orphéan bard
Of whom it is reported,
That nightingales sung o'er his tomb, ♣
Whilst lovers came and courted.

CORA LINN, OR THE FALLS OF
THE CLYDE.

WRITTEN ON REVISITING IT IN 1837.

HE time I saw thee, Cora, last,
'Twas with congenial friends ;
And calmer hours of pleasure past—
My memory seldom sends.

It was as sweet an Autumn day
As ever shone on Clyde,
And Lanark's orchards all the way
Put forth their golden pride ;

Ev'n hedges, busk'd in bravery,
Look'd rich that sunny morn ;
The scarlet hip and blackberry
So prank'd September's thorn.

In Cora's glen the calm how deep !
That trees on loftiest hill
Like statues stood, or things asleep,
All motionless and still.

The torrent spoke, as if his noise
Bade earth be quiet round,
And give his loud and lonely voice
A more commanding sound.

His foam, beneath the yellow light
Of noon, came down like one
Continuous sheet of jaspers bright,
Broad rolling by the sun.

Dear Linn ! let loftier falling floods
Have prouder names than thine;
And king of all, enthroned in woods,
Let Niagara shine.

Barbarian, let him shake his coasts
With reeking thunders far,
Extended like th' array of hosts
In broad, embattled war !

His voice appals the wilderness :
Approaching thine, we feel
A solemn, deep melodiousness,
That needs no louder peal.

More fury would but disenchant
Thy dream-inspiring din ;
Be thou the Scottish Muse's haunt,
Romantic Cora Linn.

SONG ON OUR QUEEN.

SET TO MUSIC BY CHARLES NEATE, ESQ.

VICTORIA'S sceptre o'er the deep
    Has touch'd, and broken slavery's
       chain;
    Yet, strange magician ! she enslaves
Our hearts within her own domain.

Her spirit is devout, and burns
  With thoughts averse to bigotry;
Yet she herself, the idol, turns
  Our thoughts into idolatry.

CHAUCER AND WINDSOR.

LONG shalt thou flourish, Windsor!
          bodying forth
     Chivalric times, and long shall live
          around
Thy Castle—the old oaks of British birth,
Whose gnarled roots, tenacious and profound,
As with a lion's talons grasp the ground.
But should thy towers in ivied ruin rot,
There's one, thine inmate once, whose strain re-
          nown'd
Would interdict thy name to be forgot;
For Chaucer loved thy bowers and trode this very
          spot.
Chaucer! our Helicon's first fountain-stream,
Our morning star of song—that led the way
To welcome the long-after coming beam
Of Spenser's light and Shakspeare's perfect day.
Old England's fathers live in Chaucer's lay,
As if they ne'er had died.   He group'd and drew
Their likeness with a spirit of life so gay,
That still they live and breathe in Fancy's view,
Fresh beings fraught with truth's imperishable hue.

TO THE UNITED STATES OF NORTH AMERICA.

UNITED STATES, your banner wears
  Two emblems—one of fame; ·
Alas, the other that it bears
  Reminds us of your shame.

Your standard's constellation types
  White freedom by its stars;
But what's the meaning of the stripes?
  They mean your negroes' scars.

LINES

SUGGESTED BY THE STATUE OF ARNOLD VON WINKELRIED,[1]

STANZ-UNTERWALDEN.

INSPIRING and romantic Switzers'
    land,
    Though mark'd with majesty by Na-
    ture's hand,
What charm ennobles most thy landscape's face?—
Th' heroic memory of thy native race—
Who forced tyrannic hosts to bleed or flee,
And made their rocks the ramparts of the free;
Their fastnesses roll'd back th' invading tide
Of conquest, and their mountains taught them
      pride.
Hence they have patriot names—in fancy's eye,
Bright as their glaciers glittering in the sky;

[1] For an account of this patriotic Swiss and his heroic death at the battle of Sempach, see Dr. Beattie's "Switzerland Illustrated," vol. ii. pp. 111-115. See also Note at the end of this Volume.

Patriots who make the pageantries of kings
Like shadows seem and unsubstantial things.
Their guiltless glory mocks oblivion's rust,
Imperishable, for their cause was just.

Heroes of old ! to whom the Nine have strung
Their lyres, and spirit-stirring anthems sung;
Heroes of chivalry ! whose banners grace
The aisles of many a consecrated place,
Confess how few of you can match in fame
The martyr Winkelried's immortal name !

TO A YOUNG LADY

WHO ASKED ME TO WRITE SOMETHING ORIGINAL FOR

HER ALBUM.

AN original something, fair maid, you would win me
   To write—but how shall I begin ?
   For I fear I have nothing original in me—
Excepting Original Sin.

LINES ON MY NEW CHILD-SWEET-HEART.

I HOLD it a religious duty
   To love and worship children's beauty;
   They've least the taint of earthly clod,
   They're freshest from the hand of God;
With heavenly looks they make us sure
The heaven that made them must be pure;
We love them not in earthly fashion,
But with a beatific passion.

I chanced to, yesterday, behold
A maiden child of beauty's mould;
"Twas near, more sacred was the scene,
The palace of our patriot Queen.
The little charmer to my view
Was sculpture brought to life anew,
Her eyes had a poetic glow,
Her pouting mouth was Cupid's bow :
And through her frock I could descry
Her neck and shoulders' symmetry.
'Twas obvious from her walk and gait
Her limbs were beautifully straight ;
I stopp'd th' enchantress, and was told,
Though tall, she was but four years old.
Her guide so grave an aspect wore
I could not ask a question more ;
But follow'd her.   The little one
Threw backward ever and anon
Her lovely neck, as if to say,
" I know you love me, Mister Grey ;"
For by its instinct childhood's eye
Is shrewd in physiognomy ;
They well distinguish fawning art
From sterling fondness of the heart.

And so she flirted, like a true
Good woman, till we bade adieu.
'Twas then I with regret grew wild,
Oh, beauteous, interesting child !
Why ask'd I not thy home and name ?
My courage fail'd me—more's the shame.
But where abides this jewel rare ?
Oh, ye that own her, tell me where !
For sad it makes my heart and sore
To think I ne'er may meet her more.

THE LAUNCH OF A FIRST-RATE.

WRITTEN ON WITNESSING THE SPECTACLE.

ENGLAND hails thee with emotion,
　Mightiest child of naval art,
Heaven resounds thy welcome ! Ocean
　Takes thee smiling to his heart.

Giant oaks of bold expansion
　O'er seven hundred acres fell,
All to build thy noble mansion,
　Where our hearts of oak shall dwell.

'Midst those trees the wild deer bounded,
　Ages long ere we were born,
And our great-grandfathers sounded
　Many a jovial hunting-horn.

Oaks that living did inherit
　Grandeur from our earth and sky,
Still robust, the native spirit
　In your timbers shall not die.

Ship to shine in martial story,
　Thou shalt cleave the ocean's path
Freighted with Britannia's glory
　And the thunders of her wrath.

Foes shall crowd their sails and fly thee,
　Threat'ning havoc to their deck,
When afar they first descry thee,
　Like the coming whirlwind's speck.

Gallant bark ! thy pomp and beauty
　Storm or battle ne'er shall blast,
Whilst our tars in pride and duty
　Nail thy colours to the mast.

EPISTLE, FROM ALGIERS, TO HORACE SMITH.

DEAR HORACE! be melted to tears,
    For I'm melting with heat as I
        rhyme;
Though the name of the place is All-
        jeers,
  'Tis no joke to fall in with its clime.

With a shaver[1] from France who came o'er,
  To an African inn I ascend;
I am cast on a barbarous shore,
  Where a barber alone is my friend.

Do you ask me the sights and the news
  Of this wonderful city to sing?
Alas! my hotel has its mews,
  But no muse of the Helicon's spring.

My windows afford me the sight
  Of a people all diverse in hue;
They are black, yellow, olive, and white,
  Whilst I in my sorrow look blue.

Here are groups for the painter to take,
  Whose figures jocosely combine,—
The Arab disguised in his haik,[2]
  And the Frenchman disguised in his wine.

---

[1] On board the vessel from Marseilles to Algiers I met with a fellow passenger whom I supposed to be a physician from his dress and manners, and the attentions which he paid me to alleviate the sufferings of my sea-sickness. He turned out to be a perruquier and barber in Algeria—but his vocation did not lower him in my estimation—for he continued his attentions until he passed my baggage through the customs, and helped me, when half dead with exhaustion, to the best hotel.

[2] A mantle worn by the natives.

In his breeches of petticoat size
  You may say, as the Mussulman goes,
That his garb is a fair compromise
  'Twixt a kilt and a pair of small-clothes.

The Mooresses, shrouded in white,
  Save two holes for their eyes to give room,
Seem like corpses in sport or in spite
  That have slily whipp'd out of their tomb.

The old Jewish dames make me sick:
  If I were the devil—I declare
Such hags should not mount a broom-stick
  In my service to ride through the air.

But hipp'd and undined as I am,
  My hippogriff's course I must rein—
For the pain of my thirst is no sham,
  Though I'm bawling aloud for Champagne.

Dinner's brought; but their wines have no pith—
  They are flat as the statutes at law;
And for all that they bring me, dear Smith!
  Would a glass of brown stout they could draw!

O'er each French trashy dish as I bend,
  My heart feels a patriot's grief!
And the round tears, O England! descend
  When I think on a round of thy beef.

Yes, my soul sentimentally craves
  British beer.—Hail, Britannia, hail!
To thy flag on the foam of the waves,
  And the foam on thy flagons of ale.

Yet I own, in this hour of my drought,
  A dessert has most welcomely come;
Here are peaches that melt in the mouth,
  And grapes blue and big as a plum.

There are melons too, luscious and great,
   But the slices I eat shall be few,
For from melons incautiously eat
   Melancholic effects may ensue.

Horrid pun! you'll exclaim; but be calm,
   Though my letter bears date, as you view,
From the land of the date-bearing palm,
   I will palm no more puns upon you.

FRAGMENT OF AN ORATORIO, FROM

THE BOOK OF JOB.

[Having met my illustrious friend the Composer Neukomm, at Algiers, several years ago, I commenced this intended Oratorio at his desire, but he left the place before I proceeded farther in the poem; and it has been thus left unfinished.]

CRUSH'D by misfortune's yoke,
   Job lamentably spoke—
   " My boundless curse be on
   The day that I was born;
Quench'd be the star that shone
Upon my natal morn.
In the grave I long
To shroud my breast;
Where the wicked cease to wrong,
And the weary are at rest."
Then Eliphaz rebuked his wild despair:
" What Heaven ordains, 'tis meet that man should
      bear.
Lately, at midnight drear,
A vision shook my bones with fear;
A spirit pass'd before my face,
And yet its form I could not trace;

It stopp'd—it stood—it chill'd my blood,
The hair upon my flesh uprose
With freezing dread!
Deep silence reign'd, and, at its close,
I heard a voice that said—
' Shall mortal man be more pure and just
Than God, who made him from the dust?
Hast thou not learnt of old, how fleet
Is the triumph of the hypocrite;
How soon the wreath of joy grows wan
On the brow of the ungodly man?
By the fire of his conscience he perisheth
In an unblown flame:
The Earth demands his death,
And the Heavens reveal his shame.' "

JOB.

Is this your consolation?
Is it thus that ye condole
With the depth of my desolation,
And the anguish of my soul?
But I will not cease to wail
The bitterness of my bale.—
Man that is born of woman,
Short and evil is his hour;
He fleeth like a shadow,
He fadeth like a flower.
My days are pass'd—my hope and trust
Is but to moulder in the dust.

CHORUS.

Bow, mortal, bow, before thy God,
Nor murmur at his chastening rod;
Fragile being of earthly clay,
Think on God's eternal sway!
Hark! from the whirlwind forth
Thy Maker speaks—" Thou child of earth,

Where wert thou when I laid
Creation's corner-stone ?
When the sons of God rejoicing made,
And the morning stars together sang and shone ?
Hadst thou power to bid above
Heaven's constellations glow ;
Or shape the forms that live and move
On Nature's face below ?
Hast thou given the horse his strength and pride?
He paws the valley with nostril wide,
He smells far off the battle ;
He neighs at the trumpet's sound—
And his speed devours the ground,
As he sweeps to where the quivers rattle,
And the spear and shield shine bright,
'Midst the shouting of the captains
And the thunder of the fight.

TO MY NIECE, MARY CAMPBELL.

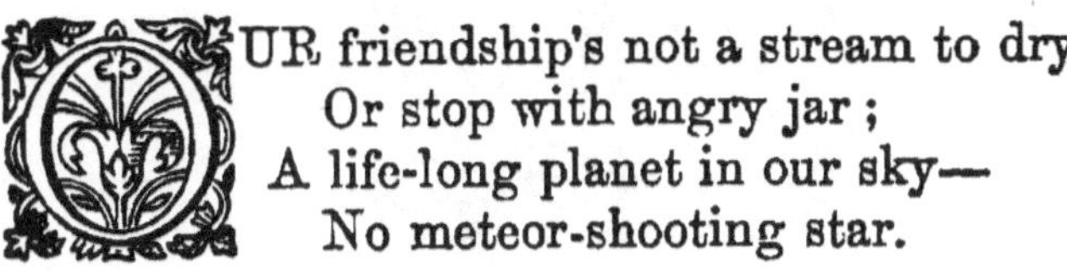

OUR friendship's not a stream to dry,
   Or stop with angry jar ;
A life-long planet in our sky—
   No meteor-shooting star.

Thy playfulness and pleasant ways
   Shall cheer my wintry track,
And give my old declining days
   A second summer back !

Proud honesty protects our lot,
   No dun infests our bowers ;
Wealth's golden lamps illumine not
   Brows more content than ours.

270. TO MY NIECE, MARY CAMPBELL.

To think, too, thy remembrance fond
   May love me after death,
Gives fancied happiness beyond
   My lease of living breath.

Meanwhile thine intellects presage
   A life-time rich in truth,
And make me feel th' advance of age
   Retarded by thy youth !

Good night ! propitious dreams betide
   Thy sleep !—awaken gay,
And we will make to-morrow glide
   As cheerful as to-day !

NOTES.

Page 4, line 27.

And such thy strength-inspiring aid that bore
The hardy Byron to his native shore—

THE following picture of his own distress, given by Byron in his simple and interesting narrative, justifies the description given in the poem.

After relating the barbarity of the Indian cacique to his child, he proceeds thus :—"A day or two after we put to sea again, and crossed the great bay I mentioned we had been at the bottom of when we first hauled away to the westward. The land here was very low and sandy, and something like the mouth of a river which discharged itself into the sea, and which had been taken no notice of by us before, as it was so shallow that the Indians were obliged to take everything out of their canoes, and carry them over land. We rowed up the river four or five leagues, and then took into a branch of it that ran first to the eastward, and then to the northward : here it became much narrower, and the stream excessively rapid, so that we gained but little way, though we wrought very hard. At night we landed upon its banks, and had a most uncomfortable lodging, it being a perfect swamp, and we had nothing to cover us, though it rained excessively. The Indians were little better off than we, as there was no wood here to make their wigwams ; so that all they could do was to prop up the bark, which they carry in the bottom of their canoes, and shelter themselves as well as they could to the leeward of it. Knowing the difficulties they had to encounter here, they had provided themselves with some seal ; but we had not a morsel to eat, after the heavy fatigues of the day, excepting a sort of root we saw the Indians make use of, which was very disagreeable to the taste. We laboured all next day against the stream, and fared as we had done the day before. The next day brought us to the carrying-place. Here was plenty of wood, but nothing to be got for sustenance. We passed this night, as we had frequently done, under a tree; but what we suffered at this time is not easy to be expressed. I had been three days at the oar without any kind of nourishment except the wretched root above-mentioned. I had no shirt, for it had rotted off by bits. All my clothes consisted of a short grieko (something like a bear-skin), a piece of red cloth which had once been a waistcoat, and a ragged pair of trousers, without shoes or stockings."

Page 5, line 9.

————a Briton and a friend!

Don Patricio Gedd, a Scotch physician in one of the Spanish settlements, hospitably relieved Byron and his wretched associates, of which the commodore speaks in the warmest terms of gratitude.

Page 5, line 23.

Or yield the lyre of Heaven another string.

The seven strings of Apollo's harp were the symbolical representation of the seven planets. Herschel, by discovering an eighth, might be said to add another string to the instrument.

Page 5, line 24.

The Swedish sage.——

Linnæus.

Page 6, line 10.

Deep from his vaults, the Loxian murmurs flow.

Loxius is the name frequently given to Apollo by Greek writers; it is met with more than once in the Choephoroi of Æschylus.

Page 7, line 8.

Unlocks a generous store at thy command,
Like Horeb's rocks beneath the prophet's hand.

See Exodus, chap. xvii. 3, 5, 6.

Page 11, line 19.

Wild Obi flies—

Among the negroes of the West Indies, Obi, or Orbiah, is the name of a magical power, which is believed by them to affect the object of its malignity with dismal calamities. Such a belief must undoubtedly have been deduced from the superstitious mythology of their kinsmen on the coast of Africa. I have, therefore, personified Obi as the evil spirit of the African, although the history of the African tribes mentions the evil spirit of their religious creed by a different appellation.

Page 11, line 23.

————Sibir's dreary mines.

Mr. Bell of Antermony, in his Travels through Siberia, informs us that the name of the country is universally pronounced Sibir by the Russians.

Page 12, line 2.

Presaging wrath to Poland—and to man !

The history of the partition of Poland, of the massacre in the suburbs of Warsaw, and on the bridge of Prague, the triumphant entry of Suwarrow into the Polish capital, and the insult offered to human nature, by the blasphemous thanks offered up to Heaven, for victories obtained over men fighting in the sacred cause of liberty, by murderers and oppressors, are events generally known.

Page 16, line 23.

The shrill horn blew.

The negroes in the West Indies are summoned to their morning work by a shell or horn.

Page 17, line 5.

How long was Timour's iron sceptre sway'd.

To elucidate this passage, I shall subjoin a quotation from the preface to " Letters from a Hindoo Rajah," a work of elegance and celebrity·

" The impostor of Mecca had established, as one of the principles of his doctrine, the merit of extending it either by persuasion or the sword, to all parts of the earth. How steadily this injunction was adhered to by his followers, and with what success it was pursued, is well known to all who are in the least conversant in history.

"The same overwhelming torrent which had inundated the greater part of Africa burst its way into the very heart of Europe; and covering many kingdoms of Asia with unbounded desolation, directed its baneful course to the flourishing provinces of Hindostan. Here these fierce and hardy adventurers, whose only improvement had been in the science of destruction, who added the fury of fanaticism to the ravages of war, found the great end of their conquest opposed by objects which neither the ardour of their persevering zeal, nor savage barbarity, could surmount. Multitudes were sacrificed by the cruel hand of religious persecution, and whole countries were deluged in blood, in the vain hope that by the destruction of a part the remainder might be persuaded, or terrified, into the profession of Mahomedism. But all these sanguinary efforts were ineffectual; and at length, being fully convinced that, though they might extirpate, they could never hope to convert, any number of the Hindoos, they relinquished the impracticable idea with which they had entered upon their career of conquest, and contented themselves with the acquirement of the civil dominion and almost universal empire of Hindostan."—*Letters from a Hindoo Rajah, by Eliza Hamilton.*

Page 17, line 19.

And braved the stormy Spirit of the Cape;

See the description of the Cape of Good Hope, translated from Camöens, by Mickle.

Page 17, line 33.

While famish'd nations died along the shore.

The following account of British conduct, and its consequences, in Bengal, will afford a sufficient idea of the fact alluded to in this passage :—

After describing the monopoly of salt, betel-nut, and tobacco, the historian proceeds thus :—"Money in this current came but by drops; it could not quench the thirst of those who waited in India to receive it. An expedient, such as it was, remained to quicken its pace. The natives could live with little salt, but could not want food. Some of the agents saw themselves well situated for collecting the rice into stores; they did so. They knew the Gentoos would rather die than violate the principles of their religion by eating flesh. The alternative would therefore be between giving what they had, or dying. The inhabitants sunk ;—they that cultivated the land, and saw the harvest at the disposal of others, planted in doubt—scarcity ensued. Then the monopoly was easier managed—sickness ensued. In some districts the languid living left the bodies of their numerous dead unburied."—*Short History of the English Transactions in the East Indies*, p. 145.

Page 18, line 13.

Nine times have Brama's wheels of lightning hurl'd
His awful presence o'er the alarmed world.

Among the sublime fictions of the Hindoo mythology, it is one article of belief, that the Deity Brama has descended nine times upon the world in various forms, and that he is yet to appear a tenth time, in the figure of a warrior upon a white horse, to cut off all incorrigible offenders. Avatar is the word used to express his descent.

Page 18, last line.

Shall Seriswattee wave her hallow'd wand !
And Camdeo bright, and Ganesa sublime.

Camdeo is the God of Love in the mythology of the Hindoos. Ganesa and Seriswattee correspond to the pagan deities, Janus and Minerva.

Page 21, line 10.

The noon of manhood to a myrtle shade !

" Sacred to Venus is the myrtle shade."—DRYDEN.

Page 23, line 27.

Thy woes, Arion !

Falconer, in his poem " The shipwreck," speaks of himself by the name of Arion.
See Falconer's " Shipwreck," Canto III.

Page 24, line 6.

The robber Moor !

See Schiller's tragedy of " The Robbers," Scene v.

Page 24, line 24.

What millions died—that Cæsar might be great!

The carnage occasioned by the wars of Julius Cæsar has been usually estimated at two millions of men.

Page 24, line 25.

Or learn the fate that bleeding thousands bore,
March'd by their Charles to Dnieper's swampy shore.

"In this extremity," (says the biographer of Charles XII. of Sweden, speaking of his military exploits before the battle of Pultowa,) "the memorable winter of 1709, which was still more remarkable in that part of Europe than in France, destroyed numbers of his troops; for Charles resolved to brave the seasons as he had done his enemies, and ventured to make long marches during this mortal cold. It was in one of these marches that two thousand men fell down dead with cold before his eyes."

Page 25, line 14.

———As Iona's saint.

The natives of the island of Iona have an opinion, that on certain evenings every year the tutelary saint Columba is seen on the top of the church spires counting the surrounding islands, to see that they have not been sunk by the power of witchcraft.

Page 25, line 33.

And part, like Ajut—never to return!

See the history of Ajut and Anningait, in "The Rambler."

Page 33, line 3.

That gave the glacier tops their richest glow.

The sight of the glaciers of Switzerland, I am told, has often disappointed travellers who had perused the accounts of their splendour and sublimity given by Bourrit and other describers of Swiss scenery. Possibly Bourrit, who had spent his life in an enamoured familiarity with the beauties of Nature in Switzerland, may have leaned to the romantic side of description. One can pardon a man for a sort of idolatry of those imposing objects of Nature which heighten our ideas of the bounty of Nature or Providence, when we reflect that the glaciers—those seas of ice—are not only sublime, but useful: they are the inexhaustible reservoirs which supply the principal rivers of Europe; and their annual melting is in proportion to the summer heat which dries up those rivers and makes them need that supply.

.That the picturesque grandeur of the glaciers should sometimes disappoint the traveller, will not seem surprising to any one who has been much in a mountainous country, and recollects that the beauty of Nature in such countries is not only variable, but capriciously dependent on the weather and sunshine. There are about four hundred different glaciers,[1] according to the computation of M. Bourrit, between Mont Blanc and the frontiers of the Tyrol. The full effect of the most lofty and picturesque of them can, of course, only be produced by the richest and warmest lights of the atmosphere; and the very heat which illuminates them must have a changing influence on many of their appearances. I imagine it is owing to this circumstance, namely, the casualty and changeableness of the appearance of some of the glaciers, that the impressions made by them on the minds of other and more transient travellers have been less enchanting than those described by M. Bourrit. On one occasion M. Bourrit seems even to speak of a past phenomenon, and certainly one which no other spectator attests in the same terms, when he says that there once existed, between Kandersteg and Lauterbrunnen, " a passage amidst singular glaciers, sometimes resembling magical towns of ice, with pilasters, pyramids, columns, and obelisks, reflecting to the sun the most brilliant hues of the finest gems."—M. Bourrit's description of the Glacier of the Rhone is quite enchanting:—" To form an idea," he says, " of this superb spectacle, figure in your mind a scaffolding of transparent ice, filling a space of two miles, rising to the clouds, and darting flashes of light like the sun. Nor were the several parts less magnificent and surprising. One might see, as it were, the streets and buildings of a city, erected in the form of an amphitheatre, and embellished with pieces of water, cascades, and torrents. The effects were as prodigious as the immensity and the height;—the most beautiful azure—the most splendid white—the regular appearance of a thousand pyramids of ice, are more easy to be imagined than described."—BOURRIT, iii. 163.

[1] Occupying, if taken together, a surface of 130 square leagues.

Page 33, line 9.

From heights browsed by the bounding bouquetin.

Laborde, in his " Tableau de la Suisse," gives a curious account of this animal, the wild sharp cry and elastic movements of which must heighten the picturesque appearance of its haunts :—" Nature," says Laborde, " has destined it to mountains covered with snow: if it is not exposed to keen cold, it becomes blind. Its agility in leaping much surpasses that of the chamois, and would appear incredible to those who have not seen it. There is not a mountain so high or steep to which it will not trust itself, provided it has room to place its feet; it can scramble along the highest wall, if its surface be rugged."

Page 33, line 15.

—enamell'd moss.

The moss of Switzerland, as well as that of the Tyrol, is remarkable for a bright smoothness approaching to the appearance of enamel.

Page 37, line 9.

How dear seem'd ev'n the waste and wild Shreckhorn.

The Shreckhorn means, in German, the Peak of Terror.

Page 37, line 14.

Blindfold his native hills he could have known.

I have here availed myself of a striking expression of the Emperor Napoleon respecting his recollections of Corsica, which is recorded in Las Cases' History of the Emperor's abode at St. Helena.

Page 57, line 9.

Innisfail, the ancient name of Ireland.

Page 58, st. ii. line 9.

Kerne, the plural of Kern, an Irish foot-soldier. In this sense the word is used by Shakespeare. Gainsford, in his " Glories of England," says, " They (the Irish) are desperate in revenge, and their kerne think no man dead *until his head be off.*"

Page 58, st. iii. line 12.

Shieling, a rude cabin or hut.

Page 58, st. iv. line 2.

In Erin's yellow vesture clad.

Yellow, dyed from saffron, was the favourite colour of the ancient Irish. When the Irish chieftains came to make terms with Queen Elizabeth's lord-lieutenant, we are told by Sir John Davis, that they came to court in saffron-coloured uniforms.

Page 59, st. iv. line 16.

Mórat, a drink made of the juice of mulberry mixed with honey.

Page 60, st. vi. line 13.

Their tribe, they said, their high degree,
Was sung in Tara's psaltery.

The pride of the Irish in ancestry was so great, that one of the O'Neals being told that Barrett of Castlemone had been there only 400 years, he replied—that he hated the clown as if he had come there but yesterday.

Tara was the place of assemblage and feasting of the petty princes of Ireland. Very splendid and fabulous descriptions are given by the Irish historians of the pomp and luxury of those meetings. The psaltery of Tara was the grand national register of Ireland. The grand epoch of political eminence in the early history of the Irish is the reign of their great and favourite monarch, Ollam Fodlah, who reigned, according to Keating, about 950 years before the Christian era. Under him was instituted the great Fes at Tara, which it is pretended was a triennial convention of the states, or a parliament ; the members of which were the Druids, and other learned men, who represented the people in that assembly. Very minute accounts are given by Irish annalists of the magnificence and order of these entertainments; from which, if credible, we might collect the earliest traces of heraldry that occur in history. To preserve order and regularity in the great number and variety of the members who met on such occasions, the Irish historians inform us that, when the banquet was ready to be served up, the shield-bearers of the princes, and other members of the convention, delivered in their shields and targets, which were readily distinguished by the coats of arms emblazoned upon them. These were arranged by the grand marshal and principal herald, and hung upon the walls on the right side of the table; and, upon entering the apartments, each member took his seat under his respective shield or target, without the slightest disturbance. The concluding days of the meeting, it is allowed by the Irish antiquaries, were spent in 'very free excess of conviviality; but the first six, they say, were devoted to the examination and settlement of the annals of the kingdom. These were publicly rehearsed. When they had passed the approbation of the assembly, they were transcribed into the authentic chronicles of the nation, which was called the Register, or Psalter, of Tara.

Col. Vallancey gives a translation of an old Irish fragment found in Trinity-College, Dublin, in which the palace of the above assembly is thus described, as it existed in the reign of Cormac :—

"In the reign of Cormac the palace of Tara was nine hundred feet square; the diameter of the surrounding rath, seven dice or casts of a dart; it contained one hundred and fifty apartments; one hundred and fifty dormitories, or sleeping-rooms for guards, and sixty men in each; the height was twenty-seven cubits; there were one hundred and fifty common drinking-horns, twelve doors, one thousand guests daily, besides princes, orators, and men of science, engravers of gold and silver, carvers, modellers, and nobles." The Irish description of the banqueting-hall is thus translated: "Twelve stalls or divisions in each wing; sixteen attendants on each side, and two to each table; one hundred guests in all."

Page 60, st. vii. line 4.

And stemm'd De Bourgo's chivalry!

The house of O'Connor had a right to boast of their victories over the English. It was a chief of the O'Connor race who gave a check to the English champion De Courcy, so famous for his personal strength, and for cleaving a helmet at one blow of his sword, in the presence of the kings of France and England, when the French champion declined the combat with him. Though ultimately conquered by the English under De Bourgo, the O'Connors had also humbled the pride of that name on a memorable occasion: viz., when Walter De Bourgo, an ancestor of that De Bourgo, who won the battle of Athunree, had become so insolent as to make excessive demands upon the territories of Connaught, and to bid defiance to all the rights and properties reserved by the Irish chiefs. Eath O'Connor, a near descendant of the famous Cathal, surnamed of the Bloody Hand, rose against the usurper, and defeated the English so severely, that their general died of chagrin after the battle.

Page 60, st. vii. line 7.

Or beal-fires for your jubilee.

The month of May is to this day called Mi Beal tiennie, *i. e.* the month of Beal's fire, in the original language of Ireland, and hence, I believe, the name of the Beltan festival in the Highlands. These fires were lighted on the summits of mountains (the Irish antiquaries say) in honour of the sun; and are supposed, by those conjecturing gentlemen, to prove the origin of the Irish from some nation who worshipped Baal or Belus. Many hills in Ireland still retain the name of Cnoc Greine, *i. e.* the Hill of the Sun; and on all are to be seen the ruins of druidical altars.

Page 61, st. viii. line 12.

And play my clarshech by thy side.

The clarshech, or harp, the principal musical instrument of the Hibernian bards, does not appear to be of Irish origin, nor indigenous to any of the British islands.—The Britons undoubtedly were not acquainted with it during the residence of the Romans in their country, as in all their coins, on which musical instruments are represented, we see only the Roman lyre, and not the British teylin, or harp.

Page 61, st. ix. line 3.

And saw at dawn the lofty bawn.

Bawn, from the Teutonic Bawen—to construct and secure with branches of trees, was so called because the primitive Celtic fortifications were made by digging a ditch, throwing up a rampart, and on the latter fixing stakes, which were interlaced with boughs of trees. This word is used by Spenser, but it is inaccurately called by Mr. Todd, his annotator, an eminence.

Page 63, st. xiii. line 16.

To speak the malison of heaven.

If the wrath which I have ascribed to the heroine of this little piece should seem to exhibit her character as too unnaturally stripped of patriotic and domestic affections, I must beg leave to plead the authority of Corneille in the representation of a similar passion: I allude to the denunciation of Camille, in the tragedy of " Horace." When Horace, accompanied by a soldier bearing the three swords of the Curiatii, meets his sister, and invites her to congratulate him on his victory, she expresses only her grief, which he attributes at first only to her feelings for the loss of her two brothers; but when she bursts forth into reproaches against him as the murderer of her lover, the last of the Curiatii, he exclaims:

> " O ciel ! qui vit jamais une pareille rage !
> Crois-tu donc que je sois insensible à l'outrage,
> Que je souffre en mon sang ce mortel déshonneur ?
> Aime, aime cette mort qui fait notre bonheur ?
> Et préfère du moins au souvenir d'un homme
> Ce que doit ta naissance aux intérêts de Rome."

At the mention of Rome, Camille breaks out into this apostrophe :

> " Rome, l'unique objet de mon ressentiment !
> Rome, à qui vient ton bras d'immoler mon amant !
> Rome qui t'a vu naître et que ton cœur adore !
> Rome enfin que je hais parce qu'elle t'honore !
> Puissent tous ses voisins ensemble conjurés
> Saper ses fondements encore mal assurés ;
> Et si ce n'est assez de toute l'Italie,
> Que l'Orient contre elle à l'Occident s'allie ;
> Que cent peuples unis des bouts de l'univers
> Passent pour la détruire et les monts et les mers ;
> Qu'elle-même sur soi renverse ses murailles,
> Et de ses propres mains déchire ses entrailles !
> Que le courroux du ciel allumé par mes vœux
> Fasse pleuvoir sur elle un déluge de feux !
> Puissé-je de mes yeux y voir tomber ce foudre,
> Voir ses maisons en cendre et tes lauriers en poudre,
> Voir le dernier Romain à son dernier soupir,
> Moi seule en être cause, et mourir de plaisir !"

Page 64, st. xiv. line 5.

And go to Athunree! (I cried).

In the reign of Edward the Second, the Irish presented
to Pope John the Twenty-second a memorial of their
sufferings under the English, of which the language exhibits all the strength of despair. " Ever since the English,"
say they, "first appeared upon our coasts, they entered our
territories under a certain specious pretence of charity, and
external hypocritical show of religion, endeavouring at the
same time, by every artifice malice could suggest, to extirpate us root and branch, and without any other right than
that of the strongest; they have so far succeeded by base
fraudulence and cunning, that they have forced us to quit
our fair and ample habitations and inheritances, and to take
refuge like wild beasts in the mountains, the woods, and the
morasses of the country:—nor even can the caverns and
dens protect us against their insatiable avarice. They
pursue us even into these frightful abodes; endeavouring
to dispossess us of the wild uncultivated rocks, and arro-
gate to themselves the property of every place on which we
can stamp the figure of our feet."

The greatest effort ever made by the ancient Irish to
regain their native independence was made at the time
when they called over the brother of Robert Bruce from
Scotland. William De Bourgo, brother to the Earl of
Ulster, and Richard de Bermingham, were sent against
the main body of the native insurgents, who were headed
rather than commanded by Felim O'Connor. The impor
tant battle which decided the subjection of Ireland took
place on the 10th of August, 1315.   It was the bloodiest
that ever was fought between the two nations, and continued throughout the whole day, from the rising to the
setting sun. The Irish fought with inferior discipline, but
with great enthusiasm. They lost ten thousand men,
among whom were twenty-nine chiefs of Connaught. Tradition states that, after this terrible day, the O'Connor
family, like the Fabian, were so nearly exterminated, that
throughout all Connaught not one of the name remained,
except Felim's brother, who was capable of bearing arms.

Page 65, line 15.

Lochiel, the chief of the warlike clan of the Camerons,
and descended from ancestors distinguished in their narrow
sphere for great personal prowess, was a man worthy of a
better cause and fate than that in which he embarked, the

enterprise of the Stuarts in 1745. His memory is still fondly cherished among the Highlanders, by the appellation of the "*gentle Lochiel;*" for he was famed for his social virtues as much as his martial and magnanimous (though mistaken) loyalty. His influence was so important among the Highland chiefs, that it depended on his joining with his clan whether the standard of Charles should be raised or not in 1745. Lochiel was himself too wise a man to be blind to the consequences of so hopeless an enterprise, but his sensibility to the point of honour overruled his wisdom. Charles appealed to his loyalty, and he could not brook the reproaches of his Prince. When Charles landed at Borrodale, Lochiel went to meet him, but on his way called at his brother's house (Cameron of Fassafern), and told him on what errand he was going; adding, however, that he meant to dissuade the Prince from his enterprise. Fassafern advised him in that case to communicate his mind by letter to Charles. "No," said Lochiel, "I think it due to my Prince to give him my reasons in person for refusing to join his standard."—"Brother," replied Fassafern, "I know you better than you know yourself: if the Prince once sets eyes on you, he will make you do what he pleases." The interview accordingly took place; and Lochiel, with many arguments, but in vain, pressed the Pretender to return to France, and reserve himself and his friends for a more favourable occasion, as he had come, by his own acknowledgment, without arms, or money, or adherents: or, at all events, to remain concealed till his friends should meet and deliberate what was best to be done. Charles, whose mind was wound up to the utmost impatience, paid no regard to this proposal, but answered, " that he was determined to put all to the hazard." " In a few days," said he, " I will erect the royal standard, and proclaim to the people of Great Britain, that Charles Stuart is come over to claim the crown of his ancestors, and to win it, or perish in the attempt. Lochiel, who, my father has often told me was our firmest friend, may stay at home and learn from the newspapers the fate of his Prince."— " No," said Lochiel, "I will share the fate of my Prince, and so shall every man over whom nature or fortune hath given me any power."

The other chieftains who followed Charles embraced his cause with no better hopes. It engages our sympathy most strongly in their behalf, that no motive, but their fear to be reproached with cowardice or disloyalty, impelled them to the hopeless adventure. Of this we have an example in the interview of Prince Charles with Clanronald, another leading chieftain in the rebel army.

" Charles," says Home, " almost reduced to despair, in his discourse with Boisdale, addressed the two Highlanders with great emotion, and summing up his arguments for taking arms, conjured them to assist their Prince, their countryman, in his utmost need. Clanronald and his friend, though well inclined to the cause, positively refused, and told him that to take up arms without concert or support was to pull down certain ruin on their own heads. Charles persisted, argued, and implored. During this conversation (they were on shipboard) the parties walked backwards and forwards on the deck; a Highlander stood near them, armed at all points, as was then the fashion of his country. He was a younger brother of Kinloch Moidart, and had come off to the ship to inquire for news, not knowing who was aboard. When he gathered from their discourse that the stranger was the Prince of Wales, when he heard his chief and his brother refuse to take arms with their Prince, his colour went and came, his eyes sparkled, he shifted his place, and grasped his sword. Charles observed his demeanour, and turning briskly to him, called out, ' Will you assist me ? '—' I will, I will,' said Ronald : ' though no other man in the Highlands should draw a sword, I am ready to die for you ! ' Charles, with a profusion of thanks to his champion, said, he wished all the Highlanders were like him. Without further deliberation, the two Macdonalds declared that they would also join, and use their utmost endeavours to engage their countrymen to take arms."— HOME'S *Hist. Rebellion*, p. 40.

Page 66, line 6.

Weep, Albin!

The Gaelic appellation of Scotland, more particularly the Highlands.

Page 67, line 23.

Lo, anointed by Heaven with the vials of wrath,
Behold, where he flies on his desolate path !

The lines allude to the many hardships of the royal sufferer.

An account of the second sight, in Irish called Taish, is thus given in Martin's description of the Western Isles of Scotland :—

" The second sight is a singular faculty of seeing an otherwise invisible object, without any previous means used by the person who sees it for that end. The vision makes such a lively impression upon the seers, that they neither see nor think of anything else except the vision as long as it continues ; and then they appear pensive or jovial according to the object which was represented to them.

" At the sight of a vision the eyelids of the person are erected, and the eyes continue staring until the object vanishes. This is obvious to others who are standing by when the persons happen to see a vision ; and occurred more than once to my own observation, and to others that were with me.

" There is one in Skie, of whom his acquaintance observed, that when he sees a vision the inner part of his eyelids turn so far upwards, that, after the object disappears, he must draw them down with his fingers, and sometimes employ others to draw them down, which he finds to be much the easier way.

" This faculty of the second sight does not lineally descend in a family, as some have imagined ; for I know several parents who are endowed with it, and their children are not, and *vice versâ*. Neither is it acquired by any previous compact. And after strict inquiry, I could never learn from any among them, that this faculty was communicable to any whatsoever. The seer knows neither the object, time, nor place of a vision before it appears ; and the same object is often seen by different persons living at a considerable distance from one another. The true way of judging as to the time and circumstances is by observation ; for several persons of judgment who are without this faculty are more capable to judge of the design of a vision than a novice that is a seer. If an object appear in the day or night, it will come to pass sooner or later accordingly.

" If an object is seen early in a morning, which is not frequent, it will be accomplished in a few hours afterwards ; if at noon, it will probably be accomplished that very day ; if in the evening, perhaps that night ; if after candles be lighted, it will be accomplished that night : the latter always an accomplishment by weeks, months, and sometimes years, according to the time of the night the vision is seen.

" When a shroud is seen about one, it is a sure prognostic of death. The time is judged according to the height of it about the person ; for if it is not seen above the middle,

death is not to be expected for the space of a year, and
perhaps some months longer: and as it is frequently seen
to ascend higher towards the head, death is concluded to
be at hand within a few days, if not hours, as daily experience confirms.   Examples of this kind were shown me,
when the person of whom the observations were then made
was in perfect health.

" It is ordinary with them to see houses, gardens, and
trees in places void of all these, and this in process of time
is wont to be accomplished: as at Mogslot, in the Isle of
Skie, where there were but a few sorry low houses, thatched
with straw; yet in a few years the vision, which appeared
often, was accomplished by the building of several good
houses in the very spot represented to the seers, and by
the planting of orchards there.

" To see a spark of fire is a forerunner of a dead child,
to be seen in the arms of those persons; of which there are
several instances.   To see a seat empty at the time of
sitting in it, is a presage of that person's death quickly after
it.

" When a novice, or one that has lately obtained the
second sight, sees a vision in the night-time without doors,
and comes near a fire, he presently falls into a swoon.

" Some find themselves as it were in a crowd of people,
having a corpse, which they carry along with them; and
after such visions the seers come in sweating, and describe
the vision that appeared.   If there be any of their acquaintance among them, they give an account of their names,
as also of the bearers; but they know nothing concerning
the corpse."

Horses and cows (according to the same credulous author)
have certainly sometimes the same faculty; and he endeavours to prove it by the signs of fear which the animals
exhibit, when second-sighted persons see visions in the
same place.

" The seers (he continues) are generally illiterate and
well-meaning people, and altogether void of design : nor
could I ever learn that any of them ever made the least
gain by it; neither is it reputable among them to have that
faculty.   Besides, the people of the Isles are not so credulous as to believe implicitly before the thing predicted
is accomplished; but when it is actually accomplished
afterwards, it is not in their power to deny it, without
offering violence to their own sense and reason.   Besides,
if the seers were deceivers, can it be reasonable to imagine
that all the islanders who have not the second sight should

combine together, and offer violence to their understandings and senses, to enforce themselves to believe a lie from age to age? There are several persons among them whose title and education raise them above the suspicion of concurring with an impostor merely to gratify an illiterate contemptible set of persons; nor can reasonable persons believe that children, horses, and cows, should be pre-engaged in a combination in favour of the second sight."—MARTIN'S *Description of the Western Isles of Scotland,* pp. 3-11.

Page 95, st. iii. line 6.

From merry mock-bird's song——

" The mocking-bird is of the form of, but larger than, the thrush; and the colours are a mixture of black, white, and grey.   What is said of the nightingale by its greatest admirers is what may with more propriety apply to this bird, who, in a natural state, sings with very superior taste. Towards evening I have heard one begin softly, reserving its breath to swell certain notes, which, by this means, had a most astonishing effect.   A gentleman in London had one of these birds for six years.   During the space of a minute he was heard to imitate the woodlark, chaffinch, blackbird, thrush, and sparrow.   In this country (America) I have frequently known the mocking-birds so engaged in this mimicry, that it was with much difficulty I could ever obtain an opportunity of hearing their own natural note, Some go so far as to say, that they have neither peculiar notes nor favourite imitations.   This may be denied.   Their few natural notes resemble those of the (European) nightingale.   Their song, however, has a greater compass and volume than the nightingale's, and they have the faculty of varying all intermediate notes in a manner which is truly delightful."—ASHE'S *Travels in America,* vol. ii. p. 73.

Page 96, st. v. line 9.

And distant isles that hear the loud Corbrechtan roar!

The Corybrechtan, or Corbrechtan, is a whirlpool on the western coast of Scotland, near the island of Jura, which is heard at a prodigious distance.   Its name signifies the whirlpool of the Prince of Denmark; and there is a tradition that a Danish prince once undertook, for a wager, to cast anchor in it.   He is said to have used woollen instead of hempen ropes, for greater strength, but perished in the attempt. On the shores of Argyleshire, I have often listened with great delight to the sound of this vortex, at the distance of many leagues. When the weather is calm, and the adjacent sea is scarcely heard on these picturesque shores, its sound, which is like the sound of innumerable chariots, creates a magnificent and fine effect.

Page 98 st. xiii. line 4.

Of buskin'd limb, and swarthy lineament ;

" In the Indian tribes there is a great similarity in their colour, stature, &c. They are all, except the Snake Indians, tall in stature, straight, and robust. It is very seldom they are deformed, which has given rise to the supposition that they put to death their deformed children. Their skin is of a copper colour : their eyes large, bright, black, and sparkling, indicative of a subtle and discerning mind : their hair is of the same colour, and prone to be long, seldom or never curled. Their teeth are large and white ; I never observed any decayed among them, which makes their breath as sweet as the air they inhale."—*Travels through America, by Captains Lewis and Clarke in* 1804-5-6.

Page 98, st. xiv. line 6.

Peace be to thee! my words this belt approve.

" The Iudians of North America accompany every formal address to strangers, with whom they form or recognize a treaty of amity, with the present of a string, or belt, of wampum. Wampum (says Cadwallader Colden) is made of the large whelk shell, *buccinum*, and shaped like long beads : it is the current money of the Indians." —*History of the Five Indian Nations*, p. 34. *New York Edition.*

Page 98, st. xiv. line 7.

The paths of peace my steps have hither led.

In relating an interview of Mohawk Indians with the Governor of New York, Colden quotes the following passage as a specimen of their metaphorical manner: " Where shall I seek the chair of peace ? Where shall I find it but upon our path ? and whither doth our path lead us but unto this house ?"

U

Page 99, st. xv. line 2.

Our wampum league thy brethren did embrace.

" When they solicit the alliance, offensive or defensive, of a whole nation, they send an embassy with a large belt of wampum and a bloody hatchet, inviting them to come and drink the blood of their enemies. The wampum made use of on these and other occasions, before their acquaintance with the Europeans, was nothing but small shells which they picked up by the sea-coasts, and on the banks of the lakes ; and now it is nothing but a kind of cylindrical beads, made of shells, white and black, which are esteemed among them as silver and gold are among us. The black they call the most valuable, and both together are their greatest riches and ornaments ; these among them answering all the end that money does amongst us. They have the art of stringing, twisting, and interweaving them into their belts, collars, blankets, and moccasons, &c. in ten thousand different sizes, forms, and figures, so as to be ornaments for every part of dress, and expressive to them of all their important transactions. They dye the wampum of various colours and shades, and mix and dispose them with great ingenuity and order, and so as to be significant among themselves of almost everything they please; so that by these their words are kept, and their thoughts communicated to one another, as ours are by writing. The belts that pass from one nation to another in all treaties, declarations, and important transactions, are very carefully preserved in the cabins of their chiefs, and serve not only as a kind of record or history, but as a public treasure." —*Major Rogers's Account of North America.*

Page 99, st. xvii. line 5.

As when the evil Manitou——

" It is certain the Indians acknowledge one Supreme Being, or Giver of Life, who presides over all things ; that is, the Great Spirit, and they look up to him as the source of good, from whence no evil can proceed. They also believe in a bad Spirit, to whom they ascribe great power ; and suppose that through his power all the evils which befall mankind are inflicted. To him, therefore, they pray in their distresses, begging that he would either avert their troubles, or moderate them when they are no longer avoidable.

" They hold also that there are good Spirits of a lower degree who have their particular departments, in which they are constantly contributing to the happiness of mortals. These they suppose to preside over all the extraordinary productions of Nature, such as those lakes, rivers, and mountains that are of an uncommon magnitude ; and likewise the beasts, birds, fishes, and even vegetables or stones, that exceed the rest of their species in size or singularity."—*Clarke's Travels among the Indians.*

The Supreme Spirit of Good is called by the Indians Kitchi Manitou ; and the Spirit of Evil, Matchi Manitou.

Page 100, st. xix. line 2.

Of fever-balm and sweet sagamité.

The fever-balm is a medicine used by these tribes ; it is a decoction of a bush called the Fever Tree. Sagamité is a kind of soup administered to their sick.

Page 100, st. xx. line 1.

And I, the eagle of my tribe, have rush'd
With this lorn dove.

The testimony of all travellers among the American Indians who mention their hieroglyphics, authorizes me in putting this figurative language in the mouth of Outalissi. The dove is among them, as elsewhere, an emblem of meekness ; and the eagle, that of a bold, noble, and liberal mind. When the Indians speak of a warrior who soars above the multitude in person and endowments, they say, " He is like the eagle, who destroys his enemies, and gives protection and abundance to the weak of his own tribe."

Page 101, st. xxiii. line 2.

Far differently, the mute Oneyda took, &c.

" They are extremely circumspect and deliberate, in every word and action ; nothing hurries them into any intemperate wrath, but that inveteracy to their enemies which is rooted in every Indian's breast. In all other instances they are cool and deliberate, taking care to suppress the emotions of the heart. If an Indian has discovered that a friend of his is in danger of being cut off by a lurking enemy, he does not tell him of his danger in direct terms as though he were in fear, but he first coolly asks him which way he is going that day, and having his answer, with the same indifference tells him that he

has been informed that a noxious beast lies on the route
he is going. This hint proves sufficient, and his friend
avoids the danger with as much caution as though every
design and motion of his enemy had been pointed out to
him.

"If an Indian has been engaged for several days in the
chase and by accident continued long without food, when
he arrives at the hut of a friend, where he knows that his
wants will be immediately supplied, he takes care not to
show the least symptoms of impatience, or betray the extreme hunger that he is tortured with: but on being invited
in, sits contentedly down, and smokes his pipe with as much
composure as if his appetite was cloyed and he was perfectly at ease. He does the same if among strangers.
This custom is strictly adhered to by every tribe; as they
esteem it a proof of fortitude, and think the reverse would
entitle them to the appellation of old women.

"If you tell an Indian that his children have greatly
signalized themselves against an enemy, have taken many
scalps, and brought home many prisoners, he does not
appear to feel any strong emotions of pleasure on the
occasion; his answer generally is, 'They have done well,'
and he makes but very little inquiry about the matter; on
the contrary, if you inform him that his children are slain
or taken prisoners, he makes no complaints; he only
replies, 'It is unfortunate:'—and for some time asks no
questions about how it happened."—*Lewis and Clarke's
Travels.*

Page 101, st. xxiii. line 3.

His calumet of peace, &c.

"Nor is the calumet of less importance or less revered
than the wampum in many transactions relative both to
peace and war. The bowl of this pipe is made of a kind
of soft red stone, which is easily wrought and hollowed
out; the stem is of cane, alder, or some kind of light wood,
painted with different colours, and decorated with the
heads, tails, and feathers of the most beautiful birds. The
use of the calumet is to smoke either tobacco or some bark,
leaf, or herb, which they often use instead of it, when they
enter into an alliance on any serious occasion, or solemn
engagements; this being among them the most sacred oath
that can be taken, the violation of which is esteemed most
infamous, and deserving of severe punishment from Heaven.
When they treat of war, the whole pipe and all its orna-

ments are red; sometimes it is red only on one side, and by the disposition of the feathers, &c. one acquainted with their customs will know at first sight what the nation who presents it intends or desires. Smoking the calumet is also a religious ceremony on some occasions, and in all treaties is considered as a witness between the parties, or rather as an instrument by which they invoke the sun and moon to witness their sincerity, and to be as it were a guarantee of the treaty between them. This custom of the Indians, though to appearance somewhat ridiculous, is not without its reasons; for as they find that smoking tends to disperse the vapours of the brain, to raise the spirits, and to qualify them for thinking and judging properly, they introduce it into their councils, where, after their resolves, the pipe was considered as a seal of their decrees, and as a pledge of their performance thereof it was sent to those they were consulting, in alliance or treaty with;—so that smoking among them at the same pipe is equivalent to our drinking together and out of the samecup."—*Major Rogers's Account of North America*, 1766.

" The lighted calumet is also used among them for a purpose still more interesting than the expression of social friendship. The austere manners of the Indians forbid any appearance of gallantry between the sexes in the day-time; but at night-time the young lover goes a-calumetting, as his courtship is called. As these people live in a state of equality, and without fear of internal violence or theft in their own tribes, they leave their doors open by night as well as by day. The lover takes advantage of this liberty, lights his calumet, enters the cabin of his mistress, and gently presents it to her. If she extinguish it, she admits his addresses; but if she suffer it to burn unnoticed, he retires with a disappointed and throbbing heart."—*Ashe's Travels.*

Page 101, st. xxiii. line 6.

Train'd from his tree-rock'd cradle to his bier.

" An Indian child, as soon as he is born, is swathed with clothes, or skins; and being laid on his back, is bound down on a piece of thick board, spread over with soft moss. The board is somewhat larger and broader than the child, and bent pieces of wood, like pieces of hoops, are placed over its face to protect it, so that if the machine were suffered to fall the child probably would not be injured. When the women have any business to transact at home, they hang the boards on a tree, if there be one at hand, and set them a swinging from side to side, like a pendulum, in order to exercise the children."—*Weld*, vol. ii. p. 46.

Page 101, st. xxiii. line 7.

The fierce extreme of good and ill to brook
Impassive———

Of the active as well as passive fortitude of the Indian character, the following is an instance related by Adair in his Travels :—

" A party of the Seuekah Indians came to war against the Katahba, bitter enemies to each other. In the woods the former discovered a sprightly warrior belonging to the latter, hunting in their usual light dress : on his perceiving them, he sprang off for a hollow rock four or five miles distant, as they intercepted him from running homeward. He was so extremely swift and skilful with the gun, as to kill seven of them in the running fight before they were able to surround and take him. They carried him to their country in sad triumph ; but though he had filled them with uncommon grief and shame for the loss of so many of their kindred, yet the love of martial virtue induced them to treat him, during their long journey, with a great deal more civility than if he had acted the part of a coward. The women and children, when they met him at their several towns, beat him and whipped him in as severe a manner as the occasion required, according to their law of justice, and at last he was formally condemned to die by the fiery torture. It might reasonably be imagined that what he had for some time gone through, by being fed with a scanty hand, a tedious march, lying at night on the bare ground, exposed to the changes of the weather, with his arms and legs extended in a pair of rough stocks, and suf-fering such punishment on his entering into their hostile towns, as a prelude to those sharp torments for which he was destined, would have so impaired his health and affected his imagination, as to have sent him to his long sleep, out of the way of any more sufferings. Probably this would have been the case with the major part of the white people under similar circumstances ; but I never knew this with any of the Indians ; and this cool-headed, brave warrior did not deviate from their rough lessons of martial virtue, but acted his part so well as to surprise and sorely vex his numerous enemies :—for when they were taking him, unpinioned, in their wild parade, to the place of torture, which lay near to a river, he suddenly dashed down those who stood in his way, sprang off, and plunged into the water, swimming underneath like an otter, only rising to take breath till he reached the opposite shore. He now ascended the steep bank, but though he had good reason to be in a hurry, as many of the enemy were in the water, and others running, very like bloodhounds, in pursuit of him, and the bullets flying around him from the time he took to the river, yet his heart did not allow him to leave them abruptly, without taking leave in a formal manner, in return for the extraordinary favours they had done and intended to do him. After slapping a part of his body in defiance to them (continues the author), he put up the shrill war-whoop, as his last salute, till some more convenient opportunity offered, and darted off in the manner of a beast broke loose from its torturing enemies. He continued his speed, so as to run by about midnight of the same day as far as his eager pursuers were two days in reaching. There he rested till he happily discovered five of those Indians who had pursued him :—he lay hid a little way off their camp, till they were sound asleep. Every circumstance of his situation occurred to him, and inspired him with heroism. He was naked, torn, and hungry, and his enraged enemies were come up with him ; —but there was now everything to relieve his wants, and a fair opportunity to save his life, and get great honour and sweet revenge, by cutting them off. Resolution, a convenient spot, and sudden surprise, would effect the main object of all his wishes and hopes. He accordingly crept, took one of their tomahawks, and killed them all on the spot,—clothed himself, took a choice gun, and as much ammunition and provisions as he could well carry in a running march. He set off afresh with a light heart, and did not sleep for several successive nights, only when he reclined, as usual, a little before day, with his back to a tree. As it were by instinct, when he found he was free from the pursuing enemy, he made directly to the very place where he had killed seven of his enemies, and was taken by them for the fiery torture. He digged them up, burnt their bodies to ashes, and went home in safety with singular triumph. Other pursuing enemies came, on the evening of the second day, to the camp of their dead people, when the sight gave them a greater shock than they had ever known before. In their chilled war-council they concluded that as he had done such surprising things in his defence before he was captured, and since that in his naked condition, and now was well armed, if they continued the pursuit he would spoil them all, for he surely was an enemy wizard,—and therefore they returned home."— *Adair's General Observations on the American Indians,* p. 394.

" It is surprising," says the same author, " to see the long-continued speed of the Indians. Though some of us have often run the swiftest of them out of sight for about the distance of twelve miles, yet afterwards, without any seeming toil, they would stretch on, leave us out of sight, and out-wind any horse."—*Ibid.* p. 318.

" If an Indian were driven out into the extensive woods, with only a knife and a tomahawk, or a small hatchet, it is not to be doubted but he would fatten even where a wolf would starve. He would soon collect fire by rubbing two dry pieces of wood together, make a bark hut, earthen vessels, and a bow and arrows; then kill wild game, fish, fresh-water tortoises, gather a plentiful variety of vege-tables, and live in affluence,"—*Ibid.* p. 410.

Page 102, st. xxiv. line 7.

Moccasons are a sort of Indian buskins.

Page 102, st. xxv. line 1.

Sleep, wearied one ! and in the dreaming land
Shouldst thou to-morrow with thy mother meet.

" There is nothing," says Charlevoix, " in which these bar-barians carry their superstitions farther than in what regards dreams; but they vary greatly in their manner of explaining themselves on this point. Sometimes it is the reasonable soul which ranges abroad, while the sensitive continues to animate the body. Sometimes it is the fa-miliar genius who gives salutary counsel with respect to what is going to happen. Sometimes it is a visit made by the soul of the object of which he dreams. But in whatever manner the dream is conceived, it is always looked upon as a thing sacred, and as the most ordinary way in which the gods make known their will to men. Filled with this idea, they cannot conceive how we should pay no regard to them. For the most part they look upon them either as a desire of the soul, inspired by some genius, or an order from him, and in consequence of this principle they hold it a religious duty to obey them.   An Indian having dreamt of having a finger cut off, had it really cut off as soon as he awoke, having first prepared himself for this important action by a feast.   Another having dreamt of being a prisoner, and in the hands of his enemies, was much at a loss what to do. He consulted the jugglers, and by their advice caused himself to be tied to a post, and burnt in several parts of the body."—*Charlevoix, Journal of a Voyage to North America.*

Page 102, st. xxv. line 9.

From a flower shaped like a horn, which Chateaubriand presumes to be of the lotus kind, the Indians in their travels through the desert often find a draught of dew purer than any water.

Page 102, st. xxvi. line 5.

The crocodile, the condor of the rock.

" The alligator, or American crocodile, when full grown," says Bertram, " is a very large and terrible creature, and of prodigious strength, activity, and swiftness in the water. I have seen them twenty feet in length, and some are supposed to be twenty-two or twenty-three feet in length. Their body is as large as that of a horse, their shape usually resembles that of a lizard, which is flat, or cuneiform, being compressed on each side, and gradually diminishing from the abdomen to the extremity, which, with the whole body, is covered with horny plates, or squamæ, impenetrable when on the body of the live animal, even to a rifle-ball, except about their head, and just behind their forelegs or arms, where, it is said, they are only vulnerable.   The head of a full-grown one is about three feet, and the mouth opens nearly the same length.   Their eyes are small in proportion, and seem sunk in the head, by means of the prominency of the brows ; the nostrils are large, inflated, and prominent on the top, so that the head on the water resembles, at a distance, a great chunk of wood floating about : only the upper jaw moves, which they raise almost perpendicular, so as to form a right angle with the lower one.   In the fore-part of the upper jaw, on each side, just under the nostrils, are two very large, thick, strong teeth, or tusks, not very sharp, but rather the shape of a cone : these are as white as the finest polished ivory, and are not covered by any skin or lips, but always in sight, which gives the creature a frightful appearance ; in the lower jaw are holes

opposite to these teeth to receive them; when they clap
their jaws together, it causes a surprising noise, like that
which is made by forcing a heavy plank with violence upon
the ground, and may be heard at a great distance. But
what is yet more surprising to a stranger, is the incredibly
loud and terrifying roar which they are capable of making,
especially in breeding time. It most resembles very heavy
distant thunder, not only shaking the air and waters, but
causing the earth to tremble; and when hundreds are
roaring at the same time, you can scarcely be persuaded
but that the whole globe is violently and dangerously
agitated. An old champion, who is, perhaps, absolute
sovereign of a little lake or lagoon, (when fifty less than
himself are obliged to content themselves with swelling and
roaring in little coves round about,) darts forth from the
reedy coverts, all at once, on the surface of the waters in a
right line, at first seemingly as rapid as lightning, but
gradually more slowly, until he arrives at the centre of
the lake, where he stops. He now swells himself by drawing in wind and water through his mouth, which causes a
loud sonorous rattling in the throat for near a minute; but
·it is immediately forced out again through his mouth and
nostrils with a loud noise, brandishing his tail in the air,
and the vapour running from his nostrils like smoke. At
other times, when swoln to an extent ready to burst, his
head and tail lifted up, he spins or twirls round on the
surface of the water. He acts his part like an Indian chief,
when rehearsing his feats of war."—*Bertram's Travels in
North America.*

Page 103, st. xxvii. line 4.

Then forth uprose that lone wayfaring man.

" They discover an amazing sagacity, and acquire, with
the greatest readiness, anything that depends upon the attention of the mind. By experience, and an acute observation, they attain many perfections to which the Americans
are strangers. For instance, they will cross a forest or a
plain, which is two hundred miles in breadth, so as to reach
with great exactness the point at which they intend to
arrive, keeping, during the whole of that space, in a direct
line, without any material deviations; and this they will
do with the same ease, let the weather be fair or cloudy.
With equal acuteness they will point to that part of the
heavens the sun is in, though it be intercepted by clouds

or fogs. Besides this, they are able to pursue, with incredible facility, the traces of man or beast, either on leaves or grass; and on this account it is with great difficulty they escape discovery. They are indebted for these talents not only to nature, but to an extraordinary command of the intellectual qualities, which can only be acquired by an unremitted attention, and by long experience. They are, in general, very happy in a retentive memory. They can recapitulate every particular that has been treated of in councils, and remember the exact time when they were held. Their belts of wampum preserve the substance of the treaties they have concluded with the neighbouring tribes for ages back, to which they will appeal and refer with as much perspicuity and readiness as Europeans can to their written records.

" The Indians are totally unskilled in geography, as well as all the other sciences, and yet they draw on their birch-bark very exact charts or maps of the countries they are acquainted with. The latitude and longitude only are wanting to make them tolerably complete.

" Their sole knowledge in astronomy consists in being able to point out the polar star, by which they regulate their course when they travel in the night.

" They reckon the distance of places not by miles or leagues, but by a day's journey, which, according to the best calculation I could make, appears to be about twenty English miles. These they also divide into halves and quarters, and will demonstrate them in their maps with great exactness by the hieroglyphics just mentioned, when they regulate in council their war-parties, or their most distant hunting excursions."—*Lewis and Clarke's Travels.*

" Some of the French missionaries have supposed that the Indians are guided by instinct, and have pretended that Indian children can find their way through a forest as easily as a person of maturer years; but this is a most absurd notion. It is unquestionably by a close attention to the growth of the trees, and position of the sun, that they find their way. On the northern side of a tree there is generally the most moss; and the bark on that side, in general, differs from that on the opposite one. The branches towards the south are, for the most part, more luxuriant than those on the other sides of trees, and several other distinctions also subsist between the northern and southern sides, conspicuous to Indians, being taught from their infancy to attend to them, which a common observer would, perhaps, never notice. Being accustomed from their infancy likewise to pay great attention to the position of the sun, they learn to make the most accurate allowance for its apparent motion from one part of the heavens to another, and in every part of the day they will point to the part of the heavens where it is, although the sky be obscured by clouds or mists.

" An instance of their dexterity in finding their way through an unknown country came under my observation when I was at Staunton, situated behind the Blue Mountains, Virginia. A number of the Creek nation had arrived at that town on their way to Philadelphia, whither they were going upon some affairs of importance, and had stopped there for the night. In the morning, some circumstance or other, which could not be learned, induced one half of the Indians to set off without their companions, who did not follow until some hours afterwards. When these last were ready to pursue their journey, several of the townspeople mounted their horses to escort them part of the way. They proceeded along the high road for some miles, but, all at once, hastily turning aside into the woods, though there was no path, the Indians advanced confidently forward. The people who accompanied them, surprised at this movement, informed them that they were quitting the road to Philadelphia, and expressed their fears lest they should miss their companions who had gone on before. They answered that they knew better, that the way through the woods was the shortest to Philadelphia, and that they knew very well that their companions had entered the wood at the very place where they did. Curiosity led some of the horsemen to go on ; and to their astonishment, for there was apparently no track, they overtook the other Indians in the thickest part of the wood. But what appeared most singular was, that the route which they took was found, on examining a map, to be as direct for Philadelphia as if they had taken the bearings by a mariner's compass. From others of their nation, who had been at Philadelphia at a former period, they had probably learned the exact direction of that city from their villages, and had never lost sight of it, although they had already travelled three hundred miles through the woods, and had upwards of four hundred miles more to go before they could reach the place of their destination.—Of the exactness with which they can find out a strange place to which they have been once directed by their own people, a striking example is furnished, I think, by Mr. Jefferson, in his account of the . Indian graves in Virginia. These graves are nothing more than large mounds of earth in the woods, which, on being opened, are found to contain skeletons in an erect posture : the Indian mode of sepulture has been too often described to remain unknown to you. But to come to my story. A party of Indians that were passing on to some of the seaports on the Atlantic, just as the Creeks above mentioned were going to Philadelphia, were observed, all on a sudden, to quit the straight road by which they were proceeding, and without asking any questions to strike through the woods, in a direct line, to one of these graves, which lay at the distance of some miles from the road. Now very near a century must have passed over since the part of Virginia in which this grave was situated had been inhabited by Indians, and these Indian travellers, who were to visit it by themselves, had unquestionably never been in that part of the country before; they must have found their way to it simply from the description of its situation, that had been handed down to them by tradition."—*Weld's Travels in North America,* vol. ii.

Page 106, st. ix. line 5.

Their fathers' dust————

It is a custom of the Indian tribes to visit the tombs of their ancestors in the cultivated parts of America, who have been buried for upwards of a century.

Page 108, st. xvi. line 8.

Or wild-cane arch high flung o'er gulf profound.

The bridges over narrow streams in many parts of Spanish America are said to be built of cane, which, however strong to support the passenger, are yet waved in the agitation of the storm, and frequently add to the effect of a mountainous and picturesque scenery.

Page 116, st. xvi. line 4.

The Mammoth comes————

That I am justified in making the Indian chief allude to the mammoth as an emblem of terror and destruction, will be seen by the authority quoted below. Speaking of the mammoth or big buffalo, Mr. Jefferson states, that a tradition is preserved among the Indians of that animal still existing in the northern parts of America.

" A delegation of warriors from the Delaware tribe

having visited the governor of Virginia during the revolution, on matters of business, the governor asked them some questions relative to their country, and among others, what they knew or had heard of the animal whose bones were found at the Salt-licks, on the Ohio. Their chief speaker immediately put himself into an attitude of oratory, and with a pomp suited to what he conceived the elevation of his subject, informed him that it was a tradition handed down from their fathers, that in ancient times a herd of these tremendous animals came to the Bigbone-licks, and began a universal destruction of the bear, deer, elk, buffalo, and other animals which had been created for the use of the Indians. That the Great Man above looking down and seeing this, was so enraged, that he seized his lightning, descended on the earth, seated himself on a neighbouring mountain, on a rock on which his seat and the prints of his feet are still to he seen, and hurled his bolts among them, till the whole were slaughtered, except the big bull, who, presenting his forehead to the shafts, shook them off as they fell, but missing one, at length it wounded him in the side, whereon, springing round, he bounded over the Ohio, over the Wabash, the Illinois, and finally over the great lakes, where he is living at this day."—*Jefferson's Notes on Virginia.*

Page 117, st. xvii. line 1.

Scorning to wield the hatchet for his bribe,
'Gainst Brandt himself I went to battle forth.

I took the character of Brandt, in the poem of Gertrude, from the common Histories of England, all of which represented him as a bloody and bad man (even among savages), and chief agent in the horrible desolation of Wyoming. Some years after this poem appeared, the son of Brandt, a most interesting and intelligent youth, came over to England, and I formed an acquaintance with him, on which I still look back with pleasure. He appealed to my sense of honour and justice, on his own part and on that of his sister, to retract the unfair aspersions which, unconscious of their unfairness, I had cast on his father's memory.

He then referred me to documents, which completely satisfied me that the common accounts of Brandt's cruelties at Wyoming, which I had found in books of Travels and in Adolphus's and similar Histories of England, were gross errors, and that in point of fact Brandt was not even present at that scene of desolation.

It is, unhappily, to Britons and Anglo-Americans that we must refer the chief blame in this horrible business. I published a letter expressing this belief in the *New Monthly Magazine*, in the year 1822, to which I must refer the reader—if he has any curiosity on the subject—for an antidote to my fanciful description of Brandt. Among other expressions to young Brandt, I made use of the following words:—" Had I learnt all this of your father when I was writing my poem, he should not have figured in it as the hero of mischief." It was but bare justice to say thus much of a Mohawk Indian, who spoke English eloquently, and was thought capable of having written a history of the Six Nations. I ascertained, also, that he often strove to mitigate the cruelty of Indian warfare. The name of Brandt, therefore, remains in my poem a pure and declared character of fiction.

Page 117, st. xvii. line 8.

To whom nor relative nor blood remains,
No!—not a kindred drop that runs in human veins!

Every one who recollects the specimen of Indian elo-quence given in the speech of Logan, a Mingo chief, to the governor of Virginia, will perceive that I have attempted to paraphrase its concluding and most striking expression : —" There runs not a drop of my blood in the veins of any living creature." The similar salutation of the fictitious personage in my story and the real Indian orator, makes it surely allowable to borrow such an expression ; and if it appears, as it cannot but appear, to less advantage than in the original, I beg the reader to reflect how difficult it is to transpose such exquisitely simple words, without sacrificing a portion of their effect.

In the spring of 1774, a robbery and murder were com-mitted on an inhabitant of the Frontiers of Virginia, by two Indians of the Shawanee tribe. The neighbouring whites, according to their custom, undertook to punish this outrage in a summary manner. Colonel Cresap, a man infamous for the many murders he had committed on those much injured people, collected a party and proceeded down the Kanaway in quest of vengeance : unfortunately, a canoe, with women and children, with one man only, was seen coming from the opposite shore unarmed, and unsus-pecting an attack from the whites. Cresap and his party concealed themselves on the bank of the river, and the moment the canoe reached the shore, singled out their objects, and at one fire killed every person in it. This happened to be the family of Logan, who had long been distinguished as a friend to the whites. This unworthy return provoked his vengeance; he accordingly signalized himself in the war which ensued. In the autumn of the same year a decisive battle was fought at the mouth of the great Kanaway, in which the collected forces of the Shawanees, Mingoes, and Delawares, were defeated by a detachment of the Virginian militia. The Indians sued for peace. Logan, however, disdained to be seen among the suppliants; but lest the sincerity of a treaty should be disturbed, from which so distinguished a chief abstracted himself, he sent, by a messenger, the following speech to be delivered to Lord Dunmore:—

"I appeal to any white man if ever he entered Logan's cabin hungry, and he gave him not to eat; if ever he came cold and naked, and he clothed him not. During the course of the last long and bloody war, Logan remained idle in his cabin, an advocate for peace. Such was my love for the whites, that my countrymen pointed as they passed, and said, 'Logan is the friend of the white men.' I have even thought to have lived with you, but for the injuries of one man. Colonel Cresap, the last spring, in cold blood, murdered all the relations of Logan, even my women and children.

"There runs not a drop of my blood in the veins of any living creature:—this called on me for revenge. I have fought for it. I have killed many. I have fully glutted my vengeance. For my country I rejoice at the beams of peace;—but do not harbour a thought that mine is the joy of fear. Logan never felt fear. He will not turn his heel to save his life.—Who is there to mourn for Logan? not one!"—*Jefferson's Notes on Virginia.*

Page 134, line 4.

The dark-attired Culdee.

The Culdees were the primitive clergy of Scotland, and apparently her only clergy from the sixth to the eleventh century. They were of Irish origin, and their monastery on the Island of Iona, or Icolmkill, was the seminary of Christianity in North Britain. Presbyterian writers have wished to prove them to have been a sort of Presbyters, strangers to the Roman Church and Episcopacy. It seems to be established that they were not enemies to Episcopacy: but that they were not slavishly subjected to Rome, like the clergy of later periods, appears by their resisting the Papal ordinances respecting the celibacy of religious men, on which account they were ultimately displaced by the Scottish sovereigns to make way for more Popish canons.

Page 136, line 27.

And the shield of alarm was dumb.

Striking the shield was an ancient mode of convocation to war among the Gaël.

Page 141, line 5.

The tradition which forms the substance of these stanzas is still preserved in Germany. An ancient tower on a height, called the Rolandseck, a few miles above Bonn on the Rhine, is shown as the habitation which Roland built in sight of a nunnery, into which his mistress had retired, on having heard an unfounded account of his death. Whatever may be thought of the credibility of the legend, its scenery must be recollected with pleasure by every one who has visited the romantic landscape of the Drachenfels, the Rolandseck, and the beautiful adjacent islet of the Rhine, where a nunnery still stands.

Page 147, line 4.

That erst the advent'rous Norman wore.

A Norman leader, in the service of the King of Scotland, married the heiress of Lochow, in the twelfth century, and from him the Campbells are sprung.

Page 173, line 3.

Whose lineage, in a raptured hour.

Alluding to the well-known tradition respecting the origin of painting, that it arose from a young Corinthian female tracing the shadow of her lover's profile on the wall, as he lay asleep.

Page 180, line 24.

Where the Norman encamp'd him of old.

What is called the East Hill, at Hastings, is crowned with the works of an ancient camp; and it is more than probable it was the spot which William I. occupied between

X

his landing and the battle which gave him England's crown. It is a strong position; the works are easily traced.

Page 185, line 27.

France turns from her abandon'd friends afresh.

The fact ought to be universally known, that France is at this moment indebted to Poland for not being invaded by Russia. When the Grand Duke Constantine fled from Warsaw, he left papers behind him, proving that the Russians, after the Parisian events in July, meant to have marched towards Paris, if the Polish insurrection had not prevented them.

Page 191, line 10.

Thee, Niemciewitz, ————

This venerable man, the most popular and influential of Polish poets, and president of the academy in Warsaw, was in London when this poem was written: he was then seventy-four years old; but his noble spirit was rather mellowed than decayed by age. He was the friend of Fox, Kosciusko, and Washington. Rich in anecdote like Franklin, he had also a striking resemblance to him in countenance.

Page 192, line 18.

Nor church-bell ————

In Catholic countries you often hear the church-bells rung to propitiate Heaven during thunder-storms.

Page 203, line 21.

Regret the lark that gladdens England's morn.

Mr. P. Cunningham, in his interesting work on New South Wales, gives the following account of its song-birds:— " We are not moved here with the deep mellow note of the blackbird, poured out from beneath some low stunted bush, nor thrilled with the wild warblings of the thrush perched on the top of some tall sapling, nor charmed with the blithe carol of the lark as we proceed early a-field; none of our birds rivalling those divine songsters in realizing the poetical idea of '*the music of the grove:*' while '*parrots*' *chattering*' must supply the place of ' nightingales' singing' in the future amorous lays of our sighing Celadons. We have our lark, certainly ; but both his appearance and note are a most wretched parody upon the bird about which our English poets have made so many fine similes. He will mount from the ground, and rise, fluttering upwards in the same manner, and with a few of the starting notes of the English lark ; but, on reaching the height of thirty feet or so, down he drops suddenly and mutely. diving into concealment among the long grass, as if ashamed of his pitiful attempt. For the pert frisky robin, pecking and pattering against the windows in the dull days of winter, we have the lively 'superb warbler,' with his blue shining plumage and his long tapering tail, picking up the crumbs at our doors; while the pretty red-bills, of the size and form of the goldfinch, constitute the sparrow of our clime, flying in flocks about our houses, and building their soft downy pigmy nests in the orange, peach, and lemontrees surrounding them."— *Cunningham's Two Years in New South Wales*, vol. ii. p. 216.

Page 213, line 24.

Oh, feeble statesmen—ignominious times.

There is not upon record a more disgusting scene of Russian hypocrisy, and (woe that it must be written!) of British humiliation. than that which passed on board the " Talavera," when British sailors accepted money from the Emperor Nicholas, and gave him cheers. It will require the " Talavera" to fight well with the first Russian ship that she may have to encounter, to make us forget that day.

Page 222, line 12.

A palsy-stroke of Nature shook Oran.

In the year 1790, Oran, the most western city in the Algerine Regency, which had been possessed by Spain for more than a hundred years, and fortified at an immense expense, was destroyed by an earthquake; six thousand of its inhabitants were buried under the ruins.

Page 229, line 7.

The vale, by eagle-haunted cliffs o'erhung.

The valley of Glencoe, unparalleled in its scenery for gloomy grandeur, is to this day frequented by eagles. When I visited the spot within a year ago, I saw several perch at a distance. Only one of them came so near me that I did not wish him any nearer. He favoured me with a full and continued view of his noble person, and with the exception of the African eagle which I saw wheeling and hovering over a corps of the French army that were marching from Oran, and who seemed to linger over them, with delight at the sound of their trumpets, as if they were about to restore his image to the Gallic standard—I never saw a prouder bird than this black eagle of Glencoe.

I was unable, from a hurt in my foot, to leave the carriage; but the guide informed me that, if I could go nearer the sides of the glen, I should see the traces of houses and gardens once belonging to the unfortunate inhabitants. As it was, I never saw a spot where I could less suppose human beings to have ever dwelt. I asked the guide how these eagles subsisted; he replied, " on the lambs and the fawns of Lord Breadalbane."—" Lambs and fawns !" I said ; " and how do *they* subsist, for I cannot see verdure enough to graze a rabbit ? I suspect," I added, " that these birds make the cliffs only their country-houses, and that they go down to the Lowlands to find their provender."— " Ay, ay," replied the Highlander, " it is very possible, for the eagle can gang far for his breakfast."

Page 234, line 10.

Witch-legends Ronald scorn'd—ghost, kelpie, wraith.

" The most dangerous and malignant creature of Highland superstition was the kelpie, or water-horse, which was supposed to allure women and children to his subaqueous haunts, and there devour them ; sometimes he would swell the lake or torrent beyond its usual limits, and overwhelm the unguarded traveller in the flood. The shepherd, as he sat on the brow of a rock on a summer's evening, often fancied he saw this animal dashing along the surface of the lake, or browsing on the pasture-ground upon its verge."— *Brown's History of the Highland Clans*, vol. i. 106.

In Scotland, according to Dr. John Brown, it is yet a superstitious principle that the *wraith*, the omen or messenger of death, appears in the resemblance of one in danger, immediately preceding dissolution. This ominous form, purely of a spiritual nature, seems to testify that the exaction (extinction) of life approaches. It was wont to be exhibited, also, as " *a little rough dog*," when it could be pacified by the death of any other being " if crossed and conjured in time."—*Brown's Superstitions of the Highlands*, p. 182.

It happened to me, early in life, to meet with an amusing instance of Highland superstition with regard to myself. I lived in a family of the Island of Mull, and a mile or two from their house there was a burial-ground without any church attached to it, on the lonely moor.

The cemetery was enclosed and guarded by an iron railing, so high that it was thought to be unscaleable. I was, however, commencing the study of botany at the time, and thinking there might be some nice flowers and curious epitaphs among the grave-stones, I contrived, by help of my handkerchief, to scale the railing, and was soon scampering over the tombs ; some of the natives chanced to perceive me, not in the act of climbing over to—but skipping over, the burial-ground. In a day or two I observed the family looking on me with unaccountable, though not angry seriousness ; at last the good old grandmother told me, with tears in her eyes, " that I could not live long, for that my wraith had been seen."—" And, pray, where ? "— " Leaping over the stones of the burial-ground." The old lady was much relieved to hear that it was not my wraith, but myself.

Akin to other Highland superstitions, but differing from them in many essential respects, is the belief—for superstition it cannot well be called (quoth the wise author I am quoting)—in the second-sight, by which, as Dr. Johnson observes, " seems to be meant a mode of seeing superadded to that which nature generally bestows ; and consists of an impression made either by the mind upon the eye—or by the eye upon the mind, by which things distant or future are perceived and seen, as if they were present. This receptive faculty is called Traioshe in the Gaelic, which signifies a spectre or vision, and is neither voluntary nor constant ; but consists in seeing an otherwise invisible object, without any previous means used by the person that sees it for that end. The vision makes such a lively impression upon the seers, that they neither see nor think of anything else except the vision, as long as it continues ; and then they appear pensive or jovial, according to the object which was represented to them."

There are now few persons, if any (continues Dr. Brown), who pretend to this faculty, and the belief in it is almost generally exploded. Yet it cannot be denied that apparent proofs of its existence have been adduced, which have staggered minds not prone to superstition. When the connection between cause and effect can be recognized, things which would otherwise have appeared wonderful, and almost incredible, are viewed as ordinary occurrences. The impossibility of accounting for such an extraordinary phenomenon as the alleged faculty on philosophical principles, or from the laws of nature, must ever leave the matter suspended between rational doubt and confirmed scepticism.

" Strong reasons for incredulity," says Dr. Johnson, "will readily occur." This faculty of seeing things out of sight is local, and commonly useless. It is a breach of the common order of things, without any visible reason or perceptible benefit. It is ascribed only to a people very little enlightened, and among them, for the most part, to the mean and ignorant.

In the whole history of Highland superstitions, there is not a more curious fact than that Dr. James Brown, a gentleman of the Edinburgh bar, in the nineteenth century, should show himself a more abject believer in the truth of second-sight, than Dr. Samuel Johnson, of London, in the eighteenth century.

Page 235, line 18.

The pit or gallows would have cured my grief.

Until the year 1747, the Highland lairds had the right of punishing serfs even capitally, in so far that they often hanged, or imprisoned them in a pit or dungeon, where they were starved to death. But the law of 1746, for disarming the Highlanders and restraining the use of the Highland garb, was followed up the following year by one of a more radical and permanent description. This was the act for abolishing the heritable jurisdictions, which, though necessary in a rude state of society, were wholly incompatible with an advanced state of civilization. By depriving the Highland chiefs of their judicial powers, it was thought that the sway which, for centuries, they had held over their people, would be gradually impaired; and that by investing certain judges, who were amenable to the legislature for the proper discharge of their duties, with the civil and criminal jurisdiction enjoyed by the proprietors of the soil, the cause of good goverument would be promoted, and the facilities for repressing any attempts to disturb the public tranquillity increased.

By this act (20 George II. c. 43), which was made to include the whole of Scotland, all heritable jurisdictions of justiciary, all regalities and heritable bailieries and constabularies (excepting the office of high constable), and all stewartries and sheriffships of smaller districts, which were only parts of counties, were dissolved, and the powers formerly vested in them were ordained to be exercised by such of the king's courts as these powers would have belonged to, if the jurisdictions had never been granted. All sheriff-ships and stewartries not dissolved by the statute, namely, those which comprehended whole counties, where they had been granted either heritably or for life, were resumed and annexed to the crown. With the exception of the hereditary justiciaryship of Scotland, which was transferred from the family of Argyle to the High Court of Justiciary, the other jurisdictions were ordained to be vested in sheriffs-depute or stewarts-depute, to be appointed by the king in every shire or stewartry not dissolved by the act. As by the twentieth of Union, all heritable offices and jurisdictions were reserved to the grantees as rights of property ; compensation was ordained to be made to the holders, the amount of which was afterwards fixed by parliament, in terms of the act of Sederunt of the Court of Session, at one hundred and fifty thousand pounds.

Page 235, line 20.

I march'd—when, feigning royalty's command
Against the clan Macdonald, Stair's lord
Sent forth exterminating fire and sword.

I cannot agree with Brown, the author of an able work, " The History of the Highland Clans," that the affair of Glencoe has stamped indelible infamy on the government of King William III., if by this expression it be meant that William's own memory is disgraced by that massacre. I see no proof that William gave more than general orders to subdue the remaining malcontents of the Macdonald clan ; and these orders, the nearer we trace them to the government, are the more express in enjoining, that all those who would promise to swear allegiance should be spared. As these orders came down from the general government to individuals, they became more and more severe, and at last merciless, so that they ultimately ceased to be the real orders of government. Among these false agents of government, who appear with most disgrace, is the "Master of Stair," who appears in' the business more like a fiend than a man. When issuing his orders for the attack on the remainder of the Macdonalds in Glencoe, he expressed a hope in his letter " that the soldiers would trouble the government with no prisoners."

It cannot be supposed that I would for a moment palliate this atrocious event by quoting the provocations not very long before offered by the Macdonalds in massacres of the Campbells. But they may be alluded to as causes, though not excuses. It is a part of the melancholy instruction which history affords us, that in the moral as well as in the physical world there is always a reaction equal to the action.—The banishment of the Moors from Spain to Africa was the chief cause of African piracy and Christian slavery among the Moors for centuries: and since the reign of William III. the Irish Orangemen have been the Algerines of Ireland.

The affair of Glencoe was in fact only a lingering trait of horribly barbarous times, though it was the more shocking that it came from that side of the political world which professed to be the more liberal side, and it occurred at a late time of the day, when the minds of both parties had become comparatively civilized, the whigs by the triumph of free principles, and the tories by personal experience of the evils attending persecution. Yet that barbarism still subsisted in too many minds professing to act on liberal principles, is but too apparent from this disgusting tragedy.

I once flattered myself that the Argyle Campbells, from whom I am sprung, had no share in this massacre, and a direct share they certainly had not. But on inquiry I find that they consented to shutting up the passes of Glencoe through which the Macdonalds might escape; and perhaps relations of my great-grandfather—I am afraid to count their distance or proximity—might be indirectly concerned in the cruelty.

But children are not answerable for the crimes of their forefathers; and I hope and trust that the descendants of Breadalbane and Glenlyon are as much and justly at their ease on this subject as I am.

Page 242, line 19.

Chance snatch'd them from proscription and despair.

Many Highland families, at the outbreak of the rebellion in 1745, were saved from utter desolation by the contrivances of some of their more sensible members, principally the women, who foresaw the consequences of the insurrection. When I was a youth in the Highlands I remember an old gentleman being pointed out to me, who, finding all other arguments fail, had, in conjunction with his mother and sisters, bound the old laird hand and foot, and locked him up in his own cellar, until the news of the battle of Culloden had arrived.

A device pleasanter to the reader of the anecdote, though not to the sufferer, was practised by a shrewd Highland dame, whose husband was Charles Stuart mad, and was determined to join the insurgents. He told his wife at night that he should start early to-morrow morning on horseback. "Well, but you will allow me to make your breakfast before you go ? "—"Oh yes." She accordingly prepared it, and, bringing in a full boiling kettle, poured it, by intentional accident, on his legs!

Page 261, line 9.

The advocates of classical learning tell us that, without classic historians, we should never become acquainted with the most splendid traits of human character ; but one of those traits, patriotic self-devotion, may surely be heard of elsewhere, without learning Greek and Latin. There are few, who have read modern history, unacquainted with the noble voluntary death of the Switzer Winkelried. Whether he was a peasant or man of superior birth is a point not quite settled in history, though I am inclined to suspect that he was simply a peasant. But this is certain, that in the battle of Sempach, perceiving that there was no other means of breaking the heavy-armed lines of the Austrians than by gathering as many of their spears as he could grasp together, he opened a passage for his fellow-combatants, who, with hammers and hatchets, hewed down the mailed men-at-arms, and won the victory.

THE END.